# BECOMING
## *Lady Washington*

### Betty Bolté

This book is a work of fiction. Any references to historical events, real people, or real places are used fictitiously. Other names, characters, places, and events are products of the author's imagination, and any resemblance to actual events or places or persons, living or dead, is entirely coincidental.

www.MysticOwlPublishing.com

# ALSO BY BETTY BOLTÉ

Notes of Love and War

FURY FALLS INN
The Haunting of Fury Falls Inn

A MORE PERFECT UNION
Elizabeth's Hope
Emily's Vow
Amy's Choice
Samantha's Secret
Evelyn's Promise

Hometown Heroines
*True Stories of Bravery, Daring, and Adventure*

SECRETS OF ROSEVILLE
Undying Love
Haunted Melody
The Touchstone of Raven Hollow
Veiled Visions of Love
Charmed Against All Odds

you for your patience and diligence in hunting down appropriate sources for me.

I'm grateful to the professional insights given by the National Park Service personnel who work at the many sites where George and Martha resided during the American Revolution. Being able to see, hear, and feel where they lived, worked, and played proved priceless.

I'd also like to thank my beta readers who slogged through the first complete draft of my story to provide valuable feedback on where I needed to clarify the story: Tracy McMahon, Veronica Forand, Crystal Lee, Stephanie Jones, Carole Swinford, and Christine Glover.

Finally, I'd like to express my deepest thanks to my ever-patient and supportive loving husband, Chris, who went willingly to so many historical sites and asked questions I didn't think of to help me write a well-rounded and informative story. But mostly for his patience and support during the years it has taken me to bring Martha's story to life for my readers.

Betty Bolté
Huntsville, AL
2020

*To the memory of Lorel Bolté,*
*my mother-in-law and who was a great example*
*of a General's granddaughter, daughter, and wife*

# ACKNOWLEDGMENTS

Writing a story about a famous person, especially one loved and revered by so many as Martha Washington, takes more than just one person. I am indebted to so many people both known and unknown, in person and fellow writers and researchers whose work I tapped online via the internet and physical books. My list of references—sources found online and in various book stores across the eastern seaboard, as well as the many historical sites associated with George and Martha Washington—is long indeed. I've striven to portray the people and places in the story as accurately and authentically as I can, and any failure to do so is mine alone.

First, I'd like to thank Susan Shames, Decorative Arts Librarian, and Allison Heinbaugh, Circulation and Reference Librarian, of the John D. Rockefeller, Jr. Library, Colonial Williamsburg Foundation, for answering my list of questions when I stopped in unannounced while visiting Colonial Williamsburg. They also graciously answered questions submitted via email with quick and efficient grace.

Virginia Lafferty graciously opened her home, Elsing Green plantation, to me and my husband for a personal guided tour of the property. She allowed us to take photographs throughout both the hunting lodge and the manor. Thank you so much for your attention and answering my many questions.

Lavonne Allen, the "jailer" at the New Kent County Historical Society also answered a list of questions and pointed me toward sources that provided both visual and textual references. Thank

# 1

Our love nestled in my hands. Pen and ink applied to linen pages were the only tangible evidence remaining of the love I shared with my husband. He called to me, softly, urgently. I sensed him more than heard his voice, but he summoned me nonetheless. Alone in my chamber, I knew the time drew near for me to answer his command, but delayed doing so until I'd done what I'd come upstairs to my bedchamber to do. I owed him that and so much more.

Voices along with the parakeets' incessant chatter floated up from the portico below, the reassuring sounds drifting up and into my room. Another more subtle voice in my mind urged me to follow George's private secretary's circumspect example for far different reasons than to protect that awful Jefferson. I'd left everyone below to escape to my private space, using my ailment as an excuse to rest. I didn't tell any one my true intention because I'm sure they'd try to stop me.

I gripped one of the many packets of letters stacked on my bedside table, each tied with a red satin ribbon faded to dusty rose. The papers were creased and stained from their travels from one state to another, from the multitude of hands which passed on the letters, and from the repeated reading of their contents. Words of love. Of private jokes between a man and his wife. Words of anger and dismay, of fear and courage, all kept mostly secure from the eyes of strangers. Safe from being abused and published in the paper, their meaning twisted and contorted to suit nefarious aims by my husband's enemies. Men like that blasted betrayer, Thomas Jefferson. I shall never forgive him for intentionally working to defame my precious life mate. The wounds from Jefferson's actions never healed. How could Tobias Lear have wanted to protect that man's reputation? Nonetheless, I'd defend George's reputation until the day I died. Maybe longer.

I looked around my bedchamber. Not the one I had shared for so many years with my love. No, that one I'd closed up tight upon his death three long years ago before moving into this third floor chamber. I smiled at the sight of the four-post bed with its pink roses dominating against a cheery yellow backing. They brought a bit of my garden inside to keep me company, now that I no longer had the interest or strength to work among the flowers. My gaze rested on the dark wood dresser, a looking glass framed above it. The fire snapped and crackled, its flames dancing merrily along the logs. The sound of the greedy flames reminded me of my mission.

Pulling a chair away from the writing desk, I positioned it close to the fire with one hand, clutching the treasured missives against my chest. Sitting, I tugged on the ribbon, freeing the folded pages to tumble into my lap. I leaned forward, and began feeding the letters into the fire. Watched the ancient pages burn and curl as they blackened into ash. As each letter shriveled and disappeared, my mind drifted back over my life. A life of love, grief, and peril. Starting with the precocious decision that set the rest into motion.

———————

*Williamsburg, Virginia – 1746*

Which one would suit my desires best? I wouldn't let such an important decision be made by any one else. Least of all the foppish young men ogling me from across the room. Suppressing a shudder of revulsion with an effort, I skimmed the offerings in the form of the eligible men in the large open room overflowing with people. My breath caught in my throat at the very idea I'd actually be allowed to take such an important matter into my own hands. I'd convinced my parents it was time, despite only having reached the age of fifteen years to be presented to society. I knew what I did and didn't want out of marriage and had taken the reins in hand to steer the course of my future as I did my pretty mare. I'd marry, but on my terms.

The first strains of the musicians tuning drew my attention away from the array of colorful and bedecked ball gowns of the older women to the festively decorated dance floor. The large table and chairs used by the lower and upper houses of the government to discuss the colony's legal business had been removed from the upstairs of the Capitol. Not that I knew from my personal experience. No, my father had to tell me since women were not normally permitted in the upstairs meeting room. I didn't understand the reasoning behind such a silly restriction, but defying it was not worth the effort. I had little to no interest in politics. I'd rather select fabrics and ribbons for a gown than worry about ordinances and laws.

I smoothed my gloved hands down the yellow silk taffeta skirts of my gown adorned with flowers in the latest fashion with fine gold satin ribbons. The skirts split to reveal the blue quilted petticoat beneath. I tapped the toe of one of my adorable shoes, made from sequin-studded yellow satin with Louis heels, anxious to have the first dance over and done with. I had more important things to contemplate than correct dance steps. Like which of the bachelors in the room might make a suitable husband, one who could provide a finer house for a family than the simple plantation house my father had given my mother when they'd first moved to the area.

Chestnut Grove plantation overlooked the Pamunkey river and was considered to be a respectable size. Yet the manor house could not hold a candle to the house and grounds my Aunt Unity lived in upriver. Elsing Green boasted a hunting lodge, a small building for occasional use, which was about the size of my childhood home. Uncle William Dandridge had built the new manor house to dwarf the original building, which it did in grand style and elegance. Even the wood floors inside were of better construction and design. I wanted to marry a man I could respect and admire, one who had the wherewithal to elevate my status in the colony and enable me to have the brood of children I longed for. Only I wanted more than a loving relationship and a house by the river. After all, marriage is a partnership more than anything else. I'd not want an abusive or boastful man, but one I could trust to keep me safe and sheltered while I managed his household and large family. Would I find a potential life mate on the night of my first presentation to the governor and our society? Not likely, but I'd decided to begin the search.

The musicians played the first notes of a minuet to open the ball and the first couples, led by Lieutenant Governor William Gooch and his wife Rebecca, stepped off into the intricate and decorous movements. I swallowed a sigh. Ladies making their first appearance, including me, were required to participate in the dance, but not until the higher ranking guests performed for the spectators. Clasping my gloved hands together, I glanced at my parents standing a few paces from me, adorned in their finest garments.

My parents, known as Jack and Fanny Dandridge by their friends, had settled into the colony and made deep connections through his work and charitable efforts, in particular as vestryman and churchwarden for St. Peter's Church. Mother loved having the house filled with children, and hoped to have more than the six of us keeping her busy. With good fortune, one day I'd have my own husband and family. Like Mother, I longed for a flock of children to love.

My mother received glances of approval as she stood in her pale green confection with silver stomacher and scattering of seed pearls on the skirt. All around the edges of the floor, burgesses and the other respected gentility of Virginia, resplendent in their finest attire, chatted amongst themselves as the dance continued. The other ladies, all young women older than me, huddled together with their mothers as chaperones. None of my friends had the courage to make their first presentation yet, so I stayed close to my parents, grateful for their support. The Birth Night Ball, celebrating the king's birthday, was the biggest night of the year and everyone who was any one made an appearance. Fresh dampness moistened my palms and I swallowed the nervousness threatening my composure. I'd begged for this opportunity, so I better not flag in my own courage. My friends would never let me forget if I didn't go through with my plan. I prayed for the strength to make it through the festivities without embarrassing myself or my family.

The beautiful gown gave me confidence, but would I remember the steps when the time came to move onto the floor with my father? I studied the movements of those dancing, rather than comparing the dancers' attire to my own. Mother had assured me the dress, the flowing silk brocade swishing gently with each step, served the purpose, maybe even better than the others. But did my manners and movements meet the mark of a young lady? I squared my shoulders, determined to present my best self.

Keeping a smile firmly in place, I perused the crowd engaged in watching the performance. A sea of heads nodded to the beat of the music, all eyes on the dance. Except for one pair of startling eyes gazing back at me, surprise and perhaps interest apparent even across the space between us. Something in his gaze drew me, but I dismissed it as whimsy. Still, I couldn't deny the familiar man continued to study me.

Daniel Custis. Tall and strong, and so handsome in his finery my heart skipped a beat before plunging into a gallop. The suit he wore reflected his prominence in the colony. Impeccable tailoring created the very essence of wealth and esteem in the lines and quality of the fabric of the coat, the sheen of the breeches and stockings. Highly polished gold shoe buckles reflected the light from hundreds of candles. I approved his appearance, recognizing it for the statement it was. He was the most eligible bachelor in Virginia. I'd known him in passing all of my life, aware of the mature, thoughtful, and much older man. Goodness, he couldn't be interested in me, though, not at twenty years or so my senior. Could he? He angled his head ever so slightly, enough to convey his appreciation. Never had a man looked at me with such a light shining from his soul. Warmth flooded my neck and crept to my cheeks. Goodness, how should I respond? Flustered, I clutched my fan with both hands. I blinked and then returned the nod before forcing my gaze to slide away from his. It would be unseemly to express too much interest. But I must admit to curiosity regarding his intentions.

"Patsy, it is time." Father appeared at my side, holding out one gloved hand.

Four simple words set my pulse pounding in my ears, damping the sound of the music. I put my hand in his, glad for the warmth and strength flowing into my fingers. I followed Father's lead and took my position, feeling as if all eyes rested upon me. The moment had arrived for me to be judged on my comportment and grace.

Father squeezed my hand, raised a brow, and smiled. "You're a beautiful and kind young woman, a prize for any man here. This is your night. I'm honored to be your first partner."

"Thank you, Father." Heat rose to my cheeks again. Lifting my chin, I vowed to do my best. The music signaled the beginning of the set and I fell into step, mirroring my father's movements as he led me through the dance.

We circled each other, first to the left, then to the right, clasping hands and then separating. In time, the rhythm of the music and the swish of my skirts combined with the repetitive movements to calm my agitation. Faces peering at me from the sidelines blurred into an indistinct image. As long as I paid attention to my actions I would retain my composure and with good fortune not trip over my feet. My father, the man who all my life had supported and encouraged, beamed his approval and pride.

The tune ended and the dancers performed their acknowledgements to one another, the men bowing, the women curtsying. I rose from my deep curtsy and my father crooked his arm to lead me off the floor, allowing the next set of eager couples to take their positions.

"That was lovely." Mother smiled, bumping her fan closed against one gloved palm. "You've made us both proud."

"I was so very nervous. Could you tell?" I needed something to do with my hands to conceal my nervousness. I retrieved my fan from where it dangled at my wrist, opening it to move slowly before my warm face.

"Not at all." Mother dropped her fan to hang from her wrist as she folded her hands before her. "Jack, darling, I'd adore a cup of punch."

He inclined his head in acknowledgment. "Patsy, would you care for some?"

Could I keep it down? Or would I spill it on my dress? Visions of terrible and mortifying results made me shake my head. "No, thank you. I believe I'll move closer to the window for some air."

"Very well. We shall return shortly." Father wrapped his hand around my mother's elbow and propelled her toward the array of delicacies spread on tables in the open space at the top of the stairs.

I made my way through the throng of guests to stand by the open window. A cool breeze bathed my cheeks, bringing the scent of dried leaves and the smoke of many fires to tickle my nose. Moonlight splayed across the formal garden and the buildings of the town in the distance. Naked trees stood starkly against the deep black of the starry heavens in the soft light. In a few months snow would blanket the land, but for now the ground remained hard and dry, making road travel possible if not pleasant. Aunt Unity had graciously invited us to ride to Williamsburg with her in a fine coach pulled by four matched black horses. Arriving in such a high fashion leant a different level of elegance to the ensuing events I hadn't dreamed of. Maybe one day I'd have my own coach-and-four to take me places.

Turning my back to the window, I observed the crowd. Through the arched door to one side, I spotted tables surrounded by seated card-playing guests. The music changed to a lively tune, announcing the beginning of the less formal English country dances. My parents eased through the crowd, stopping often to chat. They knew most everyone in the room as a result of their involvement in the colony's church and government.

I surveyed the other guests, feeling part of the society in an entirely new way. Not as a child looking through the window, but as an active member with my own role. Then my heart leapt into my throat when Daniel Custis separated from a circle of men, probably assemblymen of one rank or another, and strolled in my direction. What did he want? What would I say to him? Oh, how I wished my mother were at my side. I wasn't as ready as I'd thought.

He seemed intent on me in a way he'd never been before. Not when I'd seen him at church, or floating past the plantation in his schooner, or even when I accompanied my parents to Williamsburg for market day. I swallowed hard, clasping my trembling hands. When I'd been preparing for the ball it never occurred to me someone like the man drawing nearer with each beat of my heart would take any interest. He'd make a fine partner, with his sterling reputation and financial security.

On the other hand, becoming involved with him would mean having to deal with his quarrelsome and volatile father. My skin itched at the thought. Where was the old man, anyway? I skimmed the crowd, finally detecting John Custis, eyes narrowed, watching his son approach me. The man had a colony-wide reputation for his temper and vengeful attitude. I'd witnessed it at church on more than one occasion, given he and my father both served as vestrymen. No love was lost between them, either.

"Good evening, Miss Dandridge." Daniel greeted me with a bow. "Congratulations on fascinating every man in the room with your dancing and your charms."

"How kind of you to say so. However, I cannot imagine you are correct, sir." I spread my fan open and moved it lazily back and forth, heat once more on my cheeks. Acting as mature and grown as possible. Having something repetitive to do with my hands also calmed my sudden anxiety. "But I appreciate the sentiment."

"Verily, I say, you bewitched the bachelors with your grace and pleasing manners." Daniel shifted his weight, subtly closing the distance between us.

"Now I know you jest." I espied a new intensity in his gaze. His nearness set my heart aflutter, stealing my breath for a moment. "Where is your companion for the evening?"

He lifted a shoulder and let it drop. "I have not the honor of a companion but have arrived alone, as usual." He shot a glance over his shoulder, in the vague direction of where his father stood observing our conversation. Then his eyes returned to me, his lips curving into a seductive grin. "I shall be honored if you'd give me the pleasure of a dance."

I couldn't help but look at the older Mr. Custis. I was not at all surprised to note disapproval in his expression. My back went up, much like I'd seen the hunting dogs do when strangers approached the property. Hackles standing away from their necks as a warning. I am not quick to anger, which proved useful in times such as this. A slow burn started in my stomach at the continuing frown from across the room. Despite his opinion, what harm would one dance possibly do? Daniel was a man and could make his own decisions. Lifting my chin to meet Daniel's gaze as much as show his father how much I thought of his opinion, I nodded. "I'd enjoy dancing with you."

He held out a gloved hand with a smile on his lips. "Miss Dandridge."

I accepted his arm and followed him onto the floor as the musicians started a new tune. I intended to thoroughly enjoy myself. The weight of the elder Custis' glare threatened to make me stumble, but I ignored him, keeping my attention instead on his charming son. Out of the corner of my eye, I saw my parents exchange a look before turning to witness the dance. Daniel extended one leg to bow—a movement designed to demonstrate the strength of his legs—as I curtsied and lowered my eyes. Daniel's leg proved nice, indeed. Returning to a standing position, we regarded each other for a beat as the music wrapped around us. The dance soon drew my entire attention and had my feet flying. My heart raced with the touch of his hand guiding me to perform a turn in first one direction and then the other before parting for several steps.

Was it the idea of me being a woman now prompting me to search his face for signs of interest? Or perhaps the question of whose wife I wanted to be? Surely, he would not be truly interested, not when my father's financial situation could not hold a candle to John Custis' wealth. Yet something had changed inside, making my breath catch each time Daniel's twinkling eyes lit upon me. Making me notice the classic qualities of his face and long, straight nose. Making me wish for some miracle to make it possible such a distinguished man would consider me a suitable life companion. I imagined he asked me to dance as a charitable action, seeing that I stood alone while the dances continued. That thought settled in my stomach like a day-old biscuit, weighting my feet as well as my heart.

When the dance ended, Daniel and I bowed and curtsied again before he offered to escort me from the floor. Feeling suddenly silly and embarrassed, I laid my fingers on his steely forearm. He led me toward my parents, while a flutter of nervousness filled me.

Father cautiously greeted Daniel as they approached. Daniel returned the greeting, including Mother in his bow. Straightening, he relinquished my hand. "I surrender your daughter to your care, Colonel Dandridge."

"Thank you, Mr. Custis." Father lifted his cup of punch in salute. "Are you enjoying the ball?"

Daniel nodded, ending with a quick sideways look at me. "Congratulations on your daughter's successful presentation."

Father inclined his head to accept the compliment. "I never doubted her ability to win over any one. She is a very special young lady in our view."

Daniel cleared his throat and shifted closer to me, keeping his gaze on my parents. "Would you object if I were to wait upon your daughter?"

I inhaled sharply, converting a gasp of surprise into a deep breath. My heart bumped in my chest with alarming speed. What would Father say to such a request?

Father's brows arched, then relaxed. "We'd have no objection to your courtship, so long as she agrees." He turned to me and waited as I grappled with the concept.

Did Daniel's father know of his desire to visit me? I refused to look toward the elder Mr. Custis. Daniel, not his father, wished to call on me. Me! The earlier flutter stretched its wings like an eagle preparing to take flight. Daniel, the handsome, kind man beside me, wanted to become better acquainted. His fortune and management skills provided a solid foundation for a couple to carve out a life together. His plantation, White House, was only four miles from Chestnut Grove, and while not nearly as comfortable and inviting as Uncle William's Elsing Green, it was a step up from my home. As long as he wanted lots of children it might work. Daniel had everything to recommend him, other than his disagreeable father. Indeed, where would I ever find a better man to be my husband?

I tilted my head so I could meet his eyes, yet again wishing I was taller. I saw only approval and hope in Daniel's expression. There was only one thing I wished to make clear. "I have no objection."

---

What had I expected, after all? I swung the straw broom harder, sending dirt careering across the wood floor, a cloud of dust rising to make me cough. I sighed, realizing my childish expectation for what it was. I had hoped he'd come riding up to the front door the very next day. But an entire month had melted away into the return to daily tasks. I could kick myself for being so wanton. The glamor of my first ball existed only as a memory. The dance with Daniel one more event to recall, one relived countless times in the ensuing weeks.

Patient. I must be patient. I didn't want to be, but apparently I had no other option. Dirt scattered again. Taking a deep breath, I forced calm into my chest and slowed the movement of the broom. Creating more work for myself would not make Daniel visit any sooner. Besides, I had other work to do after I finished sweeping the parlor. Candles to dip, for instance. A quilt to finish the edging on. My brothers' socks to darn. Unfortunately, they were all tasks requiring no dedicated thought to perform which wouldn't keep me from listening for the sound of hoof beats.

Opening the back door, I swept the dirt outside and down the steps leading into the yard. I rested the broom on the ground, my cheek pressed against the pole handle, and pondered the Pamunkey flowing past the dock in the distance. Smoke rose in separate columns from the chimneys and the smokehouse, a rising whirlpool spinning in place before drifting away. The scent of smoking hams hung heavy in the air. A flock of geese honked a chorus on their way by, their distinctive V formation wavering as they crossed the ashen sky. Snow clouds formed on the horizon and I shivered at the mere hint of the white flakes. Every winter the cold and damp seeped into my bones, refusing to be banished until the spring sun thawed the ground.

I thought back to when I'd voiced my intent to find a husband who would help me elevate my station in life and let me achieve my yearning for having many children. Mother had nodded and agreed with my intent, telling me she'd done a similar thing when she'd accepted my father's hand. Given my desires, she started teaching me what I'd need to know to become an efficient plantation mistress.

The months before my presentation had been filled with both academic and dance lessons with the itinerant tutor and the endless routine of daily tasks. But I did them with a new sense of purpose. I even paid closer attention to the subject I disliked most: managing the health of the family and slaves, including how to prepare and distill the various cordials, marmalets, and other medicines. I detested the pungent smell of the concoctions. My mother, however, insisted my duty as mistress of a plantation incorporated the wellness of every member of the family, which also meant the servants.

Mother told me of the need to oversee the food and drinks consumed by every member of the household, as well as preserving food and smoking hams, brewing beer, and knowing how much of each to give to the slaves and overseers. Doling out the precious and expensive foods and flavorings that could only be obtained via England from the West Indies or Spain, like wine, gin, raisins, bitter almonds, and ambergris. Every task, every bit of work, represented the necessary activities of a well-run plantation. There were so many tasks, too.

Mother's patient instruction would enable me to be a successful plantation mistress, but I still worried about how to be a wife. Of what exactly would happen behind the closed door of the bedchamber. Of what a husband would expect or demand from me. I wouldn't solve those mysteries until I married, a thought that shook my confidence each time it flitted through my mind.

I'd been so sure of Daniel's interest. I hoped he meant it when he'd expressed a desire to court me. Every day I listened for his approach on the wide dirt carriage-way leading up to the front door. So much so, ghost hoof beats filled my ears. When I could sneak away from a task, I'd spy out a window to see if maybe I actually did hear them. Unfortunately, only the usual slaves and kin going about their days appeared in the front yard. Even now, the sound of the distant one-two, one-two beat of a trotting horse echoed in my mind. I shook my head and chastised myself for fanciful ponderings. On a sigh, I went back inside.

Placing the broom in its place, I strode into the main hall then crossed into the parlor and took my seat to do the darning. One of my least favorite duties, I'd put it off as long as possible. What did my brothers do to their stockings? I held up one and peered at the good sized hole and grimaced. Slipping the ball into the toe, I grasped the darning needle and began the task of closing the gap in the knitted garment. As soon as I stuck the needle between the threads, hoof beats sounded in my ears again. I ignored them, chiding myself for succumbing to such childish nonsense, but they grew louder until I couldn't dismiss the sound. Raising my head, I listened closely but they stopped. Again. I bent over my work.

"Patsy, Patsy!" Nancy, my seven-year-old sister, ran into the parlor, her face alight. Little Frances, her long white baby dress dancing about her ankles, toddled in behind her. "He's here!"

Surprise. Joy. Disbelief. Dismay. All flashed through me at Nancy's declaration. Goodness, I hadn't expected him to show up now. I glanced at my day dress, relieved to see one of my prettiest ones. Fortunately, I'd heeded my mother's instruction to always be prepared for company as people journeyed past the plantation. With no decent boarding homes or road houses, hospitality required the planters to entertain and house the travelers. That expectation also made it necessary for lessons in music and dancing, so we could entertain our guests. Setting aside my sewing with trembling hands, I rose and faced my sister.

"Who is here?" I fought to suppress the insistent urge to run to the window to see for myself. I had my pride, too.

"Daniel Custis, who else?" Nancy propped her fists on her slim hips and stared at me. "Don't be pretending you haven't been praying he'd come courting."

Caught in the act of prevaricating. "I can't very well go running to the door, now can I?"

"No, but you should get ready instead of arguing with me."

Nancy's frown shifted to a grin when we heard the deep voice of the doorman invite Daniel inside. "Too late."

"Do I look all right? Is my hair in order?" I peered at Nancy, holding my breath and patting at my hair until she nodded. Thank goodness. "Take Frances and go on up to our room."

Nancy arched her brows. "You wish to be alone with him?"

"I'm sure Father will arrive in due order, but little girls do not need to be underfoot." Booted steps neared in the passageway. Heart racing, I took hold of Nancy's shoulders and spun her around. "Now go!"

Nancy recovered her balance, and grasped Frances' hand. "Don't be so high-handed."

I leveled a stern look at my sisters, hoping I'd mastered my mother's expression demanding prompt obedience. Nancy huffed and led our youngest sister out of the room at a run. I hurried to my seat by the fireplace and smoothed my skirts. Snatching up my sewing, I stared at the stocking and the needle, unable to concentrate on the simple task with the sound of boots in the passage.

Then Daniel filled the open door, his hat in his hands, and a polite smile on his lips. My father appeared behind our guest. Daniel started, glanced over his shoulder at my father, and then stepped into the room. Father strode over to stand by me and regarded the visitor with a lifted brow. Surely my heart would burst into view, it pounded so hard in my chest. Anxiety set off a flurry of butterflies in my midsection, waiting to hear what he had to say. He'd finally made an appearance. While I was overjoyed to see him, I'd give him a piece of my mind for not honoring his own request for so long.

"Hello, Miss Dandridge. You are looking fine." Daniel bowed, sweeping his hat behind him, then straightened to regard me. "Your father has given his permission for me to properly court you."

"I believe he granted the privilege a while back, Mr. Custis." I held the sewing in my lap, burying my fingers into the soft wool. I didn't want to put him off, but he must understand my feelings regarding his actions. "As did I."

Daniel had the grace to appear abashed. "Indeed, Miss Dandridge. I regret my attention has been unavoidably consumed by more pressing matters at various farms. Matters requiring my immediate attention. My thoughts, however, have not strayed from you since I last beheld your beauty."

Doubtful, what with all the responsibilities the planter managed, but a pleasing compliment. I gestured to the cushioned chairs positioned facing each other over a low cherry table to form a cozy group in front of the fireplace. Could he see how nervous I was at the thought of actually being courted by him? "Please, gentlemen, have a seat. Would you enjoy tea?"

At his nod, I rather clumsily signaled Old Sally, waiting in the passageway, to bring in the tea tray. I had yet to master the subtleties of managing the household. Mother had much to teach me yet. As the servant turned to do as bidden, Mother made her entrance into the parlor, greeting our guest with a smile as she sat beside me. We exchanged pleasantries until Old Sally returned with the oversized tray, containing a silver tea pot and an array of small plates bearing biscuits, jam, and dried fruits. She placed it on the low table and then left the room. Mother served the tea, smoothly pouring the amber fluid into the flowered china cups and handing them round. All this while I tried not to stare at Daniel, not reveal how elated I felt at his presence, and not tremble when he caught my eye.

All the lessons I had learned over the years melded in my mind as I listened to the ebb and flow of conversation. Lessons on appropriate topics and ways to make a guest comfortable. Lessons on proper posture and how to sit, hold a cup, and even position my feet. The subtle lessons of interpreting a person's social rank based on their manners and clothing, as well as how they expressed themselves, I'd learned through observation and paying careful attention. All of them blended into a seamless desire to be polite, caring, and sociable, the hallmarks of hospitality. Most of all, if I could demonstrate my ability to be a proper wife and mistress, perhaps Daniel would indeed offer for me. The first step of my life plan might be at hand.

Daniel spoke with the confidence befitting his station. His regard made me bubble inside each time his eyes turned my direction.

"I'm on my way to Williamsburg, to Six Chimneys House for several days." Daniel set his cup and saucer on the table. "May I wait on you upon my return?"

I could easily forgive his neglect after his apology and explanation. I wanted to know him better. Was he as decent a man as he seemed to be? By all accounts, the answer would prove to be a resounding yes. "I will look forward to your visit."

We engaged in the first of many conversations right there in the parlor, with my parents as chaperones. The longer we talked, the more certain I became our acquaintance could lead to a friendship and, with good fortune, mayhap something more.

---

Over the course of the next year, we grew closer as we became better acquainted. I didn't fret about the length of time, needing to assure myself and my parents Daniel would be a faithful and good husband. I took advantage of the time to refine my mannerisms, my conversational skills, and most of all my knowledge of household management.

One fall day, Daniel and I went riding along the river. I enjoyed the motion of my little gray mare with her black mane and tail. I'd chosen my favorite riding habit, its long maroon skirts with black lace trim draped over the sidesaddle, a black coat with short split skirts over a white shirt, and topped with a smart black tricorne hat with ribbons down my back. I'd put the outfit together to create an air of maturity and competence as well as to complement the coloring of my mount, Darby. Daniel's dapple gray stallion, Arrow, pranced impatiently under the control of the big man. Our horses crushed red, gold, and brown fallen leaves under their hooves with each step. Half-barren trees guarded the river banks, the forests dotted with swamps stretching away on both sides of the flowing water. We reached our favorite copse and dismounted, holding the reins and each other's hands as we strolled together.

The tenor and cadence of his voice had become my favorite sound in all the world. He had shared his plans for White House, including the horse breeding efforts, expanding the orchard, and clearing more of the forest to increase the tobacco crops. I had learned about his childhood, the animosity and arguing between his mother and father until the poor woman died of smallpox in 1715 when he was but four years old. He shared his hopes for finding a wife who would make him happy, not angry and suspicious like his father. He was the youngest child: two others had died in infancy, and his poor sister Fanny, who had died four years ago. The story he told of Fanny's former suitors and marriages had set off a warning bell in my mind.

His father, John Custis, wasn't only quarrelsome and mean, but suspicious. He eyed potential suitors with an unhealthy dose of chariness. Fanny's first suitor, a ship's captain, declared his intention to marry her. John suspected the man wanted her fortune, not her person. His suspicion was confirmed when the captain started pestering John about Fanny's dowry, specifically how much land and money would be settled on her. John declared that if she married the captain, she'd do so without any dowry, which sent the captain back to his ship and out of her life. Before long, another man claimed he wished to marry Fanny, but John again threatened to disinherit her, and the man departed two days prior to the wedding. Ultimately, Fanny chose to marry twice, both times without their father's blessing or money. She had a difficult life as a result of John Custis' miserly suspicions, until she died in 1744.

Suddenly, Daniel stopped, tugging me to a halt.

"Patsy, my darling, I have a confession." He stood calm and serious, gazing at me with an intensity unusual in his countenance.

"Yes, Daniel?"

He squeezed my fingers and leveled a solemn look at me. "I feel we make a good match. I enjoy your company, find you easy to be with, to talk to. You're pretty and capable and a pleasure to be around. I adore you and wish to marry you, if you'll consent to be my wife."

I wanted to squeal with delight, but my upbringing forbade such a childish reaction. "I agree we have a good foundation for a successful marriage." I smiled at him, happiness flooding my heart and soul. He'd finally asked for my hand, to join our families and fortunes, such as they were, together. "I'm fond of you, as well."

"If our marriage is like that of your parents, we'll grow to love each other over time." Daniel kissed me, a quick press of his lips to mine, then gazed at me for several moments before sighing. "There is only one obstacle to our marriage."

I moistened my lips, savoring the fleeting yet tantalizing touch of his to mine. My first kiss from a man and it was very pleasant. I smiled confidently at him, pleased we shared a willingness to allow our relationship to grow naturally. Joining our families benefited all parties. As for the obstacle, I could guess at the hurdle before us. "Whatever it may be, I'm sure we can overcome it."

He glanced away, shaking his head slowly. After a few seconds he snared my gaze again. "I'm not sure we will."

Curious, I raised a brow in question. "What is it?"

"My father has objected to every woman I've ever courted." He studied my expression, judging my reaction to his confession. "I know not how to tell him I fully intend to marry you. You must be patient until I can persuade him of my sincerity and receive his blessing of the union."

"Do we need his blessing? Are you not of age to make such a decision on your own?"

"My father's own bad marriage to my mother left a bitter taste in his mouth and distrust in his soul. He fears fortune hunters will steal away his wealth."

"I'm no fortune hunter, Daniel." I desired to improve myself, but I had no intention of marrying for money. I wanted friendship, security, and a large family with a kind and caring man. With *this* man. "What are you afraid of?"

"You don't understand how he is." He ran one hand down his jaw as he gazed over his horse's head, silent, thinking. Then he looked at me again. "When I told Father the slaves at White House needed shoes, he flew into such a rage over the expense, and supposedly my poor management, he tried to free his favorite son, my half-brother, Mulatto Jack, then give him a tract of land near Queens Creek, a tract which once belonged to my mother. He even tried to give Jack his own mother, young Alice." He shook his head, remembered anger evident in the furrows and tension on his face. "It took months of arguing with him, both by me and his friends, about the illegality of his actions before he rescinded his gifts and his new will that left everything to Jack. Do you understand? He tried to take my inheritance and give it to a slave, all because I dared to tell him the other slaves needed shoes."

"Over shoes?" I was aghast. The man had lost his sense.

Daniel shook his head, his expression immeasurably sad and pensive. "I detest having to reveal how malicious my father can be. I'm told he heard rumors of my courting you, then flew into yet another rage and began giving away his most precious items. Most recently, he presented to Matthew and Anne Moody, his neighbors in town, a dozen black walnut chairs and a table among other furniture, a roan horse and chair harness, and most grievously the collection of silver plate bearing the family crest."

Anger swept through me on Daniel's behalf. How dare the old man give away family heirlooms? Had he no sense of what it meant to be a family? "Did they not protest? They shouldn't have accepted such valuable and precious items."

"Mrs. Moody attempted to make him desist, but..." Daniel swiped a hand over his head, loosening a few strands from his queue.

"What is it, Daniel? What did he do?"

"He's been speaking against your father, my sweet dear, and even your caring person. He's been abusing your father's reputation, disparaging his good name and his position." He dragged in a deep breath and released it in a rush. "I must tell you, to prepare you for his claims. He said he'd dispose of his property as he pleased and throw everything into the street for any one to pick up rather than allow any Dandridge's daughter or any Dandridge have them." He shook his head again, eyes glittering as he peered at me. "I must not aggravate him further or all will be lost."

The revelation chilled me first, then fueled a fire of indignation. How dare the man spread such evil and hurtful lies regarding my father? I glanced at the river, then up at the puffy clouds drifting across the blue sky. Delaying until I had tamed my temper. All the while, my stomach churned and my cheeks flamed.

*Blast the man.* He'd prevented Daniel from having a decent childhood with all his anger and spite, and now he actively sought to ensure his son never found happiness and contentment with a companion. Well, not if I could help it. All my ability to influence another's actions or opinions may be put to the test, but I'd give it my best effort. I lifted my chin and studied Daniel's aggrieved countenance while silently counting to ten.

"But your duty is to marry and provide heirs. Doesn't your father wish for you to have a companion and children?"

"I do not believe so, not after all these years. I'm tired of trying to find someone he'd approve of, which he doesn't seem inclined to ever do. Instead I will insist upon marrying a woman who makes me happy. You, my dear, make me happy. I'll have you as my wife even if our fathers cannot get along."

Ah, there it was. The other shoe hitting the floor. The animosity John Custis had for my father, the disdain and disregard. Colonel John Dandridge commanded respect throughout New Kent County as both a military leader and eminent planter. He was commander of the militia and served as the Clerk of the Court. Yet his wealth, while sufficient for a large family on a five-hundred-acre plantation, could not match that of John Custis with his two plantations totaling more than nineteen thousand acres spread over six counties. But if I married Daniel, then our fathers would be forced to have an intercourse—to talk and engage in social contact—whether they wanted to or not. An uncomfortable situation would result in the joining of the families. On the other hand, perhaps the union would also bring an end to the animosity.

"What would you have me do?"

"Be patient. I will find a way to convince him to bestow his blessing on our union."

"And if you can't?" Patience and I did not always get along well. I searched his eyes, descrying uncertainty and concern. "What then?"

He gripped my hands and kissed my cheek. "Trust me to find a way in my own time. In due course, we will marry. You have my word as a gentleman."

"Very well. I will attempt to be patient. But heed my words." I stared at him, trying to convey the extent of how serious my next words would be. "You cannot expect me to wait forever for your father's approval. I want to start my own family while I'm young enough to do so."

He kissed my cheek again, then helped me mount. "I understand. Now it is time I return you to the safety of your home."

Did he understand how far I would go to ensure his happiness? I took up the reins and urged my mare to turn toward the stable, Daniel soon beside me. I'd bide my time, but if he didn't manage to persuade his father of our intentions, then I may have to take the matter into my own hands.

# 2

*Chestnut Grove – 1749*

"Are you certain this is a good idea?" My brother Jacky's deep voice carried to my ears over the steady beat of the Pamunkey against the skiff's quivering hull and the twitter of song birds in the trees and bushes. I clutched the wooden seat beneath me as I bit my lip to keep my unease inside.

As he went through puberty, his tenor had lowered in steps, creating an often fickle pitch to his voice until it reached its current manly tone. I would never tell him, but sometimes I had mentally played with the sound like a musical piece. I heard music in everything, the shouts of the overseers, the birds flitting by, the soughing of the wind, even the river after a heavy rain. I breathed in the warm spring air. The scent of wildflowers blooming along the banks mingled with the pleasing aroma of the river. I'd finally settled on my favorite dark green dress for our secret mission. Its classic lines and somber colors, along with the cute hat with its half veil and plume, made me feel confident and mature. Well, except for the fact that I really did not like being in a boat. Of any size.

I glanced at my brother's worried expression and chuckled, though I quaked inside at my own audacity. I had thought about what I'd do if Daniel's efforts failed. After two long years had passed, my patience ended. Two years of growing more and more fond of Daniel, and longing to become united to him as his wife and start a family. I'd had to summon all my nerve, determination, and anger to devise the plan my brother and I now engaged in. Taking the boat meant a quicker journey, but oh I wish we could have ridden. But then my father would have known what we were up to. "It's the only way I can conjure which has any hope of success to secure a future with Daniel."

"You should have told Father of your plan. He'll be upset."

"He won't even notice we're gone, what with his concern regarding Mother's well-being." Our mother was due to have another baby within the next couple of months, child number seven. Would it be a brother or sister? Either way, I'd love the little one as much as I loved all of them. I had been born first, followed by Jacky a year later, then William two years later, Bartholomew three years after that, Nancy two after Bat, followed by Frances five years after my favorite sister was born, and now this new addition, whoever it might be.

After I married Daniel, we could start our own family. I envisioned having quite a full house, perhaps seven or eight children. The joys and laughter we'd share would rock the house. I could picture it in my mind as if it were a fond memory. For now, I enjoyed the company of all of my kinsfolk. Jacky, in particular, had become my favorite brother because of his eagerness to engage in our secret missions.

I winked at him with a toss of my head. "Besides, I have you as my escort, my protector. What is there for him to worry over?"

Jacky huffed. "The fact that we're going into Williamsburg without his knowledge or permission?"

"You know he'd have forbidden me to make this overture." I looked at him, then back to the flowing river ahead. My nineteenth birthday loomed on the horizon and yet my wedding did not. I intended to do something about the situation. "I must try or suffer the pangs of regret all my days."

"You're so dramatic at times." He laughed, a rich endearing sound.

"Thank you for agreeing despite your reservations as to the sanity of this errand."

"You know I'd do anything for you, to help you, right?" Jacky regarded me with a mix of love and mischief in his eyes. "Even if it lands us in trouble with Father."

I laughed with him, recalling the many previous times our actions had brought Father's ire. We didn't try to anger him, but somehow events unfolded in ways we'd never planned. Like the night we slipped out of the house, tiptoeing over the loudest squeaky boards, to marvel at the stars scattered across the velvety sky. Then to be locked out of the house when the inside bar dropped into place. Finding no other way to enter, we'd been forced to rouse the household. Our father's stern lecture while he whipped us still smarted. Or the time when we'd ridden our horses bareback into the Pamunkey to reach the little island in the middle even though recent rains had made the river fast and deep. He'd been more than aggravated at the risks we'd taken, for ourselves and our mounts.

We glided down the river in silence for a few minutes more, the soft morning breeze cool on my clammy skin. Then the first buildings and the pier on the edge of the capitol came into view and my heart flipped up into my throat. I forced it back to its proper lodgings, drawing upon every bit of my training to remain calm and poised to face John Custis. Alone.

Soon—too soon—we docked the boat, my relief great, and then walked up the lane to Six Chimneys House. The stately home suited its owner. Built of brick and stone, surrounded by the beginnings of a formal garden, John Custis built his home to last. To stand as a testament to the man and his wealth, his social rank and power in Virginia and its government. I swallowed the fear threatening to claim my power of speech. Jacky and I paused at the end of the brick walk leading up to the front steps and door. Behind him a maple tree shaded a stone bench along the side of the road.

"I can go in with you, if you've changed your mind." Jacky smiled, his support and encouragement gleaming in his eyes. "I don't mind."

"I must do this on my own." I patted his arm, glad for the strength and unconditional support of my sixteen-year-old brother, and then turned to face the walk. "This most likely will not take long. He may even throw me out of his house." I squared my shoulders as I stepped off. "Here goes."

I rapped on the door and then turned back to smile at Jacky, waiting at the end of the walk. He raised a brow in question but I shook my head before facing the door again. I'd thought long and hard about what I would say. After months of Daniel's attempts to placate his father, he'd grown ever more fearful of the man's wrath should he defy the elder man's restrictions. A very real concern, both on a personal and a financial level. If I had any hope of winning over the irascible, hateful, suspicious old man, I had to stand on my own merits.

The door swung open to reveal a medium-height man, his shock of gray hair complementing gray eyes. The butler wore the Custis livery, including the family crest—a white spread-eagle on red ground with the head and neck of a griffin at the top—embroidered over his heart. He carried his slightly bowed shoulders with an air of patience and respect suited to his station. He didn't look particularly happy to see me but held the door only part way open as he perused my person.

"May I help you?" His voice was rough and gravelly, but kind.

"I'm Miss Martha Dandridge. I wish to speak to Mr. Custis." My voice came out stronger than I'd thought it would, bolstering my confidence.

"Is he expecting you, Miss?"

"I'm afraid I've come without sending word of my intent." Would he be offended I'd not made prior arrangements to talk to him? But if I had, surely he would have rejected such an imposition out of hand. No, it was better to show up on his door step and beg admittance.

"If you'll wait in the parlor, I'll see if he has a moment." The butler ushered me inside, closing the heavy door firmly behind me with a *thud* that echoed in the large hall extending to the back of the house.

A quick glimpse into the dining room revealed an ornate table with a collection of tea bowls and wine glasses, beautifully etched to catch the light. Left to wait in the formal parlor, I strolled around the elaborately decorated and furnished room. Here again John Custis' wealth and power made itself known no matter where I looked. The elegance and quality was evidenced by the couch and chairs flanking the graceful carved low table bearing a gleaming silver-and-ivory tea service. The mahogany-and-glass bookcase reflected it as well, its shelves of expensive leather-bound books protected by drop-down glass doors. The oil painting of the elder Custis hanging above the fireplace indicated his stature in the colony, his austere and arrogant countenance gazing down on me with condescension. Or was my imagination playing with me? Either way, being in the house made me restless, so I paced from table to chair to bookcase and back to where I started.

The thump of a cane preceded John Custis stopping in the open door. I stifled a gasp at his appearance. Daniel had mentioned his father's health had suffered, just one reason why his violent actions had become ever more bizarre. His small eyes glared at me, scraggy brows drawn together and thin lips pressed flat. His frame held little flesh, making the points and hollows of his skeleton more evident beneath his richly decorated apparel. It flitted through my mind that we may have to wait until he died to marry. Then he wouldn't have a say in the matter. I dismissed the thought as uncharitable, and studied the man who stood between me and my happiness.

Stomping his way into the parlor, he waved toward a chair as he lowered himself onto the couch facing the entrance. "What do you want?"

He was nothing if not blunt. I forced a smile as I settled on the indicated seat. I'd be kind no matter how mean he became.

"I've come to speak with you about my relationship with your son."

"Ha! You don't have a relationship with my son."

"Sir, I beg your forgiveness for disagreeing." I took a breath and went on. "You know Daniel has been courting me. That is the relationship of which I speak."

"There is no relationship, not one I will ever condone." He banged his cane on the oriental carpet. "Same thing."

I took a moment to compose myself, refusing to be drawn into arguing with Daniel's father. The old man wanted me to fight with him. I could see it in his hard expression, in the tense angles of his body. A fight would end badly for all parties concerned. Searching my mind, I hunted for a way to persuade him to be open to our courtship and eventually to our marriage.

"Mr. Custis, please consider what you are doing to your son. I want only to be a proper Christian wife to him, to provide him children who will live to carry on the Custis name into perpetuity. As his father, I'm certain you want Daniel to be happy and prosperous. And he finds my companionship pleasing. Together we will make sure your name remains in living memory and is not forgotten."

He tapped one bony finger on his cane, the polished wood knob carved into the shape of a duck's head. "I have another son. Mulatto Jack. He will carry my name with more respect and reverence than Daniel."

"I cannot speak for Daniel's feelings, sir. But Mulatto Jack does not bear your name, does he?"

John gestured it made no difference and leaned forward, resting both hands on the duck head. "Whether or no, what can you bring to this union versus what you will receive, namely access to my fortune? That is your real intent, is it not? The money?"

I hitched my chin to capture his suspicious gaze with mine. "I bring love and caring to your son, and the knowledge of how to manage the White House household as a proper plantation mistress so he may work on larger concerns. Also, I bring happiness to your son. The kind of happiness you had hoped for in your marriage but unfortunately didn't find. Would you withhold the opportunity for Daniel to be content and prosperous as a result of your unhappy experience?"

Clasping cold fingers together on my lap, I kept my gaze steady. Waited as he studied me for several excruciating minutes, his heavy frown lightening by degrees. I prayed to my loving God to grant him the strength to admit he'd been wrong, to bestow his blessing on our intended marriage. He relaxed against the couch, his considering gaze not flickering. I'd said what I came to say. As the minutes ticked by, the truth settled onto my shoulders like a heavy winter snowfall. I'd failed to convince him of my love for Daniel. Time to leave.

"Please think about what I've said, sir. I implore you to consider your son's future as well as the future of your family." I rose to my feet. "If you'll excuse me."

As I spun to make my way from the room, retaining my composure with all my might, I heard the man struggle to his feet. Glancing over my shoulder, I was surprised to see him smiling, if the slight upward curve of his lips revealing yellowed teeth could be called a smile. Still, I'd made progress in how he looked at me.

"I will contemplate your points, Miss Dandridge." He nodded, slowly bobbing his head four times. "You've given me much to consider. But do not hope for my blessing."

My heart fell at his words. I dipped a quick curtsy and said my farewells. Standing on the front step of the brick home, I paused as the butler closed the door behind me. Jacky looked my way at the sound, rising from his seat on the stone bench.

Mayhap I'd managed to begin to turn the tide of the old man's negative opinion in my favor. But then, perhaps not.

"So, good news?" Jacky straightened his coat as I neared.

"He merely said he'll think on what I said." I sent a quick prayer to the heavens. "He also said not to count on his blessing of our union."

"I'm sorry he did not succumb to your charms, sister. But for now..." He glanced at the sun beginning its descent into the western sky. "Time to hasten home. I'm sure Father has missed us by now."

We took off down the road toward the pier and the dreaded skiff. "You are correct. We should hurry."

We soon settled into the boat, and Jacky began poling to fight our way back upstream. I'd done what I came to do. I tried my best to convince the irascible man. As we neared Chestnut Grove, I studied the main house as the boat angled toward the dock. The central sturdy door had been made from poplar, like the window casings. At either end of the good-sized clapboard house rose two brick chimneys poking through the white oak shingled roof. A variety of flowering bushes and plants softened the appearance of the brick-and-board structure. Around it, smaller buildings stood: the kitchen, laundry, smokehouse, privy. Chestnut Grove was the only home I'd ever known. If I'd succeeded in my mission, the two-story frame house would become my childhood home. I'd move away, to a new home, a new husband, a new life.

---

A week or so later, I sat in the front parlor, stitching on a quilt while my mother sat across from me working on a baby dress. The breeze carried the heady combination of daffodils, manure, and the ever-present smoke from fires lit for cooking or heating water for the laundry. Mourning doves, mockingbirds, and red-winged blackbirds created a chorus of song.

The sound of galloping hooves made me look up from my work. Someone certainly was in a hurry to be traveling at such a pace. I rose and crossed to the window. A familiar gray stallion carried an equally familiar man closer with each second.

"Who is it?" Mother rested her hands on her distended belly, the sand-colored fabric hanging from her fingers.

"It's Daniel." I watched him rein in his horse, nearly making him rear in the sudden stop. "He appears to be unusually reckless in his riding this morning."

"That doesn't sound like him." She returned to her stitching, inserting the needle into the fabric and drawing the thread through to attach the lace edge to the hem. "We'll learn what drives him so in due time. Resume your work while we wait."

I did as bade, though I couldn't prevent my gaze from straying to the door where my suitor would soon appear. He'd not visited for ten very long days and now he arrived in a flurry. Had my visit to the old man yielded the opposite results I'd intended? My fingers trembled as I inserted the needle and pulled another precise stitch into place.

Booted footsteps in the hall announced his entry into the house. Catching my mother's eye, a look telling me to be patient and poised, I glanced at the door as Daniel filled the opening. He wore a wide grin, his eyes sparkling as he closed the distance between us in several long strides.

"Mrs. Dandridge." He bowed to my mother, who nodded in return. Then he approached me, his eyes puzzled. "I've missed your pretty smile."

"And I've missed you as well. Pray tell me why you arrived in such a rush." I gazed up at him, noted the relaxed yet questioning expression gracing his features. "Poor Arrow nearly reared when you commanded him to halt."

"Because of happy news." Daniel withdrew a paper from his inside coat pocket and began unfolding it. He held the missive in front of him as he aimed a bemused grin at me. "I'd asked some friends to talk with my father regarding my intentions toward you, my dear."

I swallowed and nodded, afraid my attempt to reconcile had indeed gone against our cause. "And what happened? Did they fail as well?"

"Yes, unfortunately they did." He peered at me, his smile widening. "But then I beseeched another friend, James Power, to visit Father. James is an attorney in Williamsburg, and well acquainted with my father's opinion and manners. He'd said he'd try, but not to raise my hopes of his success. I've been waiting for weeks for his report."

"And he failed as well, no doubt." My heart fell, slowing until I thought it might stop. Nothing any one could say would sway the bitter man into having a good opinion of me, or of blessing our union. I studied the growing smile on Daniel's face, hope returning with each moment.

Daniel shook his head. "I want to read you a bit, and then I have a question for you."

I dipped my head, the weight of my worry heavy, and then raised my eyes to look at him. No matter what happened, I had done my best. "Very well."

He cleared his throat, and held up the page as though reading a proclamation in the town square. "Hear ye, hear ye…"

I aimed what I hoped was a reproachful look at him, one that failed miserably when I broke into a smile. "Pray, read the letter and stop the foolishness. I cannot bear the suspense."

"As you wish." He chuckled, cleared his throat again, and then read the entire letter to his captivated audience. The main message proved startling in a very good way.

"Your father approves?" A rush of disbelief and joy swept through me as I stared at Daniel.

He laughed and nodded as he folded the letter and returned it to his coat pocket. "What did you say to him? What was the 'prudent speech' you gave?"

"That was a private conversation between him and me, and I do not wish to share it with any one." I blinked and then shrugged. I didn't remember my exact words and didn't want to share the personal details of the exchange. "It makes no matter now, as long as it worked."

"I have a better question." Mother rose from her chair and stepped closer to me, a raised brow the only indication of her darkening mood.

*Gramercy.* No one had missed me and Jack on our secret mission. I'd thought we'd gotten away with our transgression. I sighed. The cat was out of the bag now. "Yes, Mother?"

"When exactly did you speak to Mr. Custis?"

Guilt and remorse for my wayward behavior warred with delight over my success. "A while back."

Mother arched both brows, her expression stern. "Where did this conversation occur?"

A quick gulp cleared the lump in my throat. "Williamsburg."

"And how, might I ask, did you get there?"

I glanced at Daniel, his earlier carefree countenance clouded. My mother's expression did not bode well, either. "Jacky and I took the skiff."

Fanny slowly shook her head, her disappointment filling the air. "You dragged your younger brother into yet another hazardous escapade. We had no idea you'd left the house, let alone the plantation itself. What if you'd been injured, or robbed?"

"But we weren't." I pasted a weak smile on my lips. Mother spoke the truth. The world held many dangers. Still, we had returned unscathed. "And now I can marry Daniel."

She crossed her arms and speared me with the look that made even my father quake in his boots. "Do not ever believe any desire warrants employing secretive means of acquiring it. Instead of sneaking off like thieves in the night, you should have spoken to your father and me. We would have accompanied you as is proper. Am I understood?"

Repentant, I lowered my eyes to study the floor boards. The move also meant not witnessing the harsh chastisement in her regard. "Yes, Mother."

Daniel took my hands, drawing my gaze up to meet his. "I agree you took unnecessary risks but I am also glad your efforts accomplished our aim. Now I may ask your father for your hand."

I smiled into his happy eyes. "Please."

"I'm certain he will approve of your request, Daniel." Mother lowered her hands to her sides and nodded. "He's been waiting for you to speak with him."

"It's been too long already." Daniel squeezed my hands and then kissed the backs. "I'll seek him out this moment, then I must away to my father's to ensure all is well with him."

"Go and make the necessary arrangements so we can set the date for our marriage." I moved closer to my mother, a flurry of questions in my mind, not least of which centered on what gown to wear. "We don't want to delay and have him change his mind, like Mr. Powers said."

"I won't be away long." He pressed his lips to my fingers, then snared my gaze with his. "You are my happiness, Patsy Dandridge."

I smiled, recalling my conversation with his father. "We will always be happy together, Daniel Custis."

---

Summer heat surrounded me as I hovered over my brother. The pungent odor of the medicine fought the smell of disease, combining to make me cough and my stomach to churn. Tucking the quilt into place over Jacky, I prayed for a miracle. I'd never seen any one so sick before, so weakened by a virulent attack of the dreaded smallpox.

"Don't go…" Jacky's scratchy voice emerged from dry lips.

His bloodshot eyes implored me to stay, but Mother had insisted I let him rest. Besides, I hated seeing his body covered in the raised flat blisters of pus. Hated seeing him feverish and aching. The pain he must be in, to writhe and moan for days. He'd complained of his back hurting, his head aching, of bone-deep fatigue. Mother had some experience with treating the often deadly disease, so I would follow her lead. And pray.

"I'll be back soon." I gathered the soiled linens off the chair where I'd placed them earlier. "You rest, like Mother advised, and you'll pull through."

He closed his eyes and rolled his head side to side. "I pray you're right, but at the moment I have serious doubts."

I clutched the bedclothes to my chest. Memories of riding together and playing pranks on our kinsfolk floated through my mind. If only the new smallpox inoculation didn't kill as often as it saved, mayhap my brother wouldn't be so sick. The Virginia assembly had banned the use of the inoculation, believing it spread the disease. Something certainly spread it, because it seemed to be everywhere. Fortunately, not every person who contracted smallpox died. If a person only had a mild case they'd be immune to it from then on, though they were marked for life by pox scars.

"You mustn't think that way. You'll be up and about before you know it."

"You're right." He opened his eyes and stared at me for several moments. "I'm so very tired. I think I will take a nap." He struggled onto his side and closed his eyes again.

I fought the panic rising in my chest, pushing into my throat. My young, strong, full of life brother couldn't die. Even in repose, Jacky's face held lines of tension, pain, and fatigue. I couldn't do anything more at the moment. Helpless but not hopeless, all I could do was try to ease his pain, lower his fever, and help him sip water from a cup. I had no magic or miracle to heal him. Tears sprang to my eyes as I slipped out the door and pulled it closed.

The cry of two-month-old Betsy drew me down the creaking stairs and across the hall smelling of fresh flowers and furniture polish to the sitting room. Peeking inside, I spied Mother resting on her favorite rocking chair with the infant already seeking her breast. Her hair stuck out from the hastily wrapped bun and her features revealed the strain she endured. After the baby began sucking, my mother looked up and then frowned.

She indicated with her head the bundle in my arms. "Take those outside and have them boiled."

I nodded, started to turn away, and then faced my mother again. "Will he be all right?"

"Only God knows the answer to such a question." She glanced at Betsy before considering me again. "All we can do is ease his suffering and pray."

"What if that's not enough?" The words hung in the room. My eyes smarted with unshed tears.

"There's no sense dwelling on what-if's." Mother's tender

smile softened the harsh reality of her words. "Go on now. Take care of the things you can do something about and let God take care of the rest."

Choking back the tangle of emotions knotted in my throat, I hurried from the room and out the back door into the hot sunshine. The daily activities of the plantation went on as though nothing had changed. Yet inside, where love and joy usually reigned, fear and disquiet now ruled. I crossed the yard to the laundry, barely aware of the flock of brown and white chickens scurrying out of my way amidst a cloud of feathers and dust. Trudging up the two steps into the small building, I paused inside the propped open door. The two dark-skinned women, colorful kerchiefs tied over their black hair, turned from their work to greet me. The warmth of the fire coupled with the summer heat took my breath. No wonder the door and windows stood wide open.

I held out the bundle, anxious to be rid of the linens and return to the house, to Jacky. "These need to be boiled immediately."

"Are they Master Jack's?" The older slave, Dot, regarded the offering with suspicion in her eyes.

I nodded. "Please, take them and clean them now."

"Yes, Miss." The younger slave, Pansy, took the linens and dropped them into a cauldron of steaming water. Then she grabbed the long wooden paddle and submerged them while Dot added wood to the fire below the huge pot.

While the women went on with their endless task, I spun on my heel and hurried back to the house. The banter and arguing of my brothers and sisters met my ears, all the common sights and sounds around me at odds with a deep sense of unease and turmoil. Footsteps above alerted me to movement in Jacky's room. I stared at the ceiling as if I could see through the wood planks. He shouldn't be out of bed, not without assistance. His pride would have him hurting himself even more. I strode to the stairs and lifted my long skirts with one hand to enable me to hurry up to Jacky's room.

The door stood open. I hesitated only a moment, but long enough to know he was not alone. Trepidation flooded my heart and propelled me into the bedchamber. My father straightened from peering at Jacky's sleeping face.

"I didn't know you'd returned." I dropped my skirt from where I'd clenched it as I stopped by his side. I glanced at Jacky, his features relaxed and peaceful for the first time in a long while. Then I became aware of my father's silent contemplation. "Is Aunt Unity well?"

"She is fine. I came back early because I had a feeling..." He swallowed, his eyes drilling into mine, glistening. "He's dead, Patsy."

Were those tears? I frowned, not understanding. Or not wanting to. "Uncle William?"

He shook his head, a reluctant movement freeing a tear to trickle down his cheek. "Jacky."

I chuckled though the situation held no humor. Refused to believe. "No, he's just playing a joke. I'll show you." I laid a hand gently on Jacky's shoulder and nudged once, twice. "Jacky, you're scaring our father. Stop pretending."

"Patsy..." My father tried to remove my hand, but I kept it on my brother. Noticed a stillness unlike any other I'd experienced.

"Jacky, come on, wake up." I shook him again. Then again. "Jacky?"

"Patsy, please." Father again reached for my hand, this time enveloping it in his and lifting it away from the lifeless body.

I stared at my brother's still form, tears winning their battle to cascade down cold cheeks. *No, Jacky. Please don't do this. Come back.* No mischievous smile or beautiful eyes responded to my silent and desperate pleas. Never again would I be able to joke and laugh with my brother. He wouldn't grow up to take over running Chestnut Grove, nor to find a wife and have children of his own. He wouldn't see me wed Daniel, an event he'd helped make possible. He wouldn't do anything ever again. The hateful disease had stolen my brother away. I wanted to scream and cry, but instead I buried my face in my father's shoulder as he wrapped his strong arms around me, holding me and comforting me while I dampened his coat with my tears.

Pounding footsteps raced up the stairs, drew closer and closer, but I didn't look up. Not until my father eased me away with a compassionate squeeze of my arm, before wrapping his arms around Mother and moving with her as she slowly collapsed to the floor beside the bed. My mother's wails echoed in the room, bouncing off the walls and out the open window, announcing to everyone the death of her son. I sniffled, trying to gain control of my grief. I studied Jacky's chest, willing it to rise and fall, to breathe. He really was gone. A cry ripped out of my soul as the tears trailed down my face. I pressed my fist to my open mouth as one by one, William, Bat, Nancy, and even little Frances slipped into the room, their every movement revealing what they feared they'd see. Their young faces wore disbelief as they struggled to understand how their big brother could die. I needed to pull myself together, to be strong for them all, but not at that moment. I couldn't.

---

The next afternoon, we gathered under the blazing sunshine at the family cemetery, huddled around the open grave. I loved how peaceful the place was, situated in a quiet part of the forest a few miles from the main house. Daniel had ridden over as soon as word reached him of the tragedy. He'd known from his own sister's death how much I might need his comforting presence. He stood beside me after doing all he could to help bury my brother. He and my father had worked side by side with two of the slaves to dig Jacky's grave.

Reverend David Mossom, the rector from nearby St. Peter's Church, held his black leather-bound Bible in his hands. He prayed, words intended to comfort the living. Somehow they didn't appease the anguish in my soul. I listened intently, willing the words to ease my pain, praying for understanding and serenity, some form of acceptance, to fill me rather than the gnawing grief.

The pain of Jacky's death appeared etched on each visage of my family. Part of the shock came from the suddenness of his passing, but also because he'd nearly grown to be a man. Infants had a much higher chance of dying, especially before the age of five years. Once a person reached puberty, barring accidents, the likelihood of surviving into adulthood increased.

I reached out for Daniel's hand, grateful for its warmth and strength when he covered my fingers within the folds of my skirt. Keeping my voice low, I said, "I don't understand why God took him away from us at such a young age. He had so much laughter and love to share in addition to his kind soul."

"We cannot always fathom the workings of our Lord, to understand the bigger scheme of the world." Daniel gazed down at me, his tender concern flowing over me. "But we can reach out to those we love and respect as long as they are with us."

I shrugged, a gentle lift of my shoulders. "I suppose we all die when we're supposed to, but the pain of being left behind is almost more than I can bear."

Daniel sighed, his features sober. "We may be gathering to bury my father ere long. His health continues to decline."

I considered my betrothed. His serious expression said more than his words. After the old man passed, Daniel would be responsible for an almost unimaginable amount of property and wealth. "I am sorry to hear such news. What has happened to make you believe so?"

"He declined to take on the duties of acting governor because he does not feel well enough to meet the challenge." Daniel returned his gaze to the gathering as my father and brothers placed Jacky's coffin into the opening. "That's a sure sign he's realized he won't live much longer."

Mother, standing at the head of the grave holding Betsy, began to weep as my father and brothers shoveled dirt over the coffin to fill in the hole. The thud of clods dropping onto the wooden surface reverberated in my soul. Unfortunately, they could not fill in the hole left in my heart. I'd do anything to keep my family safe. Right then, I vowed to learn how to tend to the health of those I loved. I never again wanted to stand at the grave of someone who shouldn't have died. I clenched my hands into fists as the men buried my brother. I couldn't do anything more for Jacky, but there was one thing I could do for the rest of my kin.

I opened my mouth and began to sing Jacky's favorite song, a final farewell to my brother and a promise to my family.

# 3

*Chestnut Grove – May 15, 1750*

My wedding day finally arrived and every one of my thoughts and feelings centered on the night looming before me. The sweet air breezing through the lace curtains heralded spring as surely as the beginning of a new phase in my life. I'd seen all the plans and preparations put into place. Aunt Unity had arrived the day before, bringing chatter and gifts. The minister, the venerable Reverend Chickley Corbin Thacker along with his wife Elizabeth had ridden up to the house mere hours ago, in time to join the family for an early dinner. Guests arrived by boat, carriage, wagon, and on horseback. Chestnut Grove teemed with family and friends all gathered to witness my marriage to Daniel. Only two family members were missing: my brother, buried now for ten months, and Daniel's father.

The thought of the old man, who had died the previous November, filled me with disgust. Not to think ill of the dead, but he'd even reached out from his grave to make Daniel feel miserable, dismissed by his own father. John Custis' final will and testament left most of the property and monies to Daniel, while still providing generously for Daniel's half-brother, Jack. His will also demanded that Daniel order a special tombstone from London with words intended to hurt both his sons. Why? How could a father wish to denigrate his children?

The words on that tombstone remained etched in my memory, but I wished more than once for them to be erased. All I had to do was close my eyes and they appeared as though engraved in my mind.

Under this Marble Tomb Lies the Body
of the Hon. John Custis, Esq.,
of The City of Williamsburg
And Parish of Bruton,
Formerly of Hungars Parish On The
Eastern Shore
Of Virginia, and County of Northampton,
Age 71 Years and Yet Lived But Seven Years,
Which was the Space of Time He Kept
A Bachelor's Home At Arlington
On the Eastern Shore Of Virginia
This Inscription Put on His tomb Was By
His Own Positive Orders

Daniel had wanted to protest, but to do so would result in him being disinherited with only a shilling from his ungrateful father. How could the old man view his only happy times as the seven years he was a bachelor, unmarried and without children he created? How could he put such on his tombstone for all the world to see? I stared out my bedchamber window, seeking solace in the abundance of blooming flowers and fully leafed trees surrounding the house.

Over the man's last few months, his bitterness toward everyone had erupted, until I'd stayed away from him whenever possible. I didn't want to give him any reason to dislike me, nor to rescind his permission, or at least his approval, of our marriage. In one way, his debilitating illness proved fortunate.

A rap on the door preceded Nancy pushing it open, a smile on her lips. "Mother said it's time to come down to the hall." She stopped inside the door, her smile growing. "Look how beautiful you are! Wait until Daniel sees you."

"I'm grateful you helped me with my dress, Nancy." I hugged my little sister, tears stinging my eyes. We'd grown so very close over the years, and now, at almost nineteen years of age, I was putting physical distance between us. Something we'd never had before. My feelings ran high and it took everything to settle my composure. "Today I become a wife, and then move away from our home. I will miss seeing you every day, sharing in your accomplishments."

Nancy nodded, eyes brimming. "As will I. But you'll only be four miles away, so I'm sure we'll visit often."

"I will hold you to that." Another brief hug, and then I squared my shoulders. Smoothing elbow-length white gloves, I smiled at her though I quaked at the enormity of the changes about to enter my life. Known or unknown. Yet this is what I had dreamed of for years. "Lead the way."

We descended the stairs and joined the chattering throng milling about the large hall and parlor. The late afternoon sun illuminated the room. Clusters of unlit candlesticks waited around the rooms ready for lighting as evening fell. Vases of red roses and white-and-yellow jonquils perfumed the air, their sweet scents pleasing. Reverend Thacker stood by the cold fireplace, my parents to his right. Daniel spotted me as I hesitated in the open door. What a handsome man I was about to marry. My good fortune cheered me, setting my pulse pounding the longer I gazed upon him. I sent a prayer of thanks to the heavens above. He made his way through the parting crowd. I smiled when he clasped my elbow and drew me back with him to stand before the minister.

"Ladies and gentlemen, please grant me your attention." Reverend Thacker raised a hand, the crowd slowly quieting as he lowered it. "Dearly beloved, we are gathered together here in the sight of God, and in the face of this congregation, to join together this man and this woman in holy matrimony."

I looked up at Daniel, while the minister's words flowed over and around me. I'd waited years to hear the sacred words uniting me to my husband. I intended to savor each and every syllable, and strive to follow their intent to the best of my ability. Daniel's eyes twinkled though his expression remained solemn. This beautiful man, so strong and caring, had chosen me to be his life companion. Before God and my entire family he vowed to join our lives until death. I'd dreamed of this day for so long, tears swam in my eyes as the reverend speared Daniel with his gaze and solemnly read the words that would bind us.

"Daniel Custis, wilt thou have this woman to thy wedded wife, to live together after God's ordinance in the holy estate of Matrimony? Wilt thou love her, comfort her, honor, and keep her in sickness and in health; and, forsaking all other, keep thee only unto her, so long as ye both shall live?"

Those were the most moving words I'd heard in a long time. They required a promise to care for me no matter what life threw at us. To work together through all kinds of adverse as well as positive events. To do so until one of us died, which would be a very long time, if I had anything to say about it.

"I will." Daniel smiled at me, then returned his attention to the minister.

Reverend Thacker regarded me with serious eyes, and I heeded his every word as he spoke. "Wilt thou have this man to thy wedded husband, to live together after God's ordinance in the holy estate of matrimony? Wilt thou obey him, and serve him, love, honor, and keep him in sickness and in health; and, forsaking all other, keep thee only unto him, so long as ye both shall live?"

I looked to Daniel, his expectant demeanor making me smile. Did he think I might decline? Silly man. "I will."

"Who giveth this woman to be married to this man?" The minister nodded to my father, who guided me to stand by Daniel. "Daniel, please take her right hand in yours and repeat after me."

The warmth of Daniel's fingers clasping mine sent a thrill coursing through me. I swallowed, trembling with the gravity of the ceremony. My life was about to truly change with Daniel's next utterance.

"I, Daniel Custis, take thee Martha Dandridge to my wedded wife, to have and to hold from this day forward, for better for worse, for richer for poorer, in sickness and in health, to love and to cherish, till death us do part, according to God's holy ordinance; and thereto I plight thee my troth."

As Daniel released my hand, I raised another quick prayer to heaven that our marriage knew more health than sickness, and that we'd live a long time. Daniel deserved to be happy and content after all the hate and distrust he'd endured at the hands of his father. At the minister's direction, I took Daniel's right hand again and repeated after Reverend Thacker the words I'd waited to say for so long.

"I, Martha Dandridge, take thee Daniel Custis to my wedded husband, to have and to hold from this day forward, for better for worse, for richer for poorer, in sickness and in health, to love, cherish, and to obey, till death us do part, according to God's holy ordinance; and thereto I give thee my troth." My heart swelled with love.

Daniel withdrew from a small pocket a few gold coins as payment for the minister's services and placed them upon the Bible. Reverend Thacker nodded to Daniel as he pocketed the coins. The minister said a prayer, then a benediction, and a blessing. I didn't really hear what he said due to the roaring in my ears and the thundering of my heart as the ceremony drew to a close. Almost. We were almost married, joined together until death parted us.

The prayers and Bible verses seemed to drag by forever as well. I caught snippets of admonitions to be fruitful and procreate. To cleave to my husband. To live in the manner of the holy women in the Bible.

Finally, the minister smiled at me and I realized the ceremony had concluded. My parents rushed forward to shake Daniel's hand and to hug me, congratulating us both. Nancy appeared at my side, radiant in her joy over the union. One day I'd see her marry and embark on her own marital adventure. Aunt Unity was next, crushing me into her happy embrace. After everyone, from the Governor and assemblymen down to the servants, had a chance to bestow their congratulations on us, the festivities began.

Old Sally had outdone herself, exceeding my request for a plentiful array of foods. The dining room glittered with glass and silver plates, platters, and bowls filled with smoked meats, fruits, cheeses, and cakes and pastries. Champagne and Madeira flowed freely. We had quite a celebration, one I would cherish in the years to come.

Daniel kept me by his side as we mingled and sampled the delicacies. His smile held a possessiveness and elation I'd never seen before, but relished with every racing beat of my heart. Nervous eagerness for our wedding night made me quiver. Mother had not been very forthcoming as to what to expect, saying only that every woman's first experience differed and should be kept between husband and wife. She did offer that most husbands were gentle and kind in their approach, and not to worry overmuch. Such vagueness did nothing to dismiss my qualms.

I'd seen animals breed, having lived on a plantation all my life. Horses, dogs, and even the birds obeyed God's directive to be "fruitful and multiply." But the method of human procreation remained a mystery. One I'd soon experience for myself. Then I'd become a mother. Joy filled my chest at the idea of bearing Daniel's children.

"What time is it, Daniel?" I caught his eye and lifted a brow.

"I'd say about six of the clock." He smiled down at me. "Still plenty of time to celebrate."

"Too much time, perhaps. Might I have some champagne?" I regarded him with all my love and respect. "I'm parched."

"Of course, my dear." He led me to the sideboard, selecting a fresh glass of the sparkling wine and handing it to me. His fingers brushed mine and I nearly dropped the flute from the unexpected shock. Gripping the fragile vessel firmly, I sipped and swallowed as Daniel asked, "Are you content, my dear?"

"I'm perfectly content to be Mrs. Custis." I wanted nothing more than to escape the crowd and be alone with my husband. Yet, my body trembled as I tried not to worry about my naiveté concerning marital relations.

Finally, after the candles were lit and the sun had set, Daniel winked at me. "I believe we should leave the others to continue the party."

The moment I'd been simultaneously longing for and dreading had arrived. I nodded, not sure what to say, so choosing silence. He led me over to where my parents conversed with several associates.

"If you'll excuse us, we shall retire for the evening. But pray let the festivities continue." Daniel pulled me up against his side with one arm.

Father smiled, a knowing look on his face. "Take care of her."

"Of course." Daniel addressed Mother, then me. "Ready?"

I hugged Mother, a sudden burst of something akin to fear making my hands shake. Time for the mystery to be solved. "Let's go."

Amidst jokes and ribbing, we made our way through the happy gathering and up the stairs to our bedchamber. Daniel closed the door, turning to face me with a tender smile. He unbuttoned his coat, then his waistcoat, removing them one by one and draping them over the back of a chair stationed by the cheery fireplace. I was grateful for the blaze chasing the slight chill from the room. Or was my trembling not from the cold but from overwrought senses?

The sight of my husband in a state of undress did nothing to calm the agitation making my hands tremble. Indeed, when he removed his cravat, adding it to the pile, the expanse of throat with a hint of dark curls on his chest made me gulp. Dear Lord, he was removing all his clothes. What did he expect me to do? Undress in front of him?

I folded my hands and waited, feeling my eyes widen but unable to stop them. His chest proved more remarkable with only his long shirt preventing me from seeing his flesh. His gentle smile widened as he sauntered closer. With each step, the space between us diminished and warmed.

"I've wanted to do this for so long, my love." He turned me with gentle yet insistent hands to undo my stays and dress, letting each fall unceremoniously to the floor, a puddle of silk and linen around my satin clad feet. Standing in only my shift, I crossed my arms, but he slowly pulled them away to gaze at me. "You are more beautiful than I could ever have imagined. I am fortunate to have you as wife. You have no need to fear me, or to be shy about yourself."

"I—I am unsure what you expect of me." I fought the urge to hide my breasts from his hungry gaze. The fire in his eyes made me think of the stallions when they chased after a mare in season, bright with intent.

"Do not fear me, Patsy. We will go slowly. I do not wish to hurt you any more than necessary your first time." He removed his shoes, stockings, and kidskin breeches, finally standing in only his night shirt. "Trust me."

Daniel was nearly naked, his arousal apparent in my one sweeping glance. A stallion indeed. I kept my eyes on his face as my cheeks flamed. Good Lord, would he fit where I presumed he must? More to the point, *how* would he fit?

I shivered and crossed my arms. Lifting my chin with a gentle forefinger, he lowered his mouth to mine. Sampling, tasting my lips. Sensations piled atop one another deep inside me, unfamiliar and yet drawing me toward him. I pressed my palms against his chest, unsure whether to push him away or succumb to the temptation to pull him closer. He wrapped his arms around me, solving the dilemma as he crushed my breasts to his chest.

Breaking the kiss, Daniel studied my face, his gaze touching on each feature. He offered a hand, palm up, waiting for mine to cover his. "Darling, sweet wife, come to bed and I'll show you pleasures such as you've never known."

More than the kiss had evoked? Curiosity and intrigue mixed with the urge to cling to him, replacing my fears. I took his hand

and let him tug me into our marriage bed. Then I savored every moment as he lovingly answered all my questions.

———————

White House stood as a testament to the simple needs of a bachelor. When Daniel lived here alone, it's rather rustic furnishings sufficed. Now that we'd married, it became my mission to help make his home reflect his standing in the colony. Despite having lived within its walls for a month, the haphazard collection of belongings annoyed me.

Daniel had bowed to the latest fashion by designating a separate dining room, complete with beautiful mahogany chairs surrounding a large matching table. But the seats were covered with plain fabric unsuited to his station in Virginia society. Perusing the rest of the furnishings in the room, I contemplated the necessary improvements. Prints hung on the walls. Drapes hung at the windows. The rugs had been rolled up and stored for the summer, leaving the room rather bland and uninspired. Crimson damask for the seats would make the exact statement I had in mind. With matching table cloths and napkins, I could picture gilt china, or perhaps blue-and-white Chinese dinnerware to provide an elegant contrast. Then we'd also need to do something about replacing the pewter and brass vessels with silver and the utensils with silver flatware. Maybe I could persuade Daniel to order a set of the newest kind of utensils, those newfangled tined forks.

Daniel had continued to press Anne Moody to return the silver his father had rashly given to her and her husband. If my husband's recent attempt failed to produce the desired results, then he'd be forced to file a legal suit demanding they give back the Custis family silver. I shook my head, though there was no one about to witness it. The old man continued to vex from his cold grave. If only I could do something to alleviate the burden and worry caused by the elder Custis. But the matter fell squarely upon Daniel's shoulders as the heir and executor.

I thoroughly enjoyed my new role as mistress of a bustling plantation. Surrounded by a handful of servants to handle the more tiresome chores, I found it possible to accomplish more of the oversight required to ensure the orderly operation of the household. One of the more time-consuming tasks was ordering the necessary items and foods from England and other countries to complement what the extensive house garden provided. I also managed the distribution of food and drink between the manor and the other farms. I was very glad administration of the entire operation fell to Daniel, as the extent of the land holdings and other property took all of his time.

Footsteps drew my attention to the open door. Sally, my new personal maid, appeared in the opening, her forehead and cheeks glistening in the afternoon heat. Dark eyes regarded me for a moment before she slipped into the room. Daniel had insisted I needed my own servant to attend me, though I'd managed all my life without one. Still, his argument that a lady of my station was expected to have a maid to assist her made me reconsider and eventually acquiesce.

"Yes, Sally?" I swept one last glance around the dining room before joining her by the door.

"Mr. Daniel has arrived, bringing a guest with him. Will you take dinner in here?"

I wondered who had joined us and how long they'd stay. I'd need to speak to the cook about adding to the menu. "It will be cooler in the hall with the doors open as usual. Come, I wish to see Daniel, and I'd ask that you tell Doll about our new arrival."

"She was with me when Mr. Daniel arrived." Sally pulled the kerchief from around her neck and mopped her face. "It's going to be a hot summer."

"All the more reason to set up the table in the hall where there is a cross draft. I'll expect dinner at the usual time." I motioned for the maid to continue with her work.

Sally nodded and strode to the back door and outside toward the kitchen.

I waited until the door had banged shut before I moved

toward the parlor. A wave of love and happiness washed through me hearing Daniel's voice. Echoes of him guiding me through my first experiences in bed warmed my cheeks. The mysterious acts proved enjoyable indeed. Daniel had reassured me, helped me enjoy our intimate time together. I'd become more daring than I had thought possible with his sweet words and tender caresses fueling a desire inside I never imagined. With Daniel's advanced age, I prayed God would enable me to be with child soon, to give my husband the children he so deserved. I wanted a house full of children, playing and laughing, to fill my heart with even more love and joy. Which of course meant more nights in Daniel's arms. A shiver of desire flooded through me. I must stop thinking of such intimate moments. Pressing hands to my flaming skin, I calmed my breathing as well as my thoughts. I dropped my hands to rest at my waist for a moment, then strode into the parlor.

"Ah, my dear." Daniel rose from where he sat talking with a scrawny middle-aged man. He ushered me toward the gentleman, his hand pressing the small of my back. "Come, meet our guest. Mr. David Lee, allow me to introduce you to my wife, Martha."

Rangy and all hard angles, the man towered over me when he stood. Which wasn't news, since I'm not very tall. He bowed, a small smile lifting the very corners of his mouth. "Pleased to meet you, Mrs. Custis."

Despite my initial reluctance, I nodded to the elegantly clad man. "Welcome to our home. Please, make yourself comfortable."

I took my customary seat, arranging my cotton and linen skirts. Daniel and David both resumed their seats. I considered our guest, searching my memory for any hint of recognition but came up with a blank.

"How did you meet Mr. Lee?" I asked.

Daniel laughed, a rolling chuckle deep and long as thunder. "I met his horse first."

"My goodness, were you injured?" I regarded our guest, searching for signs of distress.

"Only my self-esteem." Mr. Lee shrugged off the event. "Fortunately, my unexpected dismount occurred on a grassy knoll."

"His horse took a liking to mine, so he was easy to catch." Daniel braced a hand on one breech-clad knee. "It seemed only right to give Mr. Lee a chance to catch his breath as well."

"Most assuredly. I'm pleased you've joined us for some refreshments." I relaxed, knowing he'd not suffered any injury. "Will you stay to dinner with us?"

He inclined his head with a smile. "I'd be honored."

"Now that's settled, pray tell me, Mr. Lee," Daniel said, "what brings you all this way from Williamsburg?"

"The governor has directed me to investigate the claim of savages threatening and killing settlers on the frontier." David Lee shook his head slowly, brows drawn together. "I will not share the specifics in front of your wife, as the details would weigh heavy upon her tender heart, but believe me when I say if those claims are true then retaliation is inevitable."

"Why would the Indians be attacking?" Daniel's frown matched Mr. Lee's. "Why can't the people live peaceably together?"

Mr. Lee huffed a laugh. "The Indians claim the Englishmen have no right to live on their land. Land the British empire awarded to their loyal subjects."

"I see. Would you care for a sherry before dinner?" At our guest's nod, Daniel rose and paced to the sideboard where decanters of colored liquors reflected the light. He poured the garnet liquid into three small crystal glasses and then handed them round.

"To add fuel to the fire," Mr. Lee continued, "rumor has it the French have been encouraging the Indians to attack English settlements."

I stifled a gasp, covering the sound with my hand. The political maneuverings of the French against the British were nothing unusual, but to have them operating in the colonies was news indeed. Daniel's age would prevent him from becoming directly involved, which eased my worry a smidgeon. Still, having the Indians attacking the colonists raised concern to a new level.

"Skirmishes between the indigenous people and the newcomers is to be expected, but I had hoped the conflict wouldn't lead to bloodshed."

David Lee lifted a gray eyebrow. "We're speaking of savages, are we not? Do they know any other way?"

"Surely they must." Daniel sipped his wine and glanced at me. A lift of one brow indicated he detected my aversion to the discussion. He turned back to address Mr. Lee. "But enough of politics. Will you attend the next public days this fall?"

With that, Daniel steered the conversation into safer topics. I joined in when I could, but wondered about the startling revelations David Lee had shared. How would the unrest be settled? What else might be done to resolve the discord? I listened to the men discuss the pending business before the lower house of the government, political and legal topics I struggled to understand. But by paying close attention, I endeavored to become informed enough to engage in discourse with my husband and his associates. My role as hostess required nothing less, and my growing respect and love for Daniel made my task all the more enjoyable. I'd do anything to ensure his health and happiness.

After a while I grew bored with the endless conversation. Time to mix things up. "Would you like to have some music this evening?"

Daniel set his glass down and nodded. "Will you sing for us, my dear?"

Indeed, I'd love to. Nothing gave me more pleasure than to sing for my husband. His delight in my warbling fueled an answering delight of my own. I moved to sit at the spinet, fingers poised to strike up a tune.

Mr. Lee relaxed in his seat, prepared to be entertained, while Daniel leaned back and crossed his ankles. My rapt audience waited for the impromptu concert to begin.

I sang whatever came to mind, sedate hymns and folk tunes alternating over the next hour. The men sang along, and clapped when each song ended. We passed an enjoyable evening, content with our lives and our companions. I tossed a prayer to heaven that our peaceful lives continued for many years to come. Only with the addition of children to enliven our home. Then life would be perfect.

# 4

*White House – 1751*

I stifled a sharp retort, annoyed with my own reaction. Sally had not meant to spill the box of buttons across the floor. Why did tears sting my eyes? My emotions skittered about like the buttons set loose to roll and tumble. What was wrong with me?

"Sit right there, Miss Martha. I'll have these picked up in a moment." Sally quickly picked up the discs of bone, enamel, or porcelain, dropping them into their special box.

I loved to add beautifully crafted buttons to my clothes as decoration. Mother had instructed me in their meanings and how they imparted a sense of gentility the lower classes could not achieve. Honestly, the interesting carvings or stitching or painted pictures intrigued me and made me smile. Lately, though, my mood swings had become a worry.

"I do not understand why I've been inconstant." I sifted through the last few weeks, seeing no real pattern in the wildly swinging feelings I'd experienced. Still experienced as I watched my maid crawling about the floor retrieving the precious buttons imported from England, France, and China.

Sally scooped the last of the colorful pieces back into the box. She closed the lid and latched it before turning to regard me with speculative eyes. "It's been more than a month since your last courses."

I pursed my lips, searching my memory. "About six weeks ago, but a little fluctuation isn't unusual."

Sally grinned and bobbed her head. "Maybe, but your emotions are unusual. I believe you are in the family way, Miss Martha."

I gaped at her. "What?" Her words sunk in. Of course. The symptoms spoke for themselves. The word *finally* echoed in my mind. "Do not breathe a word of this, do you hear me? I must see Mother. Have Billy bring my chair 'round in fifteen minutes. And tell him I wish for him to wait for me while I visit my mother."

Half an hour later, I perched on the sporty single-seated chair, traces in hand as my mare trotted down the rough dirt road toward Chestnut Grove, while Billy rode behind me. Daniel had surprised me with the fun and easily maneuverable conveyance, saying it would enable me to visit my family upon a whim. Like now.

With child. I hummed a ditty, using the words as lyrics. My heart soared with each repetition of the magical phrase. I'd be a mother in a matter of months, the first of our children to love and rear to be upstanding citizens of Virginia. So many questions flashed through my mind I didn't know which to ask Mother first. Observing her condition and lying in was a very different matter from experiencing the progression first hand.

Halting the chair, I stepped down as Billy held my horse's bridle. I flashed him a smile of gratitude and hurried to the porch. The door swung open as I reached for it, my mother's happy yet querying expression a welcome sight. Lines creased her face, and her shoulders bowed more than before, but otherwise she appeared fit and healthy. Love swelled in my breast as I hugged her, squeezing tighter than usual. I'd missed her more than I'd realized.

"What brings you here?" She closed the door behind me, shutting out the cool spring air.

Immediately, we were surrounded by my kinfolk. I'd missed them so much an ache spread through me. I needed to visit more regularly. The short distance, less than half an hour to traverse, shouldn't prevent me from sharing in their daily lives. Especially with my own child soon to be joining the cluster of children. Little Betsy toddled into the room after Frances. Nancy strode in, behaving more like a young woman now that she'd reached twelve years old. Less like the tomboy she used to be. Love for each member of my family pulsed through every fiber. My family was about to grow, too.

I couldn't suppress a grin. "I'm with child."

Nancy squealed and ran to wrap her arms about my waist. "I'm going to be an aunt!"

Betsy grabbed a fistful of my skirts as everyone clustered around, smiling and laughing. I reveled in the attention for a few minutes, then shushed everyone with a wave of my hand. I beamed at them. I verged on becoming a mother, and had never felt such elation.

As the commotion died down, Mother slipped an arm around my waist. "We need to talk, don't we?"

"Please." I wrapped an arm over my mother's, and we sauntered into the parlor. Taking our customary seats, I studied the concern in my mother's expression.

"Have you told Daniel?"

I shook my head. "I wonder whether I should wait until I'm absolutely certain."

"You doubt you are?"

I folded my hands in my lap. "Sally believes I am, and I must admit to feeling different. Extremes of mood unlike my normal steady way."

Mother angled forward, one brow raised. "I believe Sally has it right. You won't show for a while yet. You should tell your husband."

"I will at dinner. He's out visiting the other farms and I had to share my news with you."

We chatted for a while longer before we said our farewells

and I headed home to White House. Along the way, my thoughts cavorted through the delights awaiting my child. I'd teach him so many things. Share with him everything I knew, and perhaps some things we'd learn together. My mother had promised to send over the bassinet and baby clothes Betsy had outgrown. The bassinet would go in our bedchamber, positioned so we could see our baby whenever we desired. Mostly I thought about how pleased Daniel would be when I told him of my condition.

Upon my return, I retired to my room to freshen up for dinner. Daniel would arrive before long and I wanted to look my best. I donned a shimmery blue silk dress, and Sally dressed my hair into an elegant upswept bun. All the while, I imagined his expression at the happy news.

I descended the stairs and hurried into the dining room to ensure the table had been set for the midafternoon meal. Fortunately, we weren't entertaining guests on such a special day. My revelation would be between me and Daniel. Word would spread quickly through the servants after I told him, if indeed they didn't know already. I hoped Sally had refrained from saying anything as instructed so no slips of the tongue happened before dinner.

Heavy footsteps sounded outside the front door, drawing me into the central hall. The door swung open as Daniel pushed inside on a breath of fresh pine-scented air. I smiled at him, my heart stuttering at the visage of my husband. His dark eyes regarded me for a beat before he strode toward me, a grin forming. When he reached me, he doffed his hat and pressed a kiss to my lips.

"My dear, what is it?" Daniel searched my face with puzzled eyes. "Is everything all right?"

He knew me so well. I bobbed my head, feeling giddy with love and happiness. Fit to burst with my precious news. "Dinner is almost ready. You have time to change. Then I'll tell you what has happened."

"Good news, I hope?"

I motioned for him to go upstairs. "Hurry now. You don't want your dinner to turn cold."

Before long we sat together at the crimson covered table. Silver flatware and candlesticks graced the table. On the sideboard, an elegant silver tea service and crystal wine glasses waited.

Daniel lifted his glass, the Madeira nearly matching the color of the tablecloth. "To your health."

I inclined my head and took a sip, the hint of almond in the dry wine pleasant on my tongue. Then I raised the glass, a grin bursting onto my lips. "To the health of our child."

Daniel put his glass to his lips, then froze as his gaze rested upon me. "You are with child?" Hope flared as he studied me, a half-smile on his mouth.

"Yes." I took another sip, keeping my gaze upon his expression as emotions swept across his features. "You're going to be a father."

"My dear Patsy." He sat back, grinning ear to ear. "Thank you. I feared I would never hear those words. When do you expect to have the child?"

"Sometime this fall I estimate." I reached out and briefly clasped his hand. "I went to see my mother for her advice and counsel. She intends to send some things over."

Daniel picked up his fork and knife. "Whatever you need, my dear. Put together a list and I'll send a request to my factor in London posthaste."

"Are you happy, dear?" I lifted my own utensils, but paused before slicing into the duckling. "To become a father, I mean?"

"More than I can adequately put into words." He studied me for several moments, his love clear in his regard. "Nothing could make me happier."

"I am overjoyed God has granted my wish to provide you with a child." I sliced into the dark meat covered with brown gravy. "Now I'll pray to Him to ensure a healthy one."

"And many more." Daniel cut into his duck and popped a bite into his mouth. "Like you, I wish to fill this house with children."

"One at a time, my dear." I chewed a bite of meat and then smiled at him. "We have all the time in the world to work on your desire."

"Yes, that is true." Daniel took another bite, his gaze resting on me. "Your news raises another concern I've been negligent in addressing. We must resolve the issue concerning my brother. The legal issues continue and I have no hope of satisfying the provisions regarding him in my father's will."

I bit back my retort, scooping some spinach and eggs into my mouth to prevent me from speaking in haste. The blend of poached egg, tart orange, and stewed greens tasted heavenly and chewing slowly gave me time to consider my words. Swallowing, I studied his pensive expression. "I still do not understand why your father thought he could free Jack, going against the laws of the colony."

"How did he think Jack could own not only land but other slaves?" Daniel sighed. "And to give Jack my mother's property merely adds salt to the wound."

"The wound from the words on his tombstone?" I glanced at him, anger pushing aside some of the joy I'd felt earlier.

"Yes." Daniel chewed, his eyes on his plate. "Perhaps we should invite my half-brother to move here?" He raised his eyes to meet my shocked gaze.

I held no personal grudge against Mulatto Jack. Far from it. His station in the colony, let alone the community, was difficult at best. Daniel's heart may be in the right place, but he obviously did not consider the myriad ramifications stemming from having a slave as a relative live with us. Old man Custis surely didn't consider the results of sleeping with a Negro woman, and then keeping the bastard as his son. We couldn't have him living in the manor house, nor could we expect him to sleep with the male Negroes. The other slaves would not cotton to any preferential treatment that surely Jack would expect. Merely inviting him to a family gathering sometimes caused an air of ill will, though we did on occasion endure such an event. But to live with us? The situation would prove untenable in a very short span.

"We can't have Jack live with us." I sliced off another bite, holding it poised above my plate. "It's more fitting for him to remain at the Moody's, since that's where your father desired him to live."

"His welfare is still my concern." Daniel sipped his wine and then slowly replaced the glass on the table. "I'm duty bound to ensure his well-being."

"Sometimes I hate your father." I fought the urge to fling my silverware onto the plate, instead carefully laying them down across the top. "He has made your life a continuing ordeal, trying to unravel not only the generations-spanning ordeal of the Dunbar suit but now his own will's provisions. Provisions that defy logic or even common decency."

The Dunbar suit had provoked decades of legal proceedings and counterarguments. The suit stemmed from his aunt's inheritance and continued to vex as well as generate many heated exchanges with the lawyers. His father had wrestled with the possibility of losing not only the suit but everything he owned due to the vague wording in his grandfather's will. Something along the lines of the American properties were responsible for paying for all expenses of the other land holdings in distant countries. Absurd, and yet the extent of trouble the poorly worded sentence caused suggested an incompetence hard to fathom.

"Now, now, Patsy, don't be cross. Eat. You'll need the nourishment in order to bear a healthy child."

Reluctantly, I took up the silver. The glint of metal brought to mind the missing family silver, forcing a sigh of frustration from me. "I suppose you're right, but my appetite has fled."

Daniel laid a calming hand on my wrist. "You need not fret about these matters. I will handle them."

"But it's such a burden for you, to have to worry about not only all of the thousands of acres of property, but also these complicated legal matters. I worry for your constitution."

"None of the legal issues are going to kill me." He smiled, his eyes crinkling in the corners. "Now relax and enjoy your dinner."

"As you wish." I'd vowed to obey him so I put a bite into my mouth and chewed. I still didn't like it though.

Better to keep my mouth full and my husband happy than to add to his worries with my own diatribe against his dead father. Refraining from speaking in no way meant I wouldn't continue to worry. Especially with the deep lines etched on Daniel's face and the slight bow of his shoulders. So much rested on him. Was having his child going to add to his worries? Or give him reason to smile?

———————————

How much longer must I carry this ball in my belly? I waddled—there was no other word for the awkward gait—out the back door to check on the women working in the garden. Soon they'd finish harvesting the vegetables growing there and then I'd supervise the pickling and preserving work that followed. The cold storage in the basement would be filled with barrels and jars of victuals, pickled cucumbers, cider and small beer, as well as restoratives and other medicines.

Resting my hands on my belly, I dragged in a deep breath of fall air. My back ached from the extra weight pulling on my spine. And another trip to the privy would need to happen soon. Too soon. I always had to stop what I was doing to walk out to the little building tucked under a massive oak tree, its leaves flaming gold and scarlet. Only a month or so until my lying in. Mother and Nancy promised to attend when I was due to deliver the baby. Knowing of their experience with many successful births calmed me as the fearsome day approached.

I endeavored to think happy and positive thoughts, to not truly fear the event of birthing this child. Mother had not had many stillbirths over the years. I hoped to follow in her footsteps and not have complications during or after the delivery of the child. But many other women from church and the county had succumbed during their lying in, so many that no woman could relax as the day approached.

Time to move. I strode down the couple of steps into the dirt yard, then across the open space to the privy. Along the way, I nodded in greeting to the men and women as they went about their tasks. Each person living and working on the property constituted my family. I loved my family, even when they made mistakes. Each of them was important, like their health and contentment. As long as each member of the family did their job, the plantation would smoothly function. Even the little one I carried would have an expected role to perform as it grew.

Finishing my business in the privy, I let the door thump closed and made my way back toward the house. Daniel would be home soon for dinner and I must freshen myself. Never would he see me in a state unbefitting my role as his wife. In anticipation of my increasing condition, I'd ordered special stays and gowns which helped maintain my posture and proper silhouette. With Sally's help, I'd also managed to retain my personal appearance and dignity. Well, except mayhap the odd waddling walk I'd adopted.

"Sally?" I hurried as fast as my condition allowed into the parlor, seeking my maid's assistance when I changed my dress. I'd come to depend on the woman's talents with regard to my attire and baubles. Her ideas were indeed creative as well as pleasing. "Sally?"

The woman turned as I paused inside the room, a polishing rag in her hand. Her dark eyes smiled at me, a wilted but clean white lace cap sitting on her dark curls. "Yes? Do you need something?"

"Will you please help me change for dinner?" I leaned a hand on the doorjamb to rest and catch my breath. "I'd like your opinion, if you don't mind."

Sally shoved the rag into an apron pocket. "Of course."

In my bedchamber, I loosened the ties on my bodice while Sally opened the trunk. She rummaged inside, lifting first one and then another dress before returning to the depths of the box.

"How about this one?" Sally pulled out a russet silk with gold bows and laces, shaking it to release any wrinkles. "Your watch would be fetching on this, don't you agree?"

I tilted my head while trying to imagine the resulting outfit. The pretty gold watch Daniel had given me, with its open white enamel face, would indeed be lovely against the red-brown of the fabric. I envisioned the circle of gold inlaid around the edge, along with each of the twelve gold letters of my married name above each of the twelve numerals on the dial. "That will do very well."

Half an hour later, I descended the stairs, feet clad in low bronze satin heels, the long skirts lifted with one hand. The whispered rustle of the fabric brought a smile, the sound reflecting the quality of the material. Being Daniel Custis' wife had its perquisites. Reaching the main floor, I checked the time on the watch pinned to my bodice. Daniel had sent to London upon our union to order this precious gift. The other gift I received was the collection of recipes from Daniel's mother, may she rest in peace. The woman's receipt book contained a wealth of knowledge based on her failures and successes over the years. As a result, the tome proved invaluable on many occasions.

Daniel strode through the back door as I was about to enter the parlor to wait for his arrival. Swiping his hat from his head, he smoothed his hair into place. He seemed weary from the day's work. He stopped in front me, perusing my attire in one glance, a grin replacing the fatigued expression. "You're the most beautiful mother I've ever seen."

My cheeks warmed at the pretty compliment. "You're home early today."

Tucking my hand into his, he pulled me the rest of the way into the parlor. "I bring news. First, would you care for a sherry?"

"What sort of news?" I eased onto my customary chair by the fireplace, glad for the warmth and cheer emanating from its depths. "Good or bad?"

Daniel crossed to the sideboard and poured golden wine into crystal stemmed glasses. Then he looked at me, his expression serious. "I'm not quite certain how to answer your question." Handing me one glass, he sat on the matching chair across from mine.

"Perhaps merely state the news and I can decide for myself whether it is good or bad." I sipped the sweet wine, watching him. Whatever news he brought, deep lines around his mouth and eyes revealed it weighed heavily on his mind.

He sipped, delaying his next words. "Mulatto Jack died yesterday."

Shock reverberated through me at the tragic news. Followed quickly by relief. His death solved so many uncomfortable quandaries perplexing our lives. "Your brother is dead? What happened?"

"Mr. Moody did not know exactly. The poor boy complained of a terrible pain in his neck, and within hours lay dead." He rested one large hand on a muscled thigh. His dark breeches sported smudges from his ride around the plantation. His sadness over the loss of his half-brother hung between us. "The funeral will be to-morrow."

"I assume we will attend." I did not love the poor man, but I would grieve with his family. A family who had endured so much ill will and hatred combined with sorrow.

He frowned as he regarded me for several moments. "We must. Your wisdom has saved me. I'm sorrowful regarding his demise, but also relieved he did not die under our roof. The gossips would have made much of the cause of his death under those circumstances."

"Surely they would not tarnish your reputation with such innuendo. You'd never kill your own kin."

"With the legal issues surrounding Father's will, the tangled and conflicting provisions all resolve with Jack's death."

"How so?"

"I'm his heir. I inherit all of his property and wealth."

I gaped at him for a split second before snapping my lips together. He spoke the truth. "Then truly it is best we had not opened our home to him after all."

Daniel's gaze dropped to my belly and rested there for several moments. "My son, if God grants such a gift, will be the heir of all the Custis property, free and clear."

I rested my hands on my stomach, the movements inside reassuring and hopeful. Our child would be born soon, to take his or her place in the world as a Custis. Of course, its middle name would have to be Parke, or forfeit ever inheriting anything, per the old man's hateful will. But there were worse provisions and conditions in life than that.

"Let us have dinner and put these matters aside for a time." I rose and reached for Daniel's hand. "Come, we can face anything as long as we have each other."

———————

Biting on the clean rag muffled my scream but did nothing to alleviate the pain ripping me in half. The pains had started the night before as Daniel and I were enjoying a quiet supper with our new friend, David Lee. During a lively discussion regarding the arrival in early November of the new royal governor, Robert Dinwiddie, and his young wife Rebecca, the first twinges of discomfort rippled through me. Thinking it was merely a cramp, I'd engaged in the exchange about the changes the fiery Scot planned to make to the palace and the capitol city in general. His young wife would also bring a refreshing change to the social scene. Daniel had just said he'd need to ride in to pay his respects to the new arrivals, when the second twinge made me gasp.

Fortunately, Sally happened to be nearby and recognized the symptoms at the same time as I did. After witnessing my mother's own labor with child, I should have puzzled it out sooner. Daniel sent messengers to summon my mother and Nancy, Aunt Unity, and the most highly regarded of midwives, Sarah Jacobs.

The first spasm had been uncomfortable, but nothing like the paroxysms contorting my body now. Never in my life had I imagined such agony. I panted as the convulsion eased. I relaxed back on the birthing chair Sarah had brought the night before. My mother and sister had arrived an hour later and the three ladies set about preparing for the baby's arrival. Including shooing Daniel from the bedchamber and into the parlor where he waited for word of his child's birth. I imagined him listening to my moans and screams, clenching the arms of a chair to keep him from raging up the stairs to my side. The image almost made me smile.

When the labor had begun, Daniel walked with me to ease the discomfort, much like my father had with my mother. Watching another endure childbirth was very different from experiencing it. Daniel had been patient, concerned, and comforting. As the night wore on, and the pain grew more intense, my women took over. They clustered around me, encouraging and comforting, as the pangs became pains and then unbearable moments of agony. Nancy had taken her place by my side, offering her hand for me to mangle with each paroxysm as she'd done for our mother. Mother edged closer to mop the sweat from my brow while Nancy held my hand.

I pulled the rag from between my teeth with a free hand, spearing my mother with a frown. "How have you survived this pain so many times?" I braced for the onslaught of the next attack building inside.

Mother chuckled. "After you hold your baby in your arms, you'll forget all about the birthing."

"I'll never let Daniel near me again." I groaned and shoved the rag back into place.

My moan turned into another scream, forcing my eyes closed. Did I hear laughter while I succumbed to the unstoppable urge to push down? After several excruciating moments, the intensity eased and I could breathe again.

Opening my eyes, I glared at Sarah. "What's so funny?"

"I've heard that sentiment many times." The midwife smiled grimly as she squatted before me. "The head is crowning. It won't be long until you'll have your baby in your arms."

A baby. A new life to love and cherish. To share with my husband. Soon, the mystery would be solved as to whether I'd provided him a son, as I hoped for. While our child would be loved no matter whether male or female, financial considerations also must be taken into account. A male could inherit the plantations and all of the associated property, while a female could not. Not in the real sense of the word. Any property a woman inherited became her dowry, which her husband or other male relative managed on her behalf. After all the effort made to build up the respect and wealth of the Custis name, an heir was a necessity for carrying on in perpetuity. I'd promised the irascible old man and I would do what I could to keep my word.

Another spasm stopped my thoughts, replacing them with a mindless scream. Pushing as hard as I could, I prayed for the pain to end. Hot tears leaked out of my eyes and down my cheeks. Then blessed relief flowed through me.

"That's it." Sarah reached down and caught the newborn in a clean towel with her strong hands. Cuddling the baby, she cleaned the babe off while my mother and sister eased me back, panting.

"What is it?" Nancy asked, peering at Sarah.

"A boy." Sarah smiled at me before resuming her task of slicing the umbilical cord with a sharp knife. After a few moments, she handed him to Sally to cradle before turning her attention back to me.

"A son." Tension eased from my shoulders. I watched Sarah's ministrations as she helped deliver the afterbirth onto the layers of sheets beneath the birthing chair. When the last tug in my uterus and rush of fluid had halted, I released a long breath. The ordeal had ended. I shifted, aches and pains I'd never felt before making me wince, and pulled my gown down from where it had been bunched. "Daniel will be pleased."

"Once you're presentable, we'll bring him in to see his son." Mother hugged my shoulders. "Shall I go tell him the good news?"

I smiled up at her. "He's been so anxious."

"I'll put his mind at ease while you clean yourself and get into bed." Mother helped me stand. "You'll want to feed the little one as soon as possible." With a pat on my arm, she strode from the room.

Carefully, I crossed to the pitcher of clean water situated on the table by the fireplace and poured some into the basin. Sally helped tug the soiled gown from my sore and weary body, then bundled it up with the rest of the linens to be laundered. Using a clean rag and a bit of soap, I washed and dried myself, careful around the sorest areas. Nancy pulled a clean shift from my trunk and helped me don the sheer garment with discreet flaps sewn over each breast. I slipped under the covers, propped up against several pillows.

Sarah handed me the infant, gently placing him into my eager arms. His fingers curled around my finger and squeezed. One, two, three, four fingers and a thumb. I checked his other hand, smiling when I saw all digits in place. Pulling the light blanket aside, I counted his toes and then wrapped him back in the cover. My son. My perfect little boy. An unsettling cool shiver wiggled down my back. I clasped the baby closer. I'd never let anything happen to him. Ever.

"He's beautiful, Patsy." Nancy rested a hand on my shoulder while she examined her nephew.

"Yes, he is." I flicked a glance at Nancy, then gazed on my boy's face as he began to wiggle and murmur.

"Are you ready to introduce him to nursing, Martha?" Sarah moved to stand by the bedside, ready to help if needed.

"I suppose." I opened my gown and exposed one breast as I'd seen my mother do on countless occasions. The cool air brushed my sensitive nipple while I, with occasional help from Sarah, worked to position the baby's rooting mouth. When his gums latched on, I was surprised first by the strength of his mouth and then by the sudden spasm inside me with each tug.

A moment later the door eased open and Daniel paused in the opening, sheer joy beaming from his face. He hesitated only a second before he moved to look upon our child.

"Patsy, my dear, I love you. And I adore our boy there." He stood gazing on his son for several more moments before meeting my gaze. "I'd like to claim him as my son for all the world to know."

I saw the pride in Daniel's eyes as he examined every detail of the boy's features. The best way to announce to everyone how much the boy meant to his father was to share something very precious only his parents could give him. "Daniel Parke Custis the second?"

He nodded, but never took his gaze from our son. "Exactly."

"Then so be it." A flush of contentment washed through me. I looked at our boy, then Daniel, and then included the ladies in the room. "Thank you for helping me bring our son into this world. Daniel, will you do the honor of entering his name and birthdate in the Bible, please?"

"I will take care of the matter posthaste." Daniel couldn't drag his gaze from the infant, eyes bright with pride.

I laughed, delighted in being able to bring such joy to my husband. Lowering my gaze to the suckling babe in my arms, I silently vowed our son would always know his parents loved him. He'd want for nothing. Most of all, our affection.

# 5

The clang of steel on steel from the sword play demonstration reverberated across the square, a rhythmic beat to constant merriment of the public times. Daniel and I strolled along Gloucester Street, bedazzled by the array of splendor and chaos of the market. Vendors hawked every kind of produce imaginable, their shouts of enticement echoing in my ears.

Stalls holding grunting pigs, clucking hens, and crowing roosters added to the symphony of sound. Coming to town meant coming alive, much as a crocus emerges from the snow, all amidst the fun of dueling demonstrations, athletic contests, and street musicians. And of course the dinners and balls with the gentry of the region, an opportunity to don my finest satins and silks, with laces and ruffles dripping from my elbows and edging my gown's bodice.

Even my new bulging belly, baby number two, wouldn't deter me from enjoying the birthday celebration in honor of our king and the chance to see the new ballroom added on to the Governor's Palace. I rejoiced in the life inside of me, frequently resting a hand on the growing baby I carried as testament to the love and honor I shared with its father. If Daniel seemed more distant than previously, I had only to consider the strain he remained under with all of the worries and obligations from the many farms and hands he managed. I hoped to distract him and ease his mind while we ventured away from our day-to-day cares.

"Do you suppose Daniel is old enough to enjoy the festivities?" We'd left him at the house with his servant while we took a turn around town. I squeezed my husband's arm as we passed a gaily clad woman selling baubles and paste jewelry. The sparkle and glitter beckoned me, but I resisted. Daniel preferred I didn't wear cheap jewelry, but only the finest he could buy from London. He desired to maintain proper appearances and I could not fault him for his fancy.

"At thirteen months of age? I would not think so." He drew me closer to permit another couple to pass. "Before long, we will want to change for the play. I understand the performance of *Othello* is entertaining. William Shakespeare at his best, I'm told."

Plays were always a pleasant distraction from the daily tasks and obligations. Only twice a year did we come to town to be part of the public times and be entertained by such frivolities. I looked at the sky, noting the gathering of white puffy clouds against the azure heavens. "It is well that the open air playhouse was replaced with a building behind the Capitol. Now it won't matter if the weather is foul or fair."

Daniel glanced at the sky and then me. "It will be a fine evening, though perhaps cold. If you'd rather not attend, I will understand. Especially with regard to your condition."

"Miss the play? I think not." Why had we come to Williamsburg if not to partake of the fun? Despite his preference to refrain from the gay scene of the public times, I believed a change would benefit his mood. Help him relax and let go of his worries. Not that I'd tell him as much. Better to place the blame on myself. "I receive great pleasure from the stories performed on stage. I want to see the new playhouse, as well."

"An invitation to the ball arrived this morning." Daniel

stepped to one side to avoid a puddle, pulling me with him so my skirt missed the muddy water. "I've accepted for us."

A thrill raced through me. "I am looking forward to dancing with you in the new ballroom. I hear they have an entire room set aside for supper as well. It must be very grand."

"Yes, I was given a tour of the new addition when I called on Governor Dinwiddie upon our arrival to town."

We strolled together in companionable silence, soaking in the sights and sounds of the merry crowds on the street. The entire town came out to be part of the gathering. For me, these trips were the best parts of my year. Times when my family could enjoy being together without the daily burdens, to reconnect with distant family and friends, and to learn of recent events of note.

The weeks of preparation to move the family from the plantation to the town home had flown by. The servants had been very busy while I helped with selecting the proper clothes and necessities, and then packing everything in trunks and cases for the coach trip to town. It only took a day or two to settle in at the more refined Six Chimneys House and give us time to relax and take in the many attractions of the town gathering.

We left little Daniel playing with his servant in the extensive garden my deceased father-in-law had designed and developed. I couldn't help but smile when I thought of our strong young son. Soon the family would expand again. Our next child was due to be born in the spring, my favorite time of year. After the cold of winter, the warmth of the air carrying scents of flowers and newly turned earth ready for planting quickened my heart.

"There was news at the Raleigh this morning."

Daniel's tone hinted at some sadness. The Raleigh Tavern served as the nexus of information exchange in the capital, a place where the burgesses frequented to discuss everything from market news to family scandals. I braced myself for his next words.

"Do you recall when Bellhaven was founded a few years ago?"

"That's the pet name for Alexandria, is it not?" I briefly pursed my lips before relaxing them into a welcoming smile aimed at the elderly couple approaching us. While I hadn't traveled to Bellhaven, I recalled the port town nestled on the west bank of the Potomac. I'd heard on more than one occasion from some of our visitors that the small city had its charms, which apparently attracted artisans and merchants alike.

"Indeed." Daniel cleared his throat and swallowed as we strolled along the street. "It seems the gentleman responsible for its creation, Lawrence Washington, died from tuberculosis in July. His loss will be felt in this colony for some time."

"Have I met him? I do not recall his face." I searched my memory but could not picture the man. His name seemed familiar, though. Where had I heard it? Or the family name? I puzzled over it while Daniel shook his head.

"I do not believe so, my dear. I've mentioned him to you only because he was one of the founders of the Ohio Company in the Northern Neck, as well. The company designed to open trade with lands farther inland along the Potomac River. Without such innovations, our colony would not thrive. He did much great service for Virginia in his lifetime."

"I'm sure his family will miss him as well. My heart goes out to them." Death seemed so prevalent, surrounding me. Smallpox continued to claim lives, as did yellow fever and consumption. The receipt book from Daniel's mother had proven worth its weight in gold more than once in healing or curing an illness among my extended family. Without the instructions and hints contained in my inheritance from the woman, I'd not be so fortunate in keeping my people well.

"He didn't leave much family behind, sad to say." Daniel greeted a man in an exquisitely embroidered coat and dark breeches, his polished boots and black tricorne hat adding to his distinguished appearance. "His widow, Anne, and four children. As well as his half-brother, George."

My thoughts lingered on the grieving family until my gaze landed upon a group of children chasing their rolling hoops with sticks. I laughed at the joy evident in their expressions. I placed a hand on my slightly bulging stomach, eager to meet my unborn child and add to our family. Little Daniel would have a brother or sister in about five months to play with and confide in much like I had done with my kin. So many years of playing and romping, of secrets and promises shared. My childhood seemed ages ago when in fact I'd only been married for two and a half years. How did the years slip away so fast? Which made me think of another happening during the course of the year.

"What do you think of the Parliamentary decree to change the calendar September last?" A bolt of dismay flew through my chest as I contemplated the ramifications of the decree. "Does that change the date of our wedding anniversary?"

"The adoption of the Gregorian calendar in place of the Julian will not affect our anniversary, my dear." He chuckled. "We were married on May 15 and we shall celebrate that wonderful occasion on May 15 of each year."

We turned in front of the capitol to walk down Blair Street, after making our way through the increasing crowds. As late afternoon arrived, more people were in search of their dinners so the area back by the taverns had been very busy indeed. Blair was quieter and we sauntered the several blocks to turn on Francis Street and head back toward the northern end of town and our home.

Suddenly, Daniel guffawed, a most unusual occurrence which had me turning to him with surprise. "Whatever is the matter?"

His chuckle continued for several moments before he sobered enough to speak. "I heard that Benjamin Franklin, our most respectable diplomat, made his attempt to calm the rioting of those who feared they were losing eleven days of their lives through a joke of sorts. He wrote, if I remember correctly, 'It is pleasant for an old man to go to bed on September second, and not have to get up until September fourteenth.' What a wonderful attitude to have. But imagine all the work left undone that he must then complete."

I laughed along with my husband. Even I was aware of the famous Mr. Franklin, an inventor who had recently created what he called a lightning rod to channel lightning into the ground instead of destroying a building when it hit. Ingenious man! The riots he attempted to calm with words had rocked London. All because people feared the supposed loss of days by merely changing the numbering of them. I chuckled to myself at the folly.

We arrived at Six Chimneys House at the end of Francis Street and went inside, the warmth welcome on such a chilly afternoon. Yet the house awoke so many conflicting feelings in my breast. Daniel also seemed strained by living in his father's house, reminded of so many horrid moments they had exchanged during the old man's life.

"If you need me, I'll be in the office for a time." Daniel shrugged off his cloak and hung it on the peg by the door. He sighed as he lifted mine from my shoulders and added it to its peg.

"What is it, dear?" I peered at the concern evident on his face.

"Nothing to worry your pretty head about." He gazed at me for a moment before pressing a kiss to my forehead. "Sometimes I swear I feel his presence in this house and I long to be rid of it. But how can we?"

"If you'd prefer, we could sell the place."

"We need it when we come into town. Otherwise, we'd not have room for everyone, nor would we be as comfortable."

"We'd manage, I'm sure." I laid a hand on his arm. "Whatever pleases you."

He nodded and placed his hand on mine, then leaned down to kiss me. "For now, we'll keep it."

The imposing house was the only negative aspect of coming into town. Fiscally, it made perfect sense to retain the house for these occasions. My sentiments struggled with the reality. His father continued his tirade despite his death, as evidenced through the ongoing legalities Daniel wrestled without reprieve. The Dunbar suit stemming from his aunt's inheritance also continued to vex. I feared the anxieties he harbored inside would make him ill, but he merely pushed aside my worries as so much fluff.

————————

The next evening, we took the carriage to the palace, arriving in grand fashion befitting Daniel's position. Memories of my presentation to society played through my mind until the carriage halted. I'd chosen a silk gown with garnet skirt panels featuring silver embroidery and sequins scattered across the gold bodice for tonight's festivities. I again wore my special stays due to being with child, but they were not fully loosened as I wasn't showing much yet. I also wore my favorite watch, a piece of jewelry I seldom went without.

The carriage stopped at the front gate, the postilion handing me down into the care of Daniel. I have always been proud of my husband, but that night he looked more dashing than ever. I felt giddy taking his arm and walking with him up the steps and into the grand foyer. The walls were covered in swords, guns, shields, and the royal crest.

"Excuse me, Daniel, while I join the ladies." He let me go with a gentle smile, then turned to address the other men lingering in the foyer waiting for their women to return.

I slipped into a side room, one normally used to welcome important guests to the palace. I unfastened my cloak and added it to the growing pile on the couch. All around me, women wore elaborately coiffed and powdered hairstyles, some with jewels in their curls like the strand of small pearls I wore. Naturally, the gowns represented a rainbow of colors and the latest fashions we could import from the motherland. The other ladies chatted while I slid my leather protective shoes off of my satin slippers and placed them out of the way. My slippers had as high of a heel as I could manage to help me feel taller. I went back to Daniel, aware he wished to join the dancers as soon as possible.

Moments later we entered the new ballroom and I couldn't help the pride swelling my chest as I gazed on the beautiful floor, the soaring blue walls and white door frames intricately carved with raised motifs. Branched candlesticks hung from the ceiling, the candles ablaze. The musicians played their instruments: a harpsichord, flute, and violin. The sound filled the room and I was awed by the experience. Closing my eyes, I listened to the rhythm of the dancing couples' footsteps and the tune. Then Daniel propelled me forward, my eyes flying open as we navigated our way to the far side of the room. Truly, the ballroom was a grand addition to the palace. Well worth the expense and trouble. A young woman's first presentation in this ballroom would be a memorable event, much more so than the plainer upstairs hall of the Capitol. But if not for my own presentation there, I may not be standing with Daniel as my husband and the father of my children.

I searched the growing crowd for familiar faces. Having come to the ball most every year, I had made an increasing number of friends and acquaintances. Daniel's position and reputation ensured my reception in the highest circles of society. I nodded to several ladies and their partners standing across the large room.

Daniel guided me with a hand clasping my elbow as we passed through the open double doors into the supper hall. The warmth of his fingers seared through the fabric of my gown, lingering when he dropped his grip. Several tables stood draped in white cloths and held a variety of delicacies. The room felt more intimate but no less remarkable. My eyes were drawn to the elaborate wall paper and high ceilings. The governor's wife must have had a hand in selecting the décor and furnishings.

"Mr. Custis!"

I smiled at the sound of our good friend, David Lee. He escorted a beautiful woman over to stand with us. She regarded me with dark eyes, her light brown hair swept into a chignon. Her gown stole my breath. A pale blue satin, shot through with silver threads and set off by pale yellow ribbons and trim. I did not know her, but I guessed she was his wife he'd spoken of so fondly during his visits. Melanie, or Marinda. Something that started with an M.

Daniel shook hands with David. "Well met, my friend. Please, introduce me to your companion."

David grinned and swept a hand toward the woman. "Mr. and Mrs. Custis, may I present my wife, Melanie Lee."

Melanie dipped a curtsy, as did I. Daniel half bowed and then straightened to his full height. Which of course made me feel short again. My bane. If only God had seen fit to grant me more height perhaps I wouldn't so often feel invisible or overlooked. I heard footsteps behind me and glanced over my shoulder to determine if I recognized the new arrivals. Clapping my hands in delight, I spun in place to greet my parents.

"I'm pleased you changed your minds and came to town." Hugging my mother, then my father, I included them in our little group with proper introductions.

My heart rejoiced, as I had not had opportunity to visit with Mother over the last month and I wished to speak with her regarding the advancement of my condition.

"How did your horse fare in the races today?" Daniel addressed my father with a sly wink and a laugh. "Did your jockey win or fall off again?"

Father huffed and shook his head. "Neither. He came in second, much to my chagrin."

"Pray tell me you refrained from wagering on your placement?" David lifted a shaggy brow.

"I must remain mum then." Father shrugged and splayed his hands, palms up. "I thought he would take first place with his ancestry and clean legs."

Mother glanced at me and lifted her shoulders in a resigned shrug. Her movement and expression told me she did not begrudge Father his fun. He did love the horse races, and went to them at every opportunity. Whether he had a horse of his own in the race, or wanted to bolster a friend's attempts, he frequented the gatherings. Virginia horses were avidly sought out by breeders in the other colonies, for they were renowned for their fine confirmation and speed. Father never tired of discussing the pedigrees and offspring of his horses.

The music changed to a country dance and I laid a hand on Daniel's arm to attract his attention. He inclined his head, bringing his ear closer to me so he could hear me over the din of chatter and music. "Might we join the dance?"

He took my hand as he addressed our little group. "If you'll excuse us, my wife wishes to dance."

Soon we took our places at the foot of the line of couples. I was swept away by the beat, the clapping, the steps. We danced several hornpipes and reels, until I was flushed and breathless. But I wanted to share the pleasure of the dance with my husband while I had the chance. Ere long, my condition would prevent me from dancing, and then after the baby was born, it would be a while before I'd be able to attend the public times, let alone dance. Tonight, we'd enjoy each other's company and let to-morrow take care of itself.

---

*White House Plantation – 1754*

I have always hated the cold of the winters, so was grateful the temperatures over the last couple of months had been mild. Not hot, but at least not stinging cold with piles of snow. I enjoyed the reprieve to an extent. But the rains that fell off and on through mid-February didn't want to let the sun shine and left me unsettled and irritable. Even my ten-month-old daughter Fanny's laughter proved irksome at times.

Young Daniel, at a few months past his second birthday, was not well, which added to my anxiety. He'd been hale and hearty, his usual cheerful self, then suddenly he started vomiting and his cheeks burned with fever. When he started shaking so violently he could barely stand on his pudgy toddler legs, I put him to bed, covered him with the quilt I'd made for him, and consulted my receipt book for possible causes and cures. The clawing fear in my breast only worsened when I determined he had become ill with malaria.

My thoughts strayed to the agonizing death of Aunt Unity the year before. She'd suffered great pain and fever in her last days on earth. Carter Braxton, who served as a Burgess in the General Assembly, bought the property in short order, a great relief of the financial burden for a young woman. I would miss visiting my cousin, though.

Daniel had tried to calm my agitation regarding our son, reminding me that most everyone suffered from the ague as a result of contracting the dreaded disease. Yet, we both knew not everyone survived. With him being so young, would my son have the strength to fight it off?

My usual routine had been interrupted as a result of young Daniel's illness. I thought of him with every step of my day, keeping close by so I could hear when he cried out or moaned. His servant also stayed close to attend to the slop bucket when the poor wee boy needed to vomit. Or changing his bed linens when he sweated as his fever fluctuated. We took turns sitting with him. I'd stay as long as I could tolerate, but watching my boy struggle against the shakes and chills, the purges of his belly, and the raging heat in his body brought tears to my eyes and quaked my comportment. A quick walk to the privy or for a sip of water allowed me a moment to restore my composure so when I returned to his side I could be strong for him. The weaker he became, though, the more difficult my task.

On top of the worry about Daniel, I also realized my flow had stopped, indicating another child grew inside my womb. I rejoiced our family grew so quickly. I longed for a house full of children to love and help become wonderful people. Fanny was almost one year old, come mid-April. I figured the next baby would arrive sometime in the fall, likely November. Three beautiful children to celebrate with over the holidays starting with Christmas and ending at the boisterous festivities of Twelfth Night in January.

The days dragged by, each one much like another. Visitors came and went, staying for a night, inviting us to attend a horse race or a fish bake. I declined their invitations, refusing to leave my son's side even for a few hours. My daughter Fanny didn't comprehend why her brother stayed in his bed, and why they couldn't play together. I made sure she stayed away from him, not wishing to risk her becoming ill as well.

One afternoon while I was conferring with the cook as to a special soup I wished to try to help my son, I had an awful sensation rush through me. As though a piece of my soul had been ripped out. I grabbed up my skirts and raced to his room, uncaring as to propriety or fashion. Only reaching his side mattered. Something terrible had happened while I spoke to the cook. While I'd been away from my son's side. When I arrived in his room, the black woman tending him raised startled eyes at me. Without a word, I hurried to stand by his bed, gazing down on a silent, and too still, toddler.

I don't know what I did as the realization sunk in that my son had died. My mind clouded, refusing to process the scene before me. It couldn't be, but it was. Tears flooded my face as I gently lifted him and cuddled him to my chest. The pain inside my heart at the death of my sweet child, so young, made me gasp and close my eyes. I couldn't bear it. Definitely not alone. I opened my eyes and caught the slave's attention. My throat ached, fighting to speak around sobs. "Molly, get Mr. Custis."

"Yes'm." The woman, tears glistening on her cheeks, fled the room in search of my husband.

Ere long, heavy footsteps echoed on the wooden stairs. Daniel burst into the room, distraught and pale. He crossed to me in four long strides, wrapping his arms around me and our son as he kissed my cheek. He didn't say a word for several minutes, staring at the fans of eyelashes closed forever and the cute nose and relaxed lips. He struggled to refrain from crying himself, but I could tell the effort it took to stifle sobs eager to burst forth from his chest.

"I'll inform the carpenter so he can make the coffin." His voice broke over the last word and he swallowed once before continuing. "My son."

I leaned against him, my back to his chest, his strong arms still enveloping me. I feared if he moved away, I'd shatter into a million pieces. I heard Fanny cry downstairs and wondered what had afflicted her, but the still form in my arms needed me more. I recalled the day my brother died, how distraught I had been. But this threatened to destroy me. Sniffing back the tears, I dug into my soul for strength. Lifted a prayer for help. Rousing myself, I pulled away from Daniel, away from his loving support. I had to be strong for my family, no matter how much pain I felt inside. They needed me to help them through this tragedy. Pushing aside my deep grief enough to function, I straightened but retained a firm grip on my son.

"Go let folks know while I prepare him for burial." I gulped, forcing the acid taste from my mouth. Strong. Be strong for Daniel and Fanny.

Daniel lowered his gaze to rest on our son. Tears clung to his lashes and I had to look away or start crying again myself. "Tomorrow will be soon enough to bury him. I'll make the arrangements."

He kissed me, then, a gentle press of his lips to mine, and I knew we would survive the grief clawing through us. We had to for our daughter and unborn child. After he left the room, I asked Molly to fill the tub with warm water. While she retrieved the water from the well, lugging up bucket after bucket, and then warming it with boiling water from the kettle, I worked on removing his clothes. A task that normally took moments, but my movements had been weighted with my sorrow. Each tie to untie, each lift of fabric, tortured my soul. How would I make it through bathing him, dressing him in his clean night gown, and then laying him out for the overnight vigil? Then to sit with him all night, hoping and praying he'd resume breathing? I prayed to God to help me. My heart faltered. I had to move. To find a path through the pain.

---

The next afternoon, we gathered at the family grave yard in Queens Creek, my husband's mother's dower property. I had not visited the property often, but after we buried our son, I could imagine that would change. God understood our misery and kept the rain from falling as several men lowered the hexagonal coffin into the earth. The minister spoke words meant to comfort the small gathering of family and friends, all dressed in dark somber attire, who surrounded the grave. I held Fanny, anchored to one hip, her arms around my neck a comfort. Daniel stepped forward to scoop a handful of dirt from the pile resulting from the men's efforts, and hesitated for two heart beats before opening his hand to let the small clods fall softly on the wooden surface of our son's final bed. I had already told Daniel I could not contribute to burying our boy by adding dirt to his grave. I stood with Fanny, quietly singing a lullaby while the sound of shovels scraping and clods falling on top of my son filled my ears.

I prayed to a loving God to care for Daniel, my sweet angel, even as I wished He had not taken my first born. As we rode back to White House, a silent group in the rattling carriage, I vowed again to do all in my power to protect and provide for my children. Surely I could find a way to keep death from visiting our door.

Life went on, the day in and day out tasks of plantation life. We had our typical number of guests through the spring and summer months. David Lee made his annual visit, bringing word of Indian attacks on the frontier. Governor Dinwiddie had sent Major George Washington to try to settle the dispute, but the result was that France and Britain were at war again. I had not heard anything more about the major since Daniel had told me of his brother's death two years before. But others were starting to regard him as an important person in the Virginia colony. I figured I should be more aware of the state of affairs in the colony to make informed comments when we discussed the topics with both my husband and our guests.

Finally, after enduring the hot summer while carrying a child, another son was born in November. We named him John Parke

Custis, but we called him Jacky in honor of my brother. The Parke name was forced upon another family member in order to meet the inheritance requirements of John Custis' will. As the year approached its end, I prayed that I could fulfill my promises to my family better in the next year than in the last.

6

*White House – 1756*

The breeze flowing off the Pamunkey provided no relief from the hottest summer I could recall. I had been busy rearing my two babes and running the household while Daniel worked to increase the tobacco yield and diversify the crops on the other farms. The quality of the tobacco depended on the fertility of the fields, so he insisted on rotating which fields were planted in the wide leafed plant.

Last fall I discovered I was with child again and my heart filled to bursting with joy. But imagine how my mother felt when she also discovered she was with child at forty-six years old! She had thought her childbearing years behind her. What a unique experience we shared, the two of us with child at the same time.

I attended Mother's lying in back in April despite my being big with child, so I was one of the first to welcome my new sister, Mary, to the family. Father's pride at his beautiful daughter shown plainly on his face. I sent a quick prayer to heaven that one day I'd have such a large brood of children around me. Inside me was child number four, but my mother had birthed a total of eight children in her lifetime. I hoped to do the same. At twenty-five years old, I still had plenty of time to reach my goal.

A few months later, I delivered a little girl into the happy arms of my husband. Despite some difficulties with her delivery, she was a healthy baby. We named her after both sides of our family: Martha Parke Custis. Like me, her pet name would be Patsy. She was born with dark hair and dark eyes, features we share. Daniel said it was like seeing his wife as a baby, which made us both smile.

The heat made Patsy uncomfortable, and she cried and wailed no matter what I tried. I had thought I knew how to care for babies, but her sensitive nature made comforting her difficult. Finally, in desperation, I carried her outside, Fanny and Jacky toddling along, and sat under a shady tree while she nursed. I tried to relax on the pretty bench Daniel had placed under the sugar maple. We'd celebrated Fanny's third birthday April last, and Jacky approached his second November next. With Patsy only a few months old, coupled with the August heat wave, my hands had become full indeed. But I treasured every moment and looked forward to adding to my family.

Around us the usual comings and goings of the plantation flowed in a steady rhythm. The washer women carried bundles in and out of the laundry, the lines filled with drying clothes swaying in the breeze. The carpenter pounded on a wagon wheel in need of mending. Smoke from the kitchen fires mingled with the river scents. I loved my life and my family with every breath I took. I couldn't image a prettier way of life than the one we had created.

My family would grow in another way, too. Nancy had a beau. Burwell Bassett had asked Father if he might court my sister, and Father approved. Burwell came from a sterling family, and he seemed to have a fine head on his shoulders. I believed he'd be able to provide well for my favorite sister. If affairs sorted out, they would likely marry next year, and then there'd be more children to love and cherish.

Jacky chased Fanny across the yard to the swing their father had hung from a tree branch. His short legs were no match for her longer ones. She reached the seat first and wiggled onto it, then took several steps backward, preparing to launch the swing in its pendulum arc, even as Jacky moved in front of her.

"Fanny, watch out for your brother!" Too late. A rush akin to fear swept through me.

Fanny's feet struck Jacky in the chest, and he sat down with a thud and a gasp. Then the crying began, a high-pitched wail of hurt. I struggled to my feet, careful not to disturb my baby, and hurried over to check on him. Possible injuries raced through my mind with each stride.

"Fanny, stop that swing this minute." I reached Jacky's side and helped him up with one hand. A quick perusal revealed no blood or broken bones. "You'll be fine. Now stop that crying. Fanny, tell Jacky you're sorry you hurt him."

"But Mama..." Fanny sat on the still swing, grabbing the ropes as though she feared falling off.

"Now." She had to learn to protect her brother from harm, not cause it. "He's your younger brother, and it's your job to look out for him. Now tell him you're sorry."

She huffed a sigh and looked at the grass below her dangling feet. "I'm sorry, Jacky."

"For?" I waited for her to complete the apology. Jacky sniffled at my side, dragging the back of a hand across his nose while he clung to my hand with the other.

She sighed again. "I'm sorry for knocking you down when you got in the way."

"Frances, you know better than that."

"He did."

Her whine tugged at my heart. "I understand, but you knew if you started the swing when he was in front of you that this could happen. Now please, say you're sorry properly."

Her eyes met mine as she slowly blinked once. Then she let her gaze drop to where Jacky stood. "I'm sorry I didn't protect you, Jacky."

Love swelled my breast. "Thank you, Fanny. That was lovely. Jacky, let's move over here, and you can watch Fanny swing for a while. Do you mind keeping me company?" I talked to my sniffling son as I led him back to the bench. Fanny soon had the swing rapidly climbing in its arc, her long curls flowing out behind her with each forward movement.

"Okay, Mama. What are you doing?" He peeked at my sleeping Patsy as he squirmed onto the seat.

"I finished giving your sister her meal, and now I'm simply holding her while she sleeps." My beautiful little girl. So alike to both me and to Fanny. So different from my sons.

My grief over our first son's death had abated but I'd wondered on more than one occasion what sort of man he would have grown up to become. What kind of life would he have made for himself? I liked to pretend a future for him at first, until I realized comparing my fantasy to the reality only made me sadder. In order to nurture my children, I had to live for them instead of continuing to wallow in my sad ponderings. But that did not mean I'd ever forget my first child.

Hoof beats thundered up the lane at the back of the house, away from the river front where we sat in the shade. I rose and extended my hand to Jacky. "Come. Let's see who has arrived."

Jacky hopped off the seat and took my hand. I looked at Fanny, who seeing us moving toward the house jumped off the swing and ran to join us. We barely reached the steps before the door burst open and my brother William rushed outside.

His eyes were red and wild, his hair blown by the gallop. He drew in a long breath as he raced down the steps and grasped my arm with shaking hands. "Come inside, my dear sister. I have heartbreaking news to relay."

A dart of worry flew through me at both his appearance and the strangled tone of his voice. I glanced at the children and then nodded to him. What dreadful tale would he tell? "Very well. Come, my dears, let's find Molly, shall we? I'm sure it's time for your dinner."

Surprisingly, they did not quibble with me. Perhaps they sensed the somber attitude of William and on some level knew not to push. Within a few minutes, Molly had taken control of my children and I followed William into the parlor. The windows stood wide open but no breath of air crossed into the room. No relief from the heavy heat of the day or the concern etched onto my brother's features.

I sat on the settee and William took a seat beside me. Sweat droplets slithered down my back. His trembling vibrated the furniture beneath me and I lifted a puzzled and worried brow in his direction. "Tell me your news."

"I know not how to say it." He raked a hand through his tousled hair, which was unusually not in a queue or bag. The luxurious tresses were battered and tossed by the wind from his urgent ride.

Whatever had upset him, had indeed shaken his, or rather our world. I held my breath, expectation a sharp sword at my throat.

"Our father has died." He lifted his gaze from staring at the bare wood floor boards. "He suffered an apoplexy while at the horse race with cousin Mary Spotswood. He was buried posthaste."

I gasped and grabbed the base of my throat as my eyes smarted. I could not speak for several moments as the meaning of his words scarred my heart. I brushed tears from my cheeks. Father dead? "How – how is Mother? Why were we not told sooner? Where's he buried?"

William clutched my cold hands, his warmth searing my skin. "The heat would have decomposed the body too quickly for them to wait. Even if they had sent word, neither you nor Mother is in any condition to make such an arduous journey in the heat. They did what was right. He's buried in the church yard there, in Fredericksburg, with proper respect."

"And Mother?"

"As expected, she collapsed and has taken to her bed. I've sent for the doctor to give her a sedative to help her cope." He paused, hesitating to say the thought reflected in his solemn gaze. "This means the management of Chestnut Grove falls to me now, as the eldest son."

"Yes, that would be true." I knew we both at that moment thought of our brother, Jacky. If he'd lived, the mantle of responsibility would have fallen to him. "You are the eldest living son, and Father has taught you what you need to know in order to take his place."

William jumped to his feet and began pacing from one end of the small space to the other, avoiding the few chairs and casual tables. After several laps, he stopped and shook his head. "I'll take the reins, but no one could ever replace John Dandridge."

My grief overcame my composure and I sank back on the settee, sobbing. Colonel John Dandridge had been a larger than life force in my world. He'd built Chestnut Grove into a steady working plantation that provided for his family with abounding laughter and love. Bereft, I'd never see my father again, hear his robust voice, or feel his loving arms embrace me. At least I'd told him I loved him the last time we were together. The depth of pain I experienced in that moment could not compete with what my mother endured. I straightened my spine and wrestled my sobs into silence, dabbing my eyes with my sleeve since I had dropped my handkerchief somewhere in our hurry to come inside. I sniffed and cleared my throat, drawing William's attention.

"We will never forget our father. He will live forever in our hearts and thoughts. You will do him honor by living as the decent and loving man you have become under his tutelage and example." I stood and crossed to stand before him, lifting my damp chin so I could look into his eyes. "Together, we'll care for our mother and ensure her health and security."

He wrapped his arms around my shoulders and drew me to rest my head on his chest while we cried together. Cruel death had visited my family again, and I was not sure if I could bear the hole left in my heart with each visit.

———————

*White House – 1757*

June arrived and brought with it a highly respected itinerant portraitist to capture our likenesses in oil on canvas. The larger-than-life images would be hung in the parlor as evidence of my husband's wealth and power. Image was everything in the colonies, especially in the south. As Mother had taught me long ago, fashion applied to practically everything: clothing, furnishings, houses, and landscaping. Still, I dreaded the event more than I could adequately put into words. I went in search of my husband, finally locating him conversing with the head groom. After several minutes, the groom nodded and left, and Daniel turned toward me.

"Daniel, please send him away."

He frowned and tilted his head. "Who, my dear?"

"Mr. Wollaston."

"But he's already arrived. He's been expecting to do our portraits since last year."

"I understand, but I don't desire to sit for him." I lowered my eyes to stare at the dusty ground. Death had paid us yet another visit two months previous. I didn't want to reveal the depth of my anguish over his taking our precious little Fanny. How could I do something so frivolous as have my formal portrait painted when grief burdened my heart and soul with each breath?

He moved closer and tapped my chin with one finger. His dark eyes searched my face for a long moment. "I miss our little girl so very much, but we must live on."

"Must that include portraits?" One of each of us, and then one of our two living children, Jacky and Patsy. "It seems too soon."

The difficulties associated with grieving, such as breathing and walking without crying, seemed to increase with each occurrence. My distress over my daughter's death had only begun to ease.

"Trust me, my sweet, you shall one day be glad of my insistence on the matter."

I drew in a long breath while I reviewed all the reasons to disagree. I could see in his expression how much he desired for me to agree with his declaration. I shrugged with one shoulder. "Very well. But only because I promised to honor and obey and I always keep my promises."

His chuckle died out as he strode away to tend to the business of the plantation. I spun on my heel and marched inside, intent on taking care of my own duties as best I could even if my heart rebelled.

I had started, at my mother's urging, spending time each morning in solitude with my Bible and God, praying for the strength and courage I needed to face another day. I've always held a deep belief in the power of our father above, but I needed to lean more upon his word to bolster my ability to carry on. His word stood as a constant reminder of his love in an inconstant world.

The only joy I found in my world revolved around family. First, my children and husband, and then the rest of the family and its gains and losses. Over the last few months, I'd visited my mother every few days and was heartened that her grief over Father's passing had lessened but his memory had not. William adapted to the unwanted role of manager of the plantation's finances and activities. In fact, Chestnut Grove hummed along almost as though John Dandridge continued as owner. My mother and I had shed tears together more than once over our recent losses, but we must go on and be strong for our surviving relatives.

My beloved Nancy had married Burwell last month at Chestnut Grove. I had helped Mother and Nancy plan the decorations and supper. A festive day ensued with family and friends from all around gathering to celebrate their marriage. After the wedding festivities ended, Burwell took Nancy to live in Williamsburg where he would continue his work for the government. As a result, I no longer had frequent opportunity to visit with my sister. In effect, I gained a brother-in-law but lost my sister. At least they lived close enough to visit on occasion.

The day-to-day activities of the plantation continued to keep me busy. I welcomed the tasks as a means to distract me from my lingering grief over poor sweet Fanny. Death had taken her swiftly, so quickly I did not fathom what happened. One day she seemed fine, and the next she'd stopped breathing. Daniel had been heartbroken as well when we gathered once more in our mourning clothes beside the little grave on Queens Creek. Instead of fruitlessly dwelling on what might have caused her death, I tried to concentrate on keeping my other two children hale and hearty. As God was my witness, I never wanted to bury another of my children.

After more prayer and consideration, I realized by capturing their likenesses on canvas I'd always have Jacky and Patsy with me in one sense, unlike little Daniel and Fanny whom I'd never see again. The image of Fanny flashed in my mind, of her pattering about the house in her little red shoes, the dolly Daniel had ordered from London clutched in her arms. Her laugh and squeals as she played with Jacky. I wiped away a tear and pushed on with my work.

Mr. John Wollaston, who had arrived the day before, came highly recommended to Daniel from his acquaintances. The handsome young man with curly brown hair and refined features had worked for many distinguished families in New York, Philadelphia, and across Maryland before making his way into Virginia. He'd spent the last couple of years working at various homes, including those of the powerful Randolph family, before he came to White House.

I sat on a cushioned chair in the small parlor and watched as he worked on the children's double portrait. They were dressed in their finest attire, like tiny adults. She wore a rose-colored satin gown with red shoes, and a pretty ribbon and pearls in her wispy baby hair. Jacky looked much like a younger version of his father in his silk vest and dark coat and knickers with white hose to his knees.

"Mr. Wollaston, the pet red bird on Jacky's hand is a clever way to entice him to remain posed as you like." Heaven knows that my son would much rather be outside than standing in the parlor dressed as if attending court. The bird provided an ongoing fascination.

"I thought the young man might find it distracting." The painter kept his gaze on his canvas, dabbing and stroking with efficiency, working on the facial features of the children. Then their attire. The setting he'd fill in later from memory.

"Patsy, leave the ribbon alone." I raised one brow as I gave her a quelling look.

"Yes, Mama." She dropped her fidgety fingers back to the rose laying in her lap.

Daniel had placed the order for the ribbons with fatherly pride as well as compassion for my mother. He'd requested a pair of satin shoes for Mother in a suitable color for mourning. Also on the list was a saddle and bridle for Jacky's pony. For Fanny, he requested some little dresses and caps, and then realized she needed her own slate and pencils so she could learn her alphabet. He'd added in the ribbons at the last moment, knowing how much Patsy loved them in her hair.

Daniel went second to have his portrait done, to get it over with. June was a very busy time for plantation owners as well as the servants and slaves. He'd seemed extraordinarily concerned recently about the quality of the crops, and I couldn't help but wonder why. And worry about the unknown reasons. Still, over several days, he waited upon the demands of Mr. Wollaston, while I kept a close eye on my husband's mood and health.

At long last, my turn arrived. I chose my favorite gown, a silver laced and beribboned blue dress with yellow stomacher and petticoat. Sally fixed my hair, complete with strands of pearls woven into the smooth chignon. I strolled casually, more slowly than normal, to stand in the parlor where the light proved best for the man's work.

"Mrs. Custis, please stand over here by this chair and hold

your right hand out as if you're picking a flower from a bush."
John Wollaston demonstrated how to place my hand and angle
my person so my left shoulder and hip aimed just over his right
shoulder as he worked.

"Picking a flower? There is no bush in my parlor." I smiled at
him, knowing he'd fill in the background details from his own
imagination.

He chuckled and set to work while the children, having changed
into their every day clothes, ran about, asking me questions, teasing
me into a grin or a laugh.

"Mrs. Custis, please stay in the pose. I'm almost finished. Just
a few more strokes today and we can resume to-morrow."

"It is rather tiring to stand thus." My arm ached from holding
it out to my right, palm up and fingers closed as if gripping a
flower stem.

"You'll be pleased with the completed picture." He made a
few more strokes, then paused with his brush hand in the air.
"Enough for today."

He finished his work over the next few days, charging Daniel
56 pistoles, the Spanish gold coin used between the colonies for
payment. The expense would prove worth while in establishing
Daniel's station in Virginia, and to keep my children's presence
forever in the house.

---

On July 4, a day forever emblazoned upon my memory, Jacky
came in from playing outside and his slow steps alerted me to
trouble. Patsy crawled into the hall in her baby dress, then sat
down to watch her brother make his way to me, one thumb
finding its way into her mouth. Jacky's flushed cheeks contrasted
sharply to his pale skin. Signs of a fever. A lead weight dropped in
my stomach. Dear God, not again. Three months after taking my
daughter, I could not permit God to take my son. I'd fight with
everything I could to keep Jacky with me. Calm. I had to remain
calm so as not to upset my children with my panic.

"Jacky, come here. Let me look at you." Peering closely at his bloodshot eyes, I laid a hand on his forehead. *Gramercy.*

I lifted him up and called out to Sally to find Daniel. Before long, I had Jacky in his bed, covered with a light blanket to prevent a chill on his feverish body. My mind raced, sorting through my next steps.

"Do you hurt anywhere, my dear?" I sat on the edge of his bed, examining him for bites and other symptoms. What ailment might he have?

"My throat hurts." He wrapped his hand around his neck as he whispered to me. "Mama, I don't feel good."

"I know, my sweet. Papa is on his way. I'll be back in a minute with something to help your throat feel better. Why don't you close your eyes and rest until I return."

He did as suggested, his long dark lashes fanned on his flushed cheeks. Fear, hot and sharp, consumed me. I turned away and hurried down to the basement and the medicines stored there. Honey, vinegar, a bit of saltpeter, blended together might soothe his throat, but what if he suffered from quinsy or diphtheria? My receipts for emetics and purges would not help if that were the case. Since I didn't know what Jacky had contracted, mayhap I should send for the doctor to determine the proper treatment.

As I hurried back up the stairs to the main floor, Daniel strode into the hall passage to meet me. One look at him and I knew he too was ill. I swallowed the panic rising in my throat, clawing for release. I had to stay calm and think. Rushing to Daniel's side, I peered up into his flushed face, his eyes glittering with fever.

"My darling, you must go to bed. I shall send for the doctor posthaste." I urged him toward our bedchamber but he resisted.

"What of Jacky?" Daniel's usual powerful voice emerged raspy and faint.

"He's in bed, as you should be. Come." I tugged on his arm and he acquiesced.

"I'm cold and my throat aches." He trailed after me, his boots shuffling along the wood floor.

"I'll get you warm, don't fear." He didn't need to for I feared enough for both of us with each step we took. I didn't want Death to revisit my family, not so soon after Fanny's passing.

In a matter of moments, he'd shucked his clothes down to his night shirt and lay under the marriage ring quilt I'd made after we'd first wed. The symbol of our shared love and life warmed my companion, my heart.

I sent one of the slaves to fetch medicine from Doctor Carter in Williamsburg, detailing to him the symptoms to relay. Then I did everything in my power to comfort and soothe my son and husband while my anxiety ratcheted up with each passing hour. After an eternity, the man returned with the precious drops, which I quickly administered as directed. Relief that help had arrived made it possible for me to attend to Patsy's needs with Sally and Molly's help in between checking on my patients.

I rose from my bed the next morning before the sun. I had not slept much, listening to Daniel's rapid breathing throughout the night. At least he lived. Throwing on my robe, I performed my morning necessities before judging my husband's condition. I could hear my heart beating in my ears, my angst multiplying in my chest when I realized he fared no better. The medicine had not worked. I raced to Jacky's room, and saw at once he'd not improved either. I fairly flew down the stairs, sliding several times on the steps in my satin slippers until I slowed to prevent a fall. I drew in a deep breath to calm myself then hurried to find someone to fetch the doctor.

Ever the consummate plantation owner, Daniel insisted on continuing to monitor the work of the farms from his sick bed. Despite my protests, he received each of his farm managers and issued orders. I listened with one ear to their conversations to ensure he didn't overexert himself and also to learn what the managers were concerned about. Mostly I listened to Daniel's voice. I feared he'd sap his strength and have no constitution to fight for his life. A fight he must win for all of our sakes.

Dr. James Carter arrived a few hours later, long agonizing hours during which I did my best to control my emotions.

Seeing my husband lying in so much pain and discomfort, his throat and jaw swollen, terrified me to my very soul. The problem was far beyond my simple cures. I fretted and feared for both Daniel and Jacky. Would God take them both from me?

"If you must work, at least lie back and try to relax." I tugged the blanket up around Daniel, wanting to strap him down to prevent him from rising.

"Do not worry, my dear, I do not possess the energy to move from this bed." Daniel attempted a smile but his lips grimaced in pain.

I looked to the good doctor. "Please, Dr. Carter, stay with us until my patients improve."

"I will do so, Mrs. Custis. I want to help them recover as much as you."

"I don't believe I could manage on my own." I released a long sigh of relief and worry.

Just then, my maid strode into the room with an armload of fresh linens. "Sally, please go to my mother's to inform her of the situation and to let her know the doctor has arrived."

"Yes'm." She deposited the sheets and blankets on a trunk and then left the room.

The message would keep my mother aware of the situation. I didn't want any one to be overly concerned when I knew in my heart of hearts that my kin would overcome the disease. They had to.

My anxiety grew over the next two days as Jacky showed no improvement. Daniel's condition likewise. The doctor smeared medicinal pastes made with honey on Jacky and Daniel's gums and tongues. Nothing made any difference.

Daniel's breathing became more and more labored as his throat swelled. Slowly but surely he was being choked to death. We could only try to ease his pain and discomfort. Hours dragged by, taking my husband from me minute by minute. I stayed at his side, talking and singing to him. His eyes showed he knew his fate and the squeeze of his hand begged me to accept it. How could I? My love lay dying and there was nothing any one could do.

I clutched Daniel's hand as he exhaled for the last time, going still and silent. I stared for long agonizing moments at his closed eyes, his chest, praying for movement. My prayers went unanswered. The pressure in my chest stemming from my dismay nearly suffocated me, my heart shattering. No! My God couldn't be so cruel to one so faithful. I bowed my head, struggling to breathe as I sobbed. My tears anointed our joined hands.

God took my loving husband to heaven. Daniel was still a young man, only forty-five, but four days after taking ill he passed on to a place where he'd never feel pain again.

I became a widow on Friday, July 8, 1757, at the age of twenty-six years. I had two young children and tens of thousands of acres of property and human capital to manage alone. To add to the alarm and grief flowing like ice in my veins, Daniel had died without making a will, leaving my future worth and even where I'd live up to the court to decide. Needless to say, I was terrified.

---

My first obligation, aside from stemming my tears and composing myself, was to arrange Daniel's funeral. I asked the carpenter to build the coffin out of black walnut, one of Daniel's favorite woods. Then I sent word to the minister, family, and friends of the interment of my beloved companion on Monday afternoon. With the July heat upon us, and recalling how quickly my father was buried, I knew we couldn't delay longer the awful moment when my servants would lower Daniel into his final resting place. The awful moment when I'd say my final goodbye to him.

Next, I sent word to the seamstress to come and alter a gown for the funeral, and to sew mourning clothes for me and Patsy. Then I summoned the tailor to make black mourning suits for Jacky and the house servants as well. We'd observe the proper month or two of mourning in the latest fashions, as Daniel would have wanted.

Planning my husband's funeral based on what I thought he would want in death seemed strange to me when all I wanted was for him to be alive. I didn't want to bury him. I needed him. At my side, to talk with me, comfort me, make me laugh. He'd gone too soon for my liking. We'd only had seven years together, years filled with joys and sorrows, but I wouldn't trade a single one of them unless it would bring him back to me.

Jacky continued in bed, with no sign of improvement. Doctor Carter remained at the house, concocting other combinations to combat the disease. I prayed hourly for his success in saving my son. My heart cracked and bled each time I gazed upon his wan features and red eyes looking at me from his wasted frame. I couldn't bear the thought of another funeral.

Daniel's reputation and standing drew a crowd of mourners to his grave. The sun beat down on our covered heads while the minister spoke from his place at the head of the coffin. I imagined Daniel inside the box, eyes closed, hands folded on his chest. I'd stayed up with him each night while he was laid out in that very pose in the formal parlor. Mother had arrived before supper the night Daniel died and kept vigil with me over the weekend. We were joined at times by others, but never did I leave him alone. Sally brought my meals to me, though I barely touched anything. I had no appetite. Someone, free or slave, attended my love when I could not keep my eyes open or needed to use the privy. Worst of all, my tears wouldn't fall. I'd cried so much I didn't think I'd ever be able to again.

When the four brawny slaves took hold of the ropes to ease Daniel into the earth, trembles rocked through me. I wrapped my arms around my waist and held on for dear life. Sobs burst from me and tears fell despite my earlier conviction of that impossibility. How was I to go on without my companion? My strength? My love?

My head spun, my grief quicksand inside my chest, sucking me down into a darkness I welcomed. It would be easier to die and be with Daniel than to face the vast uncertainties of the future. I closed my eyes, willing myself to die rather than trudge through life burdened with my sorrow. I could not express how the prospect of losing my other two babies, my precious Jacky and sweet Patsy, plagued my sanity. Thinking of them stopped the downward free fall as abruptly as an acorn hitting the ground. I opened my eyes and skimmed the solemn gathering.

Fingering the fine watch pinned to my bodice, I knew what I must do. I dabbed the tears from my cheeks and sniffed. The minister gave the benediction as men used shovels to bury my husband in rich Virginia soil. The soil he had loved and worked all his life. He had gone from me, but he'd gone home, too. I'd known he'd most likely die before me, as a result of the twenty-year difference in our ages. I just hadn't known he'd die so soon, so young. My job? To care for his children and his legacy to the best of my ability. Something I'd been trained to do all my life. I straightened my back, lifted my chin, regained my composure one breath at a time. Likewise, I'd take my life one day at a time and live each day to the fullest and see what my future held. With a plan in place, I swallowed and then sang farewell to my husband. Those around me soon joined in, some with tears trailing down their cheeks.

Two weeks after the funeral, I made myself walk into Daniel's office and sit at his desk. It felt strange to occupy his chair with the high back and sturdy arms. I had to perch on the front edge of the seat in order to reach the immense mahogany desk and the ink stand and quill. I'd never been solely responsible for a home, let alone the extensive property I owned. I didn't want the job, much like my brother William had not wanted to manage my mother's plantation. I had no choice. I unpinned the ceramic watch, studied its pretty face for a moment, then placed it in the top drawer. I closed the drawer with a sharp push. With a sigh, I opened the account book and then I froze as tears smarted in my eyes.

Daniel's fine, careful script danced on the lined pages. I swallowed, clearing my throat and forcing back the tears, as I leafed through until I reached his last entry. It was dated a few days before he died, the day he took ill. I'd never forget my loving companion, but I had come to realize I must move forward. As much as I wished I could turn back time, I turned the page to a fresh sheet and dipped the quill.

I started by making a list of items the overseers and servants had informed me the plantation needed to order from Robert Cary, the London factor. As I jotted down the long list of items—two large seines or nets for shad fishing in the Pamunkey, starch, castile soap, pins, thread, cotton for the slaves' clothing, and so forth—my thoughts drifted to the largest item I needed to order. Daniel's tombstone.

With my list completed, I pulled out a page of stationary and wrote a careful letter to Mr. Cary. I added that I wanted him to acquire a handsome tombstone of the best durable marble to cost about one hundred pounds with the inscription "Here Lies the Body of Daniel Parke Custis Esquire who was born the 15th Day of Oct. of 1711 & departed this Life the 8th Day of July 1757. Aged 45 Years." I stared at the words for several minutes, my breathing shallow and quick. Then I added that I wished for Mr. Cary to have two mourning rings made using two locks of hair, one from Fanny and one from Daniel, to be covered in clear crystal. I'd have appropriate reminders of my loved ones to keep them close. I needed to feel them with me.

I don't know how long I stared at the letter before I signed and sealed it. I only know a sense of satisfaction stole over me. I could do this. I could take up the reins and continue the plans Daniel had put in place and, with the help of my brother Bat and his legal sense, I and my children would survive. It wouldn't be easy to oversee the vast property and people comprising the plantation, but I would manage. Was that enough though?

I drew in a sharp breath as reality hit me. My duty to myself and my children was dictated by societal norms. I could remain a widow, many other women had done so, but I didn't want to raise my children without a father figure. I didn't want to live alone and unloved, without a loving husband to warm my bed. What I needed to do was entertain another path forward. Because, while we might survive, for the sake of my children's future I needed to find another husband.

# 7

*White House – 1758*

The rhythmic motion of the dapple gray gelding relieved the tension inside of me. March winds whipped the skirts of my riding habit and threatened to dislodge my darling hat with each cool gust. Grief over my husband's death eight months previous had eased but lingered like an interrupted measure of a symphony. Clouds raced across the bright blue sky, resolutely obscuring the heavens. Birds flew high above, calling to one another as the weather changed from fair to foul. I turned to Nancy and Burwell, riding beside me on their bays. Both looked smart in their outfits as they sat their horses. Burwell had proved a good husband for Nancy. He smiled at me over Nancy's head on her little mare. The creak of leather joined the bird melodies floating on the breeze.

"Time to head for home before the rain arrives." I turned my horse toward the manor house.

"You just don't wish to speak about Charles Carter any more." Nancy winked at me as she followed my lead, Burwell keeping pace.

"He's besotted with you, the famously wealthy widow Custis." Burwell's stallion pranced and jigged with impatience at the sedate walk forced upon him. "He's said as much to me."

I cringed at the thought of marrying Charles. Oh, he was nice enough. Charming, educated, and not in need of my money as an enticement to marriage. Three very good reasons to say yes. But I simply could not. "If only his first two wives, may they rest in peace, hadn't left him with a dozen children to care for, I might be more receptive to his overtures."

"I believe there's another reason you head for home." Burwell grinned at me, a familiar conspiratorial expression.

"What, pray tell, might that be?" My horse paused to snatch a mouthful of grass and I kicked him on. Naughty boy, he had been better trained than that.

Burwell chuckled as he calmed the stallion with steady hands. "Why, the approaching time for when my compatriot, Colonel Washington, plans to wait upon you this afternoon."

My cheeks warmed. "From what you've told me, his curiosity is piqued by my availability. Yet, he's a second tier plantation owner and involved in the Virginia militia. Neither fact endears him to me."

"He's a tad younger than you as well, I understand, which may also put you off." Nancy paused to steer her horse away from mine. "But the gossips talk about his magnificent personality and handsome features."

Nancy's mare nipped at Burwell's when the stallion danced too close to her. I guided my gelding a little to one side as I considered the three animals. I suddenly recalled the daring day so long ago when I rode my horse up onto the front portico of Elsing Green. Jacky had dared me and I had accepted the challenge, despite knowing I'd likely be punished. The wind that day held a hint of risk and danger. Much like this one. Jacky's laughter floated in my memory, egging me on. The coming storm had blown up our horses' tails and there was only one way to help them relax. Something we hadn't engaged in since we were adolescents.

"I'll race you home!" I leaned forward and urged my gelding into a gallop. We flew down the winding lane, hooves pounding, wind whipping our hair. I let my mount blow out the friskiness the changing weather had caused in all of us.

Nancy and Burwell's horses thundered behind me and soon were vying for the lead. The woods on either side blurred past. I heard only drumming hooves. I leaned closer to the whipping mane, tears blurring my vision. It had been far too long since I'd raced and the exhilaration awoke a joy inside I hadn't experienced since before Daniel died. Being a proper lady required decorum, rather than the exuberant and ruffled woman racing down the road. But oh, what fun I was having.

I shook off any sense of guilt threatening to steal away the pleasure of the moment. I needed to laugh more, I decided as the turn for home came into view. After all the worry centered on the legal aspects of an inventory and dividing the vast property equitably between me and my children, surely I deserved a little harmless entertainment. I don't know what I'd have done if Bat hadn't stepped in to deal with the many issues and decisions following my husband dying intestate.

I glanced over my shoulder and saw Burwell lean into the race, his more powerful mount surging forward, passing me. Nancy's mare tired and started to lose ground against the two bigger horses. I kicked and my gelding started to close the distance to the stallion. Coming around the bend from the opposite direction rode a tall white man on a gangly horse with a black man on a smaller one beside him. I judged the distance and our speed as we closed in on the pine where we turned for home. We'd make it before the strangers reached the tree, but only if we sped up.

I kicked my horse and he surged forward, right behind Burwell. Turning sharply in front of the tree, I glimpsed the shocked countenance of the tall stranger but didn't slow. With a whoop, we headed down the carriage-way that ended in front of White House's manor. The wind finally won its tug of war with my hat, ripping it from my head and flinging it to the ground where it rolled and tossed into tall grasses. So be it. A hat would not cost me the race. I caught up to Burwell, his coat tails flapping with each stride and gust, our horses nose to nose. Then my gelding faltered, stumbled, pitching me up his neck. I fought for my balance and managed to keep both feet in the stirrups as I clutched the mane and pushed myself back into the saddle. Burwell raced on, reaching the yard in front of the house with a whoop of triumph.

Slowing my horse to a walk, I detected he was off on his right front hoof. I dismounted in a whirl of skirts to investigate the problem while Nancy halted beside me, flushed and disheveled. Behind her, the newcomer rode up carrying my dirty hat.

I patted the sweaty neck and then rubbed the horse's nose. "Sorry, I didn't intend for you to pay for my delight."

Lifting the hoof, I saw the shoe had pulled away from the foot. One of the short thick nails which normally held the shoe in place had worked free. Walking on such a sharp point would further aggravate if not injure my horse's hoof. "Burwell, do you have anything to reset a shoe with you?"

Burwell trotted back the short distance and halted, swinging from his saddle. "No, but we're close to the barn now. I'll pull it and we can reset it there."

While Burwell worked on removing the shoe, I held the reins of both horses. The stranger dismounted and strode toward us, his horse trailing behind him. He stood tall, taller than most men, likely more than six feet.

"Burwell, we appear to have company." Something about the man's expression captured my attention so I could not look away.

Burwell stood, brushing his hands off on his breeches, as he grinned. "Colonel Washington, it's very good to see you. Allow me to introduce the ladies."

My brother-in-law quickly performed the introductions. I took the opportunity to inspect the man. I was intrigued. And curious, but also hesitant. I lived under no obligation to marry any one. As a widow, I enjoyed the freedom to rule my own life. Marrying again would change my status from free to belonging to another man. Did I want that? Yes and no. A curious conflict shimmered through me as I contemplated the colonel.

I liked what I saw in the man standing beside the big, black horse. Well proportioned, filling out his attire in a pleasing way. His simple but elegant maroon coat was worn over a white shirt and cravat, embroidered satin waistcoat, and dark breeches, emphasizing powerful thighs above his tall black boots. His suit indeed spoke to his status and appreciation for image, indicating he understood the subtle language of clothing. He swept his hat from his head with one hand, revealing brown hair tinged red, while holding the reins in the other. Gray-blue eyes smiled at me, mirroring the grin on his firm mouth. His nose was long and straight, a sign of a fine man. All this I took in with a growing sense of familiarity never before experienced. I felt drawn to him as though I'd known him all my life, an impossibility.

"Mrs. Custis." He bowed in greeting after Burwell completed the introductions. "I'm happy to make your acquaintance."

"And I yours, sir." I nodded my head in acknowledgement of his salutation. "We're just heading in before the rains come. Will you join us for tea?"

His grin widened as he inclined his head before joining our little party. Conversation flowed around me, with me interjecting a comment here and there. Mostly, I judged the man beside Burwell as we led our horses to the barn. I listened to his speech, his comments, even his banter with his friend and colleague. I appreciated the wit and humor the two men shared, joining in with their laughter. As we approached the house, I pointed out the individual gardens for flowers, herbs, and vegetables. I'd recently decided to separate the various kinds of plants, arranging the beds to enable easier reach to pull weeds and harvest the produce.

"May I say, you have a very nice plan for your garden, Mrs. Custis. I pray you won't object should I incorporate your ideas into my own gardens at Mount Vernon." George raised a brow in query as he smiled at me before looking ahead to the two young black men who arrived, prepared to relieve us of our horses.

"Thank you, Colonel Washington." His praise warmed me but I did not understand why it should. After all, we'd only just met. "Are you enamored by horticulture?"

"Indeed, madam. I have a deep interest in all types of trees and flowers, as well as potential crops. And please, call me George."

"Of course. Then, you may call me Patsy." I couldn't suppress the smile springing onto my lips. Already we were on first name terms. What did that indicate? As Jacob took the reins from me, I caught his attention. "See that the blacksmith tends to his right front hoof. I do not wish for the horse to be further injured."

Jacob nodded and promised to relay my instructions. Nancy dismounted and handed her reins to the boy, and he led the two horses toward the stable. I took the opportunity to watch the horses' movement, checking for any lameness. Other than the gelding's limp from the lack of a shoe, they both appeared sound. George's manservant trailed along with their horses. I turned back to the conversation, noting George's thoughtful gaze resting on me.

"When I first saw the three of you galloping down the road, I feared your horse had run away with you." George winked at me, an audacious gesture from a new acquaintance but one I did not entirely object to. Somehow it suited him. He chuckled. "Until I saw Burwell take the lead. Then of course I knew you were racing."

"Patsy is quite a horsewoman in her own right, as are you." Burwell's expression turned conspiratorial again as he smirked at George. "What a pleasant coincidence."

"I do believe she exhibited a fine seat after her horse stumbled." George inclined his head in my direction, a twinkle in his eyes. "I applaud your abilities."

"Perhaps one day we shall ride together and we can compare." I smiled, though inside laughter threatened to escape. I would no more challenge the man before me to a horse race than walk into a tavern unescorted. But he didn't know that.

He chuckled again, his eyes twinkling. "Perhaps one day."

"You may wish to brush up on your horsemanship, my friend." Burwell slapped George on the back in a friendly gesture. "She nearly beat me today."

"If my horse had not pulled a shoe, you are correct, Burwell. Another day, then, we shall try again." I led the way up the few steps and through the front door. "For now, let us see if Doll has prepared the tea. I'm in need of a cup, as I'm sure we all are."

After changing out of my riding habit, I descended the stairs to join the others in the parlor. Doll had provided a plentiful array of tea cakes and sandwiches along with a carafe of tea. Sugar and cream in silver vessels flanked the carafe. I took my place as hostess and served the refreshments while the others talked and teased each other. Burwell and George joked at each other's expense while Nancy and I listened and laughed at their banter. Secretly, I observed George, enthralled by the confidence he exuded by his posture, his comments, and his demeanor.

What did I know of him, though? He was eight months younger than I was. So his views and mine aligned fairly easily as he spoke about the happenings around the colonies. George also had the reputation of an excellent equestrian, and given his earlier comments he also shared a fondness for gardening and horticulture. I wondered what other common interests we might have, and found myself eager to find out.

The hours flew by as we talked and laughed, playing music on the spinet and flute while we took turns dancing. We ate dinner and then supper. As night descended, I was grateful for my sister and her husband's presence, which enabled me to invite George to stay the night rather than ride back to Williamsburg in the dark. He demurred at first, but with only a small amount of encouragement he acquiesced. My heart sang at the prospect of conversing more with him. My hesitancy at meeting him had vanished and been replaced with an alacrity I found startling and confusing, but welcomed. What a man he proved to be. Was it possible to fall in love with a person so easily?

---

The next morning at breakfast, we sat beside each other in the dining room, Nancy and Burwell sitting across from us. The two waiters, Breechy and Mulatto Jack—not my deceased brother-in-law but a slave of the same name—served the meal, their dark skin and black eyes beautifully set off by the livery they wore. I'd ordered new suits be made for the men last year, cream colored shirts with distinctive dark blue trousers and coats bearing the Custis coat of arms over their hearts. They made a fine impression for my constant stream of family and friends stopping by to check on my health and safety. Especially important matters with the increased savage attacks by Indians on the frontier, encouraged by the French to harass the English settlers. Not that any one thought such attacks would reach so close to civilization, but one never could tell what schemes might spread among the slaves.

I buttered a roll, taking a small bite. Nancy kept glancing at me as though she suspected my feelings regarding the man beside me. Which she probably had. We were so very close, if I breathed in, she'd exhale. I needed to steer the conversation to a safe topic.

"George, you mentioned your home, Mount Vernon. Tell us more about it." I sipped hot and sweet tea, the pleasant warmth spreading down my throat to my stomach.

"Ah, the true love of George's life. Am I right?" Burwell tapped the table as he peered at George.

"My home is very dear to me, I will admit." George laid his knife on his plate, lifted his fork to stab a bite of fish. He shifted his gaze to smile at me. "Mount Vernon was named for my brother's commander when he served in Cartagena, but my father built the original small house which has been replaced over the years. It sits on a lovely hill along the Potomac River, which is part of the boundary between Virginia and Maryland. Just a few miles downriver from Alexandria."

I'd heard of the property from Daniel but did not know much about it, since we had never had opportunity or need to travel in that direction. I tried to picture the place from George's description. "How large a plantation is it?"

"Several thousand acres with a smallish mansion-house." He slipped the bite into his mouth and washed it down with a sip of tea. "I'm in the process of expanding the house, and plan to also expand the acreage after I am released from my duties with the militia this fall."

"You're resigning your command?" I was surprised. He had spoken last night of the adventures and respect he enjoyed as colonel of the Virginia militia. "What will you do?"

"It is time to settle down to being a plantation master. I am tired of public service and desire only to find a genteel wife to grace my home, have my children, and provide companionship while I put my plans into place." He gazed steadily at me for several moments. "Does that idea appeal to you?"

Of course, I knew his real question. One I could not answer. Not yet. "I enjoy living at White House with the Pamunkey flowing by, so I can appreciate your keen desire to return to your Mount Vernon."

He nodded slowly, taking another bite of fish. After he swallowed it, he lifted his cup, holding it aloft. "I understand your meaning, my lady. I—"

Whatever he prepared to say was cut off by Jacky and Patsy bursting into the room, giggling. My two beautiful children, Jacky at three and a half years, fortunately healthy as a horse, and precocious Patsy nearly 2 years old and full of spunk, presented hands and faces covered with brown smears. Mud pies, I presumed. I'd made the mistake of showing them how to make the gooey creations one pretty afternoon when they were in need of a new form of distraction. Perhaps not my best idea.

"Mama! We made our breakfast outside this morning! See?" Jacky ran toward me, Patsy toddling along behind him.

"Mama!" Patsy echoed her older brother. "Mama!"

Molly followed close behind the little ones, hands outstretched in a futile attempt to snare them before they reached me and my clean clothing. Soon, I had smudges on my skirts, but I laughed and swept them to me. The dirt would come off, but my children would not always be young and carefree. They would always know I loved them and would welcome them regardless of what they had done. They were my precious gems.

"I'm sorry, Mrs. Custis." Molly stood helplessly watching my children rub mud onto my gown. "I did try to stop them, but they're getting faster every day. Or I'm getting slower."

"It's all right, Moll. Well, Jacky, Patsy… Did you enjoy your mud pies?" I chuckled and hugged first Jacky, then Patsy. "Thank you for sharing them with me, but now it's time to go wash yourselves. You two must listen to Moll. Do you understand? You're behaving rudely in front of your aunt and uncle as well as our guest."

My son's grin told me he'd had great fun being mischievous but he soon hid it from view by looking at his shoes. "I'm sorry."

Patsy glanced at Jacky then me before imitating her brother's apparent disgrace. "'m sorry."

"Thank you. Now off with you." I shooed them toward Molly, who grasped a hand of each and led them from the room.

"You're gown is soiled." Nancy shook her head. "You indulge them too much, I fear."

I shrugged off her observation. "Mayhap I do, but what does a little dirt matter when my children need me?"

"One day you may regret being so lenient with them." Burwell sliced a bite of fish with his fork and placed it in his mouth.

"They will surely learn discretion as they grow and mature." George smiled at me, hinting he understood my reasoning. "Would you object if I were to wait upon you after my business is concluded in Williamsburg?"

"Indeed, I shall anticipate your return. When will you be able to visit again?" My heart fell despite knowing he had business to attend with the Governor.

I hoped he'd return posthaste to continue our conversation. I wanted to learn more about him, especially since he'd so openly stated he wished to find a wife. Whether or not I wanted to, I really needed to marry again so my children had a father to provide a suitable role model for them. Jacky in particular needed the strong, guiding hand of a man to help instruct him on tempering his erratic behavior, to learn to dedicate himself to a task. George might well prove the proper person.

"No more than a week from today." He smiled at me as he laid his fork down. "Will that suit?"

"Does Patsy have a choice in the matter?" Nancy asked with a wink. "If so, dare I venture she'd prefer you did not leave?"

"Be quiet, sister." I shot her a quelling look, noting Burwell's suppressed chuckle.

"I shall write you, if you'll permit my impertinence." George sipped his tea, his eyes steady on me.

"You may send me a note from time to time if you'd like." Smiling at him, I briefly inclined my head. "Though I imagine you'll have little enough time for writing while you're busy with the Governor."

George removed his napkin and laid it by his plate. Pushing back his chair, he stood and bowed to me. He reached out a hand to help me stand, which I accepted and rose to my feet. The top of my head barely reached his shoulder, making me feel shorter than ever but his steady regard also made me feel very feminine and protected. I gazed up at his solemn countenance. His grasp on my fingers tightened ever so slightly, but enough to shoot awareness of him through me like the fireworks used to celebrate the king's birthday each year at the Governor's Palace. A distinctly new sensation but one I enjoyed, though with a twinge of guilt mixed in when I considered my poor Daniel looking down upon my actions. I hoped he'd understand.

"With your permission, I will say farewell for the present." His expression softened, eyes twinkling. "Fear not, my dear Patsy. I shall carry your sweet smile with me and thus will return as soon as my business is concluded."

His departure imminent, I clung to his hand feeling like a silly child but couldn't stop myself. A sense of connection, a deep understanding of the man, flowed through me as I clasped his warm hand. "I'll see you to the door."

He squeezed my hand before releasing me, and then said

farewell to Nancy and Burwell. At the door, he gazed down at me with a gentle smile. "I will miss you, Patsy."

As I would miss him. "Fare thee well, George."

Breechy brought George's cape and hat, helping the much larger man into his outer garments. At twenty-two, Breechy exhibited strength and grace. He'd been born here at White House and had grown up helping with the endless work of the plantation. He'd impressed Daniel with his manners and sharp mind, and so had been made a house servant. We tried to ensure he and the other slaves had everything they needed to make them happy and well. He nodded to me briefly. I gave him a quick nod of thanks, then looked to George.

"Until next week." He touched two fingers to his hat brim, before his manservant opened the door and they stepped outside. Jacob waited in the yard, holding George's and his man's mount at the ready.

"Good-bye." He winked at me and then hurried away. I nearly cried as he mounted in one fluid motion and turned his horse toward Williamsburg.

My feelings were a tornado in my chest. I'd loved Daniel with all my heart, and created four adorable children with him. We'd built a wonderful life together only to have it broken apart with the death of two of our angels and then my loving husband. I thought I'd never be able to move past the grief, to love another man even if I married. I anticipated I'd find a good man to provide for my children, but that was all. Then to feel such attachment to George in so few hours, to revel in his touch and his laughter. Potential love tinged with guilt created a swirling mix in my heart. But I must move on, and I truly believed Daniel would rather I be happy in my life than to continue to grieve. He wouldn't have expected me to remain alone for the rest of my life. Of that I was certain. And George did indeed made me happy.

---

True to his word, letters arrived with visitors over the course of the next week. I read and reread each with an eagerness unknown to me. My guests, whether it was Burwell stopping in, or David Lee on his way home, teased me about the correspondence. Love letters, they called the sometimes long missives they delivered into my hands. I didn't share their contents with any one, delighting in the whimsy and observations George made of his acquaintances. They contained much more, however. His words on paper deepened my understanding of the gentleman he proved to be. He seemed a thoughtful observer of people and events, quick to judge a person's character, slow to anger. But watch out when he did get angry, at least according to my brother-in-law. I looked forward to the day when George would return and I could converse with him again. To see his eyes twinkle with mirth, his lips curve into a contagious grin, hear his voice booming with laughter. In truth, I couldn't stop thinking about the man.

When he waited upon me a week later, we enjoyed talking together about everything under the sky for one long, happy afternoon. We were forced to stay inside while the spring rains and winds battered the house. The parlor stayed cozy, a cheery fire blazing in the fireplace. Sally had fixed my hair in a neat chignon and added a fresh yellow flower behind my ear, its sweet fragrance lingering in the air around me. Sitting with George calmed me while at the same time thrilled my soul. I felt a deep connection to him, despite only knowing him for a week. I couldn't explain my feelings better than that.

He told me about his time in Williamsburg. Shared his plans for improving the house at Mount Vernon, work already in progress but which he needed funds to complete. By diversifying the types of cash crops, he hoped to keep the plantation fiscally sound. We talked about my plans, my children, my love of horses, music, and gardening. As the skies cleared and the sun showed its face on a watery landscape, he once more mounted his horse and headed for his home, so very far away. As before, he promised to write, begged me to write in response, and promised he would visit when he was due back in Williamsburg in late May. Two months. Too long.

We exchanged precious letters over the next weeks, and my feelings for George deepened and my longing for his person grew. I went about my normal routine as spring burst forth in the budding trees and flowering bushes, paths and woodlands dotted with flowers of all colors. Spring had always been my favorite time of year, and remained so even though my heart hurt for George's return. Letters did not completely fill the gap left by his absence, but they did provide a connection to the man, I finally admitted both to myself and to him, I loved.

Word arrived in May that George had completed his business with the Governor and was turning his horse toward White House. Praise be to God! I encouraged my slaves in their efforts to clean and prepare for George's arrival, which he planned for the fifth day in June. The days soon passed, filled with planning menus and then food preparations, cleaning and polishing the furniture and silver, airing of linens and trunks, storing the carpets for the summer, and other tasks. I arranged for Nancy to visit at the same time to keep things respectable, and because I needed her steady support. Monday the fifth of June would be a momentous day for me and my family.

I heard the three-beat cadence of cantering horses approaching White House. Nancy and I sat in the wide downstairs hall enjoying the gentle summer breeze. She had brought a piece of embroidery to stitch, while I worked on a new dress for Patsy. Both the front and back doors stood open, encouraging each breath of air to flow through the house. Of course, the children delighted in the easy in and out, and took advantage of the opportunity by running around and around the house. Molly had given up trying to catch them at my insistence. I wanted their childhoods to be happy and carefree. Soon enough they'd grow up and shoulder their responsibilities. Perhaps too soon.

"I expect that would be George arriving." Laying aside my sewing on the drop-leaf table between us, I rose and looked out the front door. Two riders approached. My pulse fluttered and I drew in a deep breath.

Nancy laid her work beside mine and then came to stand by me. "I'll arrange for tea." She hurried across the hall and disappeared out the back door.

I stepped onto the porch, smiling at George as he dismounted at the bottom of the steps. The black man with him took the reins and rode around the house to the stable. George bounded up the steps, taking my hands in his when he reached the top. He kissed the back of one of my hands before pressing both to his chest.

"My dear Patsy, how I've longed to see you." He searched my face with his eyes, his gaze touching on my features in rapid succession. "Have you missed me?"

"I have indeed." I noted his slightly pockmarked face, glad he'd survived the smallpox attack while he was in Barbados with his brother years ago. Glad he stood towering over me, looking at me with such intensity and emotion shining in his eyes. "Welcome back to White House, George."

Nancy strolled up behind me, her footfalls lightly thumping the wood floor. "Hello, Colonel Washington. How was your trip?"

George glanced at Nancy, then me before releasing my hands. He winked at me as he greeted my sister. Flustered by his arrival, I drew in a breath and let it out slowly, vainly attempting to calm my pounding heart.

"Hello, Mrs. Bassett." He doffed his hat and handed it to Breechy when he appeared beside Nancy. "I am pleased to see you are well."

"Thank you, sir." Nancy curtsied, a quick dip. "Doll is preparing some refreshments while Patsy makes you comfortable after your long ride."

Taking the hint, I motioned for George to follow me. "Let's go to the hall where the breeze is delightful."

"I beg your indulgence, my dear."

George's words halted my steps towards the door, and I turned to look back at him. "What do you mean?"

"Walk with me for a few minutes." George proffered his arm, waiting. "Please."

A glint in his eyes and the questioning smile on his lips spoke volumes. A shimmer of premonition wiggled through me as I lightly placed my hand on his arm and allowed him to escort me down the steps. I tossed a look over my shoulder at Nancy, who shooed me on my way. Had the moment I'd prayed for arrived?

We strolled silently toward the river, my fingers on his arm, his free hand resting on mine. Once we were out of sight of the house and any prying eyes, he stopped under a dogwood tree and faced me, grasping both of my hands. He studied me for two breaths, then smiled. "Martha Dandridge Custis, you have won my compassion, my respect, my fealty, and most of all my heart. Will you do me the honor of marrying me?"

Joy swept through me as my heart thundered in my ears. I had dreamed of this moment, and anticipated my answer should the day dawn. "Yes, I will."

George gripped me on either side of my waist, lifting and spinning me while he whooped his happiness. Laughing, I held onto his shoulders, my own happiness bubbling inside like champagne.

Several slaves came running at the commotion, sliding to a stop when they saw us laughing and cavorting like children at play. Nancy soon joined us, smiling as she crossed her arms and shook her head at our antics. I didn't care if our actions might be inappropriate or undignified. Later, perhaps I would, but at that moment nothing else mattered but our decision to join our fortunes. The future held promise again, the promise of having more children and of a loving man as my companion for the rest of my life.

George left the next morning, vowing to continue to write while he went out on one last mission for the Governor. I tried not to worry about his safety, but knowing he faced months of marching and conflict left me uneasy. At least we both knew it was the last time he would face an enemy on the battlefield. I began making plans for our wedding, though we hadn't settled on a date yet. I sent my favorite nightgown to Robert Cary to have it dyed a fashionable color. I also asked Mr. Cary to hire a seamstress to make me a new genteel suit of clothes to be grave but not extravagant and definitely not for mourning.

In July, a boat docked at the pier, bringing the tombstone for Daniel's grave. Such a flood of emotion filled me when I saw its carved marble, the inscription exactly as I'd ordered. I traced the carved lettering as tears pressed my eyes. So much had transpired over the last year. The loss of a child and husband, followed by my son recovering from his illness, as well as then meeting George. I instructed the mason to install the tombstone at Daniel's grave. When that task was completed, I could plan for the future as Martha Washington, using my given name in place of my pet name to honor the reputation of the man I would marry.

Gazing out the window, I looked beyond the physical landscape to see our plans for life together. A quiet one, filled with family and good friends, spent on Mount Vernon. George would resign his commission and pursue an active role in the Virginia House of Burgesses, but otherwise would retire from the military and be happy and safe at home. We'd begin our own family with more children soon to join mine. I couldn't imagine a better future for my family.

# 8

The longed-for day finally arrived. Snow blanketed the ground, clung to the trees and bushes. A steady stream of carriages brought more family and friends to celebrate. All of the efforts and plans had combined to create the social event of the season, my second marriage. Twelfth Night festivities, including music, dancing, wine, candies, and cakes, added to the joy of the occasion.

I'd had to push the house slaves harder than usual to stay on schedule to complete the many preparations necessary. Between the cold, snowy weather and the daily arrival of more family members, each soul tired and cold from their long journey, Sally and the other house servants ended up running most of the day and half the night. I'd make it up to them later, after everyone departed in a few days. I'd ensured plenty of food and drink, as well as beds and toiletries, waited for the guests to enjoy. I turned from gazing out my bedchamber window to watch Sally bustle about the bedroom, straightening anything out of place. Joy and expectation filled me. The time had come to begin a brand new life with the most amazing man I'd ever met.

"Will you be needing anything else?" Sally, her forehead

glistening from her labors, paused to regard me. "Oh, your hair. Let me fix it pretty for you."

"No, thank you. I've promised my sister she could attend to it on this special day." I adjusted the drape of the fine lace attached at the cuffs of my golden sleeves. I relied upon Sally's efforts nearly as much as the companionship we shared. "I'll be fine until it's time to descend to the parlor. Why don't you go ahead?"

"Yes'm." Sally made to leave the room, but the door latch yanked out of her grasp by a little boy's hand. I grinned as Jacky raced into the room, a porcelain doll with long blonde hair in his hands. He skidded to a halt behind my skirts, Patsy right behind him. Their play made my heart sing but I had no time for such behavior. I thanked God my children adored George as much as I did.

"Give me my doll!" Patsy grabbed for her doll with both little hands. "Jacky!"

"Make me…" Jacky, a devilish sparkle in his eyes, held it out of reach of his little sister's flailing hands.

I would do most anything to keep my children happy and healthy. A pang struck my heart at the memory of their tiny kin buried beside their father. My grief had eased, thanks to George and his love, but clung to my heart like the snow outside on the branches. No one should have to endure so much loss in such a short period of time.

Pushing aside my morbid ponderings, I smiled at the lovable monkeys. "Children, my dears, what's this about?" I pulled Jacky around in front of me. "Take a care with my dress. You wouldn't wish for me to look a mess, now would you?"

Contrite, Jacky shook his head. "No, Mama." He handed the doll back to Patsy. "I was just having some fun."

"Not at your sister's expense. It's not seemly for you to treat her that way." I patted the top of his head, his brown hair silky beneath my fingers. "Now run along, and take Patsy with you. I'll be downstairs momentarily."

"All right. Come on, Patsy." Jacky waited for Patsy to grab hold of his hand, then he led her from the room.

They turned as one and raced out of sight down the hall. I laughed at their antics. Jacky at four and a half years and Patsy at two years younger than him managed to be both friend and foe toward one another. They'd have every opportunity to become well educated and respected as a result of my marriage. Together, we would see to it they learned all they'd need to know to survive in the American colonies. They would never want for anything. As long as I could keep them healthy and careful, of course.

I studied my appearance in the looking glass. What did George see when he gazed at me, love in his eyes, a bemused smile on his lips? Dark brown hair lay softly about my shoulders, waiting for Nancy to arrive to arrange it. My pulse raced in expectation of becoming Mrs. George Washington. So many questions spun in my mind. How would life change as a result of marrying a colonel? What would become of White House after we moved to Mount Vernon? Would George want to keep the modest plantation on the banks of the Pamunkey River, the home I had shared with Daniel? Moving to the northern part of Virginia also meant living several days' ride from my close-knit and loving family. How often would I see them after we settled in at George's home?

I squared my shoulders and angled my chin. I wouldn't entertain such worries on my wedding day. Not with a house crammed full of family and friends waiting to witness the joining of hands and lives. Fortunes, too. Our future together stretched before me. Raising our children, running an efficient household while George pursued his many interests. Confidence settled on my shoulders like a mantle. Running the household was something I knew well how to do.

George had ambitions for bettering his properties, and from what he'd shared we'd ultimately live in a grand home upon completion of all the renovations. George had been honest about his need for my money in order to enhance and improve Mount Vernon. For me, the money was an even exchange since it meant I'd have a husband and guardian again. All I had ever wanted as I learned to sew, to play the spinet, and manage an efficient household had been to find a life companion to share the joys and sorrows of life. To have a gaggle of children to love and enjoy. To have found abiding love twice in one life was more than I could have hoped for. The thought made me smile at my reflection.

Where was Nancy? Soon I must go downstairs. I checked the lay of my deep yellow brocade overdress, arranging the silver lace trim at the edge of the bodice until satisfied with its appearance. A white silk petticoat with silver woven into the fabric peeked through the split skirt of the overdress. I stepped into purple satin heels, smiling with pleasure at the silver trimmings. I didn't often have reason to don such finery, but marrying one of the most distinguished and respected men in the colony certainly justified my choice. Fortunately, the outfit had arrived from London in time to tailor the dress to fit my small figure. Why couldn't the London factors send clothing meeting the measurements sent instead of sending garments either too big or, worse, too small?

A light rap sounded at the door to my bedroom. I turned as it swung open and Nancy beamed at me. "You're beautiful, Patsy."

"I'm glad you've arrived. Come, dress my hair for me."

"I'm sorry for being so late. Now we must hurry. It's almost time for the ceremony. Everyone is so happy for you." Nancy pranced into the room and then stopped suddenly to perform a quick pirouette. "What do you think of my gown?"

I inspected the rich green dress with rhinestones sewn across the bodice, a cream silk petticoat visible through the sheer material brushing the tips of her gold satin shoes. "It's quite lovely. But then you always dress divinely."

"How are you?" Nancy winked, a sly grin on her lips. "I noticed the mistletoe strategically placed in the hall. Ready for your wedding night?"

Heat crept into my cheeks. George's tall, lanky frame dwarfed my nearly five feet of height. What would relations be like with him? I'd only ever lain with one man. What if George didn't like what I had to offer? What if I didn't please him in bed? But no, I couldn't think such thoughts. My experience would prove sufficient. It would have to. I lifted my chin and smiled at my sister. "I am. But first, can you put these pearls in my hair? I want to look my finest with the many distinguished guests downstairs."

"This day is more wonderful than the ball in Williamsburg when you made your first appearance. In spite of the ball being a grand affair, your wedding day will put it to shame. I particularly think the pine boughs intertwined with ivy and holly are fitting decorations for the season." Nancy hurried to the dressing table where I sat on the small chair. "But come. We don't want to keep everyone waiting."

I watched in the looking glass's reflection while Nancy's hands first swept my hair up into a smooth bun and then nestled the pearls artistically along the sides. Nancy chattered as she worked, going on about the snowy weather and the exhibits of delicious foods artfully arranged on clear glass plates set upon tables. I let her prattle on, love for her swelling inside.

"How does George look in his new suit?" I met Nancy's gaze in the reflection. "He liked the blue color but worried about the fit. His agent in London apparently doesn't believe he could be as tall and broad as he is."

Nancy tucked a pearl into place and moved on to the next one. "He was tugging on the shirt collar a bit, if that's any indication. But he presents quite a fine figure in the perfectly white satin waistcoat. He's a handsome man you're marrying." Nancy stepped back, cocked her head to examine the results of her efforts. After a moment, she met my gaze in the glass. "You look beautiful."

"Thank you for helping me. I hope George isn't too uncomfortable." I grinned as a wicked thought lighted in my mind. "He might want to remove his clothes too soon for the comfort of our guests."

Nancy tapped my shoulder as she barked out a laugh. "You're terrible. He'll have his hands full to keep you in line, of that I'm sure."

"I'll make sure he's never bored." I rose and faced Nancy with a wry smirk. "It's time to go downstairs."

The wooden stairs creaked as I stepped on each tread, moving with as much grace and elegance as my form allowed. Nancy trailed behind me. If I were taller, like my sister, I would have a more elegant movement. I stifled a sigh. It wasn't the first time I'd hopelessly wished to be taller. It probably wouldn't be the last, either.

My hand slid down the rail as I perused the many ladies and gentlemen in their finest clothes milling about in the hall and parlor. Reverend Mossom had arrived in time for breakfast and had now changed into his official garb. He smiled when he saw me hesitate on the stairs. Honestly, I could become lost in the crowd, and with my height nobody would even see me. I chuckled to myself, stopping abruptly when I met George's gaze resting solely on me. Gramercy but he cut a fine figure in his wedding suit. He started toward me and I quickly made my way down the last few steps.

"My dearest Patsy, you look lovely as always." George lifted my gloved hand as if I were a queen and kissed the back.

George had powdered his reddish-brown hair for the occasion, I noticed when he dipped to kiss my hand. Then he aimed his intense blue-gray eyes at me and I could only smile at him like a silly schoolgirl. The dashing colonel loved me, respected me, and vowed to do all in his power to make me happy and content. Once we wed, my place would always be at his side. Indeed, I never wanted to be apart from him. "You are quite handsome, as well."

"Shall we?" He bent his arm and I placed my hand in the crook and then glanced up at him. His seductive smile meant solely for me made my cheeks flame and my breath catch. Yes, indeed, I'd made a sound choice of a man to be my husband.

Two steps later we were surrounded by friends and family. The house barely contained the many bodies. Everyone within a week's ride of White House flowed around me, mixing and mingling like minnows in the river. The Royal Governor Francis

Fauquier and his wife Catherine chatted by the fireplace with Burwell. Elegantly attired as always, he had succeeded Dinwiddie the year previous and enjoyed throwing frequent lavish parties complete with fine wines. A passion shared by George.

I drew in a long breath to savor the fresh scent of the pine boughs decorating the room. George guided me through the crush of well-wishers. I held fast to his steely arm, relishing the power of my solid man. Finally, we stood before Reverend Mossom. I greeted his wife, Elizabeth, before turning back to the rector.

George cleared his throat. "We are ready, Reverend."

"Very well." Reverend Mossom raised both hands to motion for silence and slowly peace settled over the gathering. "We come together on this festive day to join together the lives and fortunes of Colonel George Washington to Martha Dandridge Custis."

My hands trembled as my stomach rolled. I wanted the ceremony to end and my new life to begin. I prayed for strength and grace to make him a good wife and companion.

"Colonel George Washington, do you take this woman, Martha Dandridge Custis, to be your wife?"

"I do." George's voice shook and he glanced down at me. "Forever."

I studied his happy countenance and tried to show him how much I loved him with a beaming smile. As long as we had each other, we would survive anything. I kept my attention on the minister, raising my brows to encourage him to proceed. I needed to be Mrs. Washington and soon.

Reverend Mossom peered at me and then nodded once with a smile. Feeling a touch less tense, I waited for his question.

"Martha Dandridge Custis, do you take this man to be your husband?"

"I do." Relief flooded my soul and I looked up at George. "Forever."

"Then with the powers vested in me, I now pronounce you man and wife." The rector nodded to George.

"Now and always." George bestowed a radiant smile on me as he took both my hands in his and then bestowed a swift kiss on my lips. Swift but weighted with meaning and love.

My true life had begun, and as long as he desired me to be a part of his life, nothing would ever separate me from his side.

---

The pitter-patter of Sally's slippers the next morning forced my eyes open. Pale sunshine washed the wood floor and dappled the scatter rugs and bedclothes. Glancing to my right, I discovered an empty space where George had slept. Well, he did more than *sleep*. A grin slipped onto my lips.

"Good morning, Mrs. Washington." Sally crossed to the fireplace to stir the embers into a cheery warmth.

"Thank you, Sally. It is a very good morning." I sat up, the memory of my wedding night vivid in my mind, and pulled the blanket up to cover me. "Do you know where Colonel Washington has taken himself?"

"He's gone hunting, entertaining the guests that have left their beds so early in the morning."

"Oh dear, I forgot all about the guests." I pushed the covers aside and slipped from the bed with its heavy curtains. "Help me dress, please."

Before long, I wore the simple yet elegant pale green second day dress I'd ordered from London and had my hair fashioned into a neat bun under a white cap. After one last check in the looking glass, I hurried out of the room and down the stairs, slowing as I neared the last step. Voices sounded from the dining room. Nancy's distinctive laugh, a trill of happiness, made me smile. Other voices joined in the gaiety as I entered the room.

"Good morning." I acknowledged each person at the table in one sweeping glance. "I trust everyone had a pleasant night."

Jacky and Patsy sat on opposite sides of the long table. They grinned at me, and I wondered what they'd been up to. I'd find out soon enough. I walked to stand by my son. His suit needed a brush off. I'd have to speak to his manservant, Julius, about my son's attire. Jacky raised angelic eyes to me, and I raised a brow right back. "We'll talk later, Jacky."

He blinked twice, wide-eyed with an impish smirk. "Yes, Mama."

I kissed him on the head, then went around to kiss Patsy on the head as well. She wore a pale pink dress with matching ribbons in her hair. Her maid, Rose, deserved praise for ensuring my little one appeared clean and pretty each morning.

Having greeted my children, I paused near my chair to observe the lay of the table and its contents. Doll had prepared an elegant meal. Breechy and Mulatto Jack, handsomely attired in their livery, paid careful attention to the guests' needs, moving almost silently to deliver more tea or coffee.

"Chased your husband out the door already, Mrs. Washington?" Elizabeth Mossom asked with a knowing grin.

"I dare say, she didn't." Nancy smirked as she glanced first at me and then back at Elizabeth. She nodded her head, a gleam in her eyes. "In fact, I heard Burwell pleading with George to go hunting early this morning instead of back upstairs to his wife."

"Nancy." My cheeks warmed at the suggestive tone. Unbidden, the memory of George's very pleasing attentions with his hands and his lips as we shared a bed for the first time made my cheeks flame.

"My goodness, sister, whatever are you thinking about?" Nancy grinned as she raised a hand to forestall my reply. "You don't actually need to say a word. I think we all can imagine where your thoughts have turned."

"Really, Nancy, I have no desire to comment on your insinuations." I took my place at the table, draping the crimson napkin across my lap. "Surely you have more to attend to than our private moments. Say, for instance, your plan to depart?" I lifted a brow and pursed my lips, the jest finding its mark.

"Well rejoined, Patsy." Nancy picked up her fork and stabbed a bit of cold roasted turkey, popping it into her mouth.

"Good idea, Nancy. Keep your mouth full." I selected several pieces of cheese, a piece of bread, and an apple from the bowls and platters on the table.

Nancy swallowed and then shook her head. "It won't work. I still will share my thoughts and opinions with you. At least until we leave to-morrow for home."

I inclined my head one time to acknowledge her plan. As I'd expected, the guests would slowly depart, eventually leaving me alone with George and the children, and the servants, of course. Breechy stepped up beside me and poured tea into my cup, adding the proper amount of sugar and cream. I silently stirred the steaming liquid. Taking a sip, I regarded the others at the table. Could I perhaps hurry them along as to when they'd leave? Several possible explanations flitted through my mind and were just as quickly dismissed. My southern manners refused to allow me to be inhospitable. I'd be a gracious hostess and entertain my guests as long as they wished to stay.

"You know I'll miss you when you depart." I glanced at Nancy. "But I would like some time with George and the children alone before we leave next month for the public times."

"Is George nervous about taking his place in the House of Burgesses?" Elizabeth asked.

"No, of course not." I would keep private the reality so as not to embarrass my new husband. "I believe he's anxious to begin."

"Will you stay in the Custis house?" Nancy stared at me, waiting. "I don't know how you could."

I sighed. In truth, I did not wish to return to Six Chimneys, even for a short visit. From a practical vantage, the house belonged to me, and now to George, so lodging there for the length of time the Virginia Assembly held their session still made good sense. Emotionally, I wished to be rid of the property once and for all, a decision I needed to discuss with George.

Elizabeth dabbed her napkin at her lips and laid it back in her lap. "Will you brave the snowy roads to make the newly married visits?"

I nodded slowly, concern rising in my chest at the risks we'd face. Should I take the children on such a perilous excursion? What was I thinking? I couldn't leave them at home. I'd worry even more about them if they stayed behind. "As long as the roads are passable, yes, we discussed making the tour of family and friends."

"I do not envy you such a trip." Elizabeth reached for her cup of tea, holding it poised to take a sip. "It will be bad enough to travel from here to the parish house."

I agreed, but adhered to traditions because many of them had been established for sound reasons. The newly married couple visited the homes of family in order for all of its members to meet the newest addition to the family. Friends, likewise, needed introductions. The real purpose stemmed from a desire to bring the community together. "I'm sure George will make the proper precautions."

"Most assuredly with my precious wife." George strode into the room, a smile aimed at me as he closed the distance between us. "And our children."

Reverend Mossom strolled in behind him and spotted an empty chair beside Elizabeth, detouring around the other side of the table to join his wife.

George bowed to me, the smile never wavering. "Forgive my intrusion."

"There is nothing to forgive." Joy spread a buzzing warmth through every aspect of my being. I still couldn't believe my good fortune. This man belonged to me forever. To have and to hold, in sickness and health. Nobody would come between us. Except maybe his mother, Mary Washington, with her dislike of material wealth and thus of my finery and trappings. As far as I was concerned, though, I'd treat the woman much like I had old man Custis: politely but distantly. "Did you have a good hunt?"

"Nay, the buck won the day." George pulled out the chair beside me and sat down. He nodded his thanks when Breechy poured him a steaming cup of tea. "But it was a good ride. The Reverend proved himself a fine horseman, as well."

Reverend Mossom shook his head emphatically. "I can't hold a candle to George's expertise."

My pride regarding George's accomplishments and abilities made me grin. He could do no wrong, and seemed to succeed in everything he attempted. "Do not try to horse race with him. I can tell you, he's a wild jockey."

"My dear, I can attest that I'm in full control of my horse at all times." He regarded me, as Breechy placed two corn meal cakes on a plate in front of him. George drizzled honey over the cakes, and smiled at me. "It may not look like it, but it's true."

"Believe such if you must." I laughed at his comical expression. I loved my witty, capable, and loving man. I'd made the right decision. From this day forward, we'd never be separated.

---

A little more than a month after our marriage, I shivered as the coach struggled along the snowy road, bound for Williamsburg. I shared a seat with sleeping Patsy, her dark head resting in my lap. Across the spacious compartment, Jacky stared out the window while Sally dozed against the inside wall of the vehicle, mouth open. I chuckled at the scene, one so young and full of life, the other older and apparently exhausted.

The landscape changed steadily from wilderness to occasional farms as we jounced closer and closer to the city. It had been a good while since I last came to town for the public times. George would soon formally accept his seat in the House of Burgesses, a day my big, strong, endearing husband nervously anticipated. We would also make a decision about the future of Six Chimneys House and its contents. After very little discussion, I had agreed with George to live at Mount Vernon. I had no wish to live at White House or in old man Custis' silly house. Both places harbored too many memories, loving and sad, and the money from the sale would add to the children's inheritance.

I rested my head against the headrest, or at least tried to, with the carriage bouncing and jostling us. Events over the past weeks played behind my closed eyes. I still awoke each morning and thanked all that was holy for giving me George to love. The weeks hence had flown by as we huddled in the warmth of White House during one of the worst winters I'd ever lived through. An embarrassed flush washed my face as I recalled the quiet evenings relaxing in the parlor together, followed by holding each other close through the night. With good fortune, I'd soon be carrying his child.

Jacky and Patsy had grown fond of George, calling him "papa" and playing with him after dinner. Although initially reserved, Jacky quickly warmed to his stepfather. Jacky provided little Patsy with a fine example of how to adapt to the changes in life. He may as well grow accustomed to the reality while a young child so he'd accept the unforeseen changes lying ahead. Not all of the changes he'd face would be welcome.

When the weather and road conditions permitted, we'd made the traditional nuptial rounds to visit family and friends to receive their congratulations and benediction. However, I preferred to be at home with George, keeping him all to myself. Hoarding him seemed rather selfish, but each moment alone with him deepened my attachment to him and vice versa. I glanced outside again, where George rode his stallion alongside the carriage, his inherent energy requiring he sit astride rather than inside. I'd agreed for three reasons, even though I would prefer to have him sit with me so I could enjoy his company. First, he was an excellent horseman, and I loved the way he looked in the saddle, tall and straight and in control of his world. Second, the vehicle would have been far too crowded with such a large man crammed inside. Third, my foremost desire remained to ensure his happiness.

The coach rumbled on toward our next adventure in the city. The image of Six Chimneys rose in my mind. I'd spent a good bit of time staring out a front window at the square across the street, named in honor of my deceased father-in-law. Custis Square contained a small park in the midst of several small houses. He didn't deserve to have anything named after him. Honestly, the way he abused Daniel and his sister was beyond the pale. The house's namesake chimneys trumpeted the wealth and obstinate pride of the man who'd built it. I wouldn't think more about that man or his blasted house. I'd considered tearing it down brick by brick for worrying and hounding Daniel into his grave, but it would only serve to vindicate his original opinion of me.

I pushed aside the lingering irritation ringing in my heart and closed my eyes. My former father-in-law had done all in his power to make his family miserable, to jump to his demands, and to never be happy. I had struggled to contain my anger toward the machinations of his father, to hide my true feelings behind my usual smile. Doing so took a wealth of effort and control. I harbored no doubt the man had reached out from his grave and killed my first husband.

Returning to Williamsburg and Six Chimneys served to resurrect all the old animosities underlying the happier moments spent there with Daniel. I chose to look forward to a new life with my children and George. Keep my emphasis on building a loving home for my family, an inviting resting place for travelers, and pleasing my husband.

"Look, Mama!" Jacky bounced like a jack-in-a-box on the cushioned seat. "We're in the city."

Sally stirred, rubbing her eyes and then covering her yawn with one small hand. "We're there?"

I nodded. It had been years since our last visit, years during which my young children had allowed memories of the house and town to slip away. "Soon you'll see Six Chimneys, my—our town home. There's a yard out back where you can play, Jacky. I think you'll like it."

I ran a hand down my daughter's shoulder, lightly joggling her awake. "Come, my little Patt, it's time to sit up. We'll be at the house very soon."

Patsy snuggled deeper into my lap, squeezing her eyes closed. "Nuh-uh."

I bent over my daughter and brushed strands of dark hair from her forehead, smoothing them into place. "I'm afraid you must, my sweet."

With a groan, Patsy sat up, fists rubbing her still-closed eyes. Finally, she blinked three times and yawned. "I'm thirsty."

"We'll arrive very soon and you may have something then." I pressed the rumples from the girl's clothes. "We must be presentable when we get there, mustn't we?"

"Why, Mama?" Patsy became more animated and eager as the remaining dregs of sleep fell away.

"Because we must behave as ladies and gentlemen." Patsy made to stand in the swaying carriage and I gently encouraged her to stay seated. "Please sit down. Wait until the carriage stops and Papa or one of the postilions will hand us down from the carriage. Jacky, remember to wait until your turn, understand?"

"But I want to see what's out there, Mama." Jacky fidgeted on the seat, practically bouncing. "Why can't I get out first?"

"Ladies must be handed down before the children, dear." I softened the command with a little laugh. I didn't think there'd be any danger to them, but the mother in me wanted to verify all was safe for them to exit the coach. "You'll be out soon enough."

Moments later the vehicle stopped, the horses' harnesses jangling. The door beside me opened, and the postilion, a young black man wearing the Washington livery of scarlet and gold, bowed and stepped aside for George to take my hand. A rush of love and pride swept through me, and soon I stood beside him. The postilion assisted Patsy after Jacky bounded from his position.

"Jacky, stay with us." George's measured words halted the little boy's escape. "You'll have sufficient time later to play outside. Come here, like a good boy."

True to his word, the family's transition from the confines of the conveyance to being settled in the house occurred with rapid efficiency. I stepped through the front door again, which was all it took to stir memories best laid to rest. Everywhere I confronted another vision of Daniel. I would never forget him. He was my first love and the father of my children. I'd always remember our time together with love in my heart. George grasped my hand but remained silent at my side for a moment. I squeezed his fingers letting him know I was all right. With a nod, he strode down the hall toward the parlor.

I didn't have any illusions about my ability to stay in the house for an extended period. Not with John's ghost and Daniel's love lingering in every shadowy corner. And I detested the extensive gardens behind the house, only because the gardens was where the old man had nurtured the plants' growth with far more care than his own children.

My preference was to attend to the children and George as we prepared to stay in the house for several months while George attended the assembly session. I let my gaze sweep the condition of the house. I pirouetted, taking note of the work needing hands to accomplish as Sally joined me. I'd work to put things to rights and then move on.

"We have much to do, Sally." I pulled my gloves off and held them together in one hand. "Let us begin."

"Yes'm." Sally grinned up at me as she rubbed her hands together, indicating how anxious she was to start. "I've already set the others to tasks."

"Very good, Sally. I don't know what I'd do without your help." I slipped my traveling cloak from my shoulders and handed it to Austin, who appeared at my side for that purpose. "As you have things in hand here, I'll make sure Rose and Julius see to settling the children into their rooms."

The household servants spread through the house and set to work lighting fires in the cold hearths and removing protective linen sheets from the few pieces of furniture I had retained. The rest had been sold at auction as quickly as possible. After the Assembly's session ended, we'd send the furniture to Mount Vernon. George had described his plantation in great detail, but I longed to see it. Would I enjoy living there? I huffed at my own silent question. Of course I would love living there, as long as I stayed by George's side. In only six weeks I'd grown so attached to him I wanted nothing more than to be his adoring wife and a caring mother for our children.

---

One March afternoon, George returned home more animated than usual. He surprised me by appearing at my side while I conversed with Doll and the scullion, Beck, in the kitchen. The supply of fresh vegetables had dwindled along with my patience. Surely the servants could be more judicious in the quantities they'd used. I'd deal with them after I discovered what had brought George home midday. I strode to greet him in the open door, gazing at his happy face and grinning in return.

"What is it, Papa?" I wanted him to take both my hands in his, to connect with him, but knew he would not in front of the servants. "What brings you home so cheerful?"

George stepped closer as he smiled at me. "You will be pleased to know we've been invited to the Governor's Ball."

"Our first as husband and wife." Although we'd both attended previous balls, my heart soared at the prospect of attending on the arm of my distinguished new husband. I clapped my hands once in delight. "When will it be held?"

"Three days hence." George appeared to desire to close the space between us, but remained a respectable distance from me. "I am anxious to show off my wife to the other burgesses and the Governor, so pray wear your best gown."

"I'll not disappoint you." I perused his face, and detected a glint of hesitancy in his eyes. "You will have to trust me."

He inclined his head. "I always have faith in your judgment on such matters."

I spent the next few days going over my wardrobe with Sally's assistance. I asked my seamstress, Betty, to also attend me to have her input. My bed often appeared as though a mad seamstress had invaded my private room. Should I choose the magenta confection of organza and silk, or the dark blue satin with low bodice and two parallel rows of pale pink lace extending from the shoulders and meeting at the waist? Bah!

"What else is in the wardrobe, Sally? Surely, there must be something." I shook my head as I examined a yellow gown. "If only I'd had more notice."

"How about this one?" Sally held up a burgundy organza

gown with a silk inset panel featuring vertical rays of rose buds, with wide lace hanging from the elbows.

"Perhaps. Let me take a look." I crossed to where Sally held the gown in front of the walnut wardrobe, its doors wide open and revealing the collection of gowns and petticoats. Inspecting the condition of the fabric and lace, I found a tear in the hem. Pursing my lips, I examined the extent of the damage. I glanced at Betty and caught her attention. "This will need mending. Can you manage?"

"Yes, Madame. Fixing it should only take a few stitches." Betty gathered the gown into her arms and smiled. "You'll be the best dressed woman at the ball."

I laughed, a light sound floating on the air. I held no illusion that my stature could compete with the wisps of other women in their expensive, imported ball gowns. I more than made up for my appearance by staying informed of events and styles. I could converse with any one on most topics. "We shall see. I'll have to select the ear bobs and hair décor to accompany the gown, but that can wait until to-morrow when I dress for the ball."

---

Promptly at eight o'clock the next night, we stepped into the carriage for the short ride to the Governor's Palace. Along the way, we passed the Bruton Parish Church, with its lovely rosette windows on the gable and tall arched and sashed windows. We turned left onto Palace Green Street and slowly made our way toward the brick building in the crush of carriages teeming with animated passengers waiting for their turn. As we drew nearer to the grand entrance, George pointed out the two-story brick home of George Wythe, a fellow burgess.

"Will George and Elizabeth be attending tonight?" I liked the rectangular building with its stalwart appearance. Having lived in a clapboard house during one of the more ferocious thunderstorms that rolled through on occasion, I would also prefer to live behind sturdy brick walls.

"I'm sure they will. Probably long before us at the snail's pace we're traveling." George turned to me. "You have no call to be nervous, my dear. You look beautiful this evening. Every man shall envy me my bride."

"You're just saying so because you have an ulterior aim in mind." I fanned my warm cheeks, scrambling for something provocative to say to unsettle his too confident demeanor. It had become somewhat of a game I played, teasing him with my audacious innuendo. I tapped him on the arm with my fan as I let a slow smile lift my lips. "You're thinking to flatter me into another intimate evening after we arrive home from the ball."

His eyes widened for a moment and then he chuckled as he clasped my hand. "You know me too well."

A surge of emotion welled in my chest as I leaned against him, longing for a more private space where we could make the jest become reality. Hours must elapse, time in which my imagination would surely fuel the spark of need and bring life to my fondest hope. Perhaps tonight I'd conceive his child.

Finally, our carriage halted at the gated entrance. Two square brick pillars supported statues of a unicorn on one side and a lion on the other, guarding the walkway leading to steps into the building. The palace stood as a notable example of fine architecture in the colonies. It was made of thousands of red bricks, capped with a row of dormers on the roof and a towering cupola, a testament of the power and importance of the British governor. I had been within the walled residence on several occasions, but it never failed to impress.

As we strolled up the walk past the flanking brick houses and into the palace, George returned greetings offered by his peers and those even more powerful and important. I acknowledged the formal exchange of pleasantries as we passed through the front hall with its extensive exhibit of weapons mounted on the walls. The sound of the quartet playing a tune fit for a cotillion or square dance wafted to my ears, summoning me as forcefully as the call to prayer. I quickly doffed my protective shoes and cloak and rejoined my husband.

We crossed into the ballroom and perused the vast number of guests replete in varying jewel-toned gowns, lace draping from collars and sleeves. Shiny buckles on belts and shoes reflected the light of the candles in branching candlesticks. A string quartet occupied the far corner of the large room, bows flashing across taut strings as they played. Several couples twirled and stepped in the center of the room as the remaining guests conversed and observed the festivities.

"The dancing has begun." I flicked a glance up at George.

He laughed. "I know what that means. We shall be on the dance floor posthaste."

"Do you object to dancing with your wife?" I arched a brow. "Would you have me dance with another man?"

"Of course not, Patsy." He tucked my hand into the crook of his arm. "I wish to dance only with you."

"Maybe so." I explored the humor apparent in George's eyes and expression. "But I vow you love to dance far more than I am able to keep up with you. Then I can envision you taking another lady on the dance floor."

"Only in the event you were tired or dancing with another would the thought even cross my mind."

"What have we here?" The voice carried across the ballroom.

"George Mason." My husband grinned at the couple approaching.

"My dear friend, George, and his enthralling new bride."

I greeted the couple, noting their elegant attire as I recalled all George had shared about his dear friend. George Mason was a newly elected fellow burgess. His suit of clothes revealed his status without a spoken word. Ann, walking beside her husband, had a lovely sense of the latest fashions available from London, which also spoke for her place in our society.

George acknowledged his friend's arrival. "May I present Mrs. Washington."

George Mason inclined his head in greeting. "May I say how becoming you are this evening?"

I opened my fan, glancing at Ann's amused and curious

expression, and slowly waved it in front of my face. I decided to partake of an exchange of wit to test the waters. "Why yes, you may, kind sir."

"Then so be it." George Mason smiled. "Perhaps you'll spare a dance for me?"

"Only if I may dance with your lovely wife." George glanced my way before addressing Ann. "As long as your husband does not mind."

George Mason laughed. "Of course not, my dear friend. It's a fair exchange. However, please be so good as to return her intact and in good spirits."

I chuckled along with George. "I'm sure he will."

"Shall we dance, Mrs. Mason?" George offered his arm.

"I'd be delighted to dance with a man who actually knows the steps." Ann batted her eyes at my husband and then smiled at me. "Watch your toes if you dare dance with my husband."

I contemplated George Mason for several seconds before laughing. "Perhaps I should have worn different shoes."

George Mason barked out a laugh. "Never fear, my dear Mrs. Washington. I'll take care. Shall we?" He offered his arm, and I laid my fingers on the strong limb.

The quartet began playing a lively tune and the couples paired off, amidst much laughter, to enjoy the cotillion. Thank goodness they didn't play the old formal dances, but rather the English Country Dance tunes so easy to remember and dance to. Pale blue walls flashed past as I spun and stepped to the music. George Mason proved an adequate partner but he could not surpass my elegant and athletic husband. I paid close attention to my partner's movements so I didn't find my foot crushed under his much larger one. I sensed my husband's location without having to turn my head. Felt him move around the dance floor away from me and then closer again. I'd rather dance with him, truth be told, but my partner proved acceptable. Still, all I could think was, would the dance never end?

Keeping the smile on my face became challenging. Finally the tune ended, and my George returned to lead me into the next dance. I flowed with him among the other couples on the polished wood floor, his presence easily guiding me through the intricate movement. I savored the spark of love in his eyes and the strength in his hold on my hand. I'd found my own piece of heaven on earth.

---

The days and weeks flew by. While George attended to business, my time was filled with overseeing the children's education and activities, supervising the house slaves' chores, and paying complimentary visits to the other burgesses' wives and receiving them at Six Chimneys. Despite the whirl of parties and dances and balls, I counted the days until I'd accompany George to Mount Vernon for the first time. He frequently referred to our real life on the plantation and my keenness for settling in there grew with each passing day.

One day, George returned midday from the ongoing session, surprising me in the pantry where I was inventorying the contents.

"Why, George, what is the matter?" I searched for a hint in his expression.

Since we were closeted alone in the pantry, George dared to kiss me and then stepped back. "I cannot tolerate staying here any longer. My role in the Assembly has been fulfilled. So we shall leave for Mount Vernon in a few days."

Days? Joy and concern combined in my chest. The day neared when I'd see my new home. At the same time, there remained much to organize for the trip. "Of course. I'll see to the packing and shutting up the house."

He kissed me again, lingering in our embrace for a short span. "I knew you could manage. But inform me of any assistance you may need from me."

"Oh, George, I'm so glad to be departing this house once and for all." Glad to have him all to myself for a precious moment, I hugged him closer. "I am impatient to arrive at Mount Vernon so we can begin life together in our own home."

George pressed a kiss on my forehead, then my lips. "I am impatient as well to return there. Wait until you see the renovations I've called for to suit our needs. From all accounts the work is nearly finished. I also want to investigate a new farming method I've heard about, but I must be there to ensure it's done properly."

"Then we should make haste. If we're to leave in a few days, I must set to work." I hugged him one more time and then broke the embrace.

George nodded as a smile grew on his lips. "I'm glad you are my wife, Patsy. I don't know what I'd ever do without you by my side."

Pleased at his words, I nevertheless shooed him away. "Be off, Papa, so I can finish the myriad tasks necessary to make your plans for departure come to pass."

Delight filled my chest as I directed the servants on what to pack and what furniture to take from the house. The sooner we started for Mount Vernon the better. We'd already discussed and decided on our travel plans over the last few weeks. Unfortunately, we both had realized the trip wouldn't be direct. Instead, we would have to make several stops on the way. All the more reason to begin our journey.

First, we'd stop at White House to pack the furniture for travel by boat to the plantation, a far easier way to transport heavy and bulky items than loading them in a wagon and bouncing the contents down rough and rutted roads that frequently became impassable when it rained. I would visit my family in the area while there, as I had no idea how long it would be until I saw them again. A wave of sadness flowed through me at the thought, but I bolstered my courage and resolved to visit as often as possible. As George's wife, my place was with him, wherever he may be.

George had decided we'd visit his mother, Mary, at Ferry Farm in Fredericksburg and then go to visit his sister, Betty, and her husband, Lewis Fielding who lived nearby at Kenmore. His mother sounded an awfully lot like John Custis, with his vinegar attitude. She'd not even deigned to attend her son's wedding, claiming the trip too arduous. Thus Betty and Lewis also stayed away, caring for her needs. Would we get along? Could we? What if we didn't? In the event, it didn't make much difference. No use worrying about something I had no control over. I'd be pleasant and polite no matter how Mary treated me. In contrast, George's description of Betty and her husband had me looking forward to meeting them. After we visited for a day, we'd continue on to my new home and a simple life on the plantation where everything revolved around the crops and seasons.

The day arrived to climb into the coach, Jacky, Patsy and Sally with me, and the other servants and their luggage piled in wagons. George again mounted his restless stallion and we set off for our ultimate destination, Mount Vernon.

# 9

*Mount Vernon – April 1759*

I longed to poke my head out the carriage window. Sneak a peek at my new home as the carriage traversed the long straight approach to Mount Vernon. Only propriety kept me from indulging my curiosity. My actions would reflect upon my husband as far as the servants were concerned, and I'd not project any emotion other than patience, despite the curiosity simmering in my chest. Jacky and Patsy, however, had no such compunction, hanging out the open window set in the door. Mother would have chastised me if she were to see them behaving so indecorously, but I simply smiled and kept a close eye to make sure they didn't lean too far out. They'd only be children for a few years.

As we made our way up the lane, I studied the many outbuildings and elaborate landscaping we passed. George had described each kind of plant to me in great detail over the last few months. He'd done an excellent job of helping me visualize the many kinds of ornamental as well as useful plants and trees lining the drive. The slaves paused in their labors to watch the procession, here and there an arm raised to wipe a darkly glistening brow, then returning to their chores after the carriage had passed.

Here, on this plantation, my life truly began. Again. The previous months of our marriage had been crammed with visits by and to family and friends. Then the public days in the bustling city of Williamsburg, with the dinners and balls and meetings and more rounds of visits. I pressed my back into the cushion. Home. The sense of belonging filling my entire being eased my tension as I enjoyedd the order and balance of the building locations, architecture, and even the horticulture.

The jostling ride ended at the apex of the circular carriage-way. George dismounted from his horse, and then approached the coach with a contented grin and shining eyes. He swung open the door and then handed me down from the vehicle. The children tumbled out behind me. I turned to investigate the exterior of the mansion-house, my new home.

Sitting three stories tall with a row of windows on each floor, three dormer windows in the roof, and a chimney at either end, its clean lines presented an air of both importance and welcome. I peered closely at the walls. George had ordered the special treatment of the exterior, the planks beveled and painted to resemble white rectangular stones with sand thrown onto the wet paint to create the illusion of real stone. A ladder leaned against the half-finished wall to the right of the front door, a bucket of paint sitting at its feet in the dirt. A quick sweep of the courtyard surrounded by the outbuildings confirmed the incomplete state of the repairs and changes George had ordered months earlier.

"I'm gonna catch you!" Jacky's voice broke into my musings.

I spun around. What were they up to now?

"No!" Patsy ran down a slight hill as fast as her toddler legs would carry her toward the stables.

A small herd of horses in the pasture turned white striped noses toward the sound. Rose and Julius hurried after the children, attempting to contain them much like the nags in the field.

"Leave the horses alone, Patsy." I shaded my eyes from the bright spring sunshine. "Jacky, you be careful and don't harass your little sister."

George chuckled quietly beside me. "Do not worry, my dear. They've been cooped up far too long. They'll be fine." He proffered his arm. "Let me give you the tour. I've waited a long time to share Mount Vernon with you. My apologies for the ongoing construction mess."

"I know you'd hoped it would be completed by now." I bestowed a smile on him. "It's beautiful, even if they haven't finished painting it."

He escorted me up the front steps and through the door. I stopped, amazed by the beautiful hall stretching from the front door straight through to the rear of the mansion. A delightful breeze cooled my cheeks as I took in the grand entry, boasting a branched candlestick hanging from the ceiling and rich, dark-red wood floor. True, the floor needed cleaning after the workers finished traipsing through, but I detected a fine grain to the wood. A good waxing would be necessary to restore its luster. Based on George's ambitions, I had my work before me. I started making a mental list of required tasks along with additions and refinements to the furnishings.

"I've added this black-walnut staircase in the renovation. Don't you think it enhances the overall impression?" George indicated with a slight wave of his hand the stairs leading up to a landing and then turning to continue up to the second floor. "The old set have been taken apart and rebuilt to access the new third floor where there are small rooms, including one for the fine china, and of course for access to the cupola."

"It's all so very grand and yet has an intimate feeling. I love it." I let George lead me to the left of the front door. I drank in each detail, weighing its worth, adding to my mental list as we moved through the house.

George paused inside a large room reeking of fresh paint. "This is my new best room, where we'll entertain our visitors."

I surveyed the lavishly decorated parlor with its wood panels on the walls creating a sense of majesty in the room. An intricately carved mantel over the fireplace drew my eye, and then up to what appeared to be a coat of arms above a landscape painting. A bit more lavish than I liked, but George desired to make a good impression. Beside the parlor was another small but nicely decorated room, with, surprisingly, a bed. I stared at the anomaly, blinking slowly as I digested the remaining contents of the room. Curious, I smiled up at George. "Who is supposed to occupy that bed?"

"I asked one of my most trusted workers, John Alton, to ensure a bed was set up properly on this floor for our family's use, until such time as you determined a more fitting place." He squeezed my hand and dropped a kiss onto my upturned mouth. "This room will be for the children. Ours for now is across the way."

He led me to the other side of the hall, where I spied a makeshift bedchamber with a bed large enough for us to share. The mahogany frame had carved fluted feet and gorgeous yellow silk and worsted damask curtains. To one side stood an elegant mahogany dressing table. I turned slowly to take in the area from the front door to the temporary bedchamber on the river side of the house. Servants and slaves as well as the painters and carpenters would be coming and going past our door at all hours. "Surely you'd rather sleep upstairs where we'd have more quiet and privacy?"

"As long as we are together, my dear, it matters not to me where our bedchamber is." He tugged on my hand, and I, in total agreement with his statement, eagerly followed him toward the fair-sized room beside our bedroom.

A cherry table surrounded by matching chairs stood on what I surmised to be a fine Wilton carpet, which was positioned parallel to an elaborate fireplace. Crimson embossed paper decorated the walls while the door and window frames were painted white. On a beautiful mahogany tea table rested a Chinese porcelain tea service. A silver cruet stand and a set of porcelain china serving dishes and soup plates occupied a sideboard. Yes, George had begun to furnish his—rather, our—home to suit his intentions. Still, much more needed to be done.

Through the window at the front of the house—which

interestingly was not the river side like at both Chestnut Grove and Elsing Green—I could see men, black and white, moving past the window intent upon their numerous tasks. One pushed a wheelbarrow of bricks, another carried a ladder, and yet another led a horse toward the blacksmith's shed. So many people necessary to work a plantation, and a good number of them employed within the mansion-house. I'd have plenty to keep me busy and thus happy. Idle hands being the Devil's workshop, after all. Still, my impression was of a house waiting to fulfill its potential with the proper guidance of an intelligent and educated lady. I glanced at George. "It's wonderful. I'm sure we'll be very comfortable here, especially after I add to your simple trappings with the appropriate furnishings."

George raised a brow in question. "What sort of furnishings do you have in mind?"

"Do not worry." I waved a hand dismissively, a smile edging onto my mouth. "I'll make the list after we finish the tour."

He chuckled and a sparkle lit in his eyes. "Anything you want, my dear, I'm content to provide." He took my hand and led me back to the staircase in the wide hall. "You'll want to see the upstairs, then."

We mounted the stairs to the second floor. I made a point to poke my nose into each bedchamber. I wrinkled the very same nose at the cleaning necessary to put the rooms into service. George pointed out the extent of the renovation completed, raising the roof to add a third floor and more chambers on both of the upper floors. Bits of plaster and wood mingled with sawdust across the floors. Buckets containing whitewash and paint formed a pyramid in the second floor landing. The glass windows needed a good scrub to be able to see through them.

We skirted the debris and continued investigating. As we reached the southeast end of the house, I stopped inside the door to evaluate the space, to experience the room. Without a doubt, this would be the master's bedchamber. The room boasted high ceilings and two adjacent smaller rooms. More than that, we would enjoy being together within these four walls. I sauntered into the middle of the chamber and slowly turned in place, judging the features of the large room, and then finally catching George's attention.

"This shall be our bedchamber." I strode over to the left-hand small room and walked inside. "We could use this as a closet and storage of our personal items. Can you have shelves built on the walls?"

"My thinking exactly." George followed me into what would become a closet and took one of my hands in his. "And the other a sitting room, I believe. It has a connecting door to another bedchamber, a perfect room for Patsy."

I led him through the wood door connecting to the other bedroom. The small room we stood in had a window overlooking the circular carriage-way and the outbuildings flanking the mansion-house. "Can we put two comfortable chairs and a table with an oil lamp in there? It would be the perfect place to read my Bible and say my prayers each morning." I studied his smile and twinkling eyes, aware of his agreement before he responded.

George nodded once. "Consider it done. But there is one detail we'll have to address prior to moving into the bedchamber."

"Such as?"

"The ceiling height is several inches shorter than the first floor room where our bedstead currently stands. We'll need to order a new bed to fit the room."

"Your comfort is what is most important to me." I slipped my hand free of his and clasped both of mine together. "What do you say to blue-and-white bed curtains to complement the wallpaper? Such a color will ensure the room is peaceful and restful."

George regarded the room for a few moments before nodding. "Very well."

"I shall make a note of it." When he glanced sharply at me, I smiled. "You married me for a reason, did you not?"

He bussed my lips, then half bowed. "Indeed. Your desire is my mission."

In fact, my mental list had grown rather long during the short tour. I allowed George to lead me through each of the remaining rooms as he expounded on their design, dimensions, and intended uses. I nodded and smiled at his words, but envisioned the furniture and decorations necessary to transform the home of a bachelor into a genteel abode fit to entertain our friends and family.

---

By the end of April I had compiled my request for items to be ordered from our factors in London. When George returned for supper, I broached the topic of placing an order.

"I've determined what is needed first in order to work toward creating the impression you intend." I cut a bite of venison pie and placed it in my mouth, chewing slowly as George laid down his silverware and regarded me.

"What do you have in mind, my dear?" He sat quietly contemplating me while I swallowed and smiled.

"Well, it may sound like a lot, but really it's only the beginning." I dabbed my napkin to my lips and took a breath. "Let's see. First we'll need to order six dozen metal plates with the Washington coat of arms, dessert glasses and stands for sweetmeats. We'll also need to acquire more suitable utensils, so perhaps knives and forks with handles of ivory will suit our purpose."

He nodded his head as he listened to me rattle off items. "Very well. Anything else?"

"Oh my yes. The victuals on hand are rather plain, don't you think? We shall need pickles, olives, capers, and a bottle of Indian mangoes. Perhaps a large Cheshire cheese and green tea. Raisins, almonds, about twenty-five pounds of each. Twenty loaves of sugar, and twenty sacks of salt. Then there's what we'll need to bathe and clothe ourselves and the slaves. For that, add on twenty-five pounds of soap and fifty yards of homespun cloth. Also we'll need to be prepared to treat illness. For that, we'll need six bottles of Greenhouse Tincture."

"I see. I pray you've compiled a list?"

I nodded. "It's in my room."

"Fine. Retrieve it after we finish our meal and I will write up an order to-morrow." He resumed eating, making small and precise movements with knife and fork.

"Thank you, Papa." I smiled at him, pleased with his ready acceptance of my request, and resumed eating.

"Anything to see you smile, Patsy." He leveled an intense look on me, one which suggested he had more on his mind than improving the furnishings of the house.

I flashed a smile at him, then looked at my plate. A comfortable silence stretched between us, content in being together.

"I've been thinking." Laying down his knife and fork, George drew my attention. "We should hold an infaring party so you can meet our neighbors and they can meet you. When would be acceptable to you?"

Embarrassed dismay flooded my chest. How had I forgotten? But George had remembered and understood the importance of the tradition. And I'd finally meet his closest friends, George William Fairfax and his intriguing wife Sally. Curiosity filled me each time I thought of them. George spoke so fondly of Sally, almost as if he'd become infatuated with the wife of his best friend. The party would give me a chance to determine once and for all whether my initial impression proved accurate. The past, and any improper feelings he may have felt for Sally, held no sway for my feelings. After all, George Washington would be my husband until Death visited us. Nothing Sally had done would change that fact. Indeed, I refused to feel threatened by a married woman. For the time being, I had a party to prepare.

I beamed at George. "Three days hence? That should give us time to prepare the refreshments."

"I'll send out the invitations this evening." He pushed back from the table and came around to help me rise from my chair. "I imagine you have some plans to make, so I'll leave you for the next hour or so. But I'll be thinking of you."

I smiled at his retreating figure. I'd chosen well. His self-confidence and insight came together to make his integrity a solid foundation for our future. I'd do all in my power to keep him healthy and happy. I laid a hand on my waist, wishing with all my might I could give him the best gift of all. So far, I'd had no sign or indication of being with child. A fleeting memory of the trouble I'd had delivering Patsy gave me pause. Maybe the doctor had been right that having another child may never happen. But I'd keep trying in order to make my husband happy. Shaking off the desire to follow him, I spun on my satin heel and went to find Doll to plan the menu. We had much to do.

———————

Sun blessed the day of the party, shining upon the beds of yellow and white jonquils, red roses, and the variety of trees stretching away into the distance. I sat in my favorite chair, Bible open on my lap, as I gazed out my sitting room window. The yard and carriage-way immediately before the front doors connected to the long, straight approach to the mansion-house. Slaves hurried to tend to their various tasks, calling out to each other in a symphony of bass and treble tones, but otherwise I looked out over a peaceful, idyllic view. It wouldn't be quiet for long, though. Soon, the drive would be busy with teams of horses pulling carriages.

Indeed, a carriage suddenly appeared between the trees at the far end of the drive. The festivities had begun. Closing the Bible, I laid it reverently on the small table, my fingers lingering on the raised gold lettering on the leather cover. I'd prayed for calm and for wisdom prior to meeting the most important people in my husband's life.

A knock sounded on the closed chamber door behind me.

"Come in." I rose and strode into the bedchamber.

Sally slipped into the room, quiet but quick as always. "Misses, the colonel says he begs you to come down to him. Lord and Lady Fairfax have arrived."

Despite my resolve, a tremor threatened my composure. I pushed my shoulders back and shook off any hint of hesitancy. "Help me with my gown, please." I slipped off my dressing robe while Sally deftly retrieved the gown—a divine confection of deep purple satin skirts and pink bodice, all overlaid with cream lace—from the wardrobe. Time to prepare to receive our guests and neighbors. With good fortune, my new friends.

Reaching the main floor of the house, I followed the sound of George's voice into the parlor where he entertained George and Sally. The cool spring morning warranted the fire crackling in the fireplace. Both men rose as I entered, George quickly striding to my side. He presented me to his friends. Curiosity mixed with judgment flashed in Sally's expression and then vanished as quickly as it appeared.

"Lady Fairfax, may I present my wife, Martha Washington."

"Lady Fairfax." I curtsied in greeting. As I resumed my full height, I saw what I'd been expecting.

Lady Fairfax's sweeping rake of a possessive glance traveled over George's powerful frame then flicked back to rest on me. So it was true. I'd seen the same look a hundred times in ballrooms and parlors, the one laying stake to another for the world to see. I lifted my chin ever so slightly and commanded my composure to hold, to not reveal any uncertainty or weakness in the face of a potential adversary. I didn't want to cause a rift between George and his friends, yet I would not tolerate even the hint of impropriety to taint our marriage.

I smiled at Sally. "Thank you for joining us to welcome me to my new home as Mrs. Washington. I'm happy to meet you."

A challenge lingered in Sally's laughing eyes, in the way she flipped open her oriental fan to move lazily before her face. She slid a hand down the fan, snapping it closed. "I am pleased to meet you, Mrs. Washington, and we are well met."

My smile widened and I nodded. Sally had understood my subtle meaning. "Yes, I believe we are very well met."

She laughed, a light merry sound. "We shall get on famously, I'm sure. Please call me Sally."

"I should hope so, given we're neighbors." Lord Fairfax took my hand and placed a respectful kiss on the back of it. "Welcome."

"Our door will always be open to you both." I turned at the sound of the front door opening. "It appears others are arriving."

"From the sound of that booming voice, I'd say George and Ann Mason have joined us from Gunston Hall." George slowly shook his head. "He has a tendency to make quite the wrong impression upon his entrance."

"We haven't had the privilege of their company in some weeks." Sally leaned toward me, spreading her fan to signal a confidential revelation would soon follow. "Mr. Mason has been stirring up mischief, if you ask me."

I shook my head. "I've met Mr. Mason, and his reputation makes me believe he would never instigate any trouble."

Sally snapped her fan closed and stepped back with a knowing grin. "Wait and see."

Soon the new arrivals hurried into the parlor, smiles wreathing their mouths. I waited as George greeted them before presenting me to them.

Ann strode straight to me and embraced me. "We're so happy for you both, and for ourselves that you've caught the most eligible man in the region."

I permitted a small smile as I returned the polite embrace. "He made a proposition I could not turn down."

George came to stand beside me and I looked up to meet his gentle gaze. In his eyes I saw pride and desire, a powerful combination which sparked an answering heat. I'd lay down my very life for him.

"Martha has ensnared me with her wit, her refined manners, and her many charms." George addressed his friends with a buoyant smile. "She made a bad bargain if you consider my clumsy efforts to woo her."

George Mason guffawed. "Yet she entered into the marriage contract with you. Obviously, you did something right."

"Yes, he did." I addressed each of the gathered friends. "Now he's committed to me as long as we shall live."

"And I'm happy to be so." George audaciously slipped his arm about my waist and squeezed.

"Then we need some sherry, my friend," Lord Fairfax declared. "I'd like to make a toast."

I self-consciously stepped away from my husband and indicated to Breechy to pour sherry for everyone. While he acted on my request, the banter between the long-time friends continued. My George had relaxed into a jovial demeanor, one which recalled to mind the easy exchanges between him and Burwell. Breechy moved to each guest, carrying a silver tray bearing crystal glasses filled with the garnet-colored wine. Once everyone had been served, George nodded to Lord Fairfax.

Lord Fairfax raised his glass. "May you both live a long and contented life with one another."

We all raised our glasses and tapped their rims together in a succession of clear tones from the fine crystal.

"To a long life together here on Mount Vernon." George touched his glass to mine.

My thoughts exactly. I smiled up at him. "There's no place I'd rather be than at your side."

---

*Mount Vernon – January 1760*

"This is certainly no way to spend my wedding anniversary." I tugged the quilt closer to my chin, covering the heated bricks surrounding me. "One year ago I married George and today I feel terrible."

"You're not alone in your sentiments." Sally, my very concerned maid, shook her head slowly as she folded her arms and gazed down at me. "Jacky is none too happy to be in bed neither."

"The poor thing. I should…" I started to push the cover away, and then broke into a dry, hacking cough. My throat hurt and I ached all over. But my son needed me. I started to swing my legs out of bed and then happened to glance up. Spying Sally's crossed arms and stern frown, I relented and forced myself to lie back on the bed. It didn't hurt quite as much when I lay perfectly still. I dragged the quilt up and lifted my gaze to meet the other woman's dark eyes. "Do I look as bad as I feel?"

I hoped not, or George wouldn't come near me. Then again, he probably should stay away. The children, too. Who knew how the measles spread? A stranger walked into town and within a week half the town would be covered with little red sores. The person wouldn't have to do or say anything, simply arrive and move around. Medicine seemed more guess work than science. The Pohick Church minister had come to tend me and the others in the family sick with measles, and then left after insisting on repeated sweats and hot beverages to break the fever.

How I detested being ill. I'd much prefer to be out on my horse getting air and exercise. Or perhaps engaging in the dancing lessons from the itinerant tutor who visited to teach the children their steps. But no. I had to stay abed and be miserable. Diseases afflicted so many, repeatedly, and ultimately took scores of lives away from the colony. I'd already lost so many of my family and friends in my life, I didn't know if I could survive any more deaths in the family. One thing was certain. As long as I breathed, I'd do all in my power to protect my loved ones.

Living in the young British colony meant establishing a new way of living, a new way of surviving. Faced with previously unknown diseases, such as mysterious agues, apoplexy, and the putrid throat, everyone had to know at least the minimum of how to fight the maladies. Doctors, ministers, and midwives boiled teas and other concoctions, applied mustard plasters to sweat out the fever, or resorted to purges and bleeding. All to control disease. Or at least the signs of the disease. How would one fight the source of something one cannot see? At least the mansion-house sat on a rise, distant from the bogs and marshes where the worst illnesses seemed to lurk, but that lucky situation didn't render one immune from them. As well I knew.

"You rest, like the doctor say." Sally unfolded her arms and smoothed the covers. The lines on her face seemed to deepen as she considered me. "There's no point worrying about something you can't do nothing about, except what's prescribed by them who know more than we do."

"Easy to say, Sally." Worry was one thing I knew well how to accomplish.

Not only was I covered with the dreaded measles rash and wracked with fever and an abominable sore throat, but my only boy lay similarly afflicted in his bed. And Patsy, approaching her fourth birthday already, had started acting rather strange. I couldn't put my finger on what exactly was happening, but I needed to keep a close eye on her. But how could I when the doctor wouldn't permit me to see her? Did I want Patsy to become ill, he'd asked. Of course not. But unless I could watch over her, I'd never sort out what was different.

"I'll be up with a tray and hot tea for you in a short while." Sally paused at the open door, one hand resting on her hip as she peered at me over her shoulder. "Doctor said you're to stay in bed."

I stifled a groan, unwilling to behave in a way unbecoming the mistress of the plantation. Still, I had so many tasks to see to and the requirement to stay abed would not help accomplish them. "I'm aware, Sally. I shall do as he insists."

"Colonel Washington said Lord Fairfax and his lady will be paying a visit this evening. They want to cheer you up, he said."

"I do hope they arrive soon. I'm in need of some pleasant company. Now that the mansion-house's repairs are complete, we shall have an easier time of it to provide a nice place for our guests."

"Yes'm." Sally bobbed her head. "I've made up the blue bedchamber for their use."

"No, let's put them in the yellow one so they can look out over the river instead of the lane."

"Yes'm." Sally stopped and folded her hands demurely in front of her apron, but the expression she aimed at me was anything but demure. "But, if you hope to see them, I need for you to follow the minister's doctoring orders so you're strong enough. You hear, Mrs. Washington? I know you've got your own mind, but you stay in bed. I won't be long." The warning in the black servant's voice was clear.

"I shall do my utmost to adhere to the minister's instructions." I tried to smile, but it felt limp. "Go on with you. I'll take a little nap while you're fetching tea."

Sally strode out the door, softly closing it behind her, and then thumped down the stairs to the main floor. I closed my eyes. My thoughts drifted over the events of the last year, the first year of my marriage to George. Our life together proved idyllic. The love we shared wove through every facet of our lives. Although we spent time apart, each content to deal with the day's chores and emergencies as we saw to our individual responsibilities, I always knew he was not far away. He would return from visiting the other farms on the plantation by midafternoon for dinner. Then we'd have a quiet evening together with the family, reading, sewing, and sharing our day. After the children were taken up to be readied for bed by their servants, we lingered by the fire until time to retire for the night.

The easy flow of our life was only interrupted by the many friends and family members who would stop over for a night or longer on their way past Mount Vernon. The Fairfaxes had become close friends, and we routinely exchanged visits, alternating dinners at Gunston Hall and Mount Vernon. Williamsburg also continued to grow and thrive and George's participation in the Virginia Assembly ensured his influence would also grow. I couldn't have asked for a finer manner of living with the man I loved. A smile of contentment formed on my mouth as I drifted off to sleep.

Pounding footsteps startled me awake just as the bedroom door opened and Patsy, her black curls bouncing and ankle-length cotton dress flapping, raced inside. She took one lap around the bedroom with her short legs before jumping onto the bed. "Mama! Mama! Tell me a story!"

Taken aback by the little girl's sudden cheerful face inches from my own, I frowned. "Now Patsy, you know better than to run into my room, don't you?"

My quiet, firm words had the desired effect. The bubbly enthusiasm evaporated from the little girl's walnut brown eyes as she looked down at the quilt. "Yes, Mama."

I placed a finger under her chin and lifted it up until forcing Patsy to meet my eyes. "Now, what is the matter that you've chosen to ignore your manners and burst into my room while I'm resting?"

Patsy slid her gaze away from mine and then back. "I'm bored."

"Pray, do not whine, my sweet. Mama feels bad enough without that." I chucked her under the chin, a signal all transgressions had been forgiven. "Where is Rose? Or Moll? Surely they can find something for you to do."

The dark curls bounced as she shook her head. "They's working."

"Patsy, what have I told you?" I raised both brows at her and waited. "You should say, what?"

Chagrin dragged the corners of the girl's mouth down. "They are working, Mama."

"Thank you. Even little girls should present themselves with as much decorum as their little bodies can manage." I hugged Patsy, despite the worry of somehow transferring red spots from one to the other through close proximity. Holding my children was one pleasure nothing and no one would deprive me of except death. And Death had no business around my young daughter.

"Mama?" Patsy pushed away from me and sat cross-legged on the bed, pushing the skirt of her dress between her knees. Her eyes shone bright and her cheeks wore red patches. "When can Jacky play again?"

"I hope very soon, my dear. He's young and strong." Of course, Daniel had been a virile man and he had succumbed to the dreaded ague, along with two of our children.

Why did I have to think of that? Something about Patsy? A chill rippled across my back as I inspected each feature of the pretty little girl, her dark coloring claiming her as a Parke descendant. She would grow up into quite a beauty. She'd... I jolted to attention as I realized Patsy sat unnaturally still, her eyes vacantly staring through me. Her mouth hung slack. She didn't blink. Didn't move. I waved a hand teasingly in front of Patsy's eyes, but the silent girl didn't react. Concern flared into fear.

"Patsy? Patsy!"

Struggling to sit up, I finally gained my balance and then grasped her upper arms and shook her gently but firmly. My panicked shouts brought Sally hurrying up the last few steps carrying the tea tray, followed closely by Molly.

"Moll, she's not responding. Dear Lord, help my daughter!" I dragged Patsy's tense body onto my lap, rocking the nearly rigid frame forward and back repeatedly, as I prayed and tried to remain calm. Tried to fight the alarm building inside. "Don't take her from me. Please. It can't be her time. Not yet. Not now."

The mantel clock measured the minutes as seconds ticked away and I shared my fear with the two women hovering nearby, ready to help. If only they could. Finally, Patsy's arms and legs relaxed and her head drooped onto my chest. Tears eased down my cheeks as I hugged her with trembling arms.

"Thank you, Lord." I brushed a hand over Patsy's forehead, my palm cool against the hot skin. Stay calm, I chanted to myself. Be calm. God would not answer a prayer by sending for my youngest to join him in heaven. "Moll, please take Patsy to her room and see she's put to bed right away. She's not to step one foot from bed until the reverend sees her. Is that clear?"

"Yes, Mrs. Washington."

"Sally, send one of the others for the reverend and hurry."

I sat still as Moll picked up Patsy and strode silently out the door. Sally rushed from the room to do as bid. I let out a calming breath, allowing one moment of panic before reining in the fear. If I'd learned one important lesson it was to not let fear rule.

Calm and methodical solved problems that emotional reaction couldn't touch.

I'd talk with the minister about preventive measures we could take to ward off the known diseases. Surely with all his education and experience he'd have a recommendation. An herb. A mushroom. A talisman. Something.

Sighing, I laid my head on the pillow and closed my eyes again. With care and good fortune, I'd find a way to ensure both my children reached adulthood and lived happy and productive lives. As long as Patsy's worrisome lack of response didn't signal some new disease or ailment, all would be well.

# 10

The sound of hoof beats faded but my heart raced as I broke the seal on the letter delivered moments earlier. The last time such a messenger visited, the previous spring, the note informed us that George's beloved brother, Austin, had passed away. Augustine "Austin" Washington was George's half-brother, the second oldest son of their father Augustine and his first wife Jane Butler Washington. To say George was distraught at the news would be stating it mildly. I studied the paper in my hand, the neat cursive writing calling me to open the missive. George had not returned from his daily ride around the farms. Should I wait to open it?

Patsy practiced the spinet, the notes wafting through the house, the scales rising and falling in uneven and faltering steps. She needed to practice more in order to improve her ability. She had talent enough, but discipline proved an entirely different matter. It didn't help that she spent more time sick than well. Agues, chills, sore throats, all visited her frequently.

Studying the paper, addressed to me, I pondered whether I wanted to be alone when I read it. Making up my mind, I crossed to the settee and eased onto its deep cushion. Crackling from the fireplace helped to soften the barrenness of the lonely room. I unfolded the paper and skimmed its contents once, then again.

No. My dear lord. Not little Mary. My darling seven-year-old sister—the same age as my sweet daughter Patsy—had died at Chestnut Grove. Tears pooled in my eyes, collected and pressed hot and hard, and then cascaded down my cheeks. I slipped the lace handkerchief from my sleeve and mopped my eyes. A futile effort.

The memory of my daughter staring at nothing for minutes resurfaced in my mind's eye, of her not seeing the hand waved in front of her face, or answering the many urgent questions I had peppered her with. The doctors didn't know the reason for her actions, or rather inaction. We'd followed the doctor's instructions to prepare a special mixture for her to take regularly to ward off the strange affliction. She'd been ill frequently over the past three years. What if she died? How would I ever cope with the crushing loss of yet another of my children? How did Mother manage to put one foot in front of the other after such devastation?

"Patsy? I saw the messenger on my way in. Where are you?" George's deep, calm voice announced his arrival. Booted steps came closer to the parlor door. Then there he stood, tall and broad and in firm control of his destiny. He frowned when he spotted my tears and hurried to sit beside me. "Why, what's the matter? Come, calm yourself and tell me the news."

I sniffled, struggling to regain my composure. I inhaled and let it out slowly as I searched his eyes for his comfort and understanding. "Little Mary has died."

A burst of grief—for my young sister and for the fear over my daughter's health—rushed from me on a sob and I covered my face with both hands to hide the tears. I'd cried so often, grieved for so many family members. Would it never end? How could I continue to take such sadness and pain?

George gathered me into his strong embrace and held me while I sobbed quietly for several minutes. Finally, I sat up, away from his comforting arms.

"I'll be fine." I tried to smile, to return to my normal self, but failed as the image of my sister's smiling face passed in my mind's eye. Having George at my side eased the weight of sorrow though couldn't erase the grief it left etched in my heart. "Why have you returned so early?"

He shook his head and rose to his feet. "Something told me you might need me." He studied me for a few moments. "I'm sorry for Mary. She was a beautiful and smart girl."

"She is...was." I dabbed my tears, resolving to be strong.

I had children to see to, a household to run. I had no time to break down and cry for hours even though I could feel the grief bubbling and pulsing inside my chest, a living agony. Silence alerted me that Patsy had stopped playing. Again. Come to think of it, I hadn't heard my son playing his violin, either.

I sighed and pushed to my feet, smoothing my skirts into place as I did so. "If you'll excuse me, I need to see what the children are doing rather than practicing as I told them to do."

"A moment, my dear." George clasped both my hands in his, standing facing me as he examined my expression. "I need to send an order to Mr. Cary posthaste in order to receive the shipment from London as quickly as possible, so if there are any trifles you need, please let me know by to-morrow."

I nodded, a slow movement of my head as I pictured Patsy dressed in a new frock and bonnet. Perhaps a new riding habit. Jacky needed new books and music, as well. Still, George had informed me that the many improvements and repairs he'd made to the plantation buildings and crops, as well as land purchases, had consumed the money I'd brought to our union. It had all gone to the betterment of our situation and he expected to recoup the cost with the harvest. If not this year, then in subsequent ones. Perhaps it proved a blessing I hadn't conceived since our finances were precarious. Despite the seeming lack of funds, I trusted his ability to manage the estate with efficiency and intelligence. "I shall put together a list and have it to you shortly."

"Very well." He paused and studied my tear-stained cheeks

before thumbing away a droplet from my chin. "My deepest condolences on the loss of your sweet sister."

I received his kiss, tasting salt as he pressed his mouth to mine. "I'm sure everything ultimately happens for a reason, for the best."

"Indeed, my sweet." George gazed at me and then a slow gentle smile spread onto his face. "I will always wait on you. We shall survive together, no matter what the future may hold."

I clasped his hands and peered up at him. "Yes, and being together will make traveling these sorrowful paths easier."

Over the next few months, my grief abated bit by bit, but my concern for Patsy increased. Again and again, we had to summon the doctor to tend to another complaint or fever accosting the girl. I couldn't heal her, but I could bring a smile to her lips with one simple activity: shopping.

I placed orders with the dressmaker, Mrs. Shelbury-Millner, in London for appropriate clothing for a young maid. I specifically requested that although the dresses should be genteel and proper some measure of frugality should be used as the clothing was for a nine-year-old girl. Given our current financial situation, directing the dressmaker toward less expensive fabrics and decoration seemed appropriate.

When the ship bringing our order sailed up the Potomac several months later, the entire household turned out. The arrival of a ship at the pier was a special day indeed. Patsy jumped up and down in delight as the crates and boxes were brought into the hall and opened.

"Oh, Mama, look!" She squealed and held up a pair of green satin shoes. "My name is inside."

"Yes, my dear, your papa wanted you to have something all your own." I beamed at my precious daughter, so happy and carefree. "I think you'll find more in there if you keep looking."

She dug into the open crate, her little hands frantically pulling out packages. "Silver shoe buckles! And hair bows!"

I helped her examine each lovely thing, amused as well as

relieved by her antics. She seemed such a normal little girl. Perhaps the worst of her affliction was behind us.

---

*Gunstan Hall – 1765*

Despite our concerns regarding finances, our lives continued as normally as possible. We visited the Masons at Gunston Hall as usual one afternoon for a barbecue. Jacky and Patsy bounced up and down while their maids attempted to help them dress. Or so I was told by the frustrated servants before we boarded the carriage for the short trip to our neighbors. I couldn't blame the children for being eager. We all enjoyed a barbecue with friends.

Driving along the tree lined carriage-way, we approached the two-story brick mansion. George Mason had finished building his magnificent home the same year George and I married, six years ago. The design and details Mr. Mason employed influenced some of the choices George had made for Mount Vernon.

"I'm always impressed by Mr. Mason's ingenuity," George said as he gazed out the window at the passing landscape. "You'll find the width of the lane matches the width of the front door, the passage through the house, and on out the boxwood lined path down to the river."

"Why does that impress you?" We'd visited Gunston Hall countless times, but my husband had never mentioned being affected by the design in such a manner.

"Because, my love, the symmetry effectively unites the architecture to the grounds surrounding it." He turned to smile at me. "It's a brilliant idea."

"I see." I patted his arm and looked out the window. I did not harbor the same deep appreciation for architecture and design as my husband. Rather, I noticed the subtleties of the décor and the furnishings. Together we made a fine team as we could envision the larger picture and situation. "We're almost to the house."

On either side of the lane two rows of black heart cherry trees grew in radial lines narrowing toward the house at the far end. Off to the left, the orchards boasted ripening Newtown Pippin apple trees, a fairly new kind of apple and the same kind planted in our own orchards ever since Mr. Mason gave some to my husband. Very tasty dessert apples, too.

The carriage stopped and we all hurried to step out into the sunlight. The front door opened as we climbed the stone steps and crossed the Palladian portico. The butler greeted us before George and Ann brushed past him. After the appropriate greetings and embraces, we followed them through the house and out onto the gothic-styled porch overlooking the terraced yard and gravel path we knew ended at the river bank.

Ann had outdone herself with the spread of enticing foods. Several tables stood on the breezy porch, each featuring an assortment of meats, chutney, fruits, and desserts. George Mason had greeted us with his usual good humor, but before we'd even settled onto the chairs grouped for conversations he'd started talking about the reaction to the outrageous Stamp Tax.

Parliament had imposed the Stamp Tax in March. The tax required a payment in order to affix the appropriate tax stamp on newspapers, pamphlets, documents, playing cards, licenses, dice, and a host of other items. Then in May, the Quartering Act became law, requiring the colonists to feed and house British soldiers. The very idea of being forced to take in soldiers whether I wanted to or not appalled and worried me and everyone else. And that's when the troubles began. It was one thing to write protests against the act and to boycott all stamped papers, but when men formed mobs to intimidate those who tried to collect taxes, that's when I started to feel uneasy about what the Parliament would do in response.

No longer did George feel secure in our financial situation, and he had spent more time at the Virginia Assembly in discussion with the others in control of the colonial Virginia government. I worried more about Patsy's health and the tension in my husband's countenance as well as the uncertainty washing through the colony. Not even when we attempted to enjoy some recreation could we escape from the discourse and influence of the hated taxes. I took my seat to listen and learn but bit back my opinion with an effort.

"Have you read about the nonimportation associations formed by the Sons of Liberty and several Whig merchants?" George Mason puffed on his clay pipe, reclined in a chair facing the Potomac flowing by in the distance.

"I've heard they intend to draft agreements banning the importation of English goods until the tax is repealed." George studied the landscape for two beats and then glanced at me. "Which of course means we'll need to find local sources for food stuffs and clothing."

"Or make do without, I suppose." I dreaded the impact the nonimportation agreements would have upon our household but would do what I could to mitigate the results.

We ordered everything, from nails and pins to lumber and furniture, from England. Wine, material, and even books all came from the motherland since all products had to be shipped there before being sold to her colonies. If we didn't receive necessities from there, where would we find equally good products to eat, drink, wear, or read?

"We can't import anything under such a pact?" Ann frowned and shook her head. "It will be sorely inconvenient, I dare say."

Her husband puffed on his pipe for a moment, the smoke drifting up to dissipate into the summer sky. "I'd imagine if someone tried to import the goods, the ships would not be permitted to dock or unload the merchandise."

"Indeed." My husband selected a plump green grape from the dish on a nearby table. "I think they intend to pressure the London merchants, who would lose a lot of money as a result of such a boycott, to in turn pressure Parliament to repeal the Stamp Taxes."

"I suppose that means no more imported goods." I glanced at

my children, racing across the lawn stretching toward the start of the boxwood alley leading down to the river. "And more trips into Alexandria for our needs."

I sighed inwardly. No more extensive orders from our London factors. No more fun opening a multitude of barrels and crates to distract my daughter. I wondered how long it would take for the desired results. In the meanspace, we had to make do with what we had or do without.

---

The following June, my husband read startling and unwelcome news to me over breakfast. I couldn't believe what I heard.

"No, they wouldn't inflict more taxes upon us. Would they?" I was outraged, quivering in my very shoes at the insult. Why do they treat us as misbehaving children?

"Parliament does what they wish to their colonies." George shook the offending newspaper as he perused its contents. "Mark my words, these Townshend Revenue Acts will cause a reaction without fail."

I waved my fan before my warm face. The summer heat had returned to plague us. "What will they be taxing now?"

"Let's see." His serious gaze drifted down the page. "Glass, red and white lead, painter's colors, paper. Oh, and tea."

"What? How dare they tax such a staple of our lives?" I lifted my cup and sipped my hot and sweet tea. Did I have enough on hand or should I order more before they taxed it? "When does this burden tax go into effect?"

"Immediately." He lowered the paper to look into my eyes, worry pulling his brows into a frown. "They've also authorized the Board of Customs Commissioners in Boston to collect the taxes and enforce the other measures enacted. And most startlingly of all, they have suspended the New York Assembly for not complying with the Quartering Act."

"Oh my goodness." The assembly represented the people of the colony to the Royal Governor acting on the king's behalf.

Suspending it meant the king's representative would take over all aspects of governing the people. "That will not sit well with the people of the colony."

"This abuse of power will push many to retaliate."

"What will you do?" I waited, afraid of which direction he might take as a result of the recent decrees from England.

"The Virginia Assembly will need to determine an appropriate response." His eyes met mine. "Then we'll both know what is to be done."

All taken together, these maneuverings led to my husband becoming more closely allied with people trying to find a compromise between the Parliament and the colonies. An elusive endeavor drawing his attention and his person away from Mount Vernon more and more. My question, one I kept to myself, was where would it all end?

---

*Mount Vernon – 1768–1769*

Surely I had not heard him correctly. I laid down my fork and swallowed. Send Jacky away? All the way to Maryland? George may as well have enrolled him in a school on the moon. I'd never, or at least rarely, see him. I kept my gaze on my plate while thoughts bounced in my panicked mind. Not only did I fear losing Patsy to whatever this wicked affliction was, with its fits and shaking and staring all jumbled into a seemingly endless parade of doctors and failed treatments. But my loving husband planned to send my son to an elite school run by a man I'd never heard of, the good Reverend Jonathan Boucher. I trusted my husband to do what he thought best for our family. Yet I was not in total agreement with his decision. I cleared my throat, hoping it would function without revealing the depth of my panic.

"Are you certain that's the best place for him?" I lifted my gaze to study George, seated at the other end of the table positioned in the wide hall to catch the cooling summer breeze off the river. "Reverend Boucher provides a curriculum suited to his potential?"

George met my gaze, his eyes understanding but serious. "I believe so. I've scoured the colonies for the appropriate situation for him. We shall leave on the twenty-eighth of June."

So soon? I wished yet again the colonial assemblies had not been disbanded. If they were still holding their meetings, then George wouldn't have time to consider pursuing this aim. However, in April, the Earl of Hillsborough, Secretary of State for the colonies, had ordered all governors to dissolve their assemblies rather than allow them to support the Circular Letter. Samuel Adams' Circular Letter was issued by the Massachusetts General Assembly. The letter called for uniting the colonies to resist Great Britain's most recent policies. The Circular also claimed Parliament didn't have the *right* to tax the colonies solely for revenues. On top of such inflammatory statements, Virginia was operating with an interim governor until the new governor, Lord Botetourt, arrived in the autumn. The result was many heated conversations with our visitors regarding all of these dangerous and worrisome actions.

I glanced at Jacky, saw him contemplating his guardian with an expression of vague curiosity and a hint of hesitancy. George had grown frustrated with the boy, now fourteen years old and verging on becoming a man. We'd had more than one conversation about the need to send Jacky to boarding school in order to provide him with the structure he needed to concentrate on his efforts. To buckle down on the hard work it took to become a man worthy to inherit and manage the vast holdings George had been carefully growing for him. In my head, I knew George was right. My heart was having a much harder time accepting the reality.

Billy Lee, the young slave George bought in May from the widow of Colonel John Lee of Westmoreland County, stood to one side, waiting for his next instructions. He seemed an amiable man, and although not as tall as George, he was sturdy and strong. He also appeared to match George in horsemanship, which was a real accomplishment.

"Will you take the new carriage?" I retrieved my utensil and cut a bite of fish, held it poised as I waited for George's reply. "It would make quite an impression with the coat of arms against the green doors and gold trim. He'd arrive in style, suitable for his station."

"No, even if I wanted to it's nearly unusable, especially for long distances. I've communicated my displeasure with Mr. Cary but have received no satisfaction on the matter." George resumed eating, his gaze resting thoughtfully first on Patsy and then on Jacky. "Jacky, you'll want to take Julius along. I'd have him pack your trunks for the journey."

"Yes, Papa. I'll see to it after supper." Jacky guzzled his cider and then set the silver cup back on the white linen covered table. He wiped his mouth with the cloth napkin and then asked George several questions in quick succession. "What kind of place is Boucher's? Will I have my own room or will Julius share with me? Do they have good meals?"

While George answered Jacky's many questions, I half listened, my thoughts knotted like a ball of yarn left for the cats to play with. Of course I wanted the best for my son, wanted him to be well educated, wanted him to mature into a fine man. He'd have to leave home to obtain the education necessary, especially since his long-time tutor had thrown up his hands and walked away last year, citing Jacky's laziness and inattention. George agreed with the man so had not tried to replace him. He'd decided instead to place Jacky under the tutelage of a headmaster.

Jacky wasn't a bad boy. He might have his preferences which didn't always coincide with George's desires for him. Like studying history and mathematics. But at least he and George both relished hunting on horseback with the dogs trained to flush the game they sought, whether deer or quail or turkeys. It could be worse, though I didn't bother imagining as to how it might. The idea my son would be sent away remained difficult for me to accept. I trusted George's judgment and believed with all my heart he held my children's best interests above all. Otherwise, I'd never agree.

Patsy reached for her glass of apple cider, drawing my attention. She had grown nearly reclusive over the past years. Her fits had progressively grown more pronounced. The doctors argued various treatments but agreed on one thing: no cure existed. Ever since the family's bout with measles, Patsy had dealt with the sporadic and fickle seizures.

I thought we'd found the treatment that would control the girl's fits back in February of the previous year when Dr. William Rumney came to Mount Vernon. He'd prescribed a variety of powders and nervous drops in addition to valerian. Patsy had recovered so well George had convinced me to accompany him and the Fairfaxes, who had recently returned from a trip to England, to take the waters at Warm Springs for a couple of weeks. I'd been able to keep my worries at bay, having left the children at home in fine health and spirits. But then by the spring we'd had to seek out Dr. Rumney to attempt a different treatment. And he'd returned over the past several weeks, attempting purges and bleedings, until my heart hurt.

When would the doctors find the right treatment to manage the symptoms? How would Patsy ever live a normal life with the uncertainty and fear of the next fit hanging above her like the sword of Damocles? What if she had a fit while riding a horse, or while bathing? Who would protect her if something happened to me or George? So many unanswerable questions whirled through my mind every day.

"It's only one week until you depart. I'll confer with Old Doll about victuals you'll want to take along and make sure your garments are freshened and ready."

"Thank you, Mama." Jacky smiled at me, his eyes sparkling with good humor. "I'm convinced you believe a proper picnic is required for every journey."

"You'll be needing nutrition along the way and there are no guarantees of finding it when you want it."

"Do people in the north not believe in welcoming travelers

into their homes?" Jacky angled his head, a brow lifted in surprise.

"I cannot say as I have not journeyed so far from home." Such a very long way from southern Virginia where I'd spent most of my life. I had no expectation of ever traveling to the north, seeing no reason for such an endeavor. "All the more reason to travel prepared to fend for yourselves."

The next week flew by, filled with the preparations for the momentous journey. I longed for the time to slow, so I'd have more chance to be with my adorable son. But the day arrived despite my pleas and prayers.

"That's the last of the baggage." Jacky hugged me, standing in front of the mansion-house. "It's time for us to go."

"Listen to the reverend." I pulled back far enough to see his face. "Do your work, you hear me?"

"Yes, Mama." He placed a kiss on my cheek. "Do not fret. I'll be fine. I'll have Julius to assist me."

I nodded, the threat of tears clogging my throat. "I love you. Write often."

George had already in the privacy of our bedchamber kissed me goodbye, a passionate buss and a warm embrace. So now he gave me a brief hug and then mounted. In moments, the four men had trotted down the lane, away from home. Away from me. That's when I cried, wrenching sobs in the privacy of my chamber even as I sent silent prayers to the heavens. *Please, Lord, bring my son safely home after his travels. And of course my husband. Please, I beg of you.*

Their departure represented the first time George and I would be separated for weeks, or mayhap months. I would have stayed abed for several days, prostrate with the sadness and grief of my son's departure, if not for one thing. I had Patsy to comfort and be with me. She became my sole purpose. My reason for carrying on.

George and Billy returned from depositing Jacky at school. George settled down to attend to business related to the Virginia Assembly. His work with the assembly occupied much of his time, but improvements to Mount Vernon frequently eclipsed even the urgency of the government concerns. Yet, I sensed with growing concern George's deepening interest in the activities and opinions of the burgesses toward the royal decrees and their effects to the colonies.

One afternoon in September, George searched me out, finding me in the hall where I sewed in the brighter light the area afforded to my work. I set aside the stitching to attend to what he was about to convey. I braced myself when I noted his serious expression. "What is it?"

"I need to speak with you." George placed a chair nearby and sank onto its wood seat. "I'll be leaving in the morning to attend the assembly, but I shouldn't be gone but a month or two. Did you wish to accompany me?"

Oh, how I'd adore to travel with him to Williamsburg, as it would give me the opportunity to visit with my mother and kinfolk. But not with Patsy ill so frequently. My heart simply was not interested in the gaiety of the balls and dinners and the whirl of society in the colony's capitol.

Dr. Rumney was a necessary but not entirely wanted guest. Each time I sent for him, desperate to find a solution to my daughter's increasing fits, I prayed for strength and peace. Allowing myself to lose my composure would not help any one. Better to keep calm and seek out ways to comfort and encourage my daughter.

I smiled at George, a small rueful grin as I shook my head. "I desire nothing more than to be at your side, but I cannot leave. I do not trust any one else to attend our daughter. She's not up to traveling, either. The journey and upset might undo any strides Dr. Rumney has made." George's eyes held a wealth of compassion and concern, but I wouldn't stand between him and his obligations. I could handle the household in his absence. More importantly, I trusted he'd come home if I needed him.

"Go and do what you have to. Only do not stay away a moment longer than your business requires. I will be anxious for your return."

George enclosed my hand in his. "I give you my promise to return as soon as possible."

Two months passed while I did my utmost to remain positive. But Patsy continued to need the doctor's ministrations. I kept one eye on her and one on the door, waiting for George's return. He wrote to me weekly, sharing the gossip and that he'd been asked to lead the Virginia Militia. My pride for his stellar reputation and the resulting trust placed in his hands bolstered my flagging energy. I'd do nothing to give him cause to be less proud of me than I was of him. When George trotted his stallion up the lane in November, Billy at his side like an appendage, I met him at the door to guide him to where Dr. Rumney yet again administered nervous drops and musk to Patsy.

I caught a sharp appraising glance from George, but didn't give him chance to comment on my admittedly haggard appearance. I'd attempted to correct the ravages of months of worry, but apparently had not succeeded. A fact unsurprising when I considered the keen judgment he possessed. Whether appraising the conformation of a horse or determining the trustworthiness of a servant, he missed nothing. Hurrying him to Patsy's room, I trusted speed would blur the edges enough to avoid further commentary. No matter what else, at least George returned home to help me shoulder the burden of worry.

"How long has the doctor been here?" George asked quietly, his voice rumbling in the passage.

"This time? An hour or so." I kept my voice low as we turned the corner.

"I know you're worried, as am I. We will do all we can, Patsy." George pulled me to a halt outside the closed chamber door and embraced me, a lazy bear hug that stole my breath for a few moments. Blissful moments snug within the protection of his arms. He eased me away from him and pecked a kiss to my lips. "How frequently has Dr. Rumney been summoned?"

"Weekly." I clung to his hands, needing their strength and stability, and craned my neck back so I could search his expression. "He continues to use purges and bleedings. Ointments and drugs of various kinds. But it's all guessing. He told me they do not know what causes these terrifying visitations on a person's body." A sigh clawed its way from me. "It's a terrible thing, to watch your child suffer and be unable to alleviate or remove the cause."

The last fit had been the worst I'd ever seen, and the absolute hardest event to witness. She'd started to shake uncontrollably, biting her tongue until it bled, and then dropped unconscious. I had eased her to the floor with a bump. She'd slept in my arms for nearly ten minutes before she roused. Ten long, agonizing minutes of staring at her closed eyes and willing for her to be well. I'd sent for the doctor posthaste. I shuddered at the memory. We must find an answer.

"Let's see what he has to say today." George opened the door and ushered me inside the sunny room.

Patsy sat in a chair by the window, dark eyes in a pale face, lips brushed with pink, brunette curls hidden under a kerchief, a colorful lap blanket warming her legs. Dr. Rumney turned from where he'd been stirring yet another dosage of nervous drops into warmed sherry. Not that it had worked previously. Surely something would cure her ailment. The tension coiled inside of me would take a miracle to release. A miracle for Patsy.

"Welcome home, Colonel." Dr. Rumney tapped the spoon on the edge of the glass and laid it on the table. "I do believe we may be making a bit of progress in managing your daughter's symptoms."

George strode forward and shook the doctor's hand. "That's good to hear, doctor. We're naturally very concerned about the increased frequency of the attacks."

"It's not my fault, Father." Patsy frowned slightly. "I try to stop them but I cannot."

"We know it's outside of your control, dear." George glanced from Patsy to me and then the doctor. "We'll keep looking for a way, anything with any hope of success will be tried. Understood, Dr. Rumney?"

"Of course." Dr. Rumney hurried across the room and handed Patsy the glass. "Drink this and let's hope it will help abate the events, or at least lengthen the time between them so you can play the spinet again."

I clasped my cold hands in front of me. After the years of increasing frequency and violence in her spasms, of doctor visits, and a slew of treatments, what more could we try? "Perhaps if we took her to take of the waters at Warm Springs?"

Dr. Rumney put various tools and bottles back into his bag and snapped it closed before addressing me. "I've never heard of any one recovering from the falling sickness by doing so, but if it comes down to it, we might try that as a last resort. In the meanspace, continue giving our lovely patient sips of the musk twice a day as prescribed. If you have any further concerns, send for me."

"Thank you, doctor. I'll walk you out." George ushered the doctor from the room, casting a last glance back at me with an encouraging smile.

"Mama, please don't be sad." Patsy reached out a hand, wiggling her fingers until I wrapped them with my own. "Would you like for me to play your favorite song?"

I lifted her hand to press a kiss to the fingers. The same fingers that had reluctantly pressed the ivory keys for years. "Yes, I would like that very much."

---

Winter yielded to the crocus and daffodils of spring which bloomed and gave way to the heat and humidity of summer. Patsy seemed much bothered by the intense heat, fragile and moody. Then one blistering day in early July, she started down the mahogany staircase. We'd planned an outing to the river, with a picnic lunch and a chance to swim and cool off. She'd made it halfway, when she suddenly grabbed for the rail with both hands. Her eyes rolled up and mouth fell open as she collapsed. I raced to stop her tumbling down the stairs, my heart in my mouth. Easing her down to the landing, tears seeped onto my lips. My darling girl. She could have died in that fall. I cradled her in my lap until her eyes blinked open.

"Mama, what happened?" Patsy struggled to sit up, running a hand over her hair as she gazed at me.

"You fell, but I caught you." I laid a hand on her arm. "I'll always be here for you."

Sally and Old Doll ran into the passage and hurried to help us to our feet. A quick perusal yielded no injuries, a fact for which I was grateful. Yet I'd reached my motherly limit.

In January we had celebrated our tenth anniversary by asking our friend, Dr. Hugh Mercer, to consult with Dr. Rumney on possible cures for the mysterious affliction. After a heated discussion the doctors finally agreed Patsy suffered from a condition they called epilepsy. Small comfort came from knowing the disease. Although we had a name for it, we still had no cure.

In February, Patsy had suffered an attack at least once a week and then for months. I heard of a man with an ancient remedy, a ring clamped about one finger. Within a few days, Joshua Evans had arrived at Mount Vernon and fitted the ring, complete with a powerful inscription, to ward off the demons causing the fits. I watched for days afterwards, relieved when Patsy's frequent fits vanished. But it didn't last. A week later they returned with a vengeance.

While the doctors prescribed a new round of medicines, including mercurial pills, purges, and another decoction, I ensured she had as normal a life as possible. Patsy's new friend, Millie Posey, visited frequently. I grew very fond of the cheerful young lady, pleased with her decorum and sincerity and most importantly her companionship with Patsy. But something must be done. Someone must know a way. I went in search of George, determination propelling me through the house.

"Papa, we must take Patsy to Warm Springs." I found George

in his study, sitting at his desk perusing several papers before him. "I believe we've reached the need for that last resort."

"You're certain?" George lowered the paper to the desk and considered me with a slow nod. "I see you are. Very well. I'll begin making the arrangements."

"I'll begin packing." I turned to leave, then spun back to catch George's attention. "Thank you."

"Anything I can do for your happiness and the welfare of the children, I will do, my love." He inclined his head and smiled. "Be off. We have much to accomplish."

The children. My children. Not *ours*, despite our continued hope. I'd begun to believe the difficultly I had birthing Patsy had led to my not being able to conceive again. A flash of sadness and regret firmed my mouth into a flat line. Only the good Lord could give me a child and if He did not see fit to do so, then so be it.

I began the preparations immediately, tasking Old Doll with gathering the fresh fruits and vegetables as well as meats and cheeses we'd carry on our journey. I set Rose to preparing Patsy's trunks, and Sally to preparing mine. Then I returned to Patsy's side to relay the news. I hesitated to consider the trip as a "good" event given it represented the last option available to try to mitigate the epilepsy. I'd come to terms with the fact the doctors had no cure.

Preparing to travel in the current state of affairs proved challenging. George had grown increasingly concerned with the developing crisis between the colonies and the king. He had carried the Virginia Resolves, penned by George Mason, to the assembly in Williamsburg in April. The contents detailed the reasons for opposing taxation without representation, and argued against the infringement of Americans' rights by the Britons. He believed a serious discussion would follow his presentation, but neither of us had thought the royal governor would dissolve the assembly. That didn't stop the determined burgesses, though. They had reconvened at the Raleigh Tavern, where the ongoing heated discussion resulted in another boycott against British merchandise until the Parliament repealed the hated taxes.

I agreed in principle with the boycott, but locating local sources for the items we typically imported was difficult. We had implemented several changes at Mount Vernon to supply much of what we needed. I increased the number of and thus the output from our spinners, seamstresses, and knitters. George hired more itinerant weavers to augment those we already had, whose job was to make linen and woolen fabrics from the spun flax and wool. We'd survive, perhaps not as eloquently as with the expensive imports, but well enough. We'd do what we needed to live by our principles and stand up for what we believed right.

Altogether, we spent two months soaking in the hot springs, sipping the mineral waters, and partaking of every delicacy and advantage the resort had to offer. All to no effect. In November we reluctantly admitted the waters had failed to provide any relief and returned to Mount Vernon with heavy hearts. Was there to be no happy ending to Patsy's story? I couldn't admit defeat. Ever. I must find a way.

While mulling possibilities I had my next idea. I hurried through the house, peeking into each room until I found George seated by the fire in the small parlor, reading a book by lamplight. He laid the book on his lap as I stopped before him.

"If we cannot cure our daughter, let us at least take her to spend time with my family at Eltham." I fiddled with the lace edge of my sleeve before dropping the froth and forcing my hands to be still. "Perhaps having family around will ease the terrible anguish which has settled in my heart."

"That's a good idea, or at least part of one. While we're there, maybe Dr. de Sequeyra will grant us a consult."

The eminent Williamsburg physician did venture to Eltham to see Patsy at least six times over the course of several weeks. I fairly applauded at how well she looked, and then when Jacky made a surprise visit I nearly fainted with joy. Both my children looked hearty and well, and the holiday season fast approached.

The time we spent with my sister and family had begun the festivities on a convivial note. Shortly before Christmas, Jacky and Julius returned to school in Maryland, while the rest of the family began the trip toward home. We stopped at Kenmore in Fredericksburg to visit with George's sister Betty and her husband Fielding Lewis for Christmas. I allowed myself to relax in the comforting home as the year wound down and my children's prospects looked up. Life had finally settled into a pleasing rhythm.

# 11

*Mount Vernon – 1771*

I sat by the fireplace in my sitting room, letting its light land on the worrisome letter in my hand. The early spring air held a softness, a gentle touch soothing my cheek. If I turned my head, I'd see the flowers blooming outside my window. The sun shining. The sky blue and inviting. But I didn't turn. I closed my eyes instead, silently begging for strength and wisdom as I cared for and guided my children through the perils of life. Jacky's frightening request set my heart racing.

The year had begun with sadness and fear, bringing Dr. Rumney to visit Patsy yet again. He had offered a new possibility: Peruvian bark. A tea made from it could help epilepsy as well as malaria. I had regarded the offering with jaded hope. We'd tried absolutely everything over the past years, hadn't we? The doctor left behind more pills and powders and drops to be administered in various ways at various times for the spasms and statue-like trances as well as the increasing pain Patsy endured. The memory of the terrifying three months last summer when Patsy had a fit accompanied by raging fever and torturous ague on nearly every single day had strengthened my resolve to obtain relief for her.

In February, I couldn't take seeing her writhing any longer. At my request, George had written to Jacky's school master, Reverend Boucher, asking him to buy a quantity of ether and send it to Mount Vernon to ease the girl's agony. Fortunately, the good man had honored the request, but how much more could Patsy withstand? When and how would the illness end? Actually, I feared the answer to that last question.

Opening my eyes, I skimmed the careful script on the linen pages trembling in my fingers. Jacky desired to travel to Baltimore in order to subject himself to the smallpox inoculation. The procedure was legal there, unlike in Virginia. If only he could have it done closer to home, then I wouldn't mind to quite the same extent.

I thought of my brother, Jacky, and the horrible death he'd suffered because he didn't have the opportunity to be administered the inoculation. But what if my son received the inoculation and died? The procedure involved inserting a pustule of the disease from an infected person into a cut in the arm. He dared risk his life to avoid contracting the dreadful disease. How could I agree when he may well be the only heir if Patsy succumbed to the epilepsy? Could a mother survive her son's death, when the mother had given her permission for the potentially lethal procedure? Then again, how could I deny my son's request when the results could prove beneficial to people in general? His act served an altruistic purpose, a desirable trait in a young man.

I sighed and picked up a pen. A few minutes later I sprinkled sand over the newly inked words granting permission to fix them in place on the page. As well as in my heart. I couldn't deny my son anything.

I folded the page and sealed it, ready to send to Jacky at school. Better he experimented with preventing an illness than taking up Reverend Boucher's flight of fancy to take a European tour, with—interestingly enough—the schoolmaster as chaperone. The slew of possible ways my beloved son could die flashed in my thoughts. George had discounted the idea of a grand tour as a good one, and I had to agree. In fact, my stomach turned over at the thought of sending my precious boy over the water to England and beyond. Ships confronted foul weather, pirates, and other hazards. In any case, what would he learn by traveling with the good reverend? No, better he stayed on this side, especially in light of all the turmoil suddenly between the motherland and the American colonies.

I shook my head as I thought of the effort by the so-called Daughters of Liberty and their protest against the embargoed items. Gathering the letter and my shawl, I made my way to the stairs and descended to the first floor. The very idea of wearing homespun rather than silk or chintz made my skin crawl. I'd not be seen in public in the same material a slave would wear no matter the politics behind such an act. A lady had to maintain appearances. Since the Burgesses signed the nonimportation act last June, we could not order the finer things, like sugar and jewelry or even finer cloth for dresses. I was grateful the embargo did not last very long, except for the tax on tea, the remaining taxes under the Townshend Act were repealed by parliament. George had affixed his name to the Association's decree as to what could and could not be imported from Great Britain, and thus our entire household adhered to its restrictions until the resolution had been reached. But the underlying issue of taxation to raise revenue without representation as to how the money was used continued to aggravate the colonists.

Later in the afternoon, I sat down to enjoy a hot dinner with George and Patsy. The spread included roasted duck and fish, two cheeses, pickles, hot spoon bread, and an iced lemon cake for dessert. After we'd settled in to eat, I cleared my throat, attracting my husband's attention.

"I've given Jacky my approval." I speared George with an intense look. "I must say I'm nervous about his proceeding, but he is a young man and able to make the decision."

George swallowed a mouthful of wine. "He'll be glad to hear of your decision. Perhaps now you'll find a trip to Williamsburg pleasing?"

I shook my head without giving his suggestion a hint of consideration. "I won't journey that far away from Jacky while he's taking this dreadful chance."

"He's a strong lad, Patsy. He'll be fine." George cut a bite of duck and placed it in his mouth, chewing slowly as he studied me. Swallowing, he tilted his head, a single bob to the side, and then the gentle smile that touched my soul formed on his lips. "If you change your mind, I'd welcome your company when I go to the city for the session."

"You know very well I'd prefer to be with you. But I won't— nay, I can't—change my mind, not as long as my son's life might well be in danger." I picked up a spoonful of bread, then paused before taking a bite. "Perhaps I should not give him my consent, then I'd be free to travel with you, and I could see my family. 'Tis something to consider."

"Do you want me to send your letter or not, then?" George cut another bite of meat, dredging it through the creamy potato pudding before the tines disappeared into his mouth, coming out clean. "My dear, you must choose and let the matter unfold as it will."

He was right, but that didn't mean I had to like it. Taking a deep breath, I considered my options, knowing how much my dear son desired my consent. I let out the air and nodded. "Yes, send it."

George continued eating, a curious smile lingering as he glanced from me to Patsy and back. "The new grist mill is making good progress. Soon, there will be two mills to grind the grains to ship to foreign ports. If all goes as planned, then my effort to create a variety of ways with which to sustain the plantation will not have been in vain."

"And that pleases you." I returned his smile. "As well it should. You work hard to manage everything."

"As do you, managing the intricacies of the household." George wiped his mouth, and then folded his napkin before laying it beside his plate. "If you ladies will excuse me, I'll see to it your letter finds its way into your son's hands posthaste."

I watched him leave with mixed feelings, but I'd made my decision and I'd stand by it. At some point, a mother had to trust her children to make decisions for their own benefit.

A week later I received a letter from Jacky. Without delay, I opened it and skimmed the words marching across the paper. Then again. He'd decided not to have the inoculation, not to take a chance that the amount of live organisms in the inoculation would threaten his life by contracting full blown smallpox rather than a mere touch which his body could defend against. Relief—golden sunlight rays breaking through gray storm clouds—settled inside. My son's decision changed everything. Clasping the letter in both hands, I grinned. I could remain at my husband's side and see my family with a light heart. I went in search of George with the good news.

———————

One rainy spring afternoon several weeks after returning from our pleasant trip to Williamsburg, I sat enjoying afternoon tea with Patsy and Sally Fairfax by the cheery fireplace when a letter arrived.

I waved the folded paper in the air and regarded my two companions. "It's from Jacky."

"What's he say?" Sally studied me with curiosity plain on her countenance.

"I want to know, too, Mama." Patsy sipped from her pretty porcelain cup, but her gaze rested on me.

"Let's find out, shall we?" With a glad heart, I unfolded the paper and read aloud the lengthy missive.

As I did, my ire sparked and then blossomed into a raging fire. He'd had the inoculation after all, behind my back. He did so to save me the worry. More to the point, the deception had been George's idea. The two of them had decided to hide the truth. To save me the worry! Bah. I rose and paced the small suddenly close room. Did my own husband think me incapable of handling the truth when it came to my son's welfare?

I looked at my little audience who sat with mouths hanging open, aghast at the news. As well they should be.

"As their mother I have every right to know when my children put themselves in harm's way." What if Jacky had died? How would George have explained his reasoning then? I continued pacing, contemplating the situation and my reaction.

"What were they thinking, leaving you in the dark as to his course of action?" Sally shook her head. "I'd be angry, as well."

"They knew how worried I was when he'd first raised the question." Suddenly, I halted, my long skirts swaying to and fro until they hung still. My trembling hands calmed as I pondered a sudden realization.

George and Jacky may have conspired to hide the dangerous episode, but without any doubt they did so out of love and concern for me. For my feelings and well-being. Which had worked, hadn't it? I'd not experienced any pangs or colic as a result of being upset and worried as I had in the past.

My anger and hurt dissipated, frittering away like dogwood petals on a breeze. Fine. I'd not let on to how angry I had been, seeing how their actions revealed their love for me much as my actions stemmed from love for my family. I could live with that.

"Well, it's done now." I resumed my seat and lifted my cup. "Let's enjoy our tea knowing he's protected from at least one terrible disease."

------------------

*Mount Vernon – 1773*

Our distinguished guests proved to be great company to warm the spring days of March. My beloved son, a young man at eighteen, had come home a few days before, bringing with him Maryland's Governor Robert Eden and Jacky's school chum, Charles Calvert. But more than his friend, he brought the entire Calvert clan for a visit. Charles' parents, Benedict Swingate

Calvert, and his wife Elizabeth, swept into our home and became friends within minutes. They were a delight to have in the house, too. George engaged in more than one impassioned conversation on various lineages of thorough bred horses. For my part, I enjoyed becoming acquainted with Elizabeth, as well as her two lovely daughters, Becky, twenty-four, and Nelly, a sweet fifteen. Patsy, too, at two years Nelly's senior, had developed a fondness for the girls, spending their every waking moment together, laughing and chatting about everything under the sun.

We'd hoped that the structure and discipline at the renowned school under Boucher would prompt Jacky to attend more to his studies. His many trips home were contrary to our expectations. Indeed, I soon learned from young Charles that Jacky was a frequent visitor to the Calvert home. How did my son manage to learn when not at school? I dreaded the answer.

As the sun rose above the reddish tipped trees, I detected signs of the leaf buds preparing to unfurl along the branches. I finished my morning devotional and went downstairs to join George and the others for breakfast. Before long, I'd need to instruct the servants to serve meals in the breezy main hall, but for the moment we could enjoy our meals in the small dining room. Laughter reached my ears when I strode toward the happy party. Jacky had been particularly gay during his school holiday, and I wondered at the cause. Perhaps he was eager to start at King's College ere long. Or maybe his levity stemmed from having young Charles to show about Mount Vernon. On the other hand, I noticed he had made a point of engaging the lovely sisters in conversation on many occasions. Perhaps he had discovered the wonders of women? A thought worth pondering.

Upon entering the room, I couldn't help but smile. George stood by the sideboard, a cup held aloft in one hand. He gestured with it to emphasize the points he attempted to make with Benedict and Robert about choosing quality mares to breed to their stallions for the best issue of foals. Given that importing horses had been banned for years, the selection in Virginia had dwindled but there remained several good options. Jacky and Charles had flanked the three girls at the table, the remains of their meal cooling on the plates while they debated the merits of the latest jig the dancing tutor had taught them last evening.

"Mama, there you are!" Patsy rose from her seat to rush around the table and embrace me. "You're just in time to settle an argument."

Gently ending the exuberant hug, I regarded the group with raised brows. "What sort of disagreement would cause such laughter that I heard it all the way down the hall?" I chuckled as I took my seat, letting my good humor soften the edges of my words.

Patsy flounced onto her seat, disregarding the stern look I shot at her. "Jacky believes that ladies should perform a full curtsy at the end of each dance, but I think a shallower curtsy is sufficient. Charles agrees with me, don't you, Charles?"

"I do. It seems inefficient to require women to dip so low when the music will likely begin quickly for the next dance." Charles brushed crumbs into a pile beside his plate, his manicured hands capable and strong at only seventeen years old. "It's a dance, not a presentation to the king."

Laughter bubbled inside as my family and convivial guests continued to verbally poke at each other. "A quick curtsy is all that is required while dancing. It's intended to be a polite gesture of gratitude for dancing with you."

"There. I told you so, Jacky!" Patsy clapped her hands together, her self-satisfied grin illuminating her face.

Jacky shook his head, but his gaze stayed on Nelly. She didn't look away from him for long, her attention bouncing between Patsy and Becky and then back to Jacky. Interesting. Something must have transpired between them. I needed to keep an eye on those two.

Not that I minded if Jacky had fallen in love. Or lust. Infatuation was a normal healthy attitude for a young man to have toward a beautiful, intelligent, caring woman. He could do worse than choose Eleanor to be his wife. Her father, Benedict, held a public office, customs officer, I believe, for the Patuxent region. George told me the man was a fine planter and a gentleman. His wife and cousin, Elizabeth, came from a fine family as well. Captain Charles Calvert, her father, served as the Governor of Maryland until his untimely demise in 1734. Her mother, Rebecca, was a landed heiress, and when she also died in 1734—or was it 1735?—Elizabeth inherited the wealth and property of her parents. The Calverts of Maryland could be considered the ruling elite of the colony. Joining our two families would benefit both.

The next day the Calverts continued on their journey. The Masons, however, had arrived after breakfast, much to my delighted surprise. We enjoyed a lively conversation and a quick ride in the carriage to take some air. Then, my family and friends slowly gathered in the parlor for afternoon tea. Jacky acted nervous, anxious as he strode into the room and hurried to take a seat by my side. George lingered in the hall, continuing a discussion with George Mason. My dear friend, Ann, had been struck with a pain in her head and retreated to the bedchamber reserved for guests.

"Mama, I am bursting to tell you my news." Jacky leaned forward, his elbows resting on his knees.

His eyes were alight with barely suppressed emotion. I detected joy mixed with caution in his expression. "What, my dear? What has happened?"

"Mama, Nelly has accepted my proposal of marriage. There! I've said it out loud for the very first time." He raked a hand through his light brown locks, mussing the waves in his agitation. "Are you happy for me?"

Aghast, I could only stare at him while I struggled to breathe. My heart thundered in my chest, pounding in my ears. "When did this happen? Why did you not follow traditions like a decent man?"

"I am infatuated with Nelly, in love so deep nothing else matters in my life." Jacky grasped my hands, squeezing them as he regarded me with an intensity I rarely saw in him. "We wish to marry soon, to not be apart from one another. Will you give me your permission, Mama?"

"What about school? You're to start college soon. Have you told Papa?"

I did not know what to think. Jacky acted impulsively far too often, and while I was glad he'd found someone to be a life companion, I worried about his impetuosity and disregard for common decency. He should have discussed this with George, and then they would have approached Benedict together with the proposal, since Jacky was still but a boy.

"Not yet, but I intend to tell him when he comes in. Do you think he'll be very upset?" Jacky released my hands with one last squeeze, and then sat back to straighten his waistcoat with a sharp tug.

"I would be surprised if he were not, Jacky. But here he comes, so we shall find out."

George strode into the room, his smile sobering with each step. He stopped in the center of the oriental rug, glancing from me to Jacky. "What is amiss?"

Jacky drew in a deep breath and let it out on a rush of air. His artistic hands curled into fists at his side. "Papa, I've asked Nelly to marry me, and she has accepted. Her father has willingly given his blessing."

Everything stilled around me, as though the very chairs held their breath. My dear George struggled to present a calm exterior, but his anger and disappointment showed clearly in his expression. I rose from my seat and hurried to him, anxious to intervene for my son.

I grasped George's arm and peered up at his stern countenance. "Papa, I'm so happy for Jacky. He's found someone to love and share his life with, to start a family of his own with. Please, I beg of you, do not be very angry with him."

George laid a massive hand over my small one, and squeezed gently, but tension buzzed through him like a disturbed hornet's nest. "You are correct, my dear Patsy. I am cross that he did not see fit to consult me in such a serious matter. How did this happen, Jacky? What were you thinking?"

"Papa, I'm sorry." Jacky moved to stand closer to us. "It all happened so suddenly, while I was at school. Mr. Boucher permitted Charles and I to visit Mount Airy when we were finished our studies. That's where I met Nelly and I knew after spending one afternoon with her that I wanted to be with her for the rest of my life."

"Mr. Boucher should have informed me of this before matters got out of hand." George shook his head slowly, keeping his frown aimed squarely at our son. "I am displeased with the man, as well as with you. You've maneuvered me into an untenable position by proposing a union with the young lady without my consent. I insist you finish your education before you marry."

Jacky frowned back at George. "That will take years and would mean being farther apart for long spells. I don't know..."

"I do. You will go to King's College as planned. We can stop on our way to New York to visit the Calverts, if you'd like. But you must learn all you need to know to run your properties when you inherit them in full. There is much to learn to be a good manager."

"But Papa, must it be years?" Jacky's brows lifted, smoothing away the frown. "I do not wish to wait that long."

"Your responsibility is to be prepared to successfully take command of your own properties and the people who work on them. You may not realize it, being seventeen and still naïve about the business of the colony. Which is even more reason to wait, study, and experience the world around you before settling down with a wife and family."

My son appeared tortured by the restrictions George enforced upon him. "Your father is right, Jacky. Your education is vital to your future success. If Nelly truly loves you, and I believe she does from what I saw this week, then she'll wait for you."

George turned to me with a query in his eyes. "What did you see?"

"Subtle signs of interest between them, though I had no idea their attachment had grown to such an extent as to be planning marriage."

He inclined his head, acknowledging silently my keen observational ability. "I'll write to Benedict to convey my desire for an extended betrothal while you complete your studies."

"May I deliver it to them, Papa?" Jacky fairly glowed with eagerness.

I waited, silently encouraging my husband to allow Jacky his fondest wish of seeing his lady.

"Very well. You may ride up to Mount Airy, but wait for a reply from Benedict. I'd have his answer upon your return."

The next morning, Jacky mounted his horse and trotted down the lane, Julius beside him. I watched him go, delighted for him. Nelly would be a fine daughter-in-law, a welcome addition to the family. Perhaps I'd be a grandmother before too many years passed. Something about the sound of baby laughter and the patter of little feet through the house made me happy. I did not know why I never conceived another child after marrying George. It wasn't for lack of trying. Having a grandchild would satisfy my longing to hold a baby again. Even that would not happen for two or three years, until Jacky had graduated from college.

---

While Jacky was away, George and I had several long conversations about our son's future. George was determined to shape Jacky into a better man, one who would be more like George, if truth be told. I didn't think any one could change the light-hearted, fun-loving young man into a planter responsible for thousands of acres and hundreds of lives. Not even George. I loved my son as he was, and would always support his best interests. But I also had to be supportive of my husband's efforts. The trick was doing both with honesty and integrity, a fine line to walk.

A week passed before Jacky rode back up the lane. He brought with him letters from both Benedict and Mr. Boucher and handed them to George while we sat at supper. Jacky took his seat across from Patsy, who had been feeling rather poorly of late. Her fits had increased in both frequency and duration. The doctor had come and gone, bringing more potions and drops to try to cure or at least minimize the effects of the seizures. My concern for my lovely daughter overshadowed my happiness for the betrothed couple. I prayed every morning for an end to my daughter's affliction.

George unfolded the missive and skimmed its contents. "Good. Benedict agrees to the need for a long engagement, but he insists that Jacky keep his promise to wed the girl."

"How was your visit?" The idea of going to Mount Airy way north in Maryland seemed impossible to me. I had never traveled so far in my life. The prospect of the long, difficult journey crossing rivers and jouncing along rough roads was daunting.

Jacky launched into a long and animated account of the social life of the Maryland tidewater region. The horse races at Annapolis warranted a detailed description, one that George not surprisingly actively engaged in. Soon the pair had decided to attend the next match the following week as an opportunity for George to see for himself the caliber of family the Calverts might prove to be.

"What does Mr. Boucher have to say?" I interjected my question into the discussion on which horses to ride to Annapolis to make the best impression among the other equine experts.

"Ah, yes." George reached for the other letter and quickly read it. He huffed in disbelief. "He declares he had no knowledge of your courtship of Miss Calvert. Bah! Of course he knew, or could predict the likelihood."

"He never went to either of the Calverts' homes, so he honestly may not have known." Jacky slathered apple butter onto a hot biscuit, holding it aloft as he nodded. "Though I'd talked about the girls with him."

George laid the letters aside and picked up his fork. "This is the same man who believed a world tour with him as chaperone would benefit you. More likely, it would benefit him by my paying for him to travel the world with you as the excuse. If his tutelage had not come with a high opinion of his effectiveness, you'd have never attended that school. But the college will be a good match for you, a better place where you can further your understanding of the world."

"Yes, sir." Jacky bit into his bread, his expression revealing his doubts.

True to their word, the pair rode away Monday morning, the day after Easter. The house seemed empty without George in it. Knowing George carried an invitation to the Calverts to visit at the end of April, I began planning for a gathering of our friends and family to celebrate the happy betrothal of our son. When they returned a few days later, George confirmed that Benedict and Elizabeth, along with Nelly and Becky, would arrive on the twenty-fourth of the month. I loved to entertain my family and friends, especially for happy occasions such as this. I worked closely with Doll to prepare a feast unlike any we'd provided before. After all, we were about to celebrate my son and his intended bride.

We enjoyed four fabulous days of dancing and food and easy companionship with our guests. George and Sally Fairfax, as well as George and Ann Mason, had made a special effort to attend and help us with the festivities. The gaiety of the evenings, with parlor games, music, dancing, and lively conversation were enjoyed by everyone. After our friends and family departed, I was exhausted but very pleased with the choice our son had made for a wife.

---

The day I dreaded arrived in June, when George escorted Jacky to New York City to attend King's College. Of course, Billy and Julius went along. Billy had become George's right hand, so to speak. But New York! So very distant from Mount Vernon.

I worried something would happen to Jacky and I'd never see him again. I understood the need for him to acquire a fine education, but must it be so very far away? I held my fears close, not sharing them with any one. I wanted the best for both of my children, and George had chosen that path as being in Jacky's best interest. I could live with the choice, no matter how difficult to bear. But I asked George to press Nelly to come visit me while Jacky was away. I wanted to become better acquainted and hoped her presence would help with my loneliness for Jacky. Perhaps she and Patsy would grow closer as well, a sister to replace the one who went to live with God.

George returned on the eighth with the promise of Nelly's visit in a few days. Joy filled my heart as I ordered the bedchamber prepared for her arrival. When she arrived on the eleventh, I greeted her like a long lost relative. While it had only been a month or so since last I saw her, I treasured her company. She and Patsy indeed had similar appearance, the same dark beauty almost as though they actually were sisters. We settled into our summer routine, the days so hot walking outside in the sunshine proved unbearable. The caged birds, a handful of parakeets and a beautiful macaw, chittered and screeched from the cooler rear portico overlooking the Potomac flowing past. I kept a close eye on them, not wanting them to become overheated. We elected to sit in the breezy hall on the first floor of Mount Vernon, talking endlessly while we sewed.

One especially hot Saturday, the nineteenth, we all gathered in the hall for supper. The slight breeze blowing through the open doors at either end provided a bit of relief and carried the incessant but comforting noise from the birds. The cold supper helped cool us, along with the ladies' fans.

"Jacky seems to be settling in at college well." Nelly sliced a bite of smoked ham and placed it in her mouth.

"I do hope so." Patsy sipped her cider and set the sweating cup back on the table. "He seemed rather lonely in his last letter."

"If you'd like, I'll share my letter with you. You'll see what I mean." Nelly pushed back from the table. "Will you excuse us, Papa?"

I was surprised at the sudden desire to leave the table, but had no qualms about the girls doing so. I continued eating my dinner, thinking how healthy Patsy appeared. She hadn't had a fit in days, and I dared to harbor hope the latest medicines her doctor had brought actually worked.

"If you insist." George nodded and waved them away. "I have no control in my own house, it appears."

The girls laughed as they left us and climbed the central staircase up to Nelly's room. I cut a piece of ham, and lifted it to my mouth, listening all the while to the thud of shoes on the wood floor above our heads along with the girls' chatter as they went. Such a happy and carefree sound, the young voices pitched high and lively. Then something fell onto the floor and Nelly cried out.

"Oh no!" I pushed back from the table a second behind George. We raced upstairs to find Patsy lying unconscious at Nelly's feet.

Fear sliced me in two. Patsy did not move. George lifted Patsy and laid her on the bed. He checked for a pulse. Lifted an eye lid to peer at her pupil. Slowly, he turned to face me and I knew without him having to open his mouth to say a word. It couldn't be, but it was. Oh dear God. Why? Why my lovely daughter? Pain grabbed my heart. I opened my mouth to ask if she really were dead, but my voice choked into silence by the grief wrapped around my throat. My precious little girl. Why had God taken her?

I wobbled where I stood, dark spots blocking the horrid scene. George appeared before me, pulling me into a supportive embrace. I'd have fallen if not for his strength and calm during the storm raging within me. I could hear Nelly crying, but couldn't bear to move from the comfort my husband offered. Not yet. I couldn't see a way to push past the raw pain of losing my precious daughter.

George lifted me and carried me, crying in great wracking sobs, to our bedchamber. I couldn't think straight, didn't want to think at all, truth be told. I wanted to hide from the agony ripping my heart to shreds. He understood, murmuring soothing sounds as I wailed. He tenderly helped me change into my night clothes and put me to bed.

He kissed my forehead. "I'll send for a sedative to help you sleep. I'd stay with you, but her burial must be arranged quickly in this heat. We cannot postpone even a few days."

His words brought me to my senses. I had responsibilities. I sat up and grabbed his hands, forcing back the tears threatening to start again. There would be plenty of time to grieve, but I had to be strong for both my husband and my daughter. "I don't want to sleep. I have to prepare her to meet God."

George took care of ordering a coffin to be made by a carpenter in Alexandria by the next day. He also sent for a funeral pall to drape over my daughter's final bed. He sent for Reverend Lee Massey to perform the funeral service the following afternoon. While he was busy with the ceremonial details, Nelly and I prepared Patsy's body. All the while I sang softly to my daughter, saying good-bye.

She was laid out in the parlor, wearing one of her favorite dresses. Nelly had styled her hair to lay in curls around her angelic face. I willed her to breathe each time my weary gaze skimmed her body as I sat vigil through the long night. Nelly stayed with me, holding my cold hand in her warm one. George came and went, his loving concern and his own sorrow evident in every aspect of his countenance.

The next morning, the Fairfaxes arrived. I was bone tired and my tears had dried, but my grief had in no way subsided. Sally hugged me and we cried together. Dinner was a quiet and subdued affair, sharing memories and better times with my sweet angel. After dinner, we gathered at the family vault, thunder rumbling in the distance among the foreboding clouds boiling in the sky.

The brick structure faced the Potomac river, a calming influence on my senses. Sweat trickled between my breasts and I dabbed my face with my handkerchief. The day proved yet another hot one, even standing in the shade of the ancient trees surrounding the vault. I didn't want to be there, to hear the minister making it official, to see the coffin eased through the door into the darkness beyond. I didn't want to hear the door closed and secured, forever separating me from Patsy. Until I too made the same journey, which I wouldn't mind taking soon if it weren't for my duty to my husband and Jacky and the rest of my family. Would I ever recover from the despair and the devastation filling my heart and soul? Did I want to?

------

*Mount Vernon – 1773*

I was so pleased that Nelly entered my life. Her sister, Becky, arrived to lend her assistance during the awful days that followed. Their parents had permitted Nelly and her sister to visit for an extra week, an allowance I'd forever be grateful for. Nelly provided comfort in the days following Patsy's burial. I dragged myself through each day, tears never far from my cheeks. I ate but did not taste the morsels nourishing my body. Sally visited often, her friendship and caring helping to ease my heart. But I knew she and her husband were planning a trip to England soon. Another void in my life to endure. Nelly became very dear to me during her stay, but of course, she couldn't stay with me forever. She and Becky left for home before the end of June.

Patsy's dresses were packed up and sent along with the girls, at least those suitable for them. My heart broke to have to give her clothes to others. I handled each garment with care, wanting to go back and write a different ending to the song of my precious child's life. My only consolation was in knowing she died instantly, without pain. I sobbed into the shift I clutched in my trembling hands, my tears soaking the fine linen. The mansion-house felt so cold and empty after enjoying the vivacity of the two young women. Oh my sweet Patsy! I lost count of the number of times I started to share something with her as though she sat next to me in her usual seat. At least I still had her miniature to gaze upon when sadness overwhelmed me.

I cried also for the loss of my dear friend, Ann Mason. George had learned she died back in March at the Gunston Hall. Although we didn't have much opportunity over the last year to visit, she would be missed. She'd always been so cheerful and amiable, ready to laugh and sing with the least encouragement. As the years flowed by in my life, the pangs of grief became sharp reminders of the frailty of the human form. How easily the hand of God snuffed out a life, taken to be with Him. Some days I prayed he'd take me as well, but that prayer he ignored.

The day came when George and I went to Belvoir plantation to say farewell to George and Sally Fairfax. We stood on their dock in the blistering heat, my hair and clothes damp with perspiration. The ship tugged at its mooring lines while the trunks and crates and barrels were loaded by strong men drenched from their exertions.

"Please take care on your journey." I hugged Sally, sad and worried for her. There were pirates prowling the ocean waters, and storms that could toss the ship until it splintered and cracked open like a fresh egg fallen to the ground. "I will miss you."

"As I will miss you." Sally squeezed tighter and then ended the embrace. "We do not know how long we'll be away. It will be a long time before I'll see you again, but I will write weekly."

I tried to smile but my lips didn't want to cooperate, weighed down by my sorrow. "My old man will be overseeing the estate in your absence, so you will not need to worry about that matter."

"I may have found someone to rent the property, as long as his references prove satisfactory." George shook his friend's hand, then pulled him into a strong embrace. "Be safe on your journey."

"I will keep you informed of my progress in this blasted legal suit." George Mason stepped back and shook his head. "It's such a complicated matter I must handle the affair personally, otherwise the trip would not be necessary."

"We will miss seeing you while you're away. Please be careful and come back as soon as you can manage." I took George's arm, bringing my husband close to me for comfort and support as our dear friends prepared to board their sloop.

"I'm afraid we must away." Lord Fairfax clasped his lady's elbow. "Farewell, Colonel and Mrs. Washington."

We exchanged final farewells before the couple stepped aboard their ship. They intended to sail down to visit Sally's parents before continuing on to England. I waved until the sloop rounded the bend, until Sally's return wave could no longer be seen. Then we sighed and I climbed reluctantly into our own boat to head back to Mount Vernon.

———————

A month later, on a hot afternoon, I sat with Nelly, George, Bryan Fairfax, and Bryan's wife Elizabeth on the terrace overlooking the river. We hadn't seen much of Bryan in recent times, though he and George stayed in touch, their close friendship maintained via numerous letters. Elizabeth was Sally Fairfax's younger sister, who married Bryan the same year I married George. The two friends relaxed and cherished having time together again. I'd elected to use the breezy rear porch for our dining area because of the cooling effect of the water. Having the pretty birds in their cages nearby was entertaining to our guests. The rippling motion of the waves on the river also soothed my near constant agitation.

"I've had another letter from Jacky." Nelly lifted her sweating glass of wine, holding it gracefully aloft. "He's very anxious to start our life together. It's all he speaks of."

George shook his head in silent disapproval. "Remind him of the necessity to complete his studies in order to provide sufficiently for you and your future children."

"Yes, sir. I have done so." Nelly sipped and set the crystal glass on the white clothed table. She regarded George with kind affection. "Yet, I must admit to an urgency in my breast to be officially part of this family. My love for you all has grown remarkably in these few months."

I laid my hand on Nelly's. "I'm so pleased you've come into our lives. Your marriage to my son cannot happen soon enough to ease my heart."

I choked up, but managed to swallow the tears threatening to clog my throat and leak from my eyes. I had to be strong for my family. No doubt existed in my mind on that score. Yet the storm of grief ebbed and flowed through me, distracting and consuming my thoughts. Concentration had become difficult to maintain, but I pushed through. I had no other recourse but to carry on. Though some days were harder than others.

"We can enjoy our time together whether the vows have been exchanged or not." Nelly squeezed my hand in return. "After all, our homes are not so very far apart that distance precludes exchanging visits."

"Verily. We're pleased to journey to Mount Airy to become further acquainted." George bit into a grape and winced.

"Are your teeth bothering you again?" I worried about his ability to chew his food, an activity that seemed to become more and more difficult.

Doctor John Baker of Williamsburg had extracted two bothersome teeth months before to relieve the nearly incessant pain my husband endured. He'd also suggested George begin to use a tooth brush regularly, a new concept indeed. We used chew sticks to help clean our teeth when necessary, but to think of brushing daily seemed too much. Then again, if it would deflect the pain in my husband's mouth, perhaps he should give it a try.

George waved off my concern and resumed eating, though I noticed he took smaller bites and masticated each with more care. He'd not admit to pain or discomfort before his compatriots, and I would not press further for fear of embarrassing him. But later we would discuss the matter.

Over the course of the summer, my attachment to Nelly deepened. Her presence helped to fill the void, easing my grief. Our new connection with the eminent family in Maryland enabled worrisome communications related to the mounting tension in the colonies toward King George's and Parliament's levies and taxes. George spent many evenings discussing the situation with Bryan, right up until it was time for bed. I left the men to discuss their politics, well aware my husband would inform me of events and concerns relative to our household.

In late September, George left to meet Jacky in Annapolis for the horse races and to visit Nelly's parents. While I knew Jacky longed to spend ever more time with his betrothed, I was anxious to see my son again. On the second day in October, George and Jacky, along with their manservants, finally crossed the threshold at Mount Vernon. My exuberant son flung his arms around me the moment he saw me where I'd risen from my seat by the fire, and I welcomed his strong embrace. I clung to him, relief and joy mingled in my heart at the feel of him.

"I'm so happy to have you home again." I squeezed one last time, then stepped back to accept George's buss and hug. Both men were fair and strapping examples of gentlemen, and both loved me almost as much as I loved them. "Papa, have you told him our plan?"

George moved to face Jacky, a wry twist to his mouth. "As I must present my guardian accounts to the court as well as settle your sister's estate in Williamsburg, we thought it a fine opportunity for your mother to visit Eltham. With the social season beginning along with the fall legislative session, and you on holiday from school, we can all enjoy the festivities."

Jacky grinned and folded his arms over his chest. "When do we leave?"

"I'm almost ready. I need to pack the last of the essentials we'll need to carry with us." I glanced from one to the other of the men standing in the parlor by the cheery fire. "We can leave in two days, unless you wish me to push the servants to finish the packing?"

George shook his head. "Two days is sufficient for me to determine the state of affairs on the farms before we depart for several months."

"Then it's settled." I couldn't wait to see my sister.

———————

True to my word, we left for Williamsburg and Eltham in the coach with the men on horseback. The roads had been improved but remained rough and uncomfortable, alternating between pitted and muddy for miles on end. On our way south, we stopped for a couple of days at Mary Washington's house and the Lewises in Fredericksburg.

My relationship with my mother-in-law could be characterized as tenuous at best. We did not visit with her often. She'd recently moved from Ferry Farm across the Rappahannock into Fredericksburg. She lived alone, with a few servants to see to her needs, but close to Betty and Fielding. George showed his love and concern for his mother by managing her financial affairs and sending her money when needed.

Mary once had been known as the "rose of Epping Forest" because of her beauty and the name of her father's estate. George's father, another Augustine Washington, had married her in 1731, the same year I was born. They lived at Pope's Creek farm in Westmoreland County. Augustine had three children from a previous marriage. My husband was the first child of their union, with four younger children following.

Betty, George's only sister, married Fielding Lewis in 1750. Fielding worked as a notable merchant and storekeeper in Fredericksburg, earning a comfortable living which provided suitably for his wife and children. Fielding had worked as the commissary for a company of associators in 1756, for a time attached to the Virginia Regiment. He also handled the sale and transportation of George's tobacco crop. In fact, Fielding continued to provide merchandise to us at George's request, items such as a looking glass, salt, molasses, and blankets. He represented Spotsylvania County in the Virginia House of Burgesses, too. Fielding and George maintained a close association, working together on many business transactions.

We didn't stay long with Mary or with Betty and Fielding as I was so anxious to see Nancy and Burwell. Ere long we had arrived at Eltham and were welcomed with loving arms into my dear sister's elegant and stately home.

George wrote to Mr. Cary requesting several books he would like Jacky to take back to school with him. If only Jacky would comply, he'd most definitely benefit from reading Adam Smith's *Theory of Moral Sentiments* as well as John Locke's *Two Treatises of Government*. However, my son acted like he contemplated not returning to New York, talking and dreaming about his future with Nelly. George used some of Jacky's inheritance to purchase more land close to his other properties. The new tracts were Romancoke and Pleasant Hill, with one of them including a fine brick home. I secretly hoped they would not choose to live there after Jacky took Nelly as his wife. The great distance between us would make visiting inconsistent and thereby irksome.

As Christmas approached, it came as no surprise to any one but George when Jacky announced he would not return to school, because he and Nelly had set the date to marry. I had my work before me but managed to convince George to accept our son's decision. He yielded to my argument when I pointed out that Jacky was the sole heir to a vast fortune, and it was in everyone's best interest for him to produce children. With the uncertainties of life, and the constant threat of succumbing to an illness or injury, the sooner he married and started a family the better. February 3, 1774 would be the happy event.

---

In late January, we were startled when a rider galloped up our lane at Mount Vernon. Breechy notified George of the urgent message the courier carried with him as the rider continued on his mission. The concern on George's face informed me that he feared the worst. After all the increasing tensions related to the levy of taxes, there were many men who were ready to retaliate. George had tried to calm and placate the men he conversed with, but frequently the exchange became heated.

He opened the missive, unfolding it and angling the paper to catch the waning afternoon sunlight. His eyes flashed over the words marching across the page in a firm but hurried hand. When he raised his gaze from the letter to regard me, I knew trouble had arrived. Steeling myself against the terrible possibilities racing through my mind, I moistened my dry lips.

"What is it?" Did I want to know? George's involvement in the colony's government only increased with each passing year.

"The Sons of Liberty in Boston, under Samuel Adams's leadership, have, on the night of the sixteenth of December, boarded three British ships in the Boston harbor." George shook his head. "They threw the tea shipment into the water, an act of defiance the king will not ignore."

"What did they intend from such an act?" The reality of what this rebellion meant simmered in my thoughts. "Do they think it will go unanswered?"

George huffed a mirthless laugh. "With Mr. Adams involved, they can want nothing more than to incite the king's wrath to prove their point about the burdens the Tea Act has laid upon our shoulders."

"They should have merely rejected the shipments, as Charles Town, Philadelphia, and New York have done." I wrapped my arms around my waist and held firm. "King George may consider this to be an act of war."

"No, my sweet Patsy, do not worry yourself over such an extreme response to this petty rebellion." George folded the letter, tucked it into his coat pocket, then tugged my hands into his. "The colonies will not rebel against their king. We simply wish to clarify the relationship between the motherland and her children."

Jacky walked into the parlor and heard the last words of our conversation. He raised one brow as he stopped at my side. "What is the matter?"

George caught him up on the startling news. "It is probably well that you did not return to New York at this time with feelings running so high."

"So be it. I'd rather be helping Nelly with the wedding plans than studying or having to protect myself from the rabble in Boston."

"We'll be safe here in Virginia, far away from any retaliation from Parliament." I gazed lovingly on my son, happy to see him preparing for his wedding.

We need not fear for our safety. Even if the king retaliated, he would do so in the Massachusetts colony. Hundreds of miles separated Mount Vernon from Boston, so we had nothing to worry about.

# 12

Mount Vernon – 1774

Firm resolve held me together. The third day of February arrived as a rainy and windy morning and I tried to not regret my decision to remain at Mount Vernon rather than journey to Mount Airy. Old Doll prepared an early dinner so George and his cousin, Lund Washington, would be ready to ride to the Calvert's for the ceremony. I was grateful the rain, which helped to melt the ice, ended by the noon time so the men needn't ride in the wet. I ate my food in silence, torn between my desire to witness my son's marriage and the gnawing sorrow dampening my spirits.

"Are you certain you don't want me to have the coach readied?" George caught my eye with his loving gaze. "Doing so won't take but a few minutes."

"I can send word now, if you'd like." Lund paused in lifting his fork to spear a bite of beef. "I'm sure they'd be pleased if you made the trip."

After a long internal debate, I'd chosen to absent myself from the joy surrounding the marriage of my only remaining child to his love and my friend, Eleanor Calvert. Nelly said she understood my desire to stay away, understood that mourning my daughter consumed me in a way I never could have imagined possible. Jacky had readily comprehended my reasons for not attending, embracing me and kissing my cheek. He missed his sister nearly as much as I did, and wanted to start a family of his own so he wouldn't be alone later in life.

"I cannot inflict my grief on such a happy occasion." Laying my fork on my plate, I covered my husband's hand with mine. "Bestow my blessings on their union for me, please."

George placed his other hand on top of mine. "As you wish. I'll return at my earliest opportunity."

"I'll be fine with my sweet companion to attend me." I smiled at Nancy Carlyle where she sat between George and Lund.

Sally Fairfax's shy niece, Nancy, had graciously offered to wait on me, keeping me company while the men were away. She had arrived on the first day of February around dinner time. Her presence comforted but also provided a reason for dragging myself from my warm bed each morning. The sweet young woman deserved to have a hostess to see after her needs, and her youthful countenance helped ease my pain.

"We shall make sure Mrs. Washington is well tended in your absence." Nathaniel Gist placed a bit of ham on his fork and eased it into his mouth.

Nathaniel, a refined and able man, had arrived earlier in the afternoon, in time to join us for dinner. He had served in his father Christopher's company of George's regiment, the Seventeenth Company Rangers, during the French and Indian War. Christopher had passed from this earth before I ever met my husband. But Nathaniel and George had remained good friends ever since their time fighting together.

"I hope that the Calverts understand my reasoning, my choice to keep my grief apart from the happy ceremony." I peered at my husband, who smiled reassuringly at me.

"I'll make certain they understand, my dear."

We had discussed how torn I was about not going with him, of not being with him on such a joyous day. George remained my steadfast love and agreed to go to the wedding for us both so I needn't mask my raw grief in front of so many strangers.

Nathaniel did indeed remain to entertain me while my kin were away. George and Lund stayed in Maryland a couple of extra days after the wedding, finally returning home on the fifth in time for a late dinner to share with me the splendor of the event of the season. Naturally, we had some other guests to dinner, who also seemed glad to hear of the joyous occasion.

Valentine Crawford had showed up after breakfast, despite the cold snowy aspect of the clouds outside, and was delighted to be invited to sup with us and listen to the report regarding the wedding and the gathering afterward. Val was the younger brother of William, a trader and surveyor who worked for my husband on various projects. Val also worked for George, and in fact had come to discuss acting as his overseer and business manager for his Ohio lands.

Dr. Rumney joined us at table as well, having returned to check in on me.

"Martha, you would have enjoyed the sumptuous banquet of elaborately prepared foods." George sliced a roasted potato and lifted a morsel to his mouth.

Lund laid his knife across the top of his plate, preparing to wield his fork. "The Calverts provided a seemingly unending supply of wine and spirits."

"Yes, indeed. The liquor fueled the gaiety of the dancing and music." George chuckled, his gaze taking in the rapt attention of his audience. "But you would have been pleased most of all by the solemn happiness of Jacky and Nelly during the wedding ceremony itself."

"I can well imagine they had a beautiful ceremony." I dabbed my napkin to my mouth and laid it back on my lap. "Thank you for representing me to the newly married couple and their family."

George nodded once and then sipped his wine. "My pleasure."

I might regret having not gone in years to come, but I'd made my decision based on my love for my son. I would not rob him of a joyous occasion by sharing my sorrow.

---

The first week of March brought a bevy of visitors. Jacky and Nelly brought her parents and sister on the first and we spent a lovely time catching up on all the news from Maryland and the newly married couple's plans. The following day Messieurs Muir, Piper, and Adams joined us in time for dinner, bringing even more news from around the state. Then on the third, Nancy Carlyle, Dr. Rumney, Mr. Ramsay, Mr. Dulany, Messieurs Herbert, Brown, Fitzgerald, Harrison Campbell, and Alexander Steward came to dinner and stayed the night. Most important from George's point of view, Valentine Crawford also returned to discuss his employment. I loved having the house full of guests and family, but the news they carried worried us, George in particular.

"Why do you believe the Parliament and our king are forcing such harsh penalties in the form of taxes and acts?" Val crossed his arms across his chest.

George pinned his gaze on each man in turn. "Perhaps to finance the wars in other areas."

"We need to find some way to mitigate the growing tension between England and her colonies. This direction will lead to increasing conflict." Dr. Rumney sipped his wine, his eyes on my husband.

I swallowed a sip of Madeira to cool the burning questions in my mind. I could tell even he had begun to doubt a solution would be found. Where would all the mistrust and skepticism end?

"War?" Val raised startled eyes to gaze at the good doctor.

George laid his hands on the table, pressing the palms flat on the white linen. "Let us hope it does not go that far."

Would the colonies go to war? I did not know, but thanked my merciful God that George had retired from military service so he would not be directly involved in defending Virginia from the rabble encouraging disquiet among the people.

Dinner ended and we retired to the parlor for the men to smoke and relax. Piper, Adams, and Muir excused themselves and went on their way. The talk turned to more mundane topics.

"I see materials have begun to arrive for the major changes you started last summer." Dr. Rumney settled onto a chair by the snapping and popping fire.

"Indeed. I'm relieved to see them arrive in good order." George crossed his ankles, relaxing back in the cushioned chair, a glass of sherry in one large hand. "It's almost spring and time to put my plans for the estate into action."

Patsy's estate had reverted to me, and knowing my husband longed to improve the appearance of Mount Vernon, I had happily signed over control of the monies to him. "Yes, in fact, the new large room to be added will provide much needed space for a formal dining room which could then double as a ballroom."

"I intend to add a new bedroom on the main floor, along with a convenient private office for myself." George sipped his drink and set the glass on a side table.

He didn't mention that the carriage-way leading to the house would become a curving and elegant approach instead of the straight cut from the main road to the door. And of course, George had a host of plans for the kinds of trees to plant along the road to present the best impression to the endless stream of visitors upon their arrival. All I cared about, besides making my husband content as he met the societal demands for the proper image, was that we had plenty of room to entertain our family and friends.

---

Nancy and Burwell and their children Billy and Fanny came for a two-week visit in April. They arrived on the ninth, a Saturday, and were happy to see Robert Adam when he joined us for dinner. George had to delay a planned trip with Burwell to the Ohio Valley due to the increased tensions between whites and the Indians along with the foul weather. George, of course, took Burwell off and detailed every nuance of the plans for the renovations about to commence. The children ran outside to find entertainment, and I settled down with my sister in the parlor for a chat.

"Come, Nancy, tell me what has been happening at Eltham."

"You wouldn't believe the lack of anything worth mentioning, my dear sister." She stirred sugar into her tea.

"You are correct. Surely there is something." I smiled encouragingly.

"Why do you think I insisted we come for a visit? I am so bored at home and I needed a change of air."

"You won't be bored here, what with all the visitors stopping by every day. We've been planning an outing at Johnson's fishery, which will be diverting I'm sure."

We chatted on about upcoming plans and who we might see. The length of time between visits stretched too long for my heart, but with the many miles between our homes we did the best we could. With the public times next month in Williamsburg, we would have another opportunity to visit at Eltham. With good fortune, my mother would attend as well.

George and Burwell went up the river, visiting the fishing landings as high as Broad Creek. When he returned in the afternoon, he sent Doll to find me.

"Yes, George, what do you need?" I asked as I strode into the front hall. Then I smiled when I saw who stood with him. "Jacky! Nelly! What a surprise."

Jacky hugged me and then stepped back to address me. "We wanted to see you all so much we just had to come. You don't mind, do you?"

"Of course not! Let's get you all settled."

To say I was pleased would be minimizing my reaction. Over the next few weeks there were many outings as well as visitors. We went to the fishing landings at Posey and at Johnson's. We rode into Alexandria one afternoon, bringing home with us Walter Magowan, my children's former tutor, to dine. We tried to go to Alexandria Church but the poll broke on the chariot so we had to return home. We enjoyed rides, barbecues, fish bakes, and most of all convivial company.

Jacky and Nelly stayed until the twenty-third before heading back to Maryland. Nancy and her family stayed until the end of the month. Seeing them had lifted my mood a great deal and I actually began to anticipate seeing friends during our intended trip to the public times.

———————————

We did indeed journey to Williamsburg in May, departing on the twelfth. We stopped for a night with Betty and Fielding, so that George could complete the sale of some property to Dr. Hugh Mercer. We had a lovely visit and then we were off again the next day. All in all, it took us three days to travel from home to Eltham. I stayed at Eltham the first week while George went on to town to attend the sessions of the House of Burgesses. The distance from Eltham to Williamsburg seemed smaller than when I was a younger woman. The various trips to and from my home town area as well as from Mount Vernon up to Annapolis gave me a new understanding of distances. My stay at my sister's home flew past, and suddenly George had returned on the twenty-first, making the trip in order to carry me with him back to enjoy the entertainments of the public times.

The night he arrived, we sat down to supper with Nancy and Burwell, a delicious meal consisting of venison stew, rolls with butter, and apple spice cake. I could tell George struggled to refrain from blurting out the news and gossip from his stay in town. I know he'd spent some time with John Murray, fourth earl of Dunmore, who had arrived to serve as royal governor of Virginia. I decided to provide an opening in order to satisfy my own curiosity.

"My dear, pray tell us the latest news from Williamsburg." I smiled at him, encouraging his revelations.

He cleared his throat with a look of appreciation aimed my way. "The town is quite a stir with both good and troubling occurrences. The event most talked about is the ball to be held to welcome Governor Dunmore's wife, Lady Charlotte Stewart Dunmore."

"I'm certain it will be a grand affair. Fit for a king if I know our governor." Burwell lifted his wine glass in salute.

George chuckled and followed suit. "Indeed. The ladies spoke of nothing but their attire for the event."

"A lady's gown says a great deal about the person wearing it." I glanced at Nancy for confirmation and agreement, which she granted with a nod of her head. "Most definitely a matter to consider with due care."

"I'm sure the gentlemen will be paying extra attention to their evening attire, as well." Nancy raised her brows at Burwell who angled his head with a grin. "You wouldn't want to be shown up by your wife, now would you?"

Burwell rumbled with mirth before taking another sip and setting his glass down. "I do not harbor any hope of outshining my beautiful wife."

"Well played." George motioned to the server to refill his glass. "More disturbing news came regarding affairs in Boston."

"The Sons of Liberty?" Burwell shook his head and frowned. "They do not know the kind of mischief their actions may provoke."

"The citizens and merchants of Massachusetts will pay for their insolence." George picked up his fork and stabbed a bite of meat. "The Parliament passed an act which requires the port of Boston to close to all trade as of the first of June, and to remain closed until reparations are made for the tea destroyed last December in the so-called Boston Tea Party."

"How did the assembly react to such news?" Burwell leaned forward, anxious for the answer.

"Not well, I'm afraid." George stabbed a piece of potato, holding it poised above his bowl. "The burgesses were thoroughly indignant on behalf of our fellow colony's punishment. We spent the week discussing an appropriate response from Virginia to the heavy-handed actions of the Parliament."

"What can we do against Parliament's decrees?" I had never seen George quite so animated about the activities of the colony's government. I frowned, wondering where the colony was headed.

"That is what we discussed and we have several possibilities. We could send a formal protest, or boycott certain items imported from England until the decree is lifted." George glanced at Burwell and then back to me. "We will decide when the assembly reconvenes."

"Then since we cannot solve the issue ourselves, let us enjoy our visit and put aside business." Nancy smiled at each of us, then addressed her meal, effectively ending that topic of conversation.

My husband's slight frown spoke volumes.

---

Two days later, we made the trip to Williamsburg. We dined at the home of John Randolph, the brother of Peyton Randolph, along with a few other young burgesses. George introduced me to Thomas Jefferson, Patrick Henry, and Richard Henry Lee. During the course of the evening, the discussion inevitably turned to the pending port closure in Boston.

"Our response must send an appropriate message of determination and solidarity between the colonies." Thomas spun the pewter mug of ale in a slow circle, his hazel-eyed gaze flitting from one man to the next. I could tell he was shy and serious combined. Could his height, nearing that of George, make him uncomfortable? "Do you agree?"

I applauded to myself the sensibility of his studied approach. An intimidating scholar and a lawyer, he benefitted from a stellar reputation. He preferred music and social activities to combative or aggressive attitudes. Indeed, the young man with reddish-blonde hair and glowing complexion had been enthralled by Patrick Henry's speech against the Stamp Acts.

"We should fight back with measures intended to disrupt the revenues flowing from our shores to England's." Patrick drummed his fingers on the cloth covered table, a frown marring his pointed features which seemed to reflect his sharp view of politics. "The Parliament only decides based on their purse's weight."

Patrick's views surprised no one at the table. Back in '65 in defending his actions to repeal the Stamp Act, he expressed his belief that the king acted more like a tyrant than a royal leader. Despite cries of treason then, he'd maintained his view and managed to convince the burgesses to his argument. His temper and aggressive nature stood in direct opposition to Thomas' gentle ways.

"We don't want to antagonize Parliament into more stringent restrictions." George glanced at me and then to his compatriots. "We don't want to break off our relations with England, after all."

"Why not? They take everything from us and then overcharge for finished goods we import." Patrick slapped his palm on the table, making the salt and pepper cellars jump. "We should push for their respect as equals, as British subjects."

"They do not treat us as equals." Thomas reversed the direction of the mug though he kept his eyes on Patrick as he spoke. "Why should they? We're merely colonists to them."

"We cannot change our relationship with the motherland over the closure of one port." George shook his head slowly, hinting at a kind of weariness though he appeared wide awake. "But we do need to stand with our brothers in Boston. We need a response that is nonviolent but sends proof of our united front."

They bandied ideas back and forth and finally decided to propose on the morrow that the first of June be a day of fasting, humiliation, and prayer in support of their brethren. I wondered how Governor Dunmore would react to such action by the colony's government, but held my tongue rather than speculate. We retired later in the evening to our lodgings at Mrs. Campbell's.

A couple of nights later, we were pleased to accept an invitation from Lady Dunmore to dine at the governor's residence. They were both very gracious, but I sensed a subtle change in our friendship as the evening passed. I could not discern the cause for the shift. Perhaps the rapid success of the resolution for a day of fasting on the same day as the port closure sparked a caution between the men. Or perhaps the tension sizzling between them stemmed from a much larger alteration in the political climate of the American colonies. Either way, the strain between them evoked a sorrow in me for their once compatible relationship.

---

One morning we rode out to Governor Dunmore's farm to see the new plants and trees which had arrived over the last few months. We spent the morning enjoying a sumptuous breakfast and a tour of the farm's features and fields. George was in his element, asking for specifics on the types of crops and rotation cycles the governor employed. We were back in town before the eleven o'clock start of the session. While he went to the capitol, I went to my room. The mending still needed to be done, even though we'd come to town for some relaxation and merriment.

George returned that afternoon, bristling with disgust. "I know not what the next few days will bring after the events of today."

"What has happened to make you so vexed?" I laid aside my sewing to give him my full attention.

"Lord Dunmore dissolved the assembly when he learned of our intent to have a day of fasting and prayer."

"Can he do that?"

"He did. But we have decided to gather at the Apollo room at the Raleigh to-morrow." He raked a hand through his hair, pulling the ribbon from the tip. "We are going to create an agreement in support of the constitutional liberties of America and to protest the closure of the Boston port. I look forward to adding my name to the agreement."

"Do not act in haste, my dear." Fear washed through me. George was clearly agitated, an unusual state for him to exhibit. "You don't want to do something that might be interpreted as treason against the king."

"No, you're right. I don't want to." He stared at me for a long moment, his eyes intense and his lips pressed into a line. "But by God, I will if I have to."

I could tell he was being enmeshed in the growing controversy, and I supported him every step. I agreed with the need to defend our rights as British citizens, rights being trampled upon by the Parliament's acts and actions. If relations between the colonies and England continued on this path, my husband's life as well as all who united to the cause would be at risk for defying the king. I could support his efforts with all my heart, and yet I feared for his safety and our future.

We talked late into the evening about whether or not we should attend the ball in Lady Dunmore's honor the next night. The governor and George had been friends for many years, and now that his wife and six children had joined him, it seemed the polite thing to go and welcome them officially to Virginia. The other consideration, though, remained the appearance of endorsing the crown's actions by dancing with the British governor and his lovely wife. In the event, we decided that as a burgess and a planter, George was duty bound to attend. We went to bed more quietly than usual. For myself, the concerns of the day lingered in my thoughts well into the early morning hours.

---

The next day the burgesses did indeed pass an agreement. Although it pained me, I agreed to adhere to the stipulations to boycott all goods imported through the East India Company, including tea. So many delicacies and fashionable items flowed through their hands, items no longer to be imported for our use. All of the burgesses signed the agreement and called for a general congress of deputies from the other colonies to meet to discuss any further response. That night, George and I entered the Governor's Palace with no small measure of trepidation. How would we be received after the rebellious activity of the morning?

The musicians were already hard at work, the strains of a minuet playing grandly in the ball room. Lady Dunmore's gown, straight from the high fashions of London, was the most beautiful dress I had ever seen. I glanced down at my skirts and bodice. My gown, by contrast, appeared dull and perhaps even dowdy. The governor and his wife danced the opening minuet with so much grace and elegance that the other guests watched in awe.

We wandered around the edges of the dancers, circling and moving in time to the beat. I noticed there didn't seem to be as many guests willing to partake of the sumptuous food and drink. George led me to the supper room where tables exhibited the elaborately prepared meal. Nothing but the finest linen, silver, and porcelains for our governor.

Everyone treated each other with the utmost politeness and felicity. If it were not for the mandate of southern hospitality, the civility of the evening would be even more tested. As the night wore on and the time finally arrived that we could make our departure, I wondered how long the façade of propriety would last.

Over the next few days, the burgesses determined to hold a convention of all their members on the first of August, despite the fact that such an action was illegal. The governor solely could summon the burgesses into session, just as he had dismissed them. Where would all of this lead? My concern for the life and safety of my husband increased with each passing day, though George tried to calm my fears. But I knew without a shadow of doubt that his sense of duty would propel him into defending his homeland. Even if that meant rebelling against King George III.

---

I anticipated the arrival of Jacky and Nelly at Mount Vernon in a few days. They planned to stay most of July, which would enliven the house no end. I needed some life around the place.

"Do we have enough butter and flour? Or do I need to send out for some?" I had cornered Doll in the kitchens, where she was making rolls for our dinner.

"No, Mrs. Washington, we have enough for all them extra mouths to feed. Don't you worry."

I nodded as I perused the kitchen and her helpers hard at work. "Very well. But if you find you're running low on anything, do not hesitate to inform me."

"Maybe you could find out how much longer the repairs are going to take." Doll grunted and shook her head. "No matter where I go, there's some man and his tools in the way."

"The construction cannot finish soon enough for my liking."

George readily supervised the workers, who seemed to be everywhere and in the way of everything I attempted to do. The pounding and shouting and general commotion that went with the building effort disturbed my day. Even going to the privy proved challenging, having to find a path through the tools, supplies, and debris. How much longer would we have to endure the disruption?

I reveled in my son and daughter-in-law's company, especially on those days when George traveled to Alexandria for business. He was pleased to be re-elected to the House of Burgesses in mid-July, along with Major Charles Broadwater of Springfield. He stayed overnight, throwing a ball to celebrate his election. He made a point of serving coffee and chocolate only, adhering to the ban on drinking tea even at a celebration of his being returned to the royal governor's government. He came home on a Friday, and then after church on Sunday, George Mason paid us a visit. My husband escorted him into the parlor where I had decided to read for a while. I laid my book aside and rose to greet our good friend.

"Hello, Mrs. Washington." He performed an elaborate bow, a gesture he made out of deference and a sense of humor. The move was far too grand for mere friends to exchange, after all.

I enjoined his light-hearted greeting with a playful quick dip of a curtsy. "Hello, Mr. Mason."

He straightened with a grin. "I've come to steal your husband for a few hours."

"What business might you have on the Sabbath?" I didn't entirely approve of working on Sundays, having been raised to rest one day each week. George had explained to me that not everyone held such beliefs, including him when the demands of his business required his attention.

George regarded me for the span of two blinks and then smiled. "We've been tasked with drafting a set of resolutions to present to the burgesses on the morrow."

"Indeed. We intend to make quite a statement to the Parliament and King George." George Mason grinned but not from pleasure. "We'll boycott most British imports including slaves, as well as detail our beliefs related to English liberty, American rights, taxation and representation, and more. Our message will be abundantly clear."

"Shall we get to work?" My husband extended an arm in the direction of his office, and the two men strode away, deep in conversation.

I trusted my husband to be careful to not commit treason with ill-considered sentiments, but still I worried about the response from England.

Monday the eighteenth George departed for Alexandria again to meet with the committee. My thoughts stayed with him as I went about my daily work and visited with my family. When he finally returned home that evening, bringing Walter Magowan with him, my fears were confirmed.

"What do you mean, George?"

"The resolutions were adopted at a general meeting at the court house." He snared my attention with an intense scrutiny of my face. "And I have been chosen to lead a twenty-five man committee charged to concert and adopt other resolutions necessary and expedient."

I swallowed my fear on his behalf, knowing he was fully aware of the risks involved in these actions. Adding to his cares would not help him finish his unenviable task. "They have bestowed quite an honor upon you."

"A huge responsibility as well. I hope I am up to the challenge." He glanced at Walter, who inclined his head.

My husband had started down a path undoubtedly leading to conflict with Lord Dunmore. Although nervous, my duty was clear: support him with his aims any way I could.

———————

While George was away in Williamsburg for the convention, pretty Becky Calvert visited me, providing a lovely distraction in his absence. We settled in comfortable chairs in the airy hall, the doors open at either end to catch any hint of breeze during the hot August days. I prepared to read aloud a letter from George while Becky worked on a seat cover, a beautiful tapestry of crewel needlework featuring the tree of life surrounded by decorative birds and flowers. She had been fortunate to attend the school in New York to learn the complex stitches using silk and wool on linen to make truly beautiful designs.

"Shall I read Colonel Washington's letter?" I expected she'd agree, and I wasn't disappointed.

"Please do. He doesn't write very often, does he?" Becky paused in pulling the heavy wool thread through the fabric.

"He is so busy he has little time to write me." I skimmed the page in my hand and then summarized its contents, skipping over his endearments and personal asides. "He says the convention voted on delegates to send to a Continental Congress in Philadelphia in early September, and George was elected as one of them. They also unanimously resolved on a nonimportation and nonexportation association, which means the colony is stopping all British imports, excluding medicines, unless Britain repeals the offensive laws targeted at Boston and the Massachusetts colony."

Becky's worried eyes met mine. "When will that happen?"

I shared my companion's anxiety over the news contained in

the missive, my fingers vibrating like a plucked violin string. "He says the ban will go into effect on the first day of November for imports."

"I wonder if my father will be able to export the tobacco as planned."

"Only if he does so before next August according to this letter. That's when tobacco exports will be banned." It was a good thing George had already ordered and received the lumber and nails and all the rest of the supplies and tools necessary to complete his vision for Mount Vernon. The same items could not be acquired locally because most of our money was in the form of a credit in London, the result of the previous exported shipments of tobacco being sold by our agent. How would we manage our finances without dealing through our London factors? The consequences of the ban on importing and exporting would have an enormous impact on our daily lives.

Even with the dark cloud of worry hanging over our heads, I strove to maintain a normal routine. George and Billy returned from Williamsburg before Becky left us for her home. We enjoyed visits from several good friends over the course of the next couple of weeks, and even went up to Alexandria for dinner one afternoon. All along, the talk circled around the actions of the Virginia burgesses and the intent of the upcoming Congress. On the first of September, George and Billy departed for the meeting in Philadelphia, leaving me at home to oversee everything. He did not return this time until the thirtieth day in October, in time for dinner midafternoon.

Our new routine appeared to center around my husband journeying to different places while I remained at home to manage the household. Alone, but not really. I always had at least one young person to keep me company. The arrangement suited me as I did not enjoy traveling on the rough and uncertain roads. I no longer rode horseback, having reached an age where it was not considered proper. The problem with the arrangement, of course, was that my husband and I were frequently separated by hundreds of miles. That must change and soon.

———————————

Nelly and Elizabeth Calvert sought me out, locating me in the parlor by the fire. My hands and feet were cold, despite the crackling warmth emanating from the fireplace. I worked on stitching together a quilt on this cold December day, mainly to try to keep me warm. Jacky had brought his wife and her parents for a visit to start the holiday season on a bright note. As usual, both ladies were finely attired in their quilted day gowns.

"Martha, what plans have you made for the upcoming festivities?" Elizabeth sank onto the couch, folding her hands in her lap.

"I understand that we shall have a special guest. A good friend of my husband, Charles Lee, is due to spend New Year's with us."

"I have not had the pleasure of his acquaintance." Elizabeth glanced at Nelly, where she sat on a chair on the other side of the fireplace, then back at me. "Tell me about him."

"General Charles Lee fought alongside George during the Braddock expedition back in 1755. He is a veteran of many wars in England and Poland, but now has decided to support the American cause."

"Then I hope he arrives before we must return home ourselves." Elizabeth smiled as she tucked her skirts more snugly around her legs.

I understood the necessity, having already tucked mine. "In the meanspace, would you care for something hot to drink?"

At their nods of agreement, I asked Sally to arrange with Doll for some hot chocolate and biscuits and we enjoyed a nice long chat.

Unfortunately, the Calverts and the Custises left before our esteemed guest made an appearance. He had a rather effeminate appearance, actually, with a small, full mouth, and light curly hair pulled into a queue. His dark mocking eyes looked down his long straight nose at me. He carried himself as though he harbored no doubt of his superiority of all and everyone he surveyed. Including my George, who welcomed him with warm greetings.

The next morning, I came down early to make sure the kitchen was prepared to feed all of our guests. When my foot touched the hard wood floor board of the hall, I heard the skitter of claws coming from the parlor. Wondering what varment had gotten into the house, I hurried down the passage and into the room.

What I saw stole my breath and swept hot outrage through my chest in a single moment. Anger fueled my steps as I hurried to clear the room. "Get out, you curs!"

Lee's six big hunting dogs didn't even pause in their actions. They had ransacked my good parlor. One held a large ball of fine yarn in its drooling mouth. Another had chosen to lay upon the gold couch, its black hair visible on the expensive fabric from across the room. The others milled about, looking for other mischief to make. A mess of muddy paw prints marched across my carpets. I went in search of General Lee, fuming and forming my reprimand with as much finesse as I could muster given my temper. Fortunately, he had just entered the passage as I left the parlor. I strode up to him, seething but attempting to mollify my expression.

"General Lee, your dogs are in need of some control if they are to continue in my home." The man looked at me as though I spoke Greek or perhaps Yiddish. "Do you understand?"

"Mrs. Washington, I do not believe it your concern as to what my dogs do." He half bowed and then straightened back to his full height. "If you'll excuse me, I have important matters to discuss with Colonel Washington."

He towered above me, driving home the disparity in our size and strength. Add in that he was our guest, and my hands may as well have been tied behind my back for all the effect I'd have on his actions. I didn't like it, but that was beside the point.

"Breakfast will be served soon." Forcing a calm I didn't feel, I turned to walk away, heading for the kitchens and my morning ritual of unlocking and dispersing spices and sugar for the day. And to have one of the maids attend to putting the parlor to rights. All the while knowing that the sneer on the man's face did not bode well.

Time proved my fears well founded. His fickle nature made it difficult to like the man. I imagined nobody wished to align their fortunes with his temper and his volatility for fear they'd be sorely disappointed. As for the dogs, he never did confine them or even scold their behavior but let them run through my house causing mischief. Forcing me to keep the doors closed and my sewing locked away, an extreme inconvenience but at least I could keep some measure of peace. By the time the day arrived for the man to continue on his way to Williamsburg, I prayed he would never set foot in my home again.

I stood beside George as Lee thanked us for our hospitality. Keeping mum so as not to voice my true thoughts, I merely smiled at his pretty words.

"You're always welcome in our house, General Lee." George half bowed to the man, who returned the acknowledgement.

"I must be on my way." Lee paused, never even deigning to look at me, then cleared his throat. "I beg your pardon, sir, but might it be possible to borrow fifteen pounds to cover my travel expenses?"

George's expression shifted from relaxed and friendly to arched brows and blinking eyes. He recovered much faster than I did, however. "Why, of course. Having just arrived in the country, I'm sure your affairs are not quite in order yet. One moment."

He strode away to his office to retrieve the funds while I tried to make conversation with the man, ignoring with an effort his dogs padding about, sniffing and drooling all over my floors.

George returned in a few minutes, carrying the pouch of coins, and wearing of all things a smile on his lips. "Here you go, my friend. Repay me when you can."

Lee inclined his head in gratitude. "As soon as possible, I will return your money to you. My regards."

I'd never been so pleased to see the backside of any of our guests as I was to say farewell to General Lee and his curs. Only later did I realize peace would never again fully reside in our home. The general's presence foreshadowed the unease and disturbances that would plague us for the rest of our lives.

# 13

"Doll, would you please put together a tray of refreshments?" The kitchen bustled, with the servants hurrying to prepare the food necessary for meals later in the day.

"Yes, Madame. Would you want biscuits as well?" Doll wiped her hands on her apron, leaving smears of apple juice as evidence of her labors. "Something to complement this afternoon's light dinner?"

"A fine idea. Thank you. And have Breechy bring a table out to the lawn overlooking the Potomac in a while."

"Yes, Madame."

I turned and left the kitchen to return to my guests. The house teemed with visitors on the eve of the next Congress. I had been busy keeping everyone fed and entertained. Breakfast had been a crowded affair with several of my husband's acquaintances stopping in, most of whom had continued on their way by late morning. George had gone outside to converse with Major Horatio Gates, now retired from service. Our good friend and neighbor, Bryan Fairfax, had also come to stay the night. I could only wonder who else might join us before the day ended.

I walked out the door and crossed the lawn to where the men enjoyed the early May sunshine while sitting on the bank overlooking the river. Breechy passed me, lugging a table out to the group. He was followed by Mulatto Jack, who laid a cheery cloth on it so Doll could set down the tray of chocolate and coffee as well as a plate of biscuits. I joined the group, resting my weary feet for a few minutes. Apparently, I'd interrupted a rather intense exchange.

"We must do something to end the siege of Boston by those New England troops. The city cannot last much longer." Tension rolled off of Major Gates, belying his relaxed pose.

Major Gates, or rather Captain Gates back then, had known George since they fought together in Braddock's defeat in '55. He'd also fought in the French and Indian War before returning home to England to retire as a major. Three years ago he and his family decided to move to America, to their pretty farm, Traveler's Rest, on Opequon Creek. While not far from our home, we didn't often have the pleasure of his visits. With the recent skirmishes at Lexington and Concord, I was not surprised he made the effort to come speak with George on the situation.

"The matter is to be addressed at Congress next week." George regarded each man in turn. "We must consider every angle, every option open to us before we land upon the right course of action."

"Agreed. If any one can ensure all the possibilities have been identified it will be you, my friend." Bryan puffed on a clay pipe, the smoke rising lazily on the gentle breeze.

"I fear we may end up fighting again." Major Gates crossed his arms over his broad chest. "My retirement may be coming to an end."

George nodded slowly, his eyes troubled. "We will work to avoid a full rebellion by striving for a tactful solution to the impasse."

"Do you believe such a solution is possible?" Bryan asked.

"Providence will show us the right course to follow." George gave me a look that made my pulse race with apprehension, and then turned back to his friends. "We must defend our rights against tyranny."

Major Gates huffed and shook his head. "We may end up fighting against our old commander, General Thomas Gage. I never thought I'd be opposed to the commander of the British troops. It's quite a daunting prospect."

"Verily, but we shall do all in our power to succeed in our endeavors, including fighting against our friends who take up the king's cause."

As the sun set, the group moved inside to continue their dialogue until it was time to light the candles. Then as was our custom, we retired to our bedchamber for the night. The next day brought more visitors and saw Bryan depart for his home. Our friend and one of many Lees in the colony, Colonel Richard Henry Lee, and his brother Thomas, as well as Colonel Charles Carter arrived in the afternoon. Colonel Lee would accompany George on the morrow to Pennsylvania. As had been occurring all week, the men settled in to discuss the state of affairs with regard to the recent battles and the British response.

Colonel Lee was a long-time acquaintance who had served as a burgess along with George and had also been a delegate from Virginia for the first Congress, and again for the second. His sister, Anne, was married to George's brother Augustine.

I didn't know much about the other men, having infrequent contact with them. I did know that Colonel Carter served as a burgess representing Stafford County and so George had more occasions to be in his company than I had.

My role was not to know everything about everyone but to ensure everyone had what they desired. I also helped Billy with gathering George's things together for the imminent trip, adding a few last minute items I thought he'd require. I'd be lonely for my husband while he was away, but I had to tend to matters at home. I hoped he would not stay away any longer than necessary, to come home to me in a matter of weeks unlike the last time when he was away nearly two months. Naturally, I did not share my feelings with any one else, knowing he was well aware of my preferences.

I stood on the front step saying my farewells to my husband the next day, on the fourth of May. "I shall miss you more than I could convey in my letters."

"Write me often, my dear, as I will write you." George held my upper arms for a moment, studying my face as if to fix each of my features in his memory.

Despite the servants passing by, I wanted nothing more than to be held in George's strong embrace. We had no way of knowing the end result of the treasonous actions. When he'd return. Or, much worse thought, *if.* The king could order his hanging, after all, for participating in the dangerous rebellion. After he rode away on such a harrowing mission, he may never see his home, his family again. He must have felt the same. He flicked a glance at Billy, who moved to stand in front of us, facing the carriage-way.

George pulled me to him, wrapping his arms around me, and holding me tight. My cheek pressed against his coat, the beat of his heart reassuring in my ear. I clung to him. I wished he'd never let go, that he not leave. But my wish remained pure fancy. He'd been called to duty, a summons he heard and could never deny.

"I will be home at the earliest possible hour." He pulled far enough away to clasp our hands together between us, allowing him to study my face a few moments more. "Never doubt my love and my desire to be with you here."

I cried, hot tears of pride and fear, as George departed with his companion, heading to Philadelphia in our family coach. Traveling across the country remained a dangerous endeavor despite the progress within the colonies. George's cousin, Lund, had moved to Mount Vernon in order to supervise the workmen and, to my mind, generally make a nuisance of himself. He seemed to feel I should answer to him, but I would not tolerate such a situation. I had run the household for fifteen years without major lapses or inconveniences and I'd continue to do so. George relied upon my judgement and good sense. The younger man would have to learn his place.

---

Days and then weeks dragged by. I looked for George's letters to arrive each week. He wrote about the people with whom he dined and where he lodged, but the Congress had decided to keep its proceedings secret so I had no news on what might happen next. May became June and still I waited for his return. Then, I received a shocking letter from him. One I read quickly and then plunked down on my chair to read again.

So he'd been made commander-in-chief and wasn't coming home. Not yet. He'd reluctantly accepted the command of the army, feeling he lacked the capacity sufficient for such a trust. But also because he would rather be with me. I read the letter carefully, aware of the fact that he hoped to return in the fall. Several more long, dreary months without him. He went on to suggest how I might spend the lonely months. Either moving to the house in Alexandria or staying with my family, or whatever would produce content and a tolerable degree of tranquility.

I couldn't help the tears when I saw the will he'd enclosed with the letter. If he should die... If I never saw him alive again... An unbearable thought.

I considered my options and dismissed the idea of moving to Alexandria, staying in the town home he used when doing business in the port city. I'd stay at our home, at Mount Vernon, and hope if he could arrange a holiday from the demands of Congress and the army he now commanded, he'd come to me. Come back to his treasured home.

Lund, on the other hand, attempted to direct my actions. He concocted a foolish idea regarding our friend, Lord Dunmore.

"Mrs. Washington, you must listen to reason." Lund paced back and forth in the small parlor, hands clasped behind his back.

"I do not believe Lord Dunmore would find any benefit in

sailing a British man-of-war up the Potomac to kidnap me." I studied the jerky strides of the agitated man as he shook his head. His posture bespoke the extent of his disquiet as he continued to press.

"Capturing the wife of the commander of the American army would put George in a very tenuous and difficult position." Lund paused in his endless to and fro to glare at me. "Why do you not listen to me?"

"Because you make little sense." I resumed my stitching, attempting to end the lunacy. Trying to ignore any qualms his gossip caused in my midsection. "I'll not abandon my home and leave it unprotected."

"Not even when the general also worries about the possibility?"

"Bah, I say." I looked Lund straight in the eye, refusing to back away from what I believed to be the best course of action. "I'm staying and there's nothing you can do about it. So go about your business overseeing the workers and leave me to my sewing."

He sputtered and fumed without saying a word, and finally strode out of the parlor, shaking his head and muttering. I chuckled and concentrated on my stitching.

———————

Nelly was due to have a baby over the summer, and I spent much of the span of lonely months preparing for my grandchild's arrival. Another sweet baby to hold and to cherish. My joy at the prospect offset the loneliness I endured each day. Jacky and Nelly came to visit during the hot summer months, to enjoy the cooling breezes from the river. Sitting outside under the trees, watching the river flow by, we shared what was happening in our lives and in the country.

"When will Papa be home?" Jacky sipped his small beer and gazed out across the water.

"He hopes this fall, but with events as they are, who knows." I worried every day for his safety, but knew my old man would take all necessary precautions. "He writes me weekly, sometimes more frequently, to reassure me of his care and attention as much as keep me apprised of events he can share."

"We are living in very precarious times." Nelly shifted, searching for a more comfortable position with her bulging belly. She rested her hands on her unborn child and turned concerned eyes my way. "I'm not sure I'm ready to be a mother."

"Why would you say such a thing?" I smiled, trying to reassure her much like my husband did for me. "You're bound to be a fine mama."

She shook her head and glanced at Jacky before addressing me again. "I don't know that I'll be a good mother. Not like you or my own."

"You could not help but be a wonderful mother to your children. It's in your nature. Speaking of which..." I set down my cup of cider and cleared my throat. The sound drew Jacky's gaze from the distance to rest on me. "I have written to Papa, asking that I be permitted to join him in camp."

Surprise filtered into Jacky's eyes. I grinned at his expression, realizing the thought had never occurred to him that I might miss my husband enough to desire to change the situation in my favor. Knowing armies rested during the terrible weather of the winter, I might be able to go to George if he couldn't come to me. I hoped so at least. My duty and desire for once were in agreement.

"Do you know where camp will be?" Jacky leaned forward, clasping his hands between his knees as he stared at me.

"It doesn't matter. If he invited me to the winter camp I'd happily make the long, treacherous trip to be with him."

Although I had never traveled so far from home, and the idea of taking a stage on such a perilous journey quailed my insides, I'd go. I missed him like an amputated limb, a throbbing ache nothing but his presence could assuage. I'd face any challenge to put my heart at ease to do my duty by being at his side where I belonged.

"If you're sure..." Nelly peered at me, her hands gripping her bulge.

"Absolutely. Now, let's talk about making some baby clothes for your little one."

―――――――――――

The first week of September, Nelly went into labor and Jacky came to me, fighting his own panic. I was out in the kitchen, working alongside several servants making candles to ward off the coming dark nights of winter. Trying not to worry about the continued silence from my husband regarding my request. But oh, how I longed to hear from him.

"Mama, Nelly needs you."

I looked up from dipping candles at his frowning countenance and saw the summons clearly in his eyes. "Very well. I'll be along. Doll, send for the midwife and then heat some water and bring up some clean sheets and towels." I rested the dipping rack on its stand and then wiped my hands on my apron as I followed Jacky back to the mansion-house.

After many hours and many female hands helping with the comfort and care of my daughter-in-law, Nelly gave us all a precious little girl.

"Look, Mama, how beautiful she is." Nelly smiled tiredly up at me.

"My granddaughter is lovely." So small and cuddly. I couldn't wait to hold her, but I had to bide my time until she'd been cleaned.

The midwife took the baby to look over, inspecting its health. She caught my eye, and I hurried to her side. "What?"

"She is very weak. See how she is silent? She's not even looking to suckle." She glanced at Nelly, listening to the conversation with wide, horror-filled eyes. Then the midwife looked back to me and her expression warned me of her next words. "Prepare yourself that she may not live long."

"Oh, but she must." How could she not thrive in such loving arms as Nelly's? "What can we do?"

The midwife handed the baby to me, all swaddled in a warm blanket. "Love her while you can."

I carried her back to Nelly, who had tears trickling down her face, and nestled the babe in her mother's arms. Then I eased out of the room to find Jacky and tell him the awful tidings.

God chose to take the baby to heaven a few days later. Nelly was devastated by the loss of her first child, as were we all. In the event I relived the deaths of my wee babes, the pain a dull throb in my heart. But I consoled her with the hope of having more little ones in the near future. The pain would ease over time, but I knew it would never entirely vanish.

Waiting for George had become ever more difficult. Still he had no idea as to when he might be permitted to return home, even for a brief visit. Lund kept him informed of the progress on the improvements to the mansion-house. He proved very talented in that regard, and I had to admit my relief at not being required to supervise the workmen.

One morning at breakfast in the middle of October, Jacky cleared his throat to attract my attention.

"Is something amiss?" I sipped my coffee laced with cream and sugar to make it somewhat palatable.

"I want you to consider removing to Eltham rather than continuing here, pining away for your husband." Jacky smiled as he spoke, softening the urgency of his words.

"Leave?" The coffee warmed my throat as I swallowed another sip and glanced to Nelly. I had been contemplating visiting my sister, as a distraction and to be away from the clumsy attempts Lund made to dictate my affairs. But hadn't reached a decision. "Are you well recovered? Would you be able to make such a journey?"

"Aye, I wish to go as well. I'd enjoy visiting the Dandridge clan again." Nelly spooned porridge into her mouth.

"Very well. I'll need a couple days to pack the necessities and then we can take the family coach. I'll have Breechy see to preparing it for the journey." I finished my beverage and then rose from the table. "I have much to do so if you'll excuse me."

George's foresight in returning the coach for my use told me how much he knew my preferences. He'd bought a phaeton and team of white horses to pull it, along with three other mounts for his use in the army maneuvers. When he'd accepted the post as commander of the American army, he did so without claiming a salary as he felt it his duty to stand with his compatriots and not profit from them. Instead, he only wished to be reimbursed for expenses, such as the conveyance and horses.

On our way to Eltham, we stopped for a few nights at Mary Washington's in Fredericksburg. She fared as well as could be expected, and I was glad to have chance to speak with her. But I wanted to reach Nancy's welcoming embrace, to see for myself how she fared. Her health had been precarious for the last several years so my concern had grown with each letter I'd received. We finally arrived at Eltham and settled in to enjoy a much-needed visit with family.

"I'm so happy you're here." Nancy hugged me and then moved away to escort me into the house. "We have invitations to several merriments, including dancing, fox hunting, and fish bakes as the weather permits."

"Since I plan to stay for several weeks, we shall have ample time for everything." I linked arms with her and soon we were safely ensconced in her sitting room with a fire to warm us. She seemed to have recovered from her latest bout of indisposition, but I didn't want to overtax her strength. We had much to say to one another, catching up on her family's activities and expectations.

I'd only been at Eltham a week when on the twenty-third a dusty mounted messenger arrived from Lund. He'd obviously ridden hard to reach me so the message must be urgent. I swallowed the fears generated by an active imagination and went to meet the young man in the front hall.

I motioned the weary man into a chair with a flick of my wrist. After he'd dropped ungracefully onto the needlepointed seat, I clasped my hands together to hide the tremor that had arisen the longer I waited. "What is the news?"

He held out a folded paper to me with a quick nod. "Mr. Washington asked me to tell you that your husband has sent for you to come to him."

"I have only just arrived here, so he will have to wait a span for my journey to him." My heart soared as I took the letter and I quickly wrote a response to George's cousin, informing him I'd return to Mount Vernon in one week to pack for the long journey north. Handing the note to the man, I thanked him for his trouble, and then faced my sister who had joined us during the time it took for me to reply. "I don't know how long it might be before I see you and your family again, so if you don't mind, I'll stay at least a while longer."

"My goodness, I'm so glad for you." Nancy smiled at me as we walked to the front parlor window and watched the messenger canter away. "I can't imagine everything you'll need to pack for an extended trip north."

"Mama, we'd like to go with you, if you wouldn't mind." Jacky joined us by the window, Nelly lingering a little behind him. "I miss Papa, and we think a change of scenery will benefit us both. Would you mind?"

Relief surged through me at not having to leave behind my dear son and his lovely wife after the recent loss of their baby. "Your company will surely please Papa as much as it does me."

Our conversation turned to what to pack, what supplies would be prudent to take with us for the several months we'd be away from home. So much to consider, and I intended to do so with deliberation. Despite Lund's urgings, I'd take my time to decide what would likely be needed. Only then would I press onward to Massachusetts. And George.

---

I returned home and methodically gathered the many items I'd need while away. I hoped the change of scenery and company would take Nelly's mind off her recent loss. We had picked up my nephew, George Washington Lewis, Betty and Fielding's son, on our way through Fredericksburg as he had been offered a position on George's staff. So my trip would feel more like an excursion with family and that fact made me easier with the idea of going so far from home.

I strode through the mansion-house with a sense of despair at departing our home mingled with a deep longing to see for myself that my husband remained in good health. The advent of war changed the rhythm of our lives, even though it was an undeclared conflict that George found himself leading troops against. He prayed for a peaceable end to the matter but held no allusions based on the direction the rhetoric had taken. Our idyllic life on the plantation had been turned upside down and I was not at all certain we'd ever be able to put it to rights.

Lund, of course, tried to influence my pace, advising me to hurry through my preparations. But how could I when I needed to pack so much? The list seemed endless. Hams, bacon, preserves, olives and more were loaded up for the trip. Next I had to select appropriate clothes, cloaks, hats, gloves, ribbons and lace, as well as knitting wool and a mending kit and medicines. My favorite books including romances and plays, my Bible, stationary and ink. So very much had to be gathered and secured in trunks and other containers.

All told, it took me two weeks to finish packing, to be satisfied I had sufficient supplies for the duration of my stay in Massachusetts. On the sixteenth of November, we stepped into the loaded family coach and set out on our adventure. Jacky and George Lewis rode horses along with us, giving us plenty of space to pick up Elizabeth Gates, the wife of the adjutant general, to bring her to camp. We had quite a full coach as we continued our way north.

To my utter surprise, I was met and escorted by mounted honor guards outside of each town we approached. As we entered a town, the most eminent citizens greeted us, praising my husband in the highest terms possible. With each occasion, it slowly dawned on me that George led not only the army, but the entire nation, which had aligned behind him. He'd become more than a Virginia planter and officer, but an American leader. My heart swelled with pride and love. Concern lingered in the background, worrying over the future.

At one juncture, the coach stopped long enough for me to address the crowds gathered to greet me and my companions. The townspeople were very nice and full of compliments regarding my husband and addressed me for the first time as having been named to a station to which I had never aspired.

"Lady Washington, forgive me, but I must ask. Why are your postilions dressed in such finery when the nonimportation act is in place?"

"Pardon?" A shiver of apprehension had me clutching my cloak tighter.

"We like your simple gowns, but the servants' attire is causing much consternation."

I glanced around at my servants in their uniforms and then drifted my gaze over the small crowd, noting the plainer attire of the people. "Now I understand your concern. We imported the livery long before the resolution had been put into effect."

The man nodded, his expression relaxing from a frown into a bright smile. "We hoped for that to be the case."

The experience confirmed a new reality for me: every aspect of our lives would now be observed and commented upon, favorably or not. George and I, and by extension our entire family, had become public figures and thus subject to not only great honors but also criticism. I'd need to tread carefully in order to not leave an impression which might reflect poorly on my esteemed husband.

All in all, it took us five long days to make our first destination. We arrived in Philadelphia on the twenty-first. Such a grand city, with its beautiful red-brick buildings and churches. My party was tired, so we settled into comfortable lodgings to rest and recover from the arduous journey. I had known it would not be an easy trip, but the roads at times were next to impassable and thus we traversed them at the same speed as a dirge. During the week that we rested in town, a group organized a ball in my honor. I was flattered and pleased to accept and began to prepare for the enjoyable entertainment. It had been quite a while since the last time I'd danced and I found myself anticipating a fine evening in the beautiful city.

The day of the ball, I was enjoying a hot drink with my family in the sitting room of our lodgings. We'd been pleased with our accommodations and the various entertainments we'd attended. Fortunately, everyone remained in good health despite the trials of our excursion. We were discussing when we should depart to meet up with the army, when a group of very serious city leaders were announced by the butler. They entered the room, holding their hats before them.

"Gentlemen, what may I do for you?" The four men regarded me with serious expressions lightened only by the mere hint of a smile.

"Lady Washington, we are honored to have your presence in our fair city. We've come to bestow our great regard and affection upon you, and request that you pay our compliments to General Washington in his defense of our rights and liberties."

"I receive your words with gratitude, sirs." I set my cup and saucer on the small table and then folded my hands in my lap, waiting patiently for them to state their business.

They nodded solemnly, then looked to the tallest of the men, who squared his shoulders and cleared his throat.

"I am Mayor Bayard, Mrs. Washington." He gripped his hat with gloved hands. "We have come on a matter of no small importance."

"Pray go on." He seemed to struggle to find the appropriate words to convey his message. I waited, glancing between the committee of notable citizens before me.

"Lady Washington, we feel that a ball is an excess, in these troubled times. Please do not grace the company to which you have an invitation this evening."

The request took me by surprise, not having considered the ball as a luxury. But then, we'd never before had our country on the brink of war with all the deprivations inherent in the event.

Indeed, in 1774 the Continental Congress had passed a resolution discouraging horse racing and other gambling sports in an effort to impose a more sober and patriotic value system, as well as separate American society from that of the aristocratic social pretensions associated with England. Thus, the ball might reflect poorly on me and by extension my husband.

"Please receive my best compliments, gentlemen, and I have taken your request to heart. Your sentiments on this occasion are perfectly agreeable to me, for the reasons you've brought to mind. I shall send my regrets posthaste."

"Thank you, Lady Washington, for understanding the potential ramifications of such an event upon your husband's efforts. We wouldn't want any hint of following the lead of the British royalty and their sumptuous desires."

No, indeed. I was grateful to the men for alerting me to the new reality. A lesson well learned. I could only wonder what other sacrifices we'd have to make before the fighting ended.

---

We stayed in the city a few more days, then continued on our way on the twenty-eighth of November, taking along Betsy Gates. George had sent his aide, Captain George Baylor, to escort us from Philadelphia to Cambridge. Captain Baylor was a lusty young man, a favorite among the ladies. His familiar presence eased some of the tension from my knotted midsection. His friendship and service to my husband meant he'd insure our safe passage to the army's camp.

We had a very pleasant trip through the pretty New England countryside. As we drew closer and closer to the camp and my anxious husband, I desired nothing more than for the trip to be over and me in his arms. Finally, on the eleventh of December, we arrived at Cambridge, a very short distance from where the fighting continued in the Americans' attempt to end the siege of Boston. George led us to where George had set up his headquarters on Brattle Street.

On our way, we passed many dwellings of all descriptions, with thousands of men performing a variety of activities with an equal variety in attire. They traipsed in and out of the churches and the buildings of Harvard College, between small tents and plank huts, as well as up and down the rough streets. A ragged bunch of men unlike anything I'd ever seen before. My husband had a serious job to do to pull these men into a cohesive fighting force. Even I could tell as much with my inexperience in such matters. I tried to ignore the layer of fear lying beneath my calm, fear for the lives of the men walking past my coach as the fighting continued.

The Georgian mansion serving as headquarters dominated the rural countryside and included three stories with a balustraded expanse on the roof fit for taking the air. A set of wide steps led up to an ornately decorated door with two ionic columns on either side. Across the street, a hospital had been created for tending to ailments and battle wounds. Those poor unfortunate men already injured or dying from the battle nearby. I would visit as soon as we settled in to see what I could do to assist the patients, despite the slight tremble in my hands. For the moment, I wanted to see my husband, to judge for myself the state of his health and morale. I'd traveled a very long way to achieve my aim.

We were escorted into the entry hall. Then I saw him, dressed in his uniform, his boots shiny black. I stifled my urge to run to him, waiting with assumed patience even as my heart beat furiously in my chest. Descending the stairs hugging the left wall, George hurried to me. He appeared hale and hearty, though I could see the effects of the situation he faced in his expression. I returned his embrace, grabbing his waist for one quick squeeze but only for a moment as we had an audience and I did not wish to embarrass any one with our affections. We'd have privacy later when we could share our desperate longing for each other. An eternity from that moment.

"Welcome to Cambridge. I've heard you had a pleasant journey." George took my hand and tucked it into the crook of his elbow. "You'll want to see your temporary lodgings, I expect."

I nodded, grateful for the solid strength of his arm. "I have some ideas I'd like to discuss with you, ones the ladies and I have talked over on the way."

He chuckled and then stepped off, indicating to the others to follow. "You're always thinking and anticipating what needs doing next. Come, in here is the parlor."

We walked into the elegantly furnished room, featuring English styled furniture of a very fine craftsmanship. Skimming my gaze across the small space, I slowly nodded once. Nelly paused to my right as I turned to George.

"This room will suit my needs. Here is where the sewing circle will meet. The ladies in camp will be invited to join me to sew bandages for the hospital I saw on my way in."

"And to mend any tears in the men's uniforms." Betsy Gates paced through the room, her gaze flitting from mirror to portrait to the mahogany padded chairs flanking the marble fireplace. "We'll help with anything we can while we're here."

"Your efforts will be dearly welcomed." George laid his other hand on top of mine. "I'm pleased to see you in such fine mettle."

"And I you." Seeing his adoring and confident countenance swelled my heart with love, pride, and respect. Feelings I felt certain the men under his command shared. He smiled, though he kept his lips closed over his false teeth as was his wont. "Show us the rest of the house and then return to your work. We'll settle in with our servants' help and leave you to manage your more important affairs."

We had a hurried tour. The main floor was divided into four rooms: the parlor, dining room, kitchen, and what George called his staff room but probably had once served as a sitting room. In the latter space, desks and chairs were crammed in, providing flat surfaces for the letter copiers to do their work. George pointed this fact out to young George so he'd know where to report for duty on the morrow. The second floor was also divided into four rooms: two of which George had claimed as our private chambers, one bedroom for Jacky and Nelly to share, and one more bedchamber reserved for visiting dignitaries. We didn't venture to the third floor, as we had no pressing need to inspect the several small rooms set aside for the servants' quarters.

The servants unloaded the carriage and deposited the appropriate baggage in the designated rooms. While Sally unpacked my daily necessities, Nelly, Betsy, and I, along with our maids, ventured across the street to the hospital. Once a Presbyterian church, the stone building now had rooms designated for a surgery, medical supplies, laundry, and rows upon rows of patients in the sanctuary. I supposed it fitting to have the men fighting in this ungodly war to be sheltered within the walls of a sacred place.

The sight of the misery of the men, lying on straw mats and cots, joined to the sounds of moaning nearly made me turn away. Bolstering my courage by gripping Nelly's hand, we presented ourselves to the doctor in charge. I informed him of our intent to assist with bandages and he received the news with a ready expression of his appreciation.

"We'd like to visit with the wounded, if that meets your approval." I fully expected him to dismiss us, to say a hospital was no place for ladies. I had my arguments prepared but they were unnecessary.

"Please, I'm sure they would welcome a pretty face and a caring smile. If you want for anything, have one of the nurses fetch me." With that, he swept his arm toward the men, and bowed before hurrying away.

"Well, that was easier than I thought. Come, ladies, let's see what needs the men may have." I caught Betsy's eye and indicated for her to take the left, and then for Nelly to take the right. I went straight ahead to a back area where it appeared the more seriously wounded had been taken. Pausing at each cot, I spoke to the men, asking what I could do to help. A drink of water. A blanket straightened. A quiet word of prayer. Small tasks that meant so much to them.

I had made my way through half of the patients, when a loud boom shook the structure and rattled the windows. Startled, I glanced frantically at the nurse tending a nearby patient. "What was that?"

"You'll become accustomed to it in time. It's the bombing in Boston."

"My goodness. That sounds close." I had my doubts as to whether her prediction of growing used to the sound would come true.

I still had other patients to speak with, see what little comfort I could offer. These men, ranging in age from teens to their forties I'd guess, were fighting to secure the rights of our country, of America. They'd been injured doing dangerous work for my husband, and I would do whatever I could to thank them. I'd simply have to learn to ignore the sounds of the war in order to pay attention to the results of the fighting. I pressed my lips together and moved to the next soldier.

The following day I inspected the household management, intent on how I might improve the arrangements. I spoke with the steward and the aide charged with paying for expenses, and then made several necessary changes to smooth the running of both our home and the army headquarters. I knew my role. My duty remained with George, to support him and ensure domestic affairs didn't distract him from official business.

One afternoon I was invited to dinner with several officers and while I was out in the carriage, I managed to get a look at poor Boston and Charlestown. The shelling by cannon at Boston and Bunkers Hill had left behind a great deal of damage. Boston had a number of very fine buildings standing, but it was an open question as to how long. Charlestown had only a few chimneys visible against the sky. The wharves had been pulled up to use as firewood. All the preparations for war were terrible indeed, but I tried to keep my fears to myself as well as I could.

As the weeks passed, the routine of sewing, socializing, dinners with the other officers and their wives, and visits from the local leading citizens, became a normal rotation of events. If it were not for the fighting and the tension associated with why we had gathered in Cambridge, I could almost believe myself at home.

———————————

*Cambridge, Massachusetts – 1776*

On the first of January the Continental Army officially came into being. We went to the parade ground along with a host of others to celebrate. George had learned thousands of men had chosen to not reenlist. Tension simmered among the officers as a result. The remaining soldiers could not withstand an attack by the British. Broadsides had been distributed encouraging men to join the army, but a long span of time passed before enough had signed up to restore the army's readiness.

Indeed, the situation had become so precarious that a new acquaintance, Mercy Otis Warren, the wife of the army paymaster and Speaker of the Massachusetts House of Representatives James Warren, invited me to stay at her home for fear of a British attack on the camp. Mercy was an intelligent and educated woman, with interests as a historian, a playwright, and poetess. She also shared very strong opinions about the role women should play in our society, ideas the men did not always agree with. I was of two minds on some of them, but I could understand why she believed so strongly that women should be treated the same as men, not as property. I searched out my husband to confer on an appropriate reply to her surprising invitation.

He stood with one of his aides on the front porch discussing some task or other the young man needed to handle. I waited until they'd finished their discourse and the aide had hurried off before I spoke with George. He looked rather grim but when his eyes met mine they lit up the way they always did, relieving the strain on his features.

"I should send some response to Mercy. What do you think is the right way to tell her I cannot accept her invitation?"

"We must ensure we don't give the wrong impression. If the note were to be intercepted, we don't want any one to think we believe such an attack might occur."

I frowned at the reminder of the likelihood of others reading private correspondence as I considered possible wordings, realizing the nuances in each attempt. So many other communiques had been intercepted and read by people who shouldn't have been so nosy and disrespectful. "Perhaps you should send the reply? I'm unsure whether my writing would suffice."

"If you'd rather I send it, my love, I will take care of it this afternoon." He squeezed my hands. "If you'll pardon me, I have several pressing matters to attend."

"Of course. I'll see you at dinner." I squeezed his hands and reached up to kiss him before leaving him to his work.

George sent Mercy a very gracious response indicating if the need truly arose for me to vacate the camp, then I'd be pleased to accept her offer. With good fortune, though, I won't need to leave in fear.

---

I proposed to George that we should throw a celebration on Twelfth Night, to give the soldiers something to look forward to, to boost their morale. It was also our seventeenth wedding anniversary. Although he worried about possible misinterpretations of the event, at first thinking it frivolous, he finally agreed. In addition, several British supply ships had been captured recently by our newly formed navy. All of which added to the reasons to celebrate.

With the help of Nelly and Betsy, and the cook and quartermaster, we pulled together a holiday celebration worthy of the name. Our guests feasted upon smoked ham, roasted fish, confections and candied fruits, as well as freely flowing wine and ale. A few soldiers produced a fiddle and flutes to entertain the crowd flowing in and around headquarters.

After the festivities ended, and George and I were alone in our chambers, he sat with me in the comfortable chairs positioned in one corner. A beautifully polished teak table between us held a decanter of sherry to enjoy a small drink together before retiring. Something weighed upon my husband's thoughts. His eyes appeared tired yet steady as he gazed at me in silence for several moments. Awful possibilities of the news he prepared to relay to me filled me with dread and anxiety. Was he going to send me away after all? Finally, he shifted and cleared his throat.

"My dear, you know I value your safety and contentment above all else. Is that right?" George set his glass on the table.

"Indeed, Papa, I am aware and I am grateful for your interest on my behalf. I feel the same with regard to you."

He nodded and the corners of his mouth twitched before resuming a solemn expression. "I must beg you to favor a request."

I raised a brow and sipped my drink, intrigued. "I will certainly consider doing everything possible to please you. Pray continue."

"The incidence of smallpox within the ranks of the army greatly concerns me. With you in camp and going out among the troops you may contract the disease. I want you here with me, as I know is also your desire. So it is a dilemma. Thus I ask you to consider going to Philadelphia to be inoculated." He lifted his glass and held it aloft, torn between sipping and waiting for my response.

My brother's death from the terrible sickness lingered in my memory. Would Jacky have lived if he'd received the medicine? My son had the inoculation and he had survived the introduction of what was a small amount of the virus. Apparently with no ill effects. Would I, though?

George sipped, ever patient as I pondered my answer. I should say something to let him know I was thinking about his surprising request. "Do you believe it is safe?"

He nodded again. "The doctors assure me they are refining the methods for achieving success to make the inoculants immune to the disease. After I had smallpox in Barbados when I was there with Augustine, I've not contracted it though I've been around people who have had it. With good fortune the resulting pustules will be few and your illness mild, leaving you immune to the affliction."

"Surely I was exposed to it when my brother had it." So maybe I was already somewhat immune to it. Having another small dose would ensure my health against the disease and I'd be permitted to stay with George. A compelling reason for agreeing. "Very well, my love. For you I will comply with your request."

Eyes crinkling, George grinned, his relief evident. "My sincere gratitude is yours."

"One other matter has come to my attention, though it's a happy occasion." I waited until he tilted his head in question before revealing my news. "Nelly is expecting a child."

"Wonderful news indeed." He tapped his glass to mine and we each sipped.

"She will want to return to Maryland ere long to prepare for the baby's arrival." I so loved to see my husband with delight and happiness in his countenance. "When they go, it would be a good time for me to make the trip to Philadelphia."

"Not for a few months hence, I hope. I will not be able to leave here for a time." He set the empty glass on the silver tray. "We have more work to do to end the siege in Boston."

"Shall I be safe to stay with you?" I trembled with the possibility he'd say I must leave, but then he'd just said he wanted me to stay for a while. I relaxed and drank the rest of my sherry.

"Yes, most definitely, Cambridge is safe. The fighting is away in Boston, some distance from here. Should that change, your guard will see to your safety."

"Yes, they are a brawny pair of men you've assigned me."

Having never had any one follow my every movement, other

than my children that is, their presence took me a while to grow accustomed to. Their protection when I left the house made it possible for me to move freely around the camp, to see to the domestic needs of the men as well as check with the many wives as to their needs. I'd lost count of how many pair of socks I'd knitted, or how many bandages and packets of simples I'd handed out for their comfort.

"Are you ready for bed? I've grown weary after this long, happy day." I rose and waited while George stood and then led me to our bed, wondering what to-morrow might bring.

---

In early March, the Continental army attacked Boston, trying to end the prolonged capture of the city. The army fortified Dorchester Heights and installed field pieces under cover of darkness, so that the Britons discovered with dawn the dire predicament they'd found themselves in. From the heights, the American army could bomb both the city and the ships in the harbor, which they did with great enthusiasm and accuracy. Anything to force the enemy out. A sudden thunderstorm, bringing deafening booms of thunder and bright flashes of lightning, raged through the area and thwarted a counterattack. The British were forced to evacuate, taking as many of the Tory residents with them as they could.

I stayed at camp during the ensuing celebrations in the city because I was not immune to the smallpox which had swept through Boston during the besiegement. I did manage a carriage ride down to see the deserted lines of the enemy before returning to continue making the necessary preparations to go with George to New York where the next action would likely occur. At least, that was the expectation of George and his staff. New York would be quite a prize for the enemy to control.

As it turned out, I didn't travel with George and the army. After much discussion, George decided it would be better for me, Jacky, and Nelly to travel a different route away from the dust and noise of the troops on the march. We departed on the fourth of April on our two-hundred-mile exodus, our coach escorted by two of George's aides-de-camp, en route southwest through Connecticut. Jacky, my precious son, became ill along the way, so we stayed a few extra days in Hartford until he felt well enough to continue. As happened any time my family contracted an illness, my worry for them made me slightly ill right along with them. We arrived, finally, in the city on the seventeenth, glad to be reunited with the army and most importantly, George.

The size and design of the port city astounded and impressed me. I had thought Philadelphia a busy and industrious place, but New York far surpassed it in terms of prosperity and elegance of the houses and buildings. The wide dirt streets enabled several carriages and wagons to pass without slowing their pace. We took a rather circuitous route but the aide thought we'd benefit from a brief tour. The best part to me was passing the beautiful City Hall, with its yellow brick walls and inset rectangular windows flanking the main entry. The thirteen colonies had sent delegates there for the Stamp Act Congress, a group organized to oppose the levy of taxes. They were responsible for drafting the message claiming the colonists deserved the same rights as British citizens and demanding no taxation without representation sent to King George III, the House of Lords, and the House of Commons. In hind sight, they started the colonies down the road we, the states of America, now traveled.

I was pleased with the house George had secured for our stay. Known as the Mortier House in Manhattan, it served our needs well. We added a few items for our personal use, such as a featherbed, bolster, pillows and other furnishings. Realizing his mobile headquarters would need appropriate furniture as well, George purchased a dining marquee, a living tent with an arched chamber, some lovely walnut camp stools and table, and many other items. The work of the commander required at least the simple accoutrements for the discussion and decisions necessary to field an army.

The only aspect lacking proved to be a decent housekeeper. Definitely something that must be corrected. I found George talking to a group of aides in the downstairs office. After their discussion ended, I ventured closer to my husband.

"George, I think you need to send out word to search for a qualified woman who could oversee the cleaning and provisioning of the army household."

"We are in need of such a person?" He gazed at me. "Do you not wish to oversee the household yourself?"

"I do not want to supervise the cleaning and acquiring of necessities in an unfamiliar city." I folded my arms across my waist, determined to ensure the easy flow of the household activities. But I needed help to do so most effectively. "Please, ask for references."

"As you wish, my dear."

———————

A couple of weeks after we arrived, Jacky and Nelly confronted me while I was knitting yet another pair of socks. The serious demeanor of my son and his wife foretold news I likely wouldn't want to hear but probably could guess. I laid down my needles and yarn as the couple sat together on the settee.

"Mama, we've come to a difficult decision." Jacky tried a smile but it didn't stay in place.

"One I won't approve?" I had heard a hesitation in his speech. "Tell me."

He glanced at Nelly who nodded in encouragement. He returned his attention to me. "We're going home to Mount Airy so Nelly can be in familiar surroundings and prepare for the arrival of our child."

"Oh, that's a fine idea." A woman should be as comfortable as possible for being brought to bed. I smiled at my daughter-in-law. "Your mother will be pleased to share the blessed event with you both, I'm certain."

"Thank you for understanding, Mama." Nelly crossed the

space to embrace me. "We were a little worried you'd be upset."

"I'm not surprised you'd desire to be in your own bed with your women attending you."

"We thought we'd leave in a few days, while the weather is favorable." Jacky stood and took Nelly's hand in his affectionate grasp. "I'll tell Papa when he returns from inspecting the troops."

"He'll support your plan as I do. Now be off, and let me work." I shooed them from the room so I could accustom myself to remaining so far from my own home in private. While their departure was not unexpected, their absence would leave a hole in my heart. I carried on, following the lead of the thousands of soldiers around me who had left behind their families to fight for the cause. Surely if they could sacrifice I could as well. I lifted my chin and continued my work.

The people of New York seemed to be under the false impression that America was not at war. George worked tirelessly to meet with the leading citizens and explain the realities he faced with his army opposing the British incursions. I had little to do on an official basis while in the city, but I found ways to ensure my husband's needs and desires were met both at headquarters and in our private lives. I enjoyed having the opportunity to be at his side no matter where he chose to be.

Unfortunately, along with the army's arrival in town the smallpox spread like fire on dry grass. The need for my inoculation became imperative if I were to stay with George in the city. Yet George was needed and couldn't break away from his command to escort me to Philadelphia. We were at an impasse, as I did not wish to go alone and he would not let me stay. Then Congress sent a summons to George to attend them in Philadelphia. So, with great relief on my part, we headed to that city, arriving on the twenty-third of May. Having the recent experience of New York, Philadelphia's sturdy red brick buildings with white trim and soaring spires seemed rather subdued and quaint by comparison. In many respects, I preferred being in the city of brotherly love because it felt more welcoming with its tree-lined streets and quiet elegance.

We stayed at Joseph and Esther Reed's home, not far from the capitol where the Congress met. We chose the more private location, mainly so I'd not be expected to entertain or be entertained, rather than accept the kind invitation to stay at John Hancock's home. George had met Joseph Reed at the First Continental Congress five years earlier and they'd instantly become great comrades. Joseph had served as his secretary, then adjutant general of the army, and had helped George plan the battles at Trenton and Princeton as Joseph had great knowledge of the Delaware river. Last year, Joseph had been elected as the president of the Pennsylvania supreme executive council, a position he proved well suited to hold. As a result, Esther had the title of Mrs. President.

Esther had been quite a surprise when I first met her on a previous trip to Philadelphia. Born in England, she had married Joseph in London in 1770 before immigrating, along with her mother, Martha Symond de Berdt, to Philadelphia the next year. Her father, Dennis, had died before the wedding, which probably enabled the happy event since he'd vehemently disapproved of the union. Much like John Custis disapproved of my first marriage. What had surprised me so much about her was how zealous of an American patriot she had become, renouncing England's treatment of her colonies to all who would listen. Her sentiments aligned well with mine.

I'd waited long enough to have the infection accomplished, so we hastened to the best doctor in the city the very afternoon of our arrival.

"I should warn you that you'll feel fine and look healthy for the next two weeks or so," the doctor said. "But then you'll start to ache all over, have a fever, and might also experience severe aches in your head and back."

"That doesn't sound too difficult to endure." I thought I'd be fine if that was all I had to worry about.

"You might also vomit, and pustules will also appear on your skin and possibly in your mouth. Those pustules will fill with fluid over the next ten days."

"Is that everything?" *Please, say yes.* I swallowed my concerns. I had limits of what I could tolerate.

"Yes. All told, at least three to four weeks until the inoculation runs its course."

As we strolled back to the Reed's, I had two questions running through my mind. How ill would I become, and how many sores would scar my body?

Routine letters arrived from Mount Vernon where Lund continued to oversee the renovations with his usual efficiency. The news provided a distraction from military affairs and helped George keep his sensibilities balanced. Four new outbuildings had been built in front of the main house by the plantation's carpenters. As summer approached, they turned their attention to building a new kitchen off the southwest corner of the house. George longed to make a quick trip to our home, but the pressing events he was involved in prevented any possibility of such a jaunt for the immediate future. I could feel his frustration radiating from his person at not being able to oversee the many changes he'd ordered at the plantation.

The reforms George proposed to Congress were accepted, at least most of them. The real reason for the summons, though, was the debate over whether to declare America free from British rule. To declare independence from tyranny. George held the opinion that fielding an army amounted to just such a declaration, but the discussion continued. I didn't complain when the discussion went on for several weeks as it meant George would be with me to help bolster my morale as long as possible during the three weeks it took me to fully recover.

In the event, he had to return to New York before I was well enough to travel with him. My guard stayed when he left on the fourth of June. While the aides were nice enough, they were definitely a poor substitute for my life companion.

I received welcome news from Jacky. I settled on a chair in my room at the Randolph's to read his letter by the light flowing through the window. He congratulated me on my easy recovery, and hinted that Nelly would deliver her baby soon. He also shared that her father, Lord Calvert, was about to face troubles in Maryland based on his actions on behalf of the British monarch.

Nelly was preparing to have her baby and then they planned to move back to Mount Vernon. I indulged a moment of longing for our home so far away. When would I see it again? The memories of our time there, friends and family stopping in for a visit and a meal, the many outings to races and barbecues, flowed in my mind like the Potomac on a warm summer evening. I had never thought to travel so far north as New York and Massachusetts, and yet I'd been to both places. My past life seemed small and confined by comparison. The future, by stark contrast, held many uncertainties and dangers. Most troubling of those being that if our cause failed, every man involved, including George, faced death for treason.

The following week my recovery was complete, and I felt able to make the return trip to New York. Although happy and relieved to be back in the city, I stayed there but a couple weeks before disaster struck. On the twenty-ninth of June, fifty British ships sailed into the harbor and camped on Staten Island. Alarmed, George hurried me back to Philadelphia the very next day while he prepared to defend the city from the amassing fleet. He expected more ships to arrive, increasing the military power of the enemy and increasing the danger to civilians like me and the other officers' wives.

I returned to the Randolph's where I waited, and worried, and fretted over my husband's safety. If all went as planned, I'd be able to return to New York, so rather than journeying all the way home to Virginia, I stayed as close as was safe. With Congress in session, I'd be reasonably secure.

Intense curiosity pervaded Philadelphia at the beginning of July. John Randolph informed me that Congress had passed a new resolution on the second, put forth by Richard Henry Lee, which would change everything. Whatever that might mean. On the fourth, Congress adopted the Declaration of Independence, then John Hancock, as president of the Congress, and Charles Thompson, as secretary, both signed it. What exactly did it say? Four days later the Declaration of Independence was read for all to hear on the steps of the State House.

I stood at my open window in the upstairs of the Randolph's house. I could see the front steps of the State House and could easily hear the booming voice of the man reading the surprising and eloquent declaration. "When in the Course of human events, it becomes necessary for one people to dissolve the political bands which have connected them with another, and to assume among the powers of the earth, the separate and equal station to which the Laws of Nature and of Nature's God entitle them, a decent respect to the opinions of mankind requires that they should declare the causes which impel them to the separation."

After he finished reading the entire thing, a group of men bearing rifles fired several volleys into the air. The sharp report of the gun fire resounded through the city while people cheered and hollered their approval of the declaration. Then a rowdy parade made its way past the house, along with the constant firing of guns. I was rather sorry George wasn't there to witness the momentous event. I couldn't wait to write to him about the scene before me.

While I lingered in the city, George wrote to tell me he'd hired a seventy-two-year-old Irish woman named Elizabeth Thompson, for fifty pounds New York money a year, to keep house and negotiate favorable terms to provision the household. I anticipated with some anxiety making her acquaintance, so I could judge for myself whether she'd meet my standards.

Jacky wrote to tell me Elizabeth Parke Custis, to be called Betsy, was born on the twenty-first of August. His adoration flowed from the page, calling her "as fine and healthy, fat baby as ever was born." I longed to hold her, count her fingers and toes. My son's news provoked intense feelings of isolation and loneliness in my chest. Even surrounded by the commotion of the city, or maybe because of it, all I wished to do was flee.

And still I waited. Even while enjoying staying with friends and making excursions into the city for shows and dinners, I grew more and more restless. George wrote weekly, telling me to be patient, informing me of the many skirmishes and futile attempts at peace between the two forces. August arrived and I then watched it wane.

George sent me word of a terrible American defeat at the battle of Long Island. I could hear his disappointment and dismay over the outcome in the words on the page. The army retreated up Manhattan, attempting to regroup and stay out of reach of the pursuing British army. Then his next words struck my heart to the quick. He told me to go home as there would not likely be chance for me to return to him for some time. Sadly, I packed my belongings and Sally and I made the lonely journey home.

Before long, Jacky and Nelly arrived at Mount Vernon with my precious granddaughter, Betsy. She was indeed a beautiful little girl. Her black hair and eyes matched her mother's, with silky fair skin. Having her tiny body to hold and love distracted me from my fears for George and the American cause. For a little while. Then they returned to plague my mind.

The army had retreated to Philadelphia, chased by the British the entire way. Indeed, the British controlled all of New Jersey. In fear of being overtaken by them, Congress had fled the city, reforming in Baltimore, Maryland. Winter fell hard and bitter, snowdrifts piled high and roads froze. I waited for George to invite me to join him in winter camp, but by late December they were still on the move. Why did George not go to camp? What did he wait for?

It wasn't until January that I learned the reason. George had surprised the British by crossing the Delaware River on Christmas evening, winning a decisive battle in Trenton and followed it with one in Princeton against the Hessians stationed there. His letter abounded with new confidence in his men, their ability to fight and win, and that morale soared. The British had pulled back to New York City, and the Americans controlled New Jersey. Elated for his success, I had only one question.

When would he send for me?

# 14

I finally arrived in winter camp mid-March, so much later than I had wished. The roads were nearly impassable until the end of February so George did not want me to risk myself or the horses by attempting to traverse the distance between home and Morristown. While I champed at the bit, I kept busy gathering all of my necessities: food, sewing materials, medicines, books, and more. As soon as the rains and snows abated and the roads began to firm, I headed out with my servants.

Morristown bustled with activity the afternoon we arrived. George sent one of his aides to meet my coach and the young man led us to headquarters. A gathering of soldiers, townsfolk, and children cheered my arrival. I'd become something of a celebrity as the commander-in-chief's wife. As a result, I had to be careful about what I said and did so as not to hurt my husband's reputation by association. I'd learned during my life how to be tactful and discreet and yet manage the situation toward the desired outcome. Ever since I'd gathered the courage necessary to confront John Custis about marrying his son, I'd wielded the power of persuasive argument with deft skill. I had complete confidence in my ability to maintain the necessary decorum.

The coach halted in front of a two-story brick building. The sign hanging over the street at the door indicated we'd arrived at a tavern owned by Jacob Arnold. George emerged and strode toward me. His delight as he handed me down from the vehicle warmed me as much as the early spring sunshine.

"My sweet Patsy." He retained hold of my hand as he guided me toward the tavern. "I've been waiting for this day a long while now."

"As have I, my dear old man. If you'll show me our quarters, I wish to freshen myself."

"First, come with me. I want you to meet someone." With a lift of one brow, George led me inside, where a spry gray-haired woman in serviceable day dress and colorful apron hurried toward me. She stopped and dipped a curtsy as George drew me up beside him. "Martha, may I present Mrs. Thompson, our housekeeper."

"Pleased to meet you." I noted the frank expression performing a quick inspection of me as I did of her. Curiosity shone in her blue eyes and I found myself liking her. "If you'll show me to my chamber, I'll only be a short while."

"Yes, Lady Washington. Follow me." She spun to one side and bustled down the short hall to the stairs.

I tossed a smile at George and then I trailed after the older woman, Sally close beside me. The new title Mrs. Thompson so casually used rested uneasily on my shoulders.

An hour later I met George and his staff in the dining room for dinner. My servants had performed their duties, slipping into the flow of the household without issue. Sally had unpacked my clothes and helped me with my toilet, rearranging my hair in a neat bun. The group of men, mostly officers, turned to greet me as I stepped into their company.

"Mrs. Washington, permit me to present to you my staff." George kept me at his side as he introduced each of the men. "Major General William Alexander. Brigadier General Thomas Conway. Of course, you already know Brigadier General Nathaniel Greene. That is Brigadier General Robert Howe. Our quartermaster general Thomas Mifflin. Major General Arthur St.

Clair. Major General Adam Stephen. And this fine man is my newest aide-de-camp, Alexander Hamilton."

Each of the men greeted me as George said their names. I had met several of them during my previous stay at winter camp or as long ago as Williamsburg, but I did not remember all of their names. I had no idea that I'd find myself back in camp for yet another year. Surely the war would not last very long. Several new faces were in the group as well. Mr. Hamilton looked to be about twenty years old with intelligent eyes and a fine straight nose. Such a youth compared to the generals surrounding him. He inclined his head, his gaze fixed upon me. He stood nearly as tall as my husband. Indeed, all the men towered over me like old oaks around a rose bush.

"Mrs. Washington, I'm honored to meet you," Mr. Hamilton said.

"Thank you, sir. Gentlemen, it is my pleasure to make your acquaintance."

Dinner turned out to be a lively affair, with much discussion between the men. The rumble of deep voices in urgent discourse and uncertain laughter filled the room. I listened, absorbing the nuances, arguments, and expectations woven through the history-making conversation.

"I hope Benjamin Franklin can convince France to ally with our cause." Nathaniel lifted his cup and waggled it back and forth to give emphasis to his point.

"Although they provided support, they have only done so unofficially." Alexander speared a morsel of venison. "An official agreement to join forces surely would give the rebellion legitimacy."

"Franklin has been gone much longer than expected." George pushed some beans onto his fork. "But at least it has not proved a fruitless endeavor."

"At least not yet," Thomas Conway said with a chuckle.

"The longer this all takes, the more desperate we are for the men to stay for the spring fighting season." Adam Stephen spoke with authority ringing in his baritone voice.

"Why would they stay after their enlistment agreement ends when there is nothing to do and they don't get paid as promised?" Robert Howe shook his head.

Thomas Mifflin huffed as he picked up his wine. Glancing at the other generals, his eyes grew serious. "The shortages of necessities, such as shoes, shirts, and food, also encourage the men to return to their homes and families."

"I'm contemplating going home given how arbitrarily promotions are made. It makes no sense to me." Arthur St. Clair laid his fork on his plate and then rested his hand on the table.

"I have written to Congress with ideas on how to reform the army organization but they have not responded as of yet." George glanced at each of his staff officers. "I've received no word on whether they've even debated the suggestions. We can only wait and see what happens over time. And pray the men do not disperse when we most need them."

While we waited, I knew one thing with certainty. My role remained the same: to support George any way possible. Just by being present, he had told me, I helped to calm his agitation and bring a much needed bright spot to his day. A small measure of joy bounded in my heart knowing he relished my presence even in such a harsh and dangerous place. An equal measure of fear fought to drive me toward our home, but I'd stay with George as long as he needed me.

―――――――――

As May rolled around, the trickle of new recruits swelled to a stream as our cause became ever more known. The town and adjacent camp where the main army lived in tents could not support the increasing burden of so many thousands of men and their horses. George decided to move the army south to Bound Brook to enable better living conditions and continue training the men in preparation for the looming confrontation with the enemy. The troops left on the twenty-eighth of May, George along with them.

Shortly after they departed, Jacky wrote to share Nelly was with child. They were staying at Mount Airy as before. Home beckoned but I had several errands to attend before I could turn toward Virginia. I stayed a few more days in Morristown gathering my effects, then went to Philadelphia to do some shopping. It seemed very odd to be stopping in the city to shop for several items on my way to Virginia. When I was a girl, I had never contemplated living anywhere but in the colony I was born in. My life had certainly veered from the path I'd first set upon in ways I'd never imagined. Including the war being fought, led by my own sweet husband.

While in the city, the Assembly of Pennsylvania requested my presence at the State House. I paid particular attention to my attire and hair fashion the day I was to meet with them. Sally and my guard accompanied me to the designated area in front of the building. A group of men stood waiting as I made my way up the street. The assemblymen appeared jovial and well turned out for the occasion. I wondered what they intended.

"Good morning, Lady Washington. I am happy you could meet us here on this fine day."

"I must confess to being intrigued as to the reason behind your invitation."

"My dear Lady Washington, we have determined a special way to provide testimony of the sense of the Assembly of your husband's great and important services to the American states."

"I am grateful for your kind sentiments." I smiled at him, wondering exactly what type of testimony they had in mind even as I strove to ignore the designation of "lady," a British-sounding title.

The men parted and revealed a shiny new coach to replace the one I'd worn out with the long journey to and from home. Sleek and gleaming, the conveyance proved a welcome gift. Four white horses jangled their harnesses as they stamped a foot and swished a tail.

"Thank you so much, gentlemen. Your generosity and tribute to General Washington are appreciated in the extreme."

I enjoyed the long trip home for a change, good springs and sturdy frame keeping me dry and comfortable over the one hundred sixty miles we traveled. Despite the fact that the horses dragged me farther and farther from my love, as always Mount Vernon welcomed me with open arms.

---

George wrote to me each week, and I cherished each letter as proof he remained safe and well. With so many letters, I started dividing them into packets by year, tied with a piece of ribbon. I secreted them into a specially crafted cedar box with a lock and key. A box I kept in my wardrobe away from prying eyes or rummaging hands.

Visitors came and went and my days fell into a comfortable routine. I received a letter from my sister, Nancy, a very precious note since she so rarely wrote to me, asking me to visit in the fall. Given the uncertainties of the times, I decided to accept her invitation. She had not been well over the last several years, an ague coming and going almost as frequently as my visitors. Debating on when to make the trip, I finally responded to her that I'd visit in October. Traveling in the fall would be cooler than summer heat and the changing colors of the trees would make it pleasant as well.

I also learned from Jacky when he visited in July that Nelly's condition inflicted the same kind of misery the last one had. She endured the back aches and even the dizziness with grace, but the sudden painful spasms of her abdomen as her condition progressed proved harder to accept. The midwife had tried to comfort her, saying many women experienced similar discomfort as the baby grew inside. Still, her health worried me, more than I'd care to admit, but I could not assist her from such a distance.

By August, the army had moved to Pennsylvania to defend Philadelphia against a feared attack. George's letters included carefully worded hints as to the skirmishes and their resulting casualties. What they didn't contain was any sense of when he'd send for me. Not until the fighting ended for the season, certainly. Then where would he go? How soon could I join him? Or would the war end and he'd be able to come home?

The army tried to wrest the city from British control. On September eleventh, they fought at Brandywine and nearly won the field, but were outflanked and had to make a hasty retreat. Several weeks of skirmishes followed, making it apparent the enemy intended to take Philadelphia. The American Congress fled west to Lancaster on the eighteenth. The army fought the enemy again on the twentieth at some place called Paoli and lost again. A few days later Philadelphia was taken and occupied by three thousand British. My heart fell at the thought of the pretty city in the hands of the enemy. Only a few months ago I had been in the besieged city shopping for sundry items. What if they had captured the city while I had been still visiting the Reeds? Such an event would have been disastrous for George as well as the American cause. How quickly the tides of war changed.

In early October, on a foggy day, they clashed again, this time at Germantown, a lovely community on the outskirts of the city. George wrote me the nasty turn to the weather hampered communication and caused confusion and disorder. Although the Americans ultimately lost the battle, George noted the army held firm and resolute in the face of the adversity they encountered. They retired in good order, not in panic. A distinct improvement.

I had chosen the timing of my trip to see my sister so it wouldn't conflict with the start of winter camp. My journey proved uneventful and enjoyable. Eltham had not changed since my last visit. I arrived on a foggy morning in the middle of the month. The structure stood as before, but the shroud of moisture laden air surrounding it leant a sense of waiting, of expectation or dread.

Inside I found myself swarmed by Nancy, Burwell, and their two young boys. Embraces and greetings were shared, and then we went to the small parlor to enjoy a pot of coffee and biscuits. Everyone settled onto seats, still chatting and laughing. The odd sensation of earlier dissipated among the camaraderie and enjoyment. Young Burwell had reached the age of thirteen and strongly resembled his father, and John at eleven was beginning to show signs of the man he would grow up to become. My sister had a fine family to support and care for her, a blessing indeed. First, Nancy needed to recover her own health before she could address that of her family.

"Have you been getting the air?" I asked, as we relaxed before the welcome fire burning in the fireplace.

"I have not left the confines of this house in weeks." Nancy ruefully grinned my direction. "I'm afraid I don't have a gentle enough mount to carry me forth. I've grown too weak to ride my pretty little mare."

"You need a docile, elderly ride." I pulled my lace handkerchief from my sleeve and blew my nose. The dust from the ride to the plantation continued to tickle my senses. "I will see if I can find you an appropriate horse and have it sent down. Riding will restore your constitution."

"You are too kind, my dear sister. Please do not trouble yourself." Nancy's gaze flitted about the parlor, lighting upon every object but not meeting my eyes.

"It's not trouble. We must look out for each other, mustn't we?" I reached for the crystal glass of sherry placed on the table within grasp. "Speaking of which. Have you considered having the smallpox inoculation?" I addressed both my sister and her husband. "Or at least for the boys to have it?"

"We have considered it, but have not had opportunity to do so." Burwell crossed one ankle over the other as he glanced from me to Nancy.

"I'm afraid I have not felt well enough myself to oversee the recovery period," Nancy said. "Or to chance exposure to the disease."

Indeed, she still wore a wan countenance. Studying her features, I recalled how she helped me with my hair on my wedding day. How keen she'd been about my first presentation. Now to see her so weakened and pale stirred anxiety in my heart. My favorite sister. If I could help her now… I nodded, my thoughts spinning as I considered possibilities. Was there enough time?

"What if I carry them home with me and have them infected under my care?"

Nancy sat up straighter and glanced at her husband. "You would do that for us?"

"Certainly. I do not anticipate George's summons until the end of December at the earliest. Besides, the boys will benefit from the excursion and change of scenery and I'll enjoy having them liven up Mount Vernon."

And so it was decided that I'd take them home with me along with one of their neighbors, Samuel Claiborne, who also wanted to be inoculated. The good doctor infected them and they spent three weeks recovering under my watchful eye. On the eighteenth of November, I wrote a letter to Nancy expressing my pleasure that she had received the old gelding I had sent down to her for her daily riding and telling her of the departure of her sons and neighbor for Eltham, having not had but a small amount of symptoms to manage. The result being they no longer had to worry about contracting the disease.

After the youths left, though, the house seemed too quiet. Well, until Jacky brought Nelly home in December so I could look after her before the baby made its appearance. But I hadn't expected her to be so pale.

"Oh Nelly, dear. Let's get you up to your room."

"I am very tired, Mama." She look at me with red-rimmed eyes from an alabaster face.

"Come, my sweet, I'll help you feel strong again in no time." I walked with her, bracing her with an arm around her waist, up the stairs to the bedchamber prepared for her and Jacky's use.

While we were busily settling her in, I heard the distant sound of the rapid approach of hooves. Leaving Nelly to Jacky's tender care, I returned downstairs to see what news had arrived.

Breechy brought me a crumpled letter. I opened it and saw the missive came from Burwell's pen. I began reading, anticipating word of the boys' safe arrival at Eltham. I skimmed the contents and then nearly dropped the letter from my icy hands.

Not again. I flung a prayer to heaven for strength. My beautiful, loving sister Nancy had died the day before after a sudden bad turn to her already shaky health. My favorite sister, my closest confidante, no longer lived. My beloved friend. Tears flooded my cheeks. Oh, how hard to even think of her passing on to heaven. For surely, her sweet and kind person would be sitting with our loving God. Grief again weighed upon me. I truly understood the old saying of grieving to ones guts.

For two days I moved through my days like an automaton, a handkerchief in hand to dry the sudden bouts of tears that flowed without warning or intention down my cheeks. Nelly's presence, even though ill herself, comforted me in this desperately unhappy time. I wrote to Burwell to send my condolences and inform him I would not be able to visit until after Nelly was brought to bed and again well. Time seemed to stand still. It did not help that my beloved husband was so very far away.

Nelly anxiously awaited the day of her delivering. Finally, on New Year's Eve, she delivered a baby girl. The sounds of running feet up and down stairs with hot water and sheeting soon were replaced with the first lusty cries of a new babe.

"Will you name her now or wait?" I cuddled the wee thing as she lay with her eyes closed, sleeping after her first feeding.

"We've chosen a name. Martha Parke Custis. Or Patty as a pet name."

"She's precious." I held the wee thing in my arms, rejoicing along with the girl's parents who watched with loving smiles. The choice proved flattering, to have a namesake of my own.

Another wee babe to cuddle and love. My sadness abated somewhat when I held her, recognizing the circle of birth and death constituting life.

As the new year loomed hours away, I pondered the highs and lows of living. From the successes of the army to defeats.

From birthing of a new baby to the death of a loving sister. What would happen next? With good fortune, I'd live to see America freed from tyranny. I'd live to see my husband return to his beloved home, a place he had not set foot on since the fighting began. I'd live to see this little Patty grow up and start her own family. Or would I?

---

*Valley Forge, Pennsylvania – 1778*

Snow blanketed the ground, making it difficult for the coach to traverse the roads. At forty-six years of age, I dreaded the journey itself though never the destination. Nothing would prevent me from reaching the winter camp. I'd hire a sleigh if the wheels couldn't carry me to George through snow. I was cold, right through to my deepest center despite my heavy cloak and the once-hot brick at my feet. As in previous trips, the jouncing of the conveyance made my bones ache and complain, but I was determined to hold onto a positive attitude. After all, soon I'd be exactly where I wanted to be.

The aide-de-camp met my carriage outside of Philadelphia and led my little party out into the countryside to what was known as the Valley. Dressed in its winter attire of white, the view was charming and quaint. Small farms and villages dotted the landscape, the residents going about their lives as though the city nearby was not occupied by the enemy.

When the coach pulled into camp, the soldiers cheered and clapped, waving madly at me as I rolled past them and stopped at the Potts house by a creek. Dread made me sigh deeply. I could only hope there would be enough room in the tiny stone house for everyone in my party, what with the servants and maids. I was handed down from the vehicle by the postilion as George emerged from the house. He greeted me with a quick kiss and a matching embrace that warmed me to my toes. After so long apart, we couldn't greet each other more chastely. How I loved my husband! No one else understood me as surely as he did. No one else could love me as deeply and honestly. I had every intention to demonstrate my love and dedication to him.

Several generals and other men gathered behind George. I recognized Clement Biddle, Henry Knox, and Nathaniel Greene, each well respected and liked by my husband for their unwavering support of the cause. I wondered where their wives might be, but I'd find out after the formal greetings were exchanged.

A somber young man in a suit and tricorne greeted me. "Welcome, Lady Washington. I am one of the delegates from the committee formed in Congress to judge the true nature of the conditions in camp."

Apparently, Congress doubted George had stated the dire situation with accuracy when he'd written that the army needed help or would be forced to "starve, dissolve, or disperse." Delegates from Massachusetts, New Hampshire, Virginia, New York, and Pennsylvania welcomed me into camp.

"We've been here for the last week and have already begun to make changes to correct the deficiencies in both the supply chain and the military establishment."

"Will you address the seemingly arbitrary promotions among the officers?" From what George had told me, the changes couldn't be implemented fast enough as many had already submitted their resignations.

"Yes, we will. For now, we shall leave you to the tender care of General Washington."

I soon learned just how desperate the circumstances had become.

I set up the sewing circle as soon as possible, and before long the ladies in camp were knitting socks and sewing shirts for the men. I was glad of Caty Greene's pleasant company as well as that of Lucy Knox and Rebecca Biddle. The other generals' wives cheered me and we got along well. Little two-year-old Thomas Biddle and sweet two-year-old Lucy Knox played together on the floor while we talked. Together, we stitched and darned and chatted about everything under the sky. Including the state of affairs surrounding the status of the war. The tension in camp seemed like waiting for a thunderstorm to hit, an urgency and an expectation hovering over the camp.

"The soldiers wear rags if they have them." Lucy shook her head as she gazed at her daughter. "Their situation is deplorable."

"Indeed, I hear shoes are a luxury for many." Caty worked on knitting a pair of thick socks. "The cost to buy a pair in a nearby town is said to be equal to a month's pay for a soldier."

"We can't do much about shoes." I shook my head at Caty. "But socks, dry and without holes, are even more prized."

"Perhaps if we can provide more socks, then the disease and illness raging through camp, can be stopped."

"George said it's been awful." Between the hundreds and thousands who died and those men who did not wish to stay in the army, the strength of the army had been lessened to pitiful.

"They need food in order to survive the harsh winter."

"George and the committee raised the idea of Nathaniel becoming the quartermaster, but he is very reluctant to take the position as it would curtail his hopes for his career as a general." Caty sighed and bent her head to her work, long ringlets hugging her neck.

"We'll have to wait and see what he decides." While Nathaniel was out of camp on a foraging mission, I'd bet good money he would think long and hard about his desires versus his duties.

"I hope he returns soon and safely," Caty said quietly, studying the sewing in her hand as though it held the answer as to when he'd be back in camp.

"So much needs to be made better it's hard to know where to begin." I looked at each of my friends. "Maybe if someone could stop the rain?"

"Please, that would be a great help." Rebecca shook her head and laughed.

Shortly after my arrival, it had started to rain and had continued for days. So much water had fallen from the sky that the quartermaster had to build boats to forage for food among the neighboring farms and towns because the roads became impassable.

The evenings ended up being the most fun time of day. After the candles were lit, we'd gather in the largest room on the first floor of the house, the only space adequate for all and yet not big enough by far. Then we'd sing. Oh, how I loved to sing, singing from the song book, *The Bull-Finch*, George had presented to me shortly after we married. The book contained dozens of popular English songs. Everyone who could sing, did so. A very pleasant ending to an often harsh and horrible day. I hoped the soldiers in their huts might hear and have their hearts lightened somewhat from their troubles and strife if only for a few minutes.

George fumed about the lack of proper nutrition, proper clothing, and even proper order within the army. He urged Congress to pressure the states to contribute food and supplies to the army defending them. His strain over the dire state of his men radiated from him like heat from a bread oven. I couldn't alleviate his anxiety but I could present him with a smile and a joke to lighten his mood. My old man understood my aim and gladly played along. But then reality would return.

He also worried about Major General Horatio Gates, who thought himself a greater general and more qualified to be commander-in-chief after claiming the victory over Burgoyne at Saratoga. George knew Major General Benedict Arnold had been instrumental in that success, and had been shot in the leg and was in the hospital in Albany, New York, nursing both his leg and his wounded pride. We also knew Arnold remained bitterly disappointed when Gates, his superior officer, told everyone it was his victory. Indeed, we all desperately hoped the victory itself would convince the French to enter the war as our allies. Their aid, in the form of men, munitions, and money, could not come soon enough.

The committee moved swiftly to institute the changes they could, but several of the decisions and appointments hung over their heads for weeks. George, along with the committee, waited for word from Congress regarding the proposed reforms suggested to them. He'd surveyed his officers and compiled a report suggesting a new organization for the army. Then he'd heard the Board of War, led by those conniving generals Gates and Mifflin, had proposed another organization that separated the quartermaster role in a way that would mean the board would control the supplies to the army. This arrangement worried everyone in camp. We all knew Gates was attempting to maneuver himself into a powerful position. Would Congress allow such a blatant effort to wrest control from George and them? We could only wait and pray.

I did all I could by visiting the men in the hospital, to see to their needs, comforting them any way possible. But even with all the supplies I brought with me, shortages persisted all around. Morale plummeted to a devastating low as a result. George and his officers discussed ways to bolster their attitudes, but the best lift to their spirits would come with full bellies and clothes to wear. Commodities not easy to find in the dead of winter with an enemy army nearby.

But despite the deprivations and the cold, wet winter, the troops had a surprise in store for George on his forty-sixth birthday, a few weeks after my arrival. We heard noises outside and then a banging on the door. George sent an aide to discover the issue.

"Sir, there is a delegation of men wishing to speak to you."

"What about?" George slipped his coat on, preparing to meet the men.

"They wouldn't say, sir."

"Let's find out, then, shall we?"

Once outside, it became apparent a celebration was planned. A band consisting of fifes and drums performed outside of the Potts house, playing several merry tunes in his honor. George was asked if several of the younger officers could perform *Cato* for him, and despite Congress having banned such frivolity during the course of the war, he allowed it hoping the respite would improve morale throughout the camp.

The men escorted me and George to seats positioned at the

front and center of a clearing set up with a space for a stage and several benches for others to sit on to watch the play. As we settled onto the hard chairs, I happened to notice a number of camp followers—wives and children of the soldiers—making their way toward the site of the entertainment. Although they proved a burden on the limited resources available, the women also provided assistance to the men by doing laundry, sewing, and making meals. I fully grasped their need to be with their husbands. Smiling encouragement, I motioned for them to join in the fun. Before many minutes had passed, the actors took their positions and the audience prepared to be delighted.

We all enjoyed the play, which reinforced the idea of virtuous agrarian life over the corrupt and high-minded rulers, like a usurping Caesar. The farce proved all the more enjoyable knowing the main character of Cato corresponded to our Congress and army, and the terrible Caesar the equivalent of George III. The actors did a fine job of entertaining and easing the tension in the audience, if only for the duration of the play.

---

A distinguished Prussian professional soldier arrived in camp at Valley Forge on the twenty-third of February. Relief among the officers simmered in the air as much as celebration and huzzahs. It had been a tense few months from what I'd gathered.

"I'm hopeful that Baron von Steuben will succeed in his mission." George's shoulders settled into their proper place as he watched the man in question near.

We stood on the porch of the little stone house, waiting for the small procession of officers to escort the baron to his new commander to report for duty. Slush and puddles surrounded the headquarters. I pulled my wrap tighter about me to ward off the chill, striving to remain as stoic in the face of discomfort as my husband's example.

"Why is he here?" I glanced up at George, relieved myself at the calm in his eyes.

"He is to establish a plan for drilling the soldiers and shape them into a cohesive fighting force."

"He has his work cut out for him." The tall, elegant officer striding toward me carried an air of competence and confidence. His eyes hinted at a steely resolve as well.

"Yes, but I must believe in his experience and the skills he learned while a general staff member of the Prussian army."

Broad of shoulders, high broad forehead over dark eyes and a strong jaw, the baron impressed me with his entire attitude. Beside the baron, Alexander Hamilton strode in conversation. After several minutes, the group finally mounted the steps to the porch where we stood with others of the generals.

"General Washington, Baron Friedrich Wilhelm von Steuben reporting for duty," Alexander said. "I'm acting as the baron's translator since he does not speak English."

George received the man's salute. "I trust your travels went smoothly and you are ready to begin on the morrow."

The baron listened to Alexander's translation and then nodded. Would to-morrow be soon enough? I hoped the endless marching about to commence would unite the men and relieve their boredom at the same time. The poor men needed something to distract them from the misery in which they lived and worked. Missing their warm loving homes and families, those whose wives hadn't tagged along, could lead many to not reenlist for the new fighting season and thus cripple the army and end our bid for independence. The baron was our best hope to resolve the immediate crisis. The army teetered on the sharp edge of disbanding.

---

Nathaniel had led his foraging expedition back to camp the day before the baron arrived. A few days later, word came from Congress giving the committee authority to appoint the quartermaster at its discretion. His agreement was critical for the future of the army, and my husband's successful completion of his charge as commanding general. Hints and open queries had not convinced him before he departed. Now that he was back, the real persuasion began.

"Nathaniel, please reconsider." Caty studied her husband, doing her utmost to encourage him to accept George's nomination to be the quartermaster of the army.

"I'd prefer to stay with an active command than to lose my rank." Nathaniel's black eyebrows formed into a frown, his dark eyes serious as he glanced around the dinner table.

"You are the best man for the job, my friend." George peered at the general and nodded. "What if you retain your rank?"

Nathaniel inclined his head, considering. "I'd still rather be with my men in pursuit of the enemy. This is a national crisis, one I want a hand in winning for our cause."

"I agree, which is why I want you to be in charge of provisioning the men." George paused to drink from his wine glass. "You have the experience and the moral fortitude, along with the temperament necessary to negotiate on the army's behalf."

Nathaniel sighed and I could see he was beginning to come around to my husband's way of thinking. George could be very effective in getting others to see his point of view. I glanced at Caty and she met my gaze, a smile on her lips and in her eyes. She saw it, too.

"What about my men?" Nathaniel asked. "And fighting the enemy?"

"I will guarantee that you will retain the right to participate in the fighting when the opportunity arises." George rested his hands on the blue cloth-covered table. "Please accept, Nathaniel. We need your experience, education, and military savvy to ensure the men have the equipment and food to even have a chance at success in this great effort."

"Well..." Nathaniel blinked twice, glanced at Caty who nodded with a smile, and then peered at George. "If you're certain, then I will do my utmost to provision the men."

Relief swept through the officers at the table. Help had arrived to stabilize the uncertain and often nonexistent supply chain, and also thwarted General Gates' attempt to take over the very important lifeline of the army. The situation was beginning to look more hopeful. Whatever it took to finish what we started so we could all go home and live in peace. A prospect still very much a distant longing.

———————

I did my best that winter to keep spirits up and ease the plight of so many. Little by little, Greene's efforts paid off and a more or less steady stream of victuals flowed into camp. By establishing a little market across the river, local farmers could peddle their wares for sale to the army and soldiers. As a result, the citizens and soldiers became friendlier toward one another than they had been over the worst part of the season. A relief to everyone.

The first week of May an aide galloped into camp. He came straight to the little stone house in search of George who had just sat down at the breakfast table with me and his staff.

George opened the letter and sat back with a smile on his face. "The Treaty of Alliance was signed by France and the United States back in February."

My husband's relief and joy at the news illuminated his entire being. The staff generals shouted "huzzah" in approval, banging their fists on the table so that the cups of chocolate and coffee jumped on the wooden surface. The ladies clapped and smiled at the most welcome news.

"We need to celebrate this fortunate and timely news." George waved the paper and then laid it on the table with a flourish. "A celebration fitting of the occasion."

And what a grand festival it was! The day began with George pardoning two of his soldiers who had been sentenced to death to show his desire to reclaim rather than punish offenders. The troops marched by brigades to the area known as the Grand Parade ground in the center of the camp. The blasts of musket fire preceded three huzzahs, one each for the King of France, the friendly European powers, and the American states. The officers and George were well pleased by the fine demonstration the soldiers made in their marching and maneuvers on the parade ground, all as a result of the baron's direction and discipline. I was pleased by the fact that I didn't jump with each volley, having slowly grown accustomed to the boom and blast of guns and cannon.

A reception for the officers and their wives followed, where we all rejoiced at having a powerful ally to come to our aid.

"Did you hear? Word has it that the British are preparing to evacuate Philadelphia as a result of the alliance." Nathaniel Greene stood beside his wife, nibbling on a small spice cake.

George shifted his weight to stand square and tall. "They build fortifications to the city as a ruse, to make us believe they're preparing for battle. I'd likely do the same in Howe's position."

"When will they go, that's the main question," Henry Knox said.

"Plan to have your men ready to move with short notice, gentlemen." George glanced down at me, his expression easy and serene. "As well as your wives. We shall be breaking camp before long."

"Very well. I will begin to gather my belongings on the morrow." Would he send me home or ask me to follow the army? I could only wonder how much longer I'd have with George and the other wives I'd grown quite attached to. If he sent me to the plantation, then I would miss their friendship but I also missed my home and family.

With the better weather of spring, more recruits flowed into camp. The strength of the army increased daily; at last count it approached thirteen thousand. Spring also brought more sunshine and warmer temperatures making life in camp bearable again. But it also meant my time with George would be ending ere long as they went back to the fighting campaign.

Over the next couple of weeks, tensions increased as word came that Sir Henry Clinton had replaced General Howe, who had left the city on his merry way back to England. Would the loyalist citizens within the city go with the retreating army under Clinton's command? Or would they disperse into the countryside and quietly await the end of the war? As long as they no longer resided in what would become patriot territory, either option sufficed.

Fighting continued in sporadic attacks by both sides as May dragged on and I continued to prepare to abandon the camp to head home. Daily, I thought about my next steps, but chided myself when I became worried. I'd leave only when my husband wanted me to. Until then, I'd keep doing the things I'd been doing to help in any way I could. Finally, George and his staff had settled on their campaign opening strategy and so George set my departure for the ninth of June. When the day arrived, I bid my husband farewell with a heavy heart but determined to put a good face on it. He kissed my cheek before handing me up into the coach and I set out for home. I hoped, along with so many others, the new alliance with France would make Britain realize its colonies, now states, were lost. That would end the war and George could come home, with good fortune by fall.

# 15

Would we never arrive at winter camp? George had sent for me in November, but the weather had been so fierce I had to postpone leaving until December. Three arduous weeks after leaving Mount Vernon, we finally reached Philadelphia on the twenty-first. The roads had been treacherous with snow and then mud, then frozen ruts with more snow. My coach had left home with seven horses, in the hope of having enough sound horses to accomplish the journey. By the time we'd found our way to the city, the Delaware had frozen over. No matter. No hardship would prevent me from reaching my husband.

Just before Christmas, I arrived in camp. The roads had been barely passable and I shivered in my cloak. George had sent Captain Caleb Gibbs to lead us to headquarters. He joined my entourage in Princeton and within four days of leaving Philadelphia, I was once again at my husband's side. Never had the holidays brought more happiness as we celebrated the New Year of 1780 by the roaring fireplace with singing and a fine Madeira.

"I've attempted to improve the Ford Mansion for our purposes and comforts." George sampled his wine as we chatted by the fire. "But I fear my efforts did not fully meet the need."

"It will suffice for the time, though you're correct in saying it would be better if not so cramped."

On the other side of the cozy parlor, I could hear General Greene and Captain Gibbs engaged in a lively debate on the merits of various breeds of hunting dogs. The friendly debate rising in tone and volume as they argued.

George shook his head slowly, disappointment evident in his expression. "I added the log kitchen and a separate office beside the house, as well as had two rooms upstairs plastered, and restored the well so we'd have fresh water."

"Mrs. Ford agreed to the changes?" I could only image how I'd react to someone moving into Mount Vernon and modifying its design. Nobody best dare such an act without my consent.

"Indeed. Those, and I had to build a new stable to shelter our horses from the harsh winter storms. The army officers, aides, servants, and families will have to sleep wherever they find room."

"Yes, since all eighteen servants, both ours and Theodosia Ford's, will be sleeping in the kitchen." I clasped his hand with a gentle squeeze. "It's temporary. We'll make it work."

I had no idea how long I would stay, but planned to make the most of my time with my old man. The social life started with a whirl, dinners at headquarters as well as invitations to dine at other officers' quarters. I had much news to share with my friends, Caty Greene and Lucy Knox, while we worked on our sewing and knitting.

"Ladies, I'm pleased to tell you some joyful news." Once I had their attention, I continued. "Jacky and Nelly's third daughter, Eleanor Parke Custis, or Nelly, was born last March at Mount Airy. And they've bought their own house outside of Alexandria. They're calling it Abingdon. When I'm home, I see my three granddaughters with pleasing regularity."

"Wonderful tidings indeed." Lucy clapped her hands in delight. "Having family around you is so very important."

"Have you heard anything from your parents?" I doubted she'd ever hear from them again, given their disapproval of her marriage to a patriot. "Or your brother or sister?"

"Not a word." She sighed, her hefty bulk shifting where she sat on the brocaded sofa by the fireplace. "They each made it quite clear they'd have nothing more to do with me, a traitor to the king and all that. I don't care, as I prefer the company of my Harry over theirs."

"I cannot wait to welcome our next baby in a few weeks." Caty set her rocking chair into motion, her hands caressing her bulging stomach. "Walking becomes ever more awkward as the time nears."

"We'll attend you during your lying in, do not fear." I smiled and resumed my sewing. These ladies represented my extended family, much like George considered the men on his staff as his military family. "That's what friends and family are for, after all."

Caty delivered a healthy son the last day of January 1780. They named him Nathanael Ray Greene. Thus we added to the growing number of children living with their parents in camp. Their presence made the camp feel homier and eased my longing to see my grandchildren.

Fortunately, General Greene had established quarters on the village green where the Greene's could reside most comfortably. The Knoxes had settled on a farm outside of town, giving us an excuse to ride out to visit with them on occasion, if the weather permitted. Those occasions provided a much needed release to the tension hovering over the army camp and headquarters in particular. I'd always enjoyed riding horseback and now treasured the jaunts into the country with friends in a well-sprung carriage or phaeton. Excursions that brought us closer together as well.

The rake Alexander Hamilton, despite being indispensable to George, had developed a reputation as a flirt with the ladies. So much so that I'd named the camp tomcat "Hamilton." Every time I called its name the soldier looked up as well, making me chuckle. I wondered if he really understood why I'd chosen to name the cat as I did. Probably. Alexander most definitely prowled about looking for pretty females to sniff around. Until he met his match when the beautiful young Elizabeth Schuyler, daughter of Philip Schuyler, arrived at camp. Betsy's father was an admirer of George, so she had come to call upon him on her father's behalf. Hamilton had been sermonizing on the ideal qualities of a wife until he laid eyes on Betsy. Enthralled by her graces and wit, he became besotted. It wasn't long before the couple determined a wedding date. I approved, as Betsy seemed to have taken him in hand and settled him down. The tomcat no longer proved funny as a result, but it wasn't long before it ran off and found another home.

One evening, George and I lingered over our supper, discussing the contents of the latest newspaper. He'd grown increasingly agitated over one topic in particular. Or perhaps frustrated was a better characterization of his temperament.

"What is the matter?" I asked, laying my linen napkin beside my plate.

"Another runaway slave to be tracked down and dragged back to their owner. It's maddening." George rattled the paper in his hand as if he'd like to shake someone into action. "Poor people. I do wish there was some way to be rid of slaves and slavery once and for all."

George had expressed discontent with the institution of slavery as a labor force. Over the past few years, he'd grumbled about it, but what was there to do?

"Unless Virginia passes legislation to enforce a gradual abolition, we have no recourse, do we?"

"It's vexing to be forced to continue with an institution so repugnant to me." George raised his eyes to meet mine. "If our friend, Joseph Reed, as president of the Pennsylvania supreme executive council, cannot do anything to end it, what chance do we have in Virginia?"

"It will be a difficult transition no matter how it's accomplished. My dower slaves are tied to our children's inheritance, and so we can't free them without reimbursing the estate for their value."

"Exactly. If not for the financial burden freeing them would cause to the estate, to you, and ultimately our children, I would gladly emancipate my slaves."

"At least we can find comfort in the fact that we treat all of our servants well, providing medical attention when they become ill, and clothing and food adequate to their needs." All of my life I had worked to make sure all of my family—free and slave alike—remained hale and hearty to the best of my ability. We may have disciplined the servants a bit differently than our children but we did so with equal results in mind: to teach them what their boundaries were and what was expected of them to be decent, hard-working people. "What more could we have done?"

"Yes, my dear, but I desire nothing more than to have another option, the one my friend endorses."

The plantation, let alone a large household such as ours, could not function efficiently without the many hands of our servants. We couldn't afford to hire so many people, but we did provide them with food, shelter, and clothing. I could see why my husband was vexed, but couldn't imagine how to solve the dilemma. With a troubled heart, I wondered what he'd do, and indeed what I'd have to do, to maintain our way of life if we freed the slaves.

------

Spring finally arrived, bringing its warmer temperatures and flowers, but also rain. Still, there was no sign of the army starting the campaign. George seemed miserable, but I couldn't determine the cause for why he worried so. I suspected he meant to protect me from some harsh truth or deceit. I assumed it had a lot to do with having to order several soldiers hanged for mutiny as a result of not being paid for their service, as well as the astounding capture of Charles Town, South Carolina, by the British in May. Either would produce an infinite anxiety in my husband. I didn't press the matter. I was there to listen when he wanted me to. But I did pay more attention, seeking out my own answers.

Dinner one afternoon in May proved a delightful relief to the many burdens facing my husband and his men. Young Marquis de Lafayette, my husband's surrogate son, strode into the room and greeted everyone with a pleased smile. His full named was a mouthful: Marie-Joseph Paul Yves Roch Gilbert du Motier. He and George had bonded immediately and I knew his arrival was a welcome sight to my husband, as it was for me. The young man was dedicated to my old man.

"Gentlemen, I bring good news." Lafayette addressed each of the men surrounding the table in his smooth voice with a strong accent. At least to my ears, his speech sounded very different from the slow drawl of my compatriots. "The French fleet is on its way, along with the promise of money to pay the troops."

"Indeed?" George waved him to a chair as a smile bloomed on his mouth.

Lafayette took a seat and looked at each person listening attentively to his announcement. "Arms, ammunition, and a French army under the leadership of Comte de Rochambeau are sailing our way."

"Fantastic news." George sipped from his glass and studied his men. "How long until we should expect them?"

Lafayette accepted a glass of wine from the servant and then took a long drink before responding. "Two months until the ships arrive."

Two months? My goodness. Surely the American army could hold on until then. Despite all the deprivations of the past months. At least, I prayed they could.

General Mifflin walked into the dining room. "I've just heard word that Bernardo de Balvez led his Spanish troops to capture Mobile. So the British army in the Gulf of Mexico has another front to their fighting, distracting them from the states."

"More welcome news." George nodded, a small smile indicating his pleasure. "Although no formal alliance exists between America and the Spanish, I accept their efforts with pleasure."

When my old man took off to deal with the British in Connecticut in June, he left me at camp with my guards. I tried to have faith he would return to me, healthy and whole. He moved among so many dangers, from disease to rifles to cannon when he went out into the field. He was considered bullet proof after emerging unscathed in so many previous battles. Since I was tucked inside a stone house for the most part, I didn't worry for my own safety until one day young Captain John Steele paid me a visit.

"Lady Washington, I've heard a rumor an attack is planned on your person at this place." Captain Steele in his neatly mended uniform showed no signs of stress with his pronouncement, standing squarely on both legs but in a relaxed stance.

"Should I be concerned?" I raised my brows as I waited for his response. Hoping for reassurance.

"We have the means to keep you safe, Madam." He doffed his tricorne and smiled. "I assure you that we will protect you without fail."

"I'm certain my husband would not have placed you in charge if he could not trust you."

So I waited for the troops and my husband to return to town, praying for their success and safety. I busied myself with my usual activities, but a feeling of uselessness pervaded my breast. Surely women could do more to help the army win the war. I needed to feel like what I did mattered. But what?

———————

My prayers were answered the second week of the month. Elated with the success of their mission, the men returned to Morristown. I sensed my departure loomed on the horizon, so began to gather my belongings. I'd been away from home a very long time, and desired to return there as soon as convenient for George. My weariness left me a bit depressed. I departed camp on the nineteenth of June, having decided to boost my own morale with a visit to the Reeds for a while in Philadelphia. Esther and Joseph were such good friends, and I wished to see them before returning home. After all, we had no way of knowing when we'd see each other again.

I looked forward to arriving at their house with all the children running about. They had five of six living: Martha the oldest at nine, Joseph, Esther, Dennis, and George Washington Reed who was born in May. Poor little eighteen-month-old Theodosia had succumbed to the smallpox the year before. Such a tragic time in the Reeds' lives, Esther having been forced to flee with her family to Flemington, New Jersey, during the British occupation of Philadelphia. We had commiserated via letters on the anxiety and difficulty of being separated from our husbands during the fighting season as well as on the death of her daughter. We had both waited eagerly for the winter to arrive in order to be reunited with our men.

I arrived at the Reed house on the twenty-first of June, welcomed with open arms. Esther seemed weary but otherwise in fine health. They'd reserved the same room I had stayed in while recovering from the inoculation years earlier. About a week later, we joined a group of their friends and went to the Delaware. Boarding barges, we floated on the river for several hours.

"Look, Martha." Esther pointed at the wharves we passed. "The city is honoring your visit by draping the wharves and docks with bunting. Isn't it grand?"

I had noticed the colorful drapes, yards and yards of it, but had not realized who they feted. "I'm humbled by their recognition. It's so much more than I deserve."

Joseph shook his head. "You are the honored general's wife and deserve every bit of respect we can muster. Without you, he'd not be the great man he is."

"I wish I could do something more. I was thinking just the other week, ladies like us should find a way to help the army win this terrible war." I looked at Esther as I spoke, hoping she'd have an idea. "I sit around feeling rather useless when I'm not knitting or rolling bandages. Surely there's something?"

She smiled and lifted both brows for a moment. "I've been thinking the same thing. What if we raised money to give to the troops, a bit of spending money they can use to buy what they need?"

"To improve morale?" I sat up straighter and bobbed my head. "That's a fine idea. I'd be pleased to contribute to the cause. The men, fighting so bravely with so little, need and deserve our support."

We discussed possible ways to raise the money as we floated back to the wharf where we'd boarded. Immediately upon arriving back at the house, we started writing letters to our friends, announcing the Ladies of Philadelphia and the objective of the group. I wrote to Martha Jefferson, inviting her to participate with me, and asking her to invite others to contribute to the cause.

I stayed with my friends for another week, before deciding to head for home. I didn't set foot on Mount Vernon until the fourteenth of July, and never had I been so glad to be home. Soon a letter arrived from Esther informing me she and my old man had decided the Ladies of Philadelphia would use the three hundred thousand dollars continental—or about seventy-five hundred dollars specie—that had been raised to buy coarse linen and make shirts for the men. Apparently, George had been concerned some of the men would buy liquor instead of the necessary clothing. Her news pleased me, as I had assisted the army in my own way.

I sorely hoped my intention of leaving the plantation in the autumn before the frost set in would meet with approval from George. Traveling when the roads stood dry and hard would be much more pleasant than in the cold and snow like I experienced last time.

Then I received word from George of Benedict Arnold's betrayal, of consorting with the British to inform the enemy of our army's movements. I could well imagine George felt devastated by the man's actions. Had Benedict expected to seek revenge for being slighted by the Congress for his actions at Saratoga? He'd remained bitter over the neglect of his efforts to effect the success. George had presented him in May of '78 with a set of French epaulettes and sword knots in recognition of Benedict's courage and conduct. He'd even given Benedict command of the forces that moved into Philadelphia after the British evacuated, and then appointed him commander of West Point. Then to be repaid by Arnold's treason?

The resulting risk to George personally and to the American cause meant I could not return to camp as I'd hoped. I prepared to be summoned to my husband's side. How much longer would the war continue? How many more long journeys lay before me? I could only hope the Parliament would soon realize they'd not win back the Americans. Only then would peace be restored and my old man could come home.

---

*New Windsor, New York – 1781*

I laid in my bed, a light cover keeping me warm enough, wondering whether the bilious fever and jaundice I suffered would end me. The tiny William Ellison House where headquarters had been established provided little comfort in its cramped interior. Not a place where I'd ever thought I'd die. Yet, at that moment, it seemed a distinct possibility. I didn't want to die, of course. Not really. But I'd been ill for weeks and didn't know how much longer I could tolerate the illness. I had intended to leave camp for home in May, but I fell ill around the twenty-first while George was away in Connecticut.

The doctor told me the abdominal pain searing through me was likely caused by a stone in my gall bladder. The biliousness and yellowing of my skin did nothing to make the strain and discomfort more bearable. Five long weeks dragged past with me fearing for my life.

George had agonized about acquiring the proper medications to ease my suffering, writing the last day of May to both Jacky and Lund to see what they could do to assist. Unfortunately, those letters along with a few others from George were intercepted. How did I know? Because a letter arrived on the twenty-first of June, dated the fifteenth, from Mrs. Martha Mortier.

She not only baldly stated that his letter had been intercepted. She had the audacity to send a gift of lemons, limes, oranges, pineapples, sweetmeats, tarmarind seeds, capillaire to make a medicinal syrup from maiden hair fern, orgeat to make another syrup, and two pounds of Hyson green tea from China. A bribe or war prize. Either way, we could not accept it. Fortunately, I had recovered my health by then so could with all honesty refuse it as no longer needed. Or wanted, but that was another matter.

"The vast amount of delicacies must have cost a small fortune, what with the outrageous inflation for even common articles." I could see George's concern in the set of his jaw and the anger in his eyes.

As the war had dragged on, his health had become more my concern. He brushed aside my worries, but I have eyes and could see the subtle changes. While we both wanted to be safely at home on our beloved plantation, his duty was to his role as commander of the army. Mine was to be by his side to support him and care for him through good and bad, sickness and health.

"I cannot tolerate this blatant attempt to trick me or any one on my staff to accept favors from the enemy." George paced the office, rage pouring from him in waves. He stopped suddenly and glared at his staff member, standing rigidly at attention awaiting orders. "Major General Robert Howe, you will thwart any thing and any one from landing under such a flag of truce. I shall reject the items as politely as I can. I shall send a note thanking Mrs. Mortier but telling her you, my dear Patsy, have recovered and thus no longer need such assistance."

"That is a wise plan." In truth, while the whisper of temptation to enjoy the fruit existed for two heart beats, I'd never have succumbed.

The reason for George's tirade stemmed from learning Lund, back home at Mount Vernon, had given refreshments to the enemy in April. Lund's desperate measures proved misguided. The British had sailed up the Potomac, threatening to burn our beloved home to the ground. In order to save it, he'd offered food and drink on board the ship. He'd dared to ask for the surrender of some of our Negroes, asking a favor from the enemy! I had rarely seen my old man so livid and embarrassed in the twenty-two years we'd been married. He sent a reprimand to Lund, telling him of his displeasure with Lund's ill-judged actions. We both feared that unhappy consequences and animadversion of the General would result. I hoped no one would criticize him, not after all our sacrifices in the cause, but we'd experienced naysayers already. Then to add to that outrage his concern for my welfare, and he proved troubled indeed.

Later that afternoon, I received a letter from Jacky and sat down to read it. Caty found me reading by the light of a candle.

"What news, my friend?" Caty settled on a brocaded sofa near the fireplace.

I looked over at her, a happy smile on my face and in my heart. "Nelly delivered another baby in April. They christened him George Washington Parke Custis, and elected to nickname him Wash." Thus, I longed to set off for home to see my new grandson. My only grandson. "I miss all of my grandchildren, more each time I leave home."

"It won't be long before they break camp and we will all be on our way."

"Yes, that is true. I shall be glad to make the journey." Even as the words left my mouth, I knew them for the lie they were. I'd much prefer to stay with my husband but he wanted me away during the fighting season. Already the underlying tension in camp mounted along with the excitement of the men to be back in action instead of drilling and the endless waiting.

The years of travel had begun to wear on me, and I sincerely hoped for peace to return so we could retire to the quiet of Mount Vernon. With George preparing to force the issue at New

York, trying to wrest the city from British control, I had no other choice but to step up into my coach, heading for Virginia.

---

*Mount Vernon – 1781*

In September, I received a much-longed-for letter. George was marching his troops south and would arrive soon. He had not stepped foot home since the fighting began six years earlier. Had only heard reports of the many changes wrought to the mansion and surrounding grounds. Had not seen his new grandchildren even. I could only imagine his elation at coming home at last. I couldn't wait to see him in the flesh and judge for myself his health and state of mind.

He arrived on the ninth, late in the afternoon, along with two aides. He galloped up to the front door on Nelson, a beautiful chestnut stallion with white face and legs. He dismounted with fluid grace, as I hurried down the steps to greet him. Behind me, Jacky carried little Wash, and Nelly ushered their other children out to meet their grandfather for the first time. What a joyous reunion indeed! Much hugging and laughter followed as the children were introduced to their towering relative. Then George introduced his aides before turning back to address me.

"I'm pleased to see you in fine health." George clasped my hands, their warmth seeping through his gloves. "We shan't be able to stay but a few days, long enough for me to arrange affairs in Yorktown to our liking."

"You must be weary from your ride. Let's go in for refreshments." I had previously arranged for beds to be prepared for our guests as well as warm water supplied to remove the dust from their journey before supper. "Then tell me what has brought you home at last."

After everyone had chance to settle in, we gathered in the dining room for some light fare and wine. The conversation inevitably turned to the reason for why the army had marched to Virginia. General Cornwallis occupied Yorktown. The French fleet under de Grasse headed toward the beleaguered area, and the Americans intended to meet them there and trap Cornwallis. The generals around the table debated approaches and considerations. The more they talked, the more intently my son listened.

I darted a glance at Nelly. She stared at her husband, brows drawn together. She thought the same as I. My heart sank as a growing fear choked me. He wouldn't. He had a wife and four young children. *Please God, no.*

"Patsy, you can expect Mrs. Knox to arrive in a day or so," George said. "Her coach was following the army as usual, but I've recommended her to be under your sweet hospitality until the fighting is over."

"As Lucy is in a delicate condition, I'm pleased you invited her to stay with me." I nodded, happiness at seeing my friend again mixing with the anxiety of my thoughts. "I'll be grateful for her company."

In fact, she arrived the next day and I welcomed her with a warm embrace. As much of one as I could give her ample frame, at least. Great with child, she filled the house with life. Her buoyant attitude and determined cheerfulness helped soften my hardest worries. But they stayed in the back of my mind, stewing and swirling like a whirlpool in a lake.

The third day of George's surprise visit, as he prepared to rejoin his army, my worst fears came to pass. While standing in the front hall, my son cornered my husband with a serious expression and an erect posture he rarely assumed. Nelly had tears on her cheeks when she joined me beside my old man. She clutched my hand.

"Papa, I wish to accompany you to Yorktown." Jacky's eyes glittered with intensity. "I want to be there when you defeat Cornwallis."

I gasped, even though I had suspected the direction of his thoughts over the last several days. I remained silent with an effort. Although I disapproved, it was not my decision to make. My son was a man grown and capable of making his own choices. That did not mean I had to like it. I studied my husband's equally serious countenance, praying silently he'd deny my son's request.

George blinked twice as he studied Jacky's earnest expression. "If you'd care to be an observer, you may. I do not have need of another aide at this time, but I'd value your company."

Lucy stepped into the hall, her tentative smile revealing she'd heard the exchange from the parlor where she'd been resting. Nelly continued to cry, silent and bereft, her grasp painful to my fingers. My only child desired to accompany the army as they faced their most formidable foe. Although the generals had devised a nearly infallible plan to capture the British at Yorktown, danger abounded at every turn. What did Jacky know of strategy and fighting? Nothing that I was aware of. Yet he insisted on being present. I felt like crying as well but sniffed back the tears. He'd made his choice and my opinion wouldn't sway him.

They left the next day, a significant group of men and horses to gallop back to the army. I kept doing my daily tasks and chores, but my mind drifted to the imminent fight. Would they succeed? Would a victory in Yorktown end this awful war and bring George home for good?

Lucy and Nelly kept me from panicking over Jacky's new adventure. But we were all stricken with fear for him. He'd never once hinted at an interest in anything regarding the military and fighting. Why the sudden desire to be in the thick of it? He had no experience, no skills in surviving in such harsh conditions. My thoughts spun in circles trying to understand, and failing.

Weeks dragged by. George wrote to tell me they'd laid siege to Yorktown on the twenty-eighth of September. The American and French forces had indeed encircled Cornwallis' force and then waited for him to capitulate. But what of my son? I had not heard a line from him in several weeks and since he'd been somewhat ill before he left, I feared for his health and safety.

A week later, a messenger galloped in with a letter from my husband. Lund carried it to me where I sat with Nelly and Lucy in the small parlor, working on our sewing. I opened the paper and read the flowing script. Cornwallis had surrendered and the siege ended in victory. On the tails of that wonderful news followed a more concerning note.

"Oh my goodness." I glanced up at Nelly. My concern reflected in her frown. "Jacky has camp fever. He's at Eltham to recover. George says not to worry as it's not too serious."

"He'd not been well before he left." Nelly laid her stitching on her lap. "But his last letter said he was feeling better."

"He'll be fine under the care of his uncle and grandmother." Lucy pulled her needle through the fabric and snugged the length of thread into a precise stitch. "You must believe they will attend him to ensure he recovers."

"Yes, Nelly. Have faith." I tried to follow my own advice, but my instincts remained uneasy. "Burwell will keep us informed of Jacky's recovery."

I was right in that Burwell would ensure we knew of Jacky's progress. Within a few days a messenger again arrived, but this time with an urgent summons to go to Eltham. Jacky's condition deteriorated with each day. Frantic, Nelly and I gathered a few essentials and flew in the coach to Eltham. The horses couldn't drag us fast enough to my only surviving son's sickbed.

When we arrived, Burwell hurried us into the house. Jacky laid in bed, his skin covered in red bumps and splotches. He turned his head from one side to the other, babbling nonsense. I rushed to him, laid a hand on his head. My poor son had a raging fever. Dr. James Craik strode into the bedchamber and stopped at my side. Tentative relief filled me at his presence. Surely, he would save my son.

"How does he fare?" I gazed at the doctor, hope in my soul.

"His condition continues to fail." He shook his head, as though perplexed as to what to do. "I've done everything I can think of. I've bled him, used purges and blisters."

I laid a hand on Dr. Craik's arm, pleading with him to do something to rid my son of the camp fever. "Please, doctor."

"I have done all in my power. Now it is up to God and his mercy."

Nelly cried out and nearly collapsed to see her husband so ill. I went to her, wrapped an arm around her waist to support her as I led her to a chair. She sank onto it, her eyes never leaving Jacky.

Burwell crossed the room to stand with me. "I've sent word to the General to come as soon as he can. I'm sure he's extremely busy with all that needs to be done in Yorktown to exchange prisoners, and tend to the wounded and dead. But I feel he should be here."

I nodded, swallowing to contain my rising distress. My only child lay dying and only God could save him. The same God who hadn't saved my other children. I held out little faith he would intervene on my son's behalf. The next few days dragged by, filled with more attempts from Dr. Craik to bleed or purge Jacky back to health.

On the fifth of November, George, with Billy Lee at his side, rode up at Eltham. I ran out to meet him, desperate for his strength and comfort.

"Patsy, what are you doing here?" He held me in his embrace as I tucked my head to his chest, fighting the tears threatening to cascade down my face.

"Jacky...he's d-dying. I cannot stand it. Not again." Tears pressed for release but I blinked them back. I didn't want to give in to the grief welling up inside my gut and breast, choking me.

"What? I thought he'd be well by now." He squeezed my shoulders, lending me some of his fortitude and support. His dark eyes reflected both his surprise and concern. "Take me to him."

Pushing away from him, I quickly led him to our son's bedchamber. George hesitated at the door, a slight pause, before striding over to Jacky. Nelly rose from where she'd been sitting beside him, and stepped back to let George approach. He knelt beside the bed, and I stood near him, as my old man lifted the younger man's hand and held it to his chest.

"Jack, I'm here. I would have come sooner if I'd known."

Jacky met George's eyes, then closed his own. "I'm glad you've come. I love you, Papa. Please, I beg of you, take care of my family for me."

Tears fell with his words. With the horrible realization my son waited for his own death. How could it be God's will to take my son weeks before his twenty-seventh birthday? A loving man who cared so much for his wife and four young children. The fourth of my children to die. To be buried by his parents. My vision blurred and I turned away so he wouldn't see my tears.

"Mama? I love you. Don't cry for me. It's my time." He paused to cough, and then struggled to clear his throat. "Promise me to care for my family."

Another sob ripped from my throat at his request. I swiped my cheeks, trying to dry them before I turned around. Struggling for a calm acceptance that wouldn't come. I swallowed, delaying my response. Fighting for understanding as the tears continued to leak down my cheeks. I moved to lay my hand on the joined hands of son and father. "Of course, son. You know we will look out for them."

"Thank you..." He coughed again, spluttered, then his head fell back and his eyes closed.

"Jacky?" Nelly hurried to the other side of the bed. "Jacky!"

Sobs tore through my chest to burst from my mouth. The room spun, dark spots flashing in the maelstrom of grief convulsing my body. George turned and lifted me, carried me away from the sight but not the memory. Never the memory of my beautiful, intelligent son.

# 16

The coach trundled me and Nelly home, leaving my dear Jacky buried in the family graveyard at Eltham. The whole experience of being at what used to be one of my favorite places seemed surreal. Not only had the joy surrounding my sister Nancy's life been shuttered by her death, now my son lay near her, six feet underground. Why? Nobody seemed to have an answer to that question. Not even God. I had no more tears to cry, drained of everything except my sorrow.

"I hope George has a nice visit with his mother before he joins us at home." I peeked out the curtained window at the scenery as we passed through the countryside. The wintry landscape with barren trees and patches of snow on the rolling hills slid past. We'd left the houses and buildings of Fredericksburg behind many hours ago. The brick at my feet had cooled, leaving me chilled. I hoped we'd arrive home soon.

"How often does he visit with her?" Nelly numbly sat beside me, trying to put on a brave face at her sudden widowhood. Yet lines of tension and swollen eyes belied the effort.

"He's not seen her since before the war started, so it's good for him to take a day to spend with her before we go to the

Congress in Philadelphia." Inwardly I cringed at the stoic words, spoken as a mask of the internal pain ricocheting through me. Instead of staying home, alone with my grief, I'd chosen to go north with George as soon as possible. We'd rarely had the opportunity to travel together for what he called my "annual visit." Perhaps being away from home would help my sorrow to ease, but I had my doubts.

Finally back at Mount Vernon, Nelly and I clambered from the relative warmth of the carriage. We hurried inside and slipped off our heavy cloaks, handing them to Breechy to hang. Lund met us in the wide passage as we tugged off our gloves, a sad smile drooping his features.

"I'm so sorry for your loss, Mrs. Washington." He hesitated, halfway between offering a consoling embrace and keeping his distance.

Impatient with his uncertainty, I slapped my gloves against my palm, striving to be stalwart and not allow myself to breakdown in front of the man. "Lund, you can expect little Nelly and Wash to come live with us before ere long in order to ease Nelly's burden. The older two will remain at their home to help their mother. And please see that the servants ready my things for the trip north. George will be along in a day or so and then we will depart."

"Yes, Martha. I will see to it at once." He regarded me for a long moment, mouth falling slightly open before he pressed his lips together, and then turned to do as I'd asked.

I'm assuming he saw something in my expression that suggested I was in no mood to be questioned. Smart man.

Jacky had been a loving husband and father, but had no head for business. After some persuasion, my younger brother Bat agreed to manage the estate for Nelly, much to everyone's relief. George couldn't handle it during the war times. He had enough to do as the commander-in-chief.

George arrived home in a flurry and stayed but a week before we set off in the coach-and-six for Philadelphia. He was anxious to encourage Congress to keep to their convictions after the stunning victory at Yorktown. All along our way, the people cheered and celebrated our passing, often detaining us for a meal or a drink in our honor. While the attention proved gratifying and temporarily distracting, the delay ratcheted the urgency simmering inside us both. At long last, we arrived at the Reed's house and eagerly settled into the familiar lodgings with our dear friends.

We stayed in town for several months. George frequented the Congress, working to arrange a summer campaign to continue the fight, to force the British out of New York and Charles Town. To end the war even as peace negotiations had begun in earnest in France. While my husband took care of business, I passed the time with friends, reminiscing about my children and shopping in the fine stores. I purchased a few sundry items to send home to Nelly and the children, trinkets to perhaps bring a smile to their sad faces.

Many evenings we went out to a ball or a play, or some other entertainment held in George's honor. The parties of pleasure ran together, one much like the next. I attended but did not enjoy the revelry as much as in years past. I preferred the quiet evenings at the Reed's with my husband at my side. Those evenings gave me the most pleasure of all. I longed to return to Mount Vernon and stay there with my husband in peace. That elusive dream had flitted out of reach for far too long for either of our liking. But duty before desire unless they were one and the same. I could only shake my head at that concept. It was rare indeed to have the two coincide. How much longer before we could retire to our home for good?

————————

On the twenty-second of March, we left the city to travel to the army camp at Newburgh, New York. The trip took nine long, weary days. We were met by a military escort consisting of an officer, a sergeant, and twelve dragoons, which led us to the new headquarters set up in the Hasbrouck House. The small fieldstone farmhouse welcomed us with its pleasant situation overlooking the Hudson, but my heart quailed at the cramped accommodations.

I meandered through the building, inspecting and inventorying what was to be my home for the next several months. The furniture proved adequate if a touch shabby.

"This is the dining room." George's terse tone suggested his disapproval of the space.

Looking around, it seemed nice enough. The largest room in the house I'd seen. A good sized table and several chairs. The oddest thing about the room was that it had seven doors and only one window. Who designed this place?

In one corner, a cot leaned against the wall. I pointed to the anomaly. "Why is there a cot in here?"

"So someone has a place to sleep at night." He waved a hand in front of his nose. "I'll have someone fix that smelly, smoking fireplace posthaste."

George Augustine Washington, the eldest son of George's brother Charles, strode into the room. He was here as one of George's aides-de-camp. The poor man exhibited signs of having some illness. Pale and frail.

"Are you well?" I peered closely at the sheen of perspiration on his forehead, the tired lines between his eyes.

He gripped the back of a chair. "No, I'm not feeling well at all."

I went to him, placed a hand on his forehead. "You have a fever."

"And an intense pain in my breast." He grimaced as he glanced at George. "I'm sorry to be of so little use to you, sir."

"One cannot help others when ill, so your first concern should be to recover your health." He gripped the younger man's shoulders and spun him slowly to face the door he'd come through. "Go on with you."

"Yes, sir." He turned and made his way weakly from the room, presumably to seek out his bed.

George Augustine's work suffered from his frequent illness. I worried for his health with increasing concern over the next few months. Months of letters to and from Congress. Of trying to remain patient and supportive as the mundane matters of running an army stretched out interminably while George hoped daily for the peace treaty to be signed. We wanted to go home. But he couldn't disband the army and resign his commission until it had been signed and ratified by Congress. So we waited. My visit to camp proved rather uneventful considering the situation. But I did what I knew I had to for my husband's peace of mind if nothing else. At least there weren't any major battles to contend with, a few skirmishes here and there but nothing that involved a large part of the army.

July arrived, hot and dusty, and so did the time for my departure. Not ours, but mine alone. I was not happy but I couldn't change the situation either. Standing in the privacy of our bedchamber, we said our emotional farewells. A stubborn tear leaked from my eye, and I wiped it away.

"Oh, George, I do not wish to be parted from you."

"I hope to join you at home before long." George pressed a kiss to my lips, then regarded me with a slightly troubled expression. "But you must go on home without me because the little ones need your guidance and Lund has his hands full with the many renovations continuing on the mansion-house."

I gazed up at my darling knowing he was right to a point. "I agree the children will benefit from my presence, but Lund is pretty much on his own."

George clasped my hands to his rumbling chest as he chuckled. "Be kind to my cousin. For my sake if none other."

"Only for you, my dear." Little did he realize how much I had to work to keep patience with the man. "As long as he stays out of my way, he'll do fine."

After I arrived in Virginia, the never-ending presence of guests and visitors who came and went in a steady stream prevented me from becoming lonely. I was grateful for the distraction. Tending to their needs kept me from feeling bereft without my husband nearby. He wrote to me, of course, grumbling about the lack of troops to enable a summer campaign and the resulting boredom. The more he talked about how little they had to do while waiting for the treaty to be negotiated and then ratified, the more I clearly I saw he'd not make it home as he'd hoped. The distance between us seemed to stretch not just over miles but time as well. How much longer until I'd be with my old man again? Then he suddenly sent for me to return to Newburgh, to him. Gladly, I packed my trunks and set out without any idea as to the length of my trip this time but uncaring as long as it meant I'd be with my husband where I belonged.

---

Knowing peace hovered in the air in the spring of 1783, the French troops departed for their homes, and one by one George's aides resigned and returned to theirs. The gaiety of the previous winter camps dissipated with the evacuation of the usual officers and other staff members. As a result of the dwindling staff, George ended up putting me to work for him.

I sat at a small desk to copy several of the many letters George wrote each day, a task he previously had enough men to accomplish. He wrote to so many people, having a copy of what he wrote enabled him to recall the details. And provided a fair copy in case the original was lost or intercepted.

"My dear, here are a few more for your attention." George crossed the office and handed me a stack of papers.

"More letters to Congress to pay the men for their service?" I placed the sheaf to one side and picked up my quill again, dipping it into the inkpot.

"No, the officers have worked out a fair compromise themselves." He shook his head slowly. "A much better option than choosing to mutiny."

"Yes, it is. Do you believe the peace treaty is near to being signed?" I gazed up at him, optimism in my heart. I wanted to go home and stay there.

"It is my hope. Come, leave those for now and let's have a bite to eat." He held out his hand until I placed mine in his.

I stood and smiled at him. "Thank you for seeing to my needs."

He nodded once, his eyes serious but smiling. "I'll always wait on you and for you, my dear."

In April, a rider brought a letter directly to George where we sat at supper with his remaining staff. He opened it silently, though his eyes shone with joy at the seal, one indicating official word from Paris.

"It is done. An armistice and a provisional peace agreement are in place." He raised his eyes to meet mine, relief and happiness apparent in his entire countenance. "It's finally over."

His announcement sent his staff into joyful cheers and toasts of relief.

"Huzzah!"

"We can go home."

"Hallelujah!"

That evening, after everyone had enjoyed a celebratory dinner and dispersed to their quarters, we retired to the privacy of our chamber. George poured two small crystal glasses of Madeira. We tapped the rims together and sipped.

"Soon, we'll be able to go home for good." George gazed at me, his eyes alight. "After the treaty is accepted by Congress, then I can disband the army and we can all return to our homes and loved ones."

"That day cannot arrive soon enough." I smiled at him and sipped, relief and expectation flurrying in my chest. "We'll need to make arrangements to have our belongings sent to Mount Vernon."

He relaxed in his chair, his eyes distant. "All in good time. For tonight, let us contemplate our quiet future on the farm."

I could indeed ponder the future. Retire to the peaceful plantation in Virginia and always be together. No more of the long separations we'd endured over the last eight uncertain and dangerous years. That was the heart of our celebration.

In fact, as we passed the weeks waiting for the final acceptance of the treaty by Congress, we discussed items we'd like to have at home. George sent off for an array of new furnishings, including linen napkins, sheeting, check cloth, and twelve bed blankets of the best quality.

"When I return to Philadelphia, I will be sure to inspect the quality of those blankets myself to ensure it meets my expectations." I speared him with my gaze. "We shall also need ordinary blankets for the slaves, at least two hundred."

"Very well, I'll see that they are sent south. I will need new lenses made for my spectacles." He jotted down several items on the growing list.

"Have you ordered buff cloth to make your new breeches, vest, and coat facing?"

"It is on the list. Along with six new strong hair trunks with sturdy clasps and locks to safely pack up all my papers and books to send home."

I looked over the list, and tsked. "That's quite a number of items to acquire."

He winked at me. "With good fortune, we'll be home before many more months have passed."

I certainly hoped so. It had been far too long since he'd been able to spend much time at his beloved home.

George had to leave for a time at the end of July on army business. He was gone nineteen days, not returning until August sixth, but he left me in the care and protection of my guard. While he was gone, I fell ill again with the colic, the pain and fever prostrating me in bed for weeks. The doctor came and treated me, but the ailment had to run its course. All I could do was lie in bed and pray for my recovery.

Congress asked George to move his headquarters to Princeton. George had already sent the troops, but postponed the move until I'd recovered sufficiently to travel with him. We finally left Newburgh the middle of August, leaving General Knox in charge, and headed for New Jersey. But no appropriate residences were available in the city. We'd learned of a possible place, Rocky Hills, while in Princeton. Margaret Berrien, the widow of Judge John Berrien, had put the place up for sale but decided to rent the house, furnishings, and three-hundred or so acres to the army on a monthly basis. So we ended up moving to Rocky Hills, four miles away from the city. I was glad of the open country aspect.

The spacious farmhouse sat upon a rocky hill, with piazzas overlooking the pretty Millstone river flowing past. We had plenty of room for our small band, consisting of only three aides and our servants. George's guard, made up of three dozen dragoons, camped on the lawn in front of the house in their white tents. The entire situation made us long even more for our own plantation on the Potomac.

Unfortunately, the colic returned the end of August to plague me, a severe attack lasting into September. I detested being sick, mainly because each time I fell ill I feared I might succumb and die. I did not want to be parted from my husband and family. I didn't want to die so far from home. I had more to do, to give to each of them. Back on my feet by the tenth or so, I felt well enough to sit on the piazza and work on my sewing and watch the river flow by in the distance.

Then a few weeks later, I, George's guard, two aides, and several of the servants fell ill with some awful disease that had me back in bed for several days. That was a terrible time, but slowly I recovered. I'd had enough of being ill. I wanted nothing more than to go home. George had to wait until the peace treaty arrived at Congress before he could disband the army and be free to head south. We decided I should begin the journey without my love at my side, with a few days in Philadelphia allocated to visit with friends and inspect the linen. With mixed feelings, I said my good-byes and boarded the coach.

After inspecting the linen, and voicing my displeasure, I returned to Robert and Mary Morris' house where I would stay for a few days. "I'm glad I came to visit, Mary. Otherwise, that charlatan may have sent inferior linen."

"I'm happy to have you in town for a visit." Mary strolled

beside me down the brick sidewalks of the city. "Would you care to stop for tea and biscuits?"

"Verily. I'm famished." I followed her into an establishment boasting all manner of cakes, pies, pasties, and hot and cold beverages.

We settled at a table in the front window, overlooking the bustling streets teeming with people and conveyances of every kind. The brisk fall air had chilled me and so I was happy to order hot tea and a cream cake.

"What other merchants do you intend to visit?" Mary cut a bite of apple tart and placed it in her mouth.

"I want to see the carpenter about some furniture George and I discussed adding to our home." Eying the rich dessert before me, I stifled a moan of pleasure. It had been quite a while since I'd enjoyed such a delicate and buttery pastry.

"I'll go with you, if you'd like the company."

"My friend, I would love to have you accompany me." I smiled at her, a rather bittersweet feeling taking over my heart. "After all, when I wave farewell to you in a couple days, it may well be the last time I'm ever this far north again."

"Don't say that." Mary laid down her fork and gazed at me. "Surely we will see you here again for a visit."

"I do not know, but given George's preferences, we may never leave the plantation again."

I finished my shopping and headed for Mount Vernon days later, hoping against hope that my husband's desires became reality.

# 17

Home at last, retired—as George was so very fond of saying—to sit beneath our fig and vine tree. Work on the mansion-house continued, much to my annoyance. I'd sincerely hoped Lund would have seen we could return to live in peace, but work on the new room at the north end of the house had all but stopped during the war for lack of skilled artisans.

And so the new song of my life had begun. What I liked to refer to as the sweet rhythm of life carried us through the next several years. I really hoped it would last for the rest of our lives. Visitors came and went, a constant coming and going of friends, family, war acquaintances, and even strangers wishing to meet the great man himself. Lund married his cousin, Elizabeth Foote. Lund and Eliza moved to their own home, Hayfield, a mere five miles away. George had paid the debt to his cousin by deeding him the property. I was glad he found happiness and had his own home to go to each evening instead of hovering around me like a mosquito waiting to swoop in and make his presence known.

My niece, Fanny Bassett, finally came to live with us in February. My sister Nancy had often mentioned that if she died, she wanted me to take dear Fanny under my wing to teach her the accomplishments of a lady and help her find a decent husband. With Fanny's graceful figure, dark hair, and pretty eyes, she presented an attractive, angelic young lady. I doubted finding a husband would prove difficult, and I was right.

"Fanny, have you met Uncle George's nephew, George Augustine?" I escorted my niece over to my nephew.

George Augustine had moved to our plantation after the war. He had served as Lafayette's aide during the battle at Yorktown. He was tall, and handsome, when he was well. Unfortunately, he still suffered greatly from chest pains, fatigue, and overall debility, all of which caused him to appear gaunt and malnourished. We worried about him, recalling my husband's brother's experience with consumption.

"I've not had the pleasure." Fanny dipped a brief curtsy. She nodded her head, her dark hair bobbing once, and then she lifted her dark eyes to meet his intense gaze.

He stared at her for a long moment and then slowly smiled. "The pleasure is mine." He took her hand and kissed the back of her fingers.

Despite being a few years older than her, they immediately were attracted to one another. They spent a great deal of time in each other's company. A fact of which my heart was glad. They seemed a perfect couple. One day, it occurred to me they were becoming very attached. If so, then there was something that must be done.

"George, if your nephew and my niece have any hope of a future together, then we must try to help him recover his health."

My old man nodded and laid down the quill pen. I'd interrupted his daily diary entries, an activity almost like a religion for him. "Let me consider the matter, my dear."

"As you wish. Thank you." I was confident he'd ponder the options and then make a decision. As I was not altogether certain as to what those possibilities might include, I left it up to him to work out the solution. But I'd keep a close eye on making something happen to help George Augustine.

At dinner that afternoon, George cleared his throat and addressed his nephew. "George, I'm concerned for your well-being. I'd like to provide the funds necessary for you to seek your health in the better climes of the West Indies. Would that be agreeable?"

The man in question glanced at Fanny and then back to my husband. "Fanny and I have been discussing that very thing. I do indeed accept your generous offer as we hope to marry one day."

"That's wonderful news, George Augustine!" I was so very happy for the young people, finding each other as life companions. I fervently wished for their future together. Assuming he could defeat the lingering illness.

"Thank you, Aunt Martha. I'll begin making arrangements immediately." He smiled at me and then his uncle.

"When you depart, George Augustine, I shall go visit my father and family for a spell." Fanny folded her hands in her lap.

And after he left in May, I would be left to miss Fanny's congenial companionship. But I'd have my husband at my side, and that was all that mattered.

---

As my maid was growing older and thus approaching a point when she'd retire, I recognized the need to begin training her replacement. We chose to add a young black girl to our household staff, and she proved to be a quick study with every task we assigned. Oney Judge was only eleven and her pretty smile and pleasant demeanor soon endeared her to my heart. I welcomed her whole-heartedly to my family. She'd been born at Mount Vernon back in 1773, and had finally reached an age to work in the mansion-house. She fit seamlessly into the household and took to sewing like a bird to singing, which pleased me.

Another personal matter arose regarding our extended family. In July George wrote to Clement Biddle, his purchasing agent in Philadelphia, to ask him to arrange to have Billy's wife,

Margaret Thomas Lee, come to Mount Vernon. She was a free woman who had been a part of George's military family during the war, and who suffered from some infirmity. Billy sorely missed his wife, and we'd decided to try to bring her to Virginia to boost his morale and bring the family back together. George instructed Clement to arrange for her to come by sea or stage, but his efforts ultimately proved in vain. Poor Billy. I was depressed on Billy's behalf, knowing the full measure of sadness caused by such a separation.

On a happier note, we were excited to welcome the Marquis de Lafayette to Mount Vernon in August. George thought of him as a son, and the sentiments were returned from Lafayette as well. The lively conversations we shared will never be repeated, ranging on topics such as agriculture, philosophical and practical political aspects of individual freedom, and several sharp debates on the kind of government needed for our young republic.

Over breakfast one morning toward the end of the month, the conversation turned to practical matters.

"I'm sorry to say that I must attend to some business in my properties to the west, between the Potomac and Ohio." George cut into his favorite corn cake with honey. "Would you care to go with me, Lafayette?"

The lanky red-headed man considered for a moment, chewing his last morsel of smoked ham. "How long will you be away?"

"I'm not certain exactly, but it may be a few weeks."

Weeks? I blinked at the unexpected news but remained silent. His absence would give me time to work on a few sewing and household projects I wanted to finish. With him gone, there would be fewer visitors to stay overnight to provide for and entertain. Not that I minded having company, but at times it was tiring. The more surprising news was his intent to be away for so long. I'd have to discuss with him in private my feelings on the matter so as not to embarrass him in front of others. But discuss it we would.

"Perhaps it would be better if I were to visit a few other parts of the country in your absence."

"Where would you care to go?" George sliced into his ham and speared some with his fork.

They discussed a potential itinerary, finally deciding on departing on the twenty-ninth and heading toward Baltimore. After visiting in various northeastern locales then he'd return the end of November for another week. That settled, we finished our meal before George invited Lafayette to ride with him to inspect the progress at the farms.

After they departed, I sat for several minutes in the parlor, happy to be a simple plantation mistress again. The tranquility of our life was a balm to the soul after all the turmoil and fear of the war. If George needed to take care of business elsewhere, at least it was a short trip and he'd return ere long. A sigh escaped as I hoped we'd always have peace and calm surrounding us for the rest of our lives together.

———————————

Letters could bring happy tidings or sorrow. The paper in my hand shared the terrible news that my only surviving brother, Bat, had died. He no longer breathed the sweet April air of our beloved state. What of his children? And poor sweet Mary, his wife. No mention as to the cause of his demise, but did it matter why or how? He was gone. Gone! Tears flooded my eyes, hot and salty when they reached my mouth. I dragged my handkerchief from my skirt pocket and covered my face with it trying to stem the tidal wave of grief. My heart ached over his tragic death, all the more as it followed so closely on the heels of my beloved mother's death only nine days previous. I had not been very surprised at the news of my mother's death, for her health had suffered for some time. Still, losing my mother stabbed my heart. But Bat? A fresh wave crashed through my core.

Each time someone I loved passed on to a better place, my grief lodged in my gut and my heart, but with each passing I had become somewhat inured to the kind of sorrow that endured for an extended span of time. Otherwise, I don't know how I could have functioned. With Bat's death, Betsy remained my only living sister, and her marriage to an alcoholic man swilling brandy all day long worried me. But I didn't have time to wallow in grief as Fanny and George Augustine's wedding day would soon arrive, and I had a lot to do. I mopped my face and tucked away my handkerchief on a long breath.

Over the next months, Fanny and I plotted and planned for the ceremony. Out of respect for our mourning, she and George Augustine elected to keep the affair small and quiet. Only a few others were invited. Lund and Eliza would be there, of course, as would the Rev. Spence Grayson to perform the rite. Rev. Grayson had served as both chaplain and captain in the Revolution and became close friends with George.

Planning the event evoked so many memories and feelings from my two weddings. Each had caused quite a commotion as both of my husbands had been wealthy and important men in their own right before we joined our hands together. George's reputation and reverence far exceeded that of Daniel's, which elevated both of our stations in society. How would Fanny and George Augustine's lives change as a result of their union? I hoped they'd have a long and loving life ahead of them and I would do all in my power to help them take the first steps together as man and wife in proper fashion.

The mansion-house glowed with candlelight as they exchanged their vows on a pretty October evening. We held the ceremony on the portico, overlooking the river beyond. As intended, it was a quiet and yet beautiful moment for everyone.

Fanny had become a daughter to me. My George had been asked to give the bride away, and that moment had proved my undoing. The tears leaking down my face as Fanny and George Augustine repeated their vows warmed my skin. I'd never see my own flesh-and-blood daughter marry, but this event felt much the same. They stood together in front of the reverend and pledged to love, honor, and obey until death parted them. The moment recalled the joy I had felt when I married George, who stood at my side as a witness to the union. Our life together seemed like it would continue filled with contentment and happiness. At least, as long as we remained quietly at home at Mount Vernon.

# 18

Indeed, the happy rhythm of our life continued with each passing year. Visitors brought news of happenings across the states. George became more and more embroiled in the local politics and trade discussions between Virginia and Maryland. He even invited the delegates to come to Mount Vernon for negotiations of the particulars, which of course meant more beds in the hall and more places at the table. I didn't care as long as my husband stayed nearby and didn't venture too far or too often from home. But in 1786, Virginia called for a convention at Annapolis to discuss trade and commercial problems, and that body decided a convention of all the states would convene the following May in Philadelphia. I tried to tune out the discussions, but my fears grew that George would be drawn further and further into the public realm again.

George needed help with all his correspondence and accounts, so he asked around for recommendations for a new personal secretary and a tutor for little Nelly and Wash. Benjamin Lincoln, a Revolutionary war general, suggested a recent graduate from Harvard College, a young man named Tobias Lear. Tobias arrived in May and it took no time to realize he was an intelligent and personable man.

I perused his features while George welcomed him into our home. He was tall and graceful, with a long straight nose, kind eyes, and pretty, curly locks. He spoke with care and revealed his education through the way he phrased his replies. He'd be an asset to our family, worth every penny of the two hundred dollars annual expense.

Wash ran into the passage as Tobias removed his coat. At five years of age, the lad was full of vigor. His little sister, two years younger, wandered in after him, more composed but with as much liveliness in her expression and actions. I adored both of my grandchildren beyond words and held high hopes for their futures.

"Here are your charges, Mr. Lear." I waved at the two little ones with a smile on my lips. "Wash and Nelly, come here and meet your new teacher, Mr. Tobias Lear."

Handing his coat to Breechy, Tobias sank onto his heels and held out a hand to Wash. "I'm pleased to make your acquaintance, Master Custis."

I was rather surprised by his actions, but Wash approached him readily and extended a small pudgy hand to awkwardly clasp the elder man's. "Sir."

"And you must be Eleanor." Tobias nodded at the little girl.

She abruptly dodged behind my skirts. Gently, I tugged her trembling body around in front of me and turned her to face our new family member. I kept my hands on her shoulders for reassurance as much as to prevent her from dashing from the room. "Nelly, say hello to Mr. Lear."

"Hello." Nelly's whisper revealed her nervousness.

Tobias smiled at her as he straightened.

"I dare say you shall have your work cut out for you." George ushered Tobias farther into the passageway and Breechy shut the front door. "While I was away for so many years, I'm afraid my accounts are a mess, and the correspondence in need of copying has grown to immense proportions."

"When did you want me to begin?" Tobias glanced at the children as they ran ahead of the two men and then up the stairs to their room. "There is time today."

George shook his head, his eyes laughing. "Settle in for now and we'll start to-morrow. Come, I've promised to treat you as family, so first we'll help you find your way around."

Over the course of the next few days, I realized how seamlessly Tobias melded into the family. We learned he was from Portsmouth, New Hampshire, and his cousin was John Langdon, a powerful businessman who had attended the Continental Congress and built ships for John Paul Jones. Impressive family ties, indeed. I also discovered how kind and gentle he was with the children, endearing me to him even more. I hoped he'd be part of our family for a long time to come.

———

Early in 1787, Fanny delivered a little boy into George Augustine's delighted arms.

"Oh, Fanny, he's so beautiful." I peeked at the baby's wide eyes and tiny nose while he cuddled in his father's arms. "I've a grandnephew."

"My son." George Augustine couldn't keep a smile from his face as he stared at the child.

We shared in the joy of the boy's arrival, but only for a very short span of time. Too short for my heart to bear. He died at four days old.

I understood birth and death provided beats within the rhythm of life, but I much preferred the upbeat of a birth to the downbeat of a death. After we buried the boy, Fanny didn't recover much of her health, staying weak and developing a cough much like the consumptive cough of George Augustine. So George Augustine took her to Warm Springs for a time, though when they returned she wasn't yet fully recovered despite being five months pregnant. When George Augustine carried her to Eltham for her lying-in, I missed her greatly and longed to be with her to do all I could to help.

I tried very hard not to equate Eltham with death, but at times I was reminded of how my sister and son had both died there. Fanny was like a daughter to me. Her absence left me worried and lonesome. She gave birth to a healthy girl, Anna Maria, whom they called Maria. Late the following spring, George Augustine and Fanny finally brought their baby home to Mount Vernon and I embraced her beautiful little body, never to willingly let her go. I still wanted children in the house even if I failed at producing any with George. Children were the future and gave me great joy, even if they were not my own flesh and blood.

That year also brought more upset in the type of political conversations ringing from the newly plastered and stuccoed walls of the mansion-house. The flagstone floor had been laid on the two-story piazza facing the river on the east side of the building, and a new ceiling put in place. Many a debate filled the air as gentlemen and ladies reclined on chairs on the porch, watching the water flow by in the distance, boats and schooners sailing past. I heard more than once from many different visitors the desire to have George become the leader of our new nation. James Madison himself had written frequently with encouragement and suggestions toward that aim. Fortunately, George remained committed to staying out of the public life, overseeing his farms, building, gardening, and enjoying the companionship of Tobias and George Augustine. David Humphreys also joined our family, working on writing a biography of my husband. We led a serene, idyllic life and I wanted it to continue. But I sensed dreaded change in the air and not for the better.

One sunny day, George came to talk with me. His eyes revealed his uncertainty as much as the line his lips made. "My dear Patsy, I would like to speak with you."

A cloud shaded the brilliant sunshine at that moment. I knew what he wanted to talk about, having kept up with the many heated discussions, but made him say it. Maybe if he heard the words, he'd realize what a mistake they represented. "I'm listening."

"You know I want always to be at your side, don't you?" He paused, searching my eyes with his own clouded ones. "But I've been asked to lead the Virginia representatives at the convention in Philadelphia come May. I am aware how hard this would be for you, but I'm convinced I must go."

"Are you telling me you're going, or asking how I feel on the matter?" Stunned not by the request of others but by his expressed desire to go north again, I waited for his response. Surely not.

He took my hands in his and peered at me. "The work the convention must do to revise the Articles of Confederation is crucial to the future of America."

"Let someone else lead it. Why must it be you?" Why did he want to leave me behind? Overseeing the never-ending work on the house, the household management, as well as the education of the children. To manage without him with only the two young children and my servants for company.

"My previous role, I've been convinced, makes my presence crucial to the success of the endeavor." He squeezed my hands hard and then loosened his grip but kept my fingers in his. "You know I would not leave you were it not of the utmost importance."

The mixture of concern and hope in his expression softened my resistance. I couldn't stand in the way of his conscience and his strong sense of duty to his country. I let my fear and anger out on a sigh to dissipate into the spring air. "Write to me."

A reluctant grin curved his lips, his eyes twinkling. "Thank you for understanding, Patsy. It's one of the reasons I love you so."

With a heavy heart, I helped Tobias gather the necessities while Billy Lee packed my old man's trunk. I had no idea how long he'd be gone, but I would miss him every single day.

---

As George was preparing to leave, a rider galloped up the lane and slid to a halt at the front door. George appeared in the passage as I emerged from the parlor, anxious as to why the messenger arrived with such urgency.

"General Washington, you mother lays dying. Will you come?"

"Yes, of course." The fear and concern in his eyes as well as the tense set of his shoulders spoke volumes.

Off he went, galloping back to Fredericksburg to visit with his mother, who suffered with breast cancer, and sister, Betty, who was worn out from caring for their mother. I stayed home rather than ride on horseback all the way there at such a frantic pace, praying for both women to recover. Three days later, George came home, weary but with relief in the relaxed angles of his expression and shoulders.

I raced to the door to greet him, wondering what had transpired in Fredericksburg. "How fares your mother?"

"The ladies are somewhat better." He raked a hand through his hair, which had come loose from its usual queue. "I suppose I should be on my way to Philadelphia."

"Yes, they've been waiting for you." I nodded, my throat clogged by sudden emotion. What would the convention mean to our future here on the plantation? "Go and get this task done so you can return to me."

On the ninth of May, he and Will—as Billy Lee now desired to be called—set out for the city and the convention. I watched them canter away, knowing my husband sacrificed his cherished private time at home for the good of America. He also risked his esteemed reputation by becoming embroiled in contentious political debates. He'd asked if I'd like to go with him, but I had declined. I couldn't abandon the children nor did I want to witness the strain the convention would likely cause in my husband. I'd wait to pick up the pieces when he came home.

As promised, he wrote faithfully. He shared news of our friends in the city, as well as brief updates on the direction of the convention. George had been unanimously elected as the president of the convention. His role, he told me, was to act impartially as the most pressing of the issues were debated. However, instead of revising the Articles of Confederation as they had intended, the delegates elected to start over. Some of the main debates centered on representation of large versus small states, free versus slaveholding states, the slave trade (a topic his opinions had changed on during the war), and the form and extent of executive power in the government. The result of their efforts yielded a new document they called the United States Constitution. Next, the supporters of the Constitution had to convince nine out of thirteen states to ratify the document. Nobody expected the job to be easy as they dispersed. With their mission completed, George finally came home in September. We were ecstatic to be reunited and settled in to our quiet lives once again, the happy rhythm back in place.

But not for long.

---

*Mount Vernon – 1788*

As the debate over ratification raged over the next year, more and more people believed only one man could reassure doubters of the new form of government. The Federalists, who supported the Constitution, defended the role of president by suggesting George fill the office. Because he'd resigned his power as commander-in-chief, people seemed reassured he would not want to be king or emperor or any such dictatorial leader. Despite their confidence in his ability, which I had no doubt in either, I couldn't help believing he'd done enough. Someone else should step into the role. Hadn't he given enough years of his life for his country?

My opinions aside, a barrage of letters, visitors, and newspapers arrived daily, each touting the assumption that he would take the job. Exasperated, I desperately tried to ignore the political discussions and debates, keeping my attention instead on my granddaughter Patty Dandridge and nephew Bob Lewis.

Their youthful optimism and enthusiasm diverted my attention from other more pressing worries. Having young people around me provided a diversion like no other.

My youngest sister Betsy gave birth to her eighth child, Bartholomew Henley, in March, and a more strapping young babe never before saw the light of day. I could only hope her health would weather the bitter cold of the winter since the snow barely left the ground before more fell. Even hearing of a sniffle on the part of the wee one made me anxious he would be called to sit with the angels. Betsy's husband, Leonard Henley, worked as the overseer at White House in New Kent County, so I didn't have much chance to see any of them. Nor did I particularly want to travel at that time of year to visit.

Through all the worries and pleasing distractions, I kept my eye on my own prize, my dear spouse. I worried he'd succumb to the siren call of duty to his country.

George made my heartache ease when he declared his intention to decline the honor of being the young nation's first president. But his friends and acquaintances continued to raise the idea, to extoll his suitability for the office, and eventually wore his resolve down until he, too, became convinced his reputation and lack of self-interest in the office would best serve to join the states together. He decided to accept the election but not seek out the office.

My heart plummeted. We talked late into the night about what the first ever presidential election would mean to the country, to him, to us. Obviously, I had no doubt I'd go to be with him as soon as possible. But I had many questions and concerns about not only his role but also mine. As a general's wife, there had been certain expectations by the staff and the public. What might they be for the president's wife?

"If I do indeed become president, then I'll need to set out ahead of you and the rest of our family to establish a home as well as the office of the government."

"So then I'd stay behind until I finished my preparations." I envisioned packing clothes, books and stationery, food stuffs, servants and slaves, for the journey to New York. Much like I'd done during the war.

"Yes, if you believe you can manage?" George snuggled me close to him as we whispered our worries to each other.

"I always do, don't I?" I strived to keep any doubts to myself, not wanting to burden him with my relatively petty concerns. I had my maids to help me get through all I needed to do.

"You know that I will wait for you, long for you to be at my side." He released a breath and fell silent.

"I know. And I will hurry to be there." Silence stretched and his breathing grew steady and even.

I held no illusions. Our lives would never be the same again. Four years of public service stretched before me like a vast ocean I didn't have a boat to cross. I cried myself to sleep, wrapped in my husband's arms.

After the new year of 1789 began, we started hearing of the electors voting overwhelmingly for George. Knowing the likelihood, George sent Tobias ahead in March to find appropriate accommodations in New York. I'd given Tobias directions as to what I'd need when I chased after my husband later in the spring. I was only a little ashamed to admit that everybody could tell I reluctantly had agreed to the idea of my aging husband taking on such a major role. Despite my efforts to keep my worries to myself. His eyesight was failing, his teeth needed to be replaced again, he fatigued easily which left him prone to illness. Yet he prepared to abandon the luxury of home for the good of his country. Doing his duty as I performed mine by beginning the tasks necessary to go with him, back to a situation I supposed would be much like winter camp.

Then in April, a quorum was officially reached. Official word arrived with Charles Thompson on the fourteenth of April that George had been unanimously elected. Two days later I waved a teary good-bye as the two men, along with Will and David Humphreys, disappeared down the newly winding lane toward the main road. George was proud of the new design for the approach. A variety of flowering trees lined each path, with a bowling green stretching between the two lanes. When would he see it again?

While a beautiful sight, my sadness and resignation didn't permit me to enjoy the expanse of green lawn. I turned from the door, slipping my handkerchief from my pocket to dry my eyes. I'd decided to take with me our nephew, Bob Lewis, as well as my grandchildren, but to send my niece Patty home. The mere thought of parting with her added to my sorrow.

So much for my desire to grow old together with my husband in solitude and tranquility. But duty called and we both must answer.

# 19

*New York City, New York – 1789*

Returning to the city on the twenty-seventh of May evoked
memories of the war, despite the fresh appearance of many of the
buildings and homes, streets and alleys, the coach passed. Inside
the jostling vehicle, Nelly and Wash, as well as Bob, peered out
the windows at what would become their new home. Behind my
coach, a separate carriage held my maids, Oney Judge and Molly,
as well as Giles, Austin, Paris, and Christopher. Tobias had
informed me in a kind letter of his progress establishing the new
household, including hiring fourteen white servants who were
already at work.

To hear my nephew talk, you'd think we'd had a very
arduous journey. I suppose from his more naïve view the delays
and dangers we faced were harrowing indeed. Compared to
previous trips during the war when I'd faced real danger to be
with my husband in far more primitive vehicles and under far
more terrifying and uncertain times, we had a very agreeable
journey. We'd been met by George, Robert Morris, and David
Humphreys at the Elizabethtown point in Philadelphia where
they waited with a fine barge. The same oarsman that had
carried the president to New York returned the favor for

transporting me to that fine city as well. I boarded the barge with as little obvious trepidation as I could muster given my aversion to boats in general. The people put on quite a parade; dear little Wash nearly got lost in the throng of people and horses and conveyances. The governor even met me at the landing and escorted my party to the president's house. A fine way to arrive in this fair city.

Poor Will had been left in Philadelphia to seek medical treatment for his painful legs. Why he desired so strongly to serve George in a house reputed to have steep stairs remained a mystery to me. I would not be surprised if he didn't choose to return to Mount Vernon to retire from being a manservant to fill some other need at home.

The coach stopped in front of a three-story brick house on the corner of Cherry and Dover, with a shady square across the street. Relief filled me at the end of the journey. With the wharves only a few blocks away, the main thoroughfare in front of the house teemed with people, noisy ironclad wheels on the wagons and carriages rattling by, stray dogs barking and chasing each other, horses clattering past, and grunting hogs running loose in the street and gutters. I glanced at the children, amused by how wide their eyes had grown as they took in their new surroundings.

Before long I became abruptly aware that being the president's wife was far different from being the general's. My hope for a camp-like situation crashed against the reality of the limits proscribed by my husband and his blasted advisors. That coupled with the endless stream of callers made this experience much different from the encampments. I've always ensured my attire and hair suited the occasion. Yet I found myself reluctantly submitting to having my hair set and dressed by a hairdresser who came to the house each day for the specific purpose. Apparently Sally's attentions no longer met the demand.

George informed me upon my arrival that my first reception would be in two days, on Friday beginning at eight o'clock in the evening. Men and women dressed formally would be permitted to attend in the upstairs drawing room. I chose to sit on the sofa, while Tobias or David escorted the guests to me. Around me blazed dozens of candles in the chandelier, while spermaceti-oil lamps rested on tables scattered about the room. George greeted each person after they'd curtsied to me. Light refreshments waited on the tables as the guests mingled and enjoyed chatting with each other. Bob escorted the guests to their carriages when it was time for them to leave. The stiffly formal affair each week lasted too long for my taste, but I had no choice. The president's wife, unlike the general's, was a public figure like no other.

I'd also be hosting formal dinner parties on Thursdays at four. I balked at the formality, preferring a more relaxed and inviting attitude. However, I soon learned how little my opinion mattered. Guests were invited by hand-printed invitation and expected to arrive punctually as George signaled the start of dinner on time each week. Government officials, members of Congress, and foreign dignitaries attended. Most didn't know each other and many had no desire to. I understood, believe me.

I sat at the head of a long table, decorated with china ornaments and artificial flowers. Looking around the brightly lit room, I smiled at George where he sat halfway down on my left. His secretaries acted as deputy hosts during the two-course meal. Conversations were often stilted or arrogant, but I used my previous experiences as hostess for large groups of men with few or no ladies in the company to smooth over the discourse during dinner. Many times the discussion proved trying, but I did my best.

After dinner, I invited the ladies, if any, upstairs for coffee. A short time later, George brought the men up to the drawing room. The conversations eased into more casual topics, providing a measure of conviviality lacking during the meal. After a short time, the guests would be escorted to their carriages and I could relax.

George confided to me that he worried about appearances and impressions. Indeed, he'd posted in the newspaper we would not attend or host any private gatherings to avoid even a hint of favoritism. I'd thought winter camp and its restrictions had been harsh, but looking back I longed for the easier interactions I'd enjoyed. My first three weeks as the president's wife proved difficult, but then I shoved aside my selfish concerns when George became seriously ill.

———————

He'd started to feel feverish and had pain in his left thigh. A few days later a large carbuncle, or hard mass, appeared on his leg. Over the next several days, the mass grew larger and became hyper sensitive and excruciating. The doctors, a father and son team, were summoned.

"What is it, doctor?" Fearing the worst, I clasped my hands together to stop them from shaking.

"We believe he suffers from anthrax poisoning." The elder doctor pursed his lips.

"What can you do about it?" *Please, God, let them have a plan.* I held my breath, fearing the worst.

"The only thing we can do is to remove the mass." The younger doctor shrugged lightly. "We know no other way to cure the ailment."

"If it is the only way, then you best begin." Little did I realize what I'd given them permission to do.

With a brief nod and an encouraging glance, they closed the door and set to work.

I couldn't see what they were doing, but George's groans and screams told me exactly what they did behind that closed door. I cried with each of my husband's outbursts of pain. Pacing to and fro in front of the blessed barrier, I hugged myself and let the tears flow. Tobias stood ready to intervene if necessary, but we both recognized the necessity of the extraction. Left to continue to grow, the mass would surely kill my husband.

"Cut deeper, cut deeper."

I shuddered at the elder doctor's words seeping past the wood door. Another anguished groan followed. My heart tore in two. I wanted to be with him in spite of the doctors fretting about me fainting. I'd seen blood and injury many times during the war, but I'd acquiesced only because those injuries had not been on my husband. I wasn't entirely certain I'd survive witnessing him being cut open. To stand by and see his blood pour out, his handsome face contorted in tortured pain. I shuddered and hugged my waist tighter.

After the doctors had cleaned him up, they summoned me to enter while a couple of strong men helped to move him to bed.

"Now, President Washington, you must lie prone for several weeks to permit the leg to heal, without putting weight upon it." The younger doctor wiped off and then packed up his bloody tools.

George shifted on the mattress and cried out in pain.

"What is the matter?" I was at his side in one frantic beat of my heart.

"My head hurts and it hurts to move." His voice came out strained and thin.

"As I said, you must lie still for your leg to heal correctly." The elder doctor tsked as he put away his instruments.

"I shall do my best." But George remained in pain and discomfort, unable to change position. Any noise hurt his head. Every pang he expressed hurt me.

The doctors feared the great man would die despite the operation. I stayed by his side as much as possible. Tobias bought rope and closed the street outside George's bedchamber window, scattering straw on the cobblestones to muffle the passing foot traffic. Some thought it rather extreme, but I'd do anything to ensure George's comfort. To ensure he'd live to find his way home again.

―――――

One afternoon in June, the vice president's wife, Abigail Adams, came to pay her respects. She brought her daughter, Nabby Smith, along. The Adamses had secured a large manor house not far from the city along the Greenwich Road, I had learned from David. He'd paid a visit to Abigail earlier in the day and enjoyed breakfast with her. He'd suggested she pay her respects to me and my husband, which is why she'd come into the city. Abigail invited George and I, as well as the children, to come for a visit when my husband's condition improved enough to allow such an outing. We had a very pleasant visit, though George remained upstairs abed, unwell and unavailable for callers. Both David and Tobias assisted in entertaining Abigail, who became a dear friend over the next few weeks as George slowly recovered, gaining back his strength and good humor. The stronger he became, the easier I breathed. He'd given us all quite a scare.

One task I attended to as soon as possible was to arrange for Nelly and Wash to be educated. While Tobias had proved a wonderful tutor, his duties now tended more to the private secretary realm. Wash was a difficult student as he preferred to play, but I found a new tutor for him. Nelly desired to attend a school for girls so she could make new friends. I enrolled her in Isabella Graham's school on Maiden Lane, a highly regarded girls' school. Of course, both of the children played with other children of several members of government. Neither wanted for playmates during the time we lived in New York.

To help Nelly learn music, we replaced the spinet with a pianoforte, and she studied under the renowned Alexander Reinagle from Austria. She also learned to paint under William Dunlap's direction. Seeing Mr. Dunlap again brought back fond memories of the time he painted George at the end of the Revolution. He flattered us by saying he believed Nelly would make a fine artist.

Unfortunately, Wash did not prove an apt pupil. His tutor worked tirelessly to ensure he studied the necessary subjects, which left no time for him to try other aspects of edification such as painting or music. By the fall of our first year in New York, George and I agreed we needed to send him to school. Neither of us had forgotten how disappointed we'd felt when Jacky had eschewed school for marriage, even though we understood his reasoning. We enrolled Wash in a new boys' school, which displeased him but gave us hope for his future.

We augmented their formal lessons with excursions to enjoy the local culture. Concerts, scientific lectures, natural history exhibits, and natural curiosities each provided opportunities to expose young minds to new ideas. We went to Dr. King's exhibition of orangutans, sloths, baboons, monkeys, and porcupines, for instance. On nearby Water Street, we saw Mr. Brown's wax likenesses of the British royal family as well as one of George wearing his uniform while being crowned with laurels. Mr. Brown also included several biblical scenes, which I enjoyed immensely.

Then there was the theater and its plays, with the most fun being the rollicking comedy *School for Scandal* by Richard Sheridan. The playhouse stood on John Street, between Broadway and Nassau, the red wooden building becoming a frequented destination for our family. They designated a president's box and painted the arms of the United States upon it. We often took guests with us to enjoy a performance, and when we arrived to the rousing tune of "The President's March," the rest of the audience would stand and clap until we'd reached our seats. I had a difficult time adjusting to the attention but George helped me understand the necessity.

We attended church services more often than we had at home, where we went perhaps once or twice a month. George elected to visit two churches, St. Paul's Chapel and Trinity Church, to provide an example for others to follow. He would not take the sacrament, but I participated in the Holy Communion. The ritual calmed my soul. I carried the beautiful leather and gilt Bible George had presented to me in August with its elaborate script and beautiful illustrations. I carefully inscribed my name on the title page, claiming it as mine. His thoughtful gift provided tangible comfort as well as spiritual, a fact he knew well. The book served as a reminder of his love and caring to hold in my hands when he could not be with me.

Although we enjoyed our outings, in between we faced the

usual challenges of living far from home in an unfamiliar city. The number of men working as secretaries for George grew to five, putting more pressure on the already crowded Osgood house that served as both government offices and private residence. As fall approached, it became ever more apparent we needed a larger accommodation. But another matter took precedence.

"My dear, may I speak with you?" George stopped my progress through the main passage.

"Of course." I turned and followed him into the parlor. "What is it?"

"I've decided to make a tour of the country. I plan to make two excursions, one to the north and one to the south. Do you care to join me?"

I shook my head even as he finished his question. "I'm not inclined to make an extended trip over such rough roads any longer. And the children need my supervision. Unless you need me with you, of course."

"Not if you do not wish to endure the journey. I feel it necessary to connect with the citizens, to see their situation and condition."

I informed Abigail and she promised to visit with me, and I with her, during his extended absence. His being away deflated my happiness like nothing else could but I knew my limitations when it came to long distance coach travel. George would have people to look out for him on the journey while I stayed behind and tended to domestic matters.

Abigail and I exchanged visits as prearranged. We went to the theater one night, and shared dinner on more than one occasion. The time dragged by until finally George and his entourage returned in the middle of November, well pleased and energized by the fond receptions he'd been greeted with across the states. At least one of us was happy at being in the city.

He also came back with the welcome news that a much larger and more spacious house would become available in February. The current tenant, French Minister Plenipotentiary, the Comte de Moustier, planned to evacuate the four-story Macomb house on Broadway to return home. Our steward, Samuel Fraunces, known as Black Sam, began instructing his staff of twenty servants in the necessary preparations to make the move in a few months.

Black Sam was an excellent steward and we were fortunate to have him on staff. George had first met him in '76 when he'd visited Fraunces's Tavern upon his arrival in the city from Cambridge. He enjoyed the elegant repast enough to return several more times during the war, and even bade official farewell to his officers in the tavern after the Revolution. As our steward, he brought his excellent culinary skills to our table. We had a hard time choosing among the oysters, lobsters, and so much more.

My anxiety related to the impending move to the larger house grew with each passing day. Tobias and George, along with Black Sam, made frequent visits to the new house. George purchased several pieces of furniture, mirrors, and other furnishings that the Comte declined to carry over the ocean with his family. While we waited for the move, I worried about the frequent colds and ailments my husband seemed to battle and win. As we'd grown older, we both had a harder time recovering from a mere cold let alone the ague or fevers which abounded in the city. I prayed for divine protection of our health as long as we lived in the teeming house. I longed with all my heart to move away from the crowded, noisy dock area to a more genteel part of the city where the more fashionable families lived. Surely better health would follow.

# 20

The new year brought happier times. By the end of February we had moved into the Macomb house, grateful for the larger drawing rooms and increased number of bedchambers for our presidential family. I was relieved by the move, because living in small houses and being crowded many in a room seemed a very great cause of sickness. Everyone enjoyed the new abode, including George's staff as they had more room to perform their functions.

We also had to happily suffer along without Tobias in early April. He left for Portsmouth, New Hampshire, his home, to wed Mary Long, the daughter of a colonel and his childhood sweetheart. Joy for his new beginning with the woman he'd loved for so long filled my soul. A couple of weeks after their marriage on the eighteenth, he brought Polly back to New York to live in the presidential mansion. From all that Tobias had said about his girl, I fully anticipated loving her as much as he did. Having another young person around the house lifted my mood as well.

"Mrs. Lear, it's lovely to meet you." The pretty, blushing young woman before me appeared smitten with her new husband. As well she should be. I greeted her with open arms.

339

"Mrs. Washington, it's a pleasure." Polly dipped a curtsy, and then stood tall and erect.

"Please, call me Martha." Although my sweet husband still called me by my pet name in private, the president's wife must be addressed appropriately by others. Or so I'd been told. "I'm sure we will be good friends."

I had always enjoyed having young people around me, and this lady reminded me so much of my own Patsy, had she grown to be a woman. Or even Fanny, who I missed dearly.

"Then please call me Polly." She glanced at Tobias, her love for him shining from her eyes. "Toby has told me how much he enjoys working for you and the president."

"Tobias is not simply an employee, my dear. He's a son to me and I wouldn't survive a day without him to rely upon."

"Thank you. I hope we get along famously."

Overjoyed, I soon befriended the twenty-year-old woman and she became indispensable to me. She was my constant companion and confidante.

Then in May, George caught a horrible cold and my worst fears stirred alive.

Over the next week, he developed a terrible fever, accompanied by chest pain and a wracking cough. The awful hacking sent shudders through me each time, much as if I were the one who was ill. I prayed for my husband to get well and prayed for the doctors to succeed in helping him through the worst of it. The doctors came and went, until one day I stopped one of them after suffering through a particularly terrible coughing spell with George.

"Doctor, what is wrong with the president?"

The gray-haired man cleared his throat, eyes dark and unfathomable. "As best I can tell, I believe he's suffering from a severe case of pneumonia."

"What makes you say that after all this time?" The days and weeks had passed, and my husband had only grown weaker. I trembled inwardly each time the thought of his demise crossed my worried mind. Which proved quite often.

"Well, when he started coughing up pink sputum. That was a good indicator. Plus the high fever seems to be affecting his awareness of his surroundings, making him confused and delirious."

"Will he survive?" I held my breath. George's skin had turned somewhat blue, as if his lungs couldn't supply the air he needed to live. Holding my own breath wouldn't help him so I let mine out slowly as I stared at the elderly man, willing him to cure my husband, to keep him with me. I feared he'd die and leave me alone.

"We can only keep him comfortable and pray." The doctor shook his head and strode away, off to see another patient he couldn't help, no doubt.

I turned back to my love, a faint bitter taste in my mouth. Would I bury another husband? I covered my mouth with one hand, stifling the urgent need to either wail or vomit at the thought. Several moments passed before I could comport myself enough to return to my own duties.

I stayed by his side as much as I could, Polly with me, but so many people visited to learn how he fared that I often had to step out and confer with them. The house always had a multitude of visitors, the doctors and my husband's illness notwithstanding.

"Mrs. Washington?" One of the latest doctors summoned me from my husband's bedside.

I practically stumbled out of the bedchamber into the passage and studied the man through tired eyes. "Yes, doctor?"

"Lady Washington, I am deeply sorry but I fear your husband is dying."

I gasped and blinked. No. It couldn't be. I wouldn't let it be. I didn't want to believe such an end loomed so soon. "You mustn't give up on him."

"Yes, but I wanted you to be prepared."

"I want you to do your job and heal him." How dare he suggest relinquishing the fight to save George's life? I had not given up even if he had. I glared at him for another moment.

The doctor inclined his head but remained mute.

"You're wrong." Swallowing anger and frustration, along with a deep-seated fear they may be right, I staggered back to George's side.

As the afternoon waned, his fever climbed, he tossed and turned on our bed. Taking his hand in mine, I prayed for hours for his recovery. I talked with him, soothing a cool rag over his brow. Then suddenly he broke out into a sweat, drenching the bed linens and filling my heart with relief. The fever had broken. My tears flowed hot with joy, washing away my fears.

Recovery from such a brush with death took weeks, but by June he had returned to work and to the renewed discussion of the Residence Act, as to where the country's capital should be built. Southerners didn't want it in the north, and Northerners didn't want it in the south. That debate became tangled up in the debate over the Assumption Bill that Hamilton had proposed, whereby the government would assume the war debts of the northern states. The southern states, who had paid off half their debts, did not want to be assessed again in order to pay off the northern states' debts. A bitter debate nearly descended into fisticuffs. But by the end of the summer a compromise came about after a dinner James Madison held with Thomas Jefferson and Alexander Hamilton.

To satisfy all parties, Philadelphia would remain the nation's capital for ten years, until November 1, 1800, at which time the new capitol building and presidential mansion would be completed and ready for Congress to move into. George was authorized to find a suitable site somewhere on the Potomac and appoint a committee to conduct surveys of each to base a final decision upon. I wondered, wearily, how long it would be before we'd move again, this time to Philadelphia.

---

Because Independence Day fell on the Sabbath, a day of rest and reflection, the city celebrated on the fifth. Throughout the morning, members of the Senate, House of Representatives, public officers, foreign dignitaries, the members of the Cincinnati, and the militia paid their respects to George. They marched to the presidential mansion accompanied by the beating of drums and firing of guns and cannons. We offered them refreshments in the manner of wine, punch, and cake. I wished we could do more to revere this day above all, for the many lives and sacrifices made to establish our new country.

About one o'clock we went to St. Paul's Chapel to hear Henry Brockholst Levingston deliver a sensible oration on the occasion. Mr. Levingston was the son of the governor of New Jersey and graduated from Princeton before the Revolution started. He had served in various capacities during the war, including serving as lieutenant colonel under General Philip Schuyler, impressing George and the other general staff members.

He spoke eloquently about how different our current situation was—under a government of our choosing—as compared to what it would have been if we had not succeeded in breaking away from British rule. He also talked about how much we should cherish the blessing within our grasp and cultivate seeds of harmony and unanimity in all our public councils. I can't recall every excellent point he made, distracted as I was by the handsome figure my husband made, but the speech was well received by his avid listeners.

That afternoon I was pleased by the number of ladies and gentlemen who stopped by the mansion to pay their respects and offer their compliments to me on this most excellent day. We reveled in sharing the fourteenth anniversary of the signing of the Declaration of Independence with our friends. Our country had certainly undergone many trials and achievements during the span of years, ones we'd endured and survived to see this fine day. My small contributions paled alongside those of my fellow countrymen.

At the end of August, despite our pleas to the contrary, all the city's leading men and militia showed up outside our door early in the morning to usher us on our way home to Mount Vernon. While the house in Philadelphia was prepared, we would spend three months in Virginia. Not since the end of the war had we been so eager and anxious to make the trip to Mount Vernon. Our entourage escorted us to the wharves, where our barge awaited. As we approached, the men divided to either side and we loaded the ship to the sound of a thirteen-gun salute. I'd grown so accustomed to the blasts from our war years I barely flinched at the honor but stepping onto another boat still took all my courage. Finally, we were on our way home, where I hoped the relaxation and amusements would confirm my love's health. Now that the fighting and debate were behind us, I hoped the remaining years of his term would pass without further drama or anxiety.

---

*Philadelphia, Pennsylvania – 1791*

Life had resumed its typical rhythm after we settled into the Morris' house on High Street the previous fall. Well, perhaps I should say, the rhythm resumed after completion of the last of the renovations to the house and outbuildings. George's ire at the delays reflected the same subdued anger he exhibited when delays happened at Mount Vernon. He tried to hide his true feelings, and in large part managed admirably, but I could tell. After all, we'd been together through better or worse for thirty-two years.

"George, I have a request." I had found my old man busy at his desk, yet again. Surely he'd spare me a few minutes.

He looked up from his work and laid his quill aside. "Yes, my dear? What can I do for you?"

"I can't abide the restrictions placed upon me. I want to engage in private gatherings with my friends, both at the presidential mansion and at their homes."

He frowned at me, the fine feathers of the quill moving lazily in the draft flowing through the room. "Why the change? We must not be accused of favoritism."

"And yet, even though I'd adhered to your request in New York, we'd still been accused of the same. I was intensely unhappy and lonesome. Why not permit me to enjoy my friends' company and they mine?"

He thought on the matter for several minutes and then smiled. "I appreciate your argument. I shall consider your request."

"Thank you." I shook my head slowly, a small smile growing on my lips. "On another topic, nephew Bob Lewis wrote to share the happy news he's become engaged to Miss Judith Carter Browne, of Elsing Green."

"Do we know this young lady?"

"I don't believe so. But I know her father, William Browne, purchased the plantation a few years ago. It's rather ironic to have our nephew marry into the family who lived at my aunt and uncle's home."

He twirled his quill, his thoughts already returning to his business. "It was unfortunate we were not able to witness the wedding since it was so far away."

With a smile and a pat on his arm, I nodded. I could tell he wanted to return to the letter before him. "I'll leave you to your work."

He was as good as his word. Within a few days I had more freedom but even though I did, I still considered us to be in a presidential prison. An elegant and familiar prison, being our friends' home, but a prison notwithstanding.

My social life blossomed from another direction. Nelly and Wash attended school, and we'd hired a dance instructor to visit the house three days a week. Naturally, we'd invited our friends' children to join in the dancing, which proved very popular among the youths. Even Abigail's six-year-old niece joined the fun. George's two nephews, Lawrence and George Steptoe Washington, were making a good name for themselves studying at the University of Pennsylvania, but they made time to dance on occasion. Both Nelly and Wash had already made quite a few friends. Wash had so many that George wondered aloud whether the boy had time to study. I loved the days when the house resounded with music and youthful laughter.

Our closest friends were Samuel and Eliza Powel. George and Samuel had first worked together during the Constitutional Convention, and he often accepted Samuel's invitation to tea or dinner. Samuel and George frequented various agricultural experiments, since Samuel served as president of the Philadelphia Society for Promoting Agriculture and George appreciated anything related to the subject. I listened intently when they talked of the progress and innovations, adding a word here and there of interest and enthusiasm. I missed my gardens at home and so considered what plants I'd like to include when we returned to Virginia. I counted the days until we'd be free to sit beneath our vine and fig again.

Eliza Powel, on the other hand, was the sister of Mary Willing Byrd, of Westover, Virginia, the widow of George's friend and compatriot Colonel William Byrd III. The two men had fought together in the French and Indian War and also served as burgesses for Virginia. Eliza seemed more family than friend, as a result. I enjoyed the days when my old friend attended the dance lessons and we had time to discourse together.

"My friend, I'm pleased you could join the dancing this day." I embraced Eliza and then released her to nod a greeting to Samuel.

Eliza clasped her hands together in front of her skirts, which were gently swaying in time to the quick beat of the music. "I love to dance, especially on these cold winter days when we cannot easily go out to ride or stroll."

"Indeed. The youth all enjoy the new dances as well." Samuel returned from where he'd gone to retrieve some punch at the sideboard.

"Speaking of youths, where is dear Polly?" Eliza asked. "Is she well?"

"She is resting. She expects to be lying in before too many more months pass." I let my gaze drift over the merry children and young people performing the dance steps to the guidance of the tutor. "She's eager to have her child in this lively city."

"Do you recall believing you'd never return to this city?" Eliza smiled at me, sipping from her punch cup.

"I do. I had not anticipated the turn of events that led us here." I had never wanted to return, to leave the beloved farm. Yet here I stood with one of my dearest friends.

"Only a few more years and then you can retire out of the public life." Samuel held his cup in one massive hand, calloused from the agricultural efforts he enjoyed.

"Indeed." Only two more years in fact. But they couldn't pass quickly enough for my tastes. I looked forward to the quiet of home more than words could convey.

On the eleventh of March, my dear Polly gave birth to a boy, Benjamin Lincoln Lear, which made both parents beam with pride. They asked George to don the role of godfather, which of course he eagerly agreed to do. I loved having a baby in the house, a wee creature to love and cuddle. I gazed on the tiny nose and dimpled chin and hoped this boy would grow to manhood.

The next day, George found me in my sitting room.

"As soon as the roads clear, I plan to set out for the southern tour of the states. I wish to learn whether the rumor is true, that my national policy is unpopular with them."

"I will miss you, but now that I can visit my friends and go about town, I'll strive to be content until your return."

He closed the distance between us and pressed his lips to mine. "I shall miss you as well, but fear not that I will return to your side as quickly as possible."

He left for the southern tour on the twenty-first of March, anticipating the trip would be about seventeen hundred miles. The very idea. I had no desire to take such a long journey on terrible roads. Instead I took the children to plays and the natural wonders exhibit nearby. We went to visit some friends in New Jersey, and made a pleasant stop at the Bristol Fair on our way home. I enjoyed having my freedom to come and go as I pleased, which made the weeks of my husband's absence seem shorter. When he returned on the fourth of June, not only was I in a fine mood but his trip had been a rousing success, so his mood matched mine.

---

One afternoon in early April, I had a surprise visitor. Edmund Randolph, a long-time friend and legal advisor, served as the first U.S. Attorney General. Having come from Virginia with his slaves, he came to warn me. I listened intently, alarm building in my chest as he spoke. The financial ramifications would be large if what he said came to pass. After he departed, I went in search of George, to convey the urgent message. I found him in his office, on the third floor of the house, with several other men. After I caught my breath from climbing so many stairs, I attracted his attention with a wave of my hand. He nodded and asked the gentlemen to step out for a minute. They filed past me with a flash of a smile, closing the door behind them.

"What is the matter?" George walked around the small desk when I strode toward him. "You don't usually come up here."

"Mr. Randolph stopped by with some disturbing news. I felt you should know right away before we're beset with a similar calamity."

He frowned and took my hands as was his custom. "Tell me."

"Several of his slaves, ones he brought with him, have used the Pennsylvania law to declare themselves free."

"What?"

"If an adult slave lives in the state for at least six months, then they are free according to the law. Mr. Randolph has lost several."

"Only three of your dower slaves fit that criteria. Hercules, Austin, and Molly." Concern flashed in George's eyes as he peered into mine. "If any of them runs off, I'd owe the estate for their value. That's a significant expense I cannot meet at this moment. We'll need to send them home before they learn of this provision."

"I've promised Austin's wife he'd be sent back soon, and we could send Hercules with him." I knew I would miss Hercules' cooking, but we'd have to suffer along without him.

"What of Molly?"

"She won't run off. She's content with working for us, as are most of the ladies who work for me." The small group of Africans who waited on my needs flashed through my mind. "I can't think of one who would give up all we provide them. We treat them like family."

"Very well. I'll see to having them go back to Mount Vernon on the next boat."

---

The rhythm of our lives picked up a new beat. Tensions simmered between Hamilton and Jefferson, the animosity palpable when they found themselves in the same room. I didn't trust Jefferson, even if he was close to our mutual friend James Madison, especially when he attacked my husband's character in the press. While George tried to negotiate a middle ground between the two opponents, the usual rounds of births, illnesses, and even a few sad deaths plagued my family. Most upsetting, George Augustine, my husband's favorite nephew, seemed to be losing his battle with consumption.

I was pleased to continue my friendship with Lucy Knox and Betsy Hamilton, whose husbands served as Secretary of War and Secretary of the Treasury, respectively. We were fully aware our husbands held reservations toward each other, but the men tolerated each other as a result of not wishing to damage their ladies' relationship. I tried as best I could to keep the peace until George's term ended the next year.

The new year of 1793 brought a unique opportunity for the residents of Philadelphia. On a cold day in January, a French aeronaut, Jean Pierre Blanchard, launched a hydrogen-gas balloon from the center of the city. Actually, he launched from the center of the yard of the Walnut Street Prison a few blocks away from the presidential mansion. Although the ascension wouldn't occur until ten in the morning, two field artillery pieces fired every fifteen minutes beginning at six to remind everyone of the event. I took the family up onto the roof of the kitchen, to listen to the brass band playing the martial music from within the court yard of the prison and to watch the yellow silk balloon inflated with gas. We had a wonderful view of the massive crowds gathered for the event.

George went in his coach to deliver a handwritten pass to Blanchard, asking on his behalf for any one he met to provide assistance as needed. The pass was a necessity since Blanchard spoke little English and didn't know where exactly he might land. Once on the ground, he'd need help to bring the balloon safely back into the city. I suppressed a giggle as I imagined some startled farmer in a panic at the strange sight of a flying man in a balloon. What I wouldn't give to witness such a sight for myself.

Fifteen cannon boomed, acknowledging the president's arrival at the launch site. Another blast of the cannon several minutes later announced the launch of the apparatus, and in another minute we could see the yellow balloon gently rise into the air. Blanchard stood in the basket, waving a flag in one hand and holding his hat in the other as he nodded to the crowd's exclamations.

Indeed, every roof and steeple surrounding us teemed with astonished people, waving and mouths open in awe. The streets appeared to be impassable with the thousands of onlookers. Blanchard rose slowly in a vertical fashion until a light breeze took charge and carried him toward the Delaware and eventually out of sight. January 9, 1793 would go down in the history books as the day of the first-ever aerial voyage in our young country's history. The entire family relished witnessing history in the making. And yet my heart longed for our imminent journey home in a few short months.

---

One morning at breakfast, that scoundrel Thomas Jefferson surprised us with a visit. He had a determined look on his face, as though he'd rather be anywhere else. I had a good idea as to why he'd come, to echo the pleas of so many others. I gripped my napkin under the table and schooled my features to reflect calm despite my agitation. I'd made my opinion clear to my husband, but I feared if the men continued to press, he'd relent and agree.

As George's term approached an end in the spring of '93, I became ever more anxious to pack up our things and head home to stay. Now in our early sixties, I wanted to retire far away from public observation and criticism. I'd had enough of public opinion. With good fortune, we'd be on our way to Virginia in a few months. He'd informed Hamilton, Knox, Jefferson, and Madison he'd retire as we both longed to go home. Hamilton and Jefferson had grown so embittered toward one another they had started political parties with opposing goals and priorities. George had had enough. I couldn't put into words my relief when George asked James Madison to write the farewell address for him.

Thomas greeted me and then addressed George, refraining from glancing my way as he did. "Please, Mr. Washington, accept a second term as president. Although we have a functioning government under your leadership, enmity and dissension continue to challenge the country. I firmly believe only your continued guidance and direction will serve our nation. In short, your country needs you."

I stifled an annoyed and, yes, embittered sigh. The man cannily understood which words to use to twist a knife in my gut. George glanced at me and then addressed Jefferson.

"George, please." I hated my weakness in that moment. Yet I truly worried about my old man's health. The strain of the last years had led to two very close brushes with death. Add in the partisan battles within his cabinet and the lack of regular exercise, and I feared for his health. If he accepted another term, would he survive it?

I thought of the sad news that arrived back in February. George Augustine had succumbed to the consumption. My husband bore with much despair and grief the loss of his nephew on the fifth of the month. He'd been buried at Eltham, alongside all those others who'd gone before him. I would never be able to think of Eltham without grief pulsing through me. We recently learned poor, sweet Fanny had contracted the dreaded disease from her husband, which worried us both. I didn't want a similar fate to befall her.

George glanced at me again, resignation dimming his eyes. "I understand, my dear." He sighed the weight of the world from his lungs. "I don't see that I have a choice."

I laid my hand on his, but saved my arguments for later, out of Jefferson's hearing. If then. Our long married life together had taught me one unavoidable fact. Once George had decided where his duty lie, nothing would change his course. I had to adjust mine to best support his endeavors and his welfare. Even if I didn't cotton to the idea.

"Very well, Mr. Jefferson. If the vote is unanimous, I'll accept another term. Let the cabinet know my decision, will you?"

Jefferson placed his hat on his head. "Thank you, Mr. Washington. I know everyone appreciates your sacrifices."

Everybody, that was, except me.

# 21

My prison sentence began again in the Senate Chamber of Congress Hall on March 4, 1793. Four more years loomed before me as I watched George, in his black velvet suit with diamond knee buckles and dress sword with its ornamented hilt, be sworn in by the Honorable William Cushing. I wore a simple yet elegant gown and tried to think positive thoughts, to keep my countenance pleasant. If it weren't for love of my old man and desire to do my duty to honor our love, I'd have insisted on staying at Mount Vernon among my family. Knowing I couldn't change the situation, I reminded myself of the positive aspects of our public life.

Days after the inauguration, George came into my sitting room, a worried frown marring his handsome features.

"What is the matter?" I laid aside my Bible to hear the news.

"I've received word from France of the beheading of Louis XVI and Marie-Antoinette, both tried and convicted of treason against France. Lafayette has been imprisoned in Austria after escaping his homeland."

"Oh my word. What of his family? Are they all right?"

He shook his head, keeping his troubled eyes upon me. "I do

not know. I assume they are safe. But Lafayette wasn't the only one detained. Several other aristocratic officers who had fought in our revolution were imprisoned, facing execution."

"What can we do?" The love we held for the man who was a son to George couldn't be thwarted by politics. But our reaction to his predicament could very well be.

"Nothing. I dare not intervene for it may appear I'm acting as the president and not a concerned friend." He shook his head slowly, the black ribbon on his queue brushing his collar. "Stay the course, my dear, that is all we can do."

The next days I couldn't settle into any routine. The rhythm had been interrupted. The dangerous situation our friends faced brought home the same fears I'd experienced during the recent war. A knock at the door pushed my heart into my throat. Shouts in the street set my pulse to throb in my neck. After a while I grappled my emotions into a calmer aspect, but then George brought word of more upsetting news.

Robespierre and the Jacobins had declared war on England, the Netherlands, Russia, and Prussia. As an ally, France wanted America to join the fight on their side. The treaty of 1784 became a discussion point between the cabinet members. Some believed since the treaty was signed by Louis XVI the alliance ended with his death. Others disagreed. George held firm that America not become involved, especially because our army and navy were not ready for such an engagement. He prevailed and the Congress signed into law the Neutrality Proclamation on the twenty-second of April. America would not join the war. Relief flooded through me at the close call, knowing the strain the other eventuality would place upon my dear husband.

At the beginning of July, George made a quick trip home to see to putting to rights Fanny's estate. Left on her own to oversee the entirety of the household, she'd found managing the property and finances more than she could handle. How could the woman be so caring and yet so incapable of overseeing her own affairs? I recalled when Daniel had died intestate and left me to sort everything. Yes, I leaned on Bat for his legal advice, but the decisions and management of the property fell upon my shoulders. While George was off in Virginia, I elected to have a bit of fun on my own.

On the fourth day of July, Independence Day, Wash and Nelly stood with me on the kitchen roof. Oney had seen to having a table of desserts brought up and situated so we could partake of the cakes and tarts while we waited for the annual fireworks to begin. The sun was slowly setting beyond the various buildings of the city. Clear skies, with only a few wispy clouds, bode well for the celebration after the sun had gone to bed.

"Stay away from the edges now, Nelly." I clasped my granddaughter's hand and brought her closer to the safety of a folding chair positioned near the table. "Do you want a tart?"

She accepted the strawberry pastry and sat to nibble on the crumbly edge. Wash skipped over to stand beside me, eyeing the offerings. The boy was growing into a young man at twelve. Soon his skipping days would be behind him, but it warmed my heart to see his youthful side prevail for yet a while. A band struck up a lively patriotic tune from somewhere in the city, probably on the square though I couldn't see them from where I stood. The smell of gunpowder lingered from an earlier round of celebratory gun firings.

"May I?" Wash slanted his head and smirked at me.

"Yes, you little urchin." I teased my well-dressed grandson and tousled his hair, then turned at the sound of approaching footsteps.

"What a lovely evening." Polly carried some cushions to place on the folding chairs Breechy hauled up behind her. "Are you warm enough? The night air is a little cool, don't you think?"

"I'm comfortable for the moment." I moved to help her set the cushions on the newly provided chairs. "Thank you, Breechy, for bringing everything up here. I trust you'll stay to enjoy the show?"

"Yes, Mrs. Washington. If you don't want me to be doing something else, that is." Breechy straightened his livery after he'd mussed it with the chairs rubbing on the coat.

"You've done quite enough for the time." I wondered how George was faring and what he was doing at Mount Vernon while we all stood here to enjoy the celebrations. I longed for his return, though I understood the reason for his absence. I didn't have to like that he risked his own life on the often dangerous roads between Pennsylvania and Virginia. Just hold dear the knowledge he'd come back soon.

Tobias soon appeared as the sun slowly sank and the stars twinkled in the twilight. The first of the fireworks exploded into the sky as he reached Polly's side and little Nelly jumped at the sharp report. I hugged her close to me as the next one shot into the air.

"Don't fret, Nelly." Tobias smiled down at the girl. "They won't hurt you, they just make a lot of noise."

"Oh, look Toby, at how pretty that blue and red one is!" Polly smiled at her husband and then turned to me with rapture. "Isn't it beautiful?"

"Oh, yes. I've always enjoyed fireworks." I was elated at how well my idea of coming up on the roof had worked out. The sharing together of the best of days in our country's history would always be a happy memory. One that could only be happier if my husband had been by my side.

---

By the time George cantered back into Philadelphia, word had spread of the beginnings of the summer fevers. At least, that's what the city officials called them. But as the weeks passed, the number of cases increased dramatically. People began fleeing Philadelphia for the countryside.

Alarmingly, sweet Polly contracted a fever and took to her bed. I summoned the doctor and he prescribed some powders to ease her distress. Tobias stayed with her as much as he could, but he also had his work to do. I followed the doctor's orders in caring for her, but she didn't improve. Fear filled my chest as she fought to survive the dreaded disease. On the eighth day, Tobias pulled me aside, the strain from his wife's condition plain on his face.

"She's very weak and still hot to the touch." He rubbed his eyes with thumb and forefinger before opening them, bloodshot and worried. "I don't believe she'll last the day."

"Oh, Tobias, I'm so sorry." Losing a spouse is one of the hardest and most sorrowful events in a person's life. I pulled him into a hug, imagining how I would have comforted my own children on such a painful day. If we'd gone home, if George hadn't relented and agreed to another term, she'd not be dying. But there was no point in pondering such futile thoughts. "We've done all we could for her. God is calling her home."

"I suppose all that's left to do now is to pray." He stepped back and studied me for a moment, then nodded. "Thank you for helping me and my wife. I'll go sit with her."

He walked away, his strides measured and almost reluctant. I returned to my chores, waiting for the announcement of her death, which came after dinner. Tobias was heartbroken, but bore the pain of her death like a philosopher. I, however, did not, for Polly had been a daughter to me and I couldn't shake a sense of guilt associated with her death. We'd grown very close and the gaping hole left as a result would never be filled.

By August, the city officials changed their story, admitting an epidemic ravaged the populace. Apparently, the refugees from the slave uprising in the West Indies brought more than rum and sugar on the ships sailing up the Delaware. They'd brought yellow fever, too. More than ever, I worried about George. He'd been under such strain during the last several months, would he be able to fight off the disease should he contract it?

The fever and its horrid effects—vomiting blood, bleeding from ears, nose and eyes, as well as delirium and jaundice—spread to our part of town. The number of deaths each day multiplied. The stench of tar burning in barrels placed around the city choked me, but they were necessary to ward off the disease. Likewise, men shot guns into the air to scare off the spread of the sickness. Lists of possible ways to ward off the fever were printed in the paper. I loathed hearing the rumble of a wagon, accompanied by the gravedigger calling "bring out your dead" in a booming, sorrowful tone. More than ever, I wanted to go home, away from the crowded living conditions that surely contributed to the raging epidemic. I held my tongue, waiting for George to decide on when we should depart. I didn't have long to wait.

"Patsy, I've made a decision." George looked up from the newspaper and the latest death toll. "I'm sending you and the rest of the family to Virginia. I won't risk your lives here any longer."

"I'd be happy to go home." Then I realized what he'd said. "You're going as well?"

He shook his head. "I don't think it's right for me to leave before my stated departure date. The people will think me a coward."

I blinked several times, marshalling my thoughts. Quelling the angry retort clawing for release. "Very well. When will we leave?"

A frown lodged between his eyes. "I'll leave in September, as planned. You and the others will leave as soon as possible."

"No. I'll not leave until you do." I stood, my agitation forcing me out of my seat as my arms locked over my heaving bosom. "You must accompany me or I shall not go."

"Patsy…"

I shook my head so hard my vision blurred. "I won't have you risk your life without me here in case you need me. We go, or stay, together."

"Are you certain? You've heard the Hamiltons both have the fever?" George stood, and stepped closer to me. "The government is not doing any work since Knox and Jefferson among so many others have fled the city. Still, I cannot go. I have a few other matters to settle."

"My place is with you and I won't have you put yourself in danger without me. It's decided. We'll leave together in September. Just tell me the date and I'll make sure we're ready to go."

Before we left the city on the tenth of September, I sent a note along with several bottles of wine to the Hamiltons. After all, everyone knew wine cured most ailments. I sincerely hoped our friends would fully recover from their distressing illness but was relieved to put the city behind us for a span.

---

We spent the next two months at Mount Vernon. I felt lighter and happier than I had in years. The tension in my old man's face eased with the fresh air and his daily rides around the farms. Sometimes I went with him, but mostly I stayed at the mansion-house tending to the needs of the family. Having the opportunity to directly oversee the servants let me witness how slovenly and lazy they'd become in my absence. I had to correct their attitudes and activities on more than one occasion. Shortly after we arrived home, Fanny brought her three children to stay with us. The poor thing latched onto me as though she drowned in sorrow. Perhaps she was. George continued to advise her on how to manage her affairs, which she appreciated but the entire situation worried me. He had so much to tend to every day I feared for his health. That fear had become near constant, almost an obsession.

With cold weather approaching and thus the end to the season of disease, we journeyed north first to Philadelphia and then on to the quaint town of Germantown where Congress had chosen to reconvene. They didn't want to be in the city so ravaged from the yellow fever. The final death toll had climbed to five thousand before the epidemic subsided. George rented the Frank's two-story house across from Market Square on the main road to town, and we moved in on the first of November.

I enjoyed the elegant home with its fine front door balanced by a wall of windows that permitted light and air to flow through the entire house. Our cook, Hercules, prepared many a delicious meal in the large kitchen. Moll tended to the needs of Wash and Nelly, loving on them as though they were her children. Oney Judge served me well, with kindness and attention. As my seamstress and personal maid, I treated her with tenderness and courtesy. She wanted for nothing as a result. We all quickly settled into the new home outside of the quarantined city.

George held official meetings in the parlor, with Jefferson, Knox, Hamilton, and Randolph in attendance to discuss policies related to the war between France and England. Their voices, sometimes low and deep, sometimes raised and shrill, rang through the house. George was surprised and saddened when Jefferson resigned his position as Secretary of State. I couldn't say the same, considering his absence removed one of the contentious players in the cabinet.

George Steptoe Washington, George's nephew, shocked the entire family by eloping with Lucy Payne, insisting upon marrying the twenty-one-year-old girl at his Harewood plantation in Virginia, though we didn't know much about her parents. John and Mary Coles Payne remained a mystery to me, but I understood Lucy was one of eight children and had a sister, Dolley, whom she was very fond of. George Steptoe told me before they departed that Dolley's recently deceased husband, John Todd, had been a fine Quaker lawyer and had done some legal work for him. The poor man along with an infant son had succumbed to the fever with so very many others, leaving a widow and a son to carry on. Remembered pain shafted through me but was quickly dispelled by my husband striding into the room. As long as we were together, my life was complete.

# 22

George dashed home to Mount Vernon again in June, after Congress adjourned. The rapid jaunt to and from our home was more than I could bear, fatiguing as it was to rattle and jolt over the rough roads. However, I was shocked, to say the least, when I received his weekly letter telling me he'd nearly fallen off his horse while touring his farms. He'd wrenched his back in the effort of preventing the horse from falling and throwing him. He could have been killed in such a fall. Was he telling me all the details about his condition? I couldn't tell from this distance. He'd withheld information before when he thought it would upset me. Was he doing so now? I needed to see him, to judge for myself the true nature of his injury. I had one poor substitute.

I pulled out paper and pen and sat down to write to my niece Fanny. I encouraged her to tell me the truth of his condition, to not deceive me. I told her also that I was pleased she had decided to move the children into Alexandria so they could attend school. I hadn't predicted Tobias Lear would strike up a courtship with her from his home in Georgetown, Maryland. Within a few months, they had married. Another happy match, in my opinion.

George returned to Philadelphia a week or so after his accident. When I heard his voice, I hurried to greet him. As I neared where he stood in the front hall, I ran my gaze over every inch, inspecting for signs of distress or pain.

"Patsy, do not fuss. I'm fine." George welcomed me into his embrace, and I pressed my cheek to his chest.

The beating of his heart reassured me more than words. I withdrew slowly so I could gaze up at my love. "You scared me. Please don't do that again."

He chuckled and kissed me. "I shall do my best to heed your admonishment."

Although still somewhat sore, he went about his duties with his usual aplomb and grace. The household continued to hum along with a steady rhythm. However, all was not so complacent across the country.

---

The summer brought on the Whiskey Insurrection when farmers and distillers in western Pennsylvania rebelled against the excise tax on whiskey as well as the long journey they had to make to stand trial if accused of a crime. George fielded several state militias to quell the rebellion in September, an act that achieved its aim but also outraged so-called Republicans.

"What are you reading with such a frown upon your face?" George looked up from the letter in his hand to smile my way.

"The Aurora paper." I had right to frown at the offensive lies in my hands. Published by an outrageous man named Benjamin Franklin Bache, grandson to his namesake, he had unleashed a malicious attack on my husband. "He is using innuendo, accusations, and several forged letters from the Revolution to besmear you in the public image."

I loathed the man, though I had never met him. How dare he attack the nation's hero with lies? Using George's own letters against him out of context no less. During the war several times both official and private letters were intercepted by the enemy.

But now the enemy wasn't the British but other Americans. The very idea made my hackles rise like a bantam rooster defending his hens from a fox in the henhouse.

"Oh, do not worry about him. Although he did force both Hamilton and Knox to resign as a result of the false allegations."

"I know, and you wanted to as well. I'm relieved you held firm in your resolve to do your duty even in the face of harsh criticism." Even though we both longed for home neither of us wanted to be forced out in disgrace brought about by falsehoods.

"Perhaps, but I do weary of fending off the attacks to my personal character in service to my country." With a sigh, he returned his attention to the contents of the letter.

"So tell me, Papa. What are you reading with a frown?"

George chuckled and glanced at me. "George Steptoe says his wife's sister, Dolley, has accepted our former friend's proposal of marriage."

"James Madison?" I was sorry for the flash of anger mixed with pain that crossed my old man's face.

The two friends had parted ways based on philosophical differences as to how the country should be governed. In truth, with Jefferson's views taken into consideration it was not surprising that Madison would follow his close friend's political bent. I wondered if George and James would ever be compatriots again.

"Yes, it appears she took your advice." George shot me a glance filled with humor. "Despite her seeming reluctance to accept his hand."

I had in fact invited Dolley Todd to attend me when I'd learned Madison had proposed but she had not yet given her answer. My curiosity had proved too much. While Madison and my husband did not see eye-to-eye on politics, I saw no reason why Madison couldn't find personal happiness. "I'm glad she did not let the difference in age or religion prevent her from what appears to be a fine match."

"They plan to wed at Harewood, George Steptoe's plantation, on the fifteenth of September."

"I'm pleased James has finally found someone who will make him happy. She is a sweet person, but I wouldn't anticipate being included on the guest list."

"No, I would not hold out any hope for that event."

I didn't and thus was not disappointed when my prediction proved accurate. But I had done my duty by giving the young lady a push in the right direction.

---

In April of 1795 my granddaughter Betsy Custis came to live with us in Philadelphia. She tended to complain more than was tolerable but my chiding had little effect on her ongoing mutterings about not feeling well. As a result, she found excuses for not visiting others but seemed always fit for receiving visits. I worried about her future, knowing how important reciprocity in visits was to cementing friendships and associations whether for personal or professional advancement. I'd realized long ago how important my role as wife to first the general of the Continental Army and then the president had been to smooth over any awkward or rough spots in the communication between diverse opinions and desires.

George endured another round of criticism when he signed Jay's Treaty into law in June '95. He believed in the agreement developed by Hamilton and negotiated by John Jay. The terms of the treaty achieved one of our country's primary goals: withdrawal of British Army units from pre-Revolutionary forts that it had failed to relinquish in the Northwest Territory of the United States, the area west of Pennsylvania and north of the Ohio River. Disputes between America and Great Britain regarding the American–Canadian boundary and debts incurred during the Revolution would be settled using something called arbitration, a new term to me. American merchants would be granted limited trading rights with British-held provinces in India and the Caribbean in exchange for limits on exports of American cotton. Congress ratified it only under his insistence, but France interpreted the treaty with Great Britain, negotiated to avoid war and allow for trade, as treason. He kept his head up, despite the public's condemnation of his actions. All in all, the months that passed while these provisions were debated proved trying to every person associated with our government. Tempers flared and debates raged, but I kept a smile on my face and a joke ready to lighten the tension in the room when necessary.

I took the children and servants home for the summer, leaving in July. We had a lovely time, pursuing our usual activities. I no longer rode horseback, but did take the carriage to barbecues and plays as well as dinners with friends. I received a letter from my daughter-in-law, now Nelly Stuart after marrying Dr. David Stuart, asking for her daughter to come home because she feared the girl would become spoiled. Young Nelly had stayed with me for more than a year, so I understood the point. I would most definitely miss my confidante but a mother had the right to enjoy the company of her children. I will admit that a pang ricocheted through me at the thought.

On our way back to Philadelphia in October, Nelly clung to me in the coach. "Must I go home? Wash doesn't have to."

I clung to Nelly in turn, the closest thing to a daughter I had left. "Yes, dear, your mother needs you. Wash remains with me so he may continue his education."

"But I don't want to be left behind! I want to be with you!"

"I know, I know." I tried to soothe her but it was no use. How could I when I was just as upset to put her out of the vehicle?

We dropped her off, protesting mightily, and then continued on our way. I couldn't stem the tears coursing down my cheeks for some time. I left part of my heart with my granddaughter, a portion she'd always possess.

---

Back in the capital, the controversy surrounding the Jay Treaty continued to cause disquiet. France declared the treaty severed the pact between France and America. The French boarded

American vessels in the West Indies, taking over the cargo and the crew. The *Aurora* meanwhile published the new French minister's declaration that my husband, the hero of America, was pro-British. Nothing could be further from the truth.

In the winter of 1796, Fanny and little Maria both came down with a fever. Tobias wrote to tell us of their condition and we prayed they would recover. Illness and death seemed to haunt my life and as the years passed I grew weary and somewhat jaded about both. I also felt for Tobias, his second wife and now his child on the brink of death. What a difficult time for him. Then a letter came and I went to share its news with my husband.

"I have sad and glad news." I settled onto a chair by the fireplace in the parlor where George and his staff had gathered for refreshments. His face revealed the serious nature of the discussions which ended with my entrance. "Which would you like first?"

George sipped a cup of afternoon tea and raised one brow in question. "Start with something good."

"Tobias writes that little Maria is much better."

"That is very good news." He peered at me, his expression sobering. "What more?"

"Poor Fanny has died." I swallowed the tears, holding them at bay until I could retreat to the privacy of our bedchamber. "He says the tuberculosis had weakened her so she couldn't fight off the illness."

He nodded, his eyes dark with his own private feelings. Even though we had anticipated the eventual death of sweet Fanny, the event nevertheless brought sorrow to our hearts. I excused myself then and went to my room to weep for my niece. A long time later, I penned a thoughtful letter to Tobias, striving for words of comfort and support. A letter often ended up being the only means for conveying the depth of feeling surrounding loss.

His little orphans proved to be quite a handful over the next several months. Tobias took them to live with his mother, Mary, but Maria acted so rudely they packed her off to a boarding school. If necessary, they planned to have her live with her aunt until she married and became some poor man's problem. It saddened me even further she didn't have the kind of disposition to make friends with the people around her. The boys, little gentlemen in every sense, stayed with Mary and attended school in town.

One sunny afternoon, George sought me out where I worked with Oney to organize and mend my various costumes. "Will you walk with me?"

"I'll get my wrap." Oney thrust my wrap at me with little grace, and I shot her a sharp reproving glance as I followed my old man downstairs and outside for a pleasant stroll.

As we walked in silence for several moments, I pondered just how bad the blacks were in their nature, never showing any gratefulness for the simple kindnesses shown to them daily. I recognized they were watched and often had to be goaded into performing their duties, but they were also sufficiently provided for. More so than some free whites and free blacks who lived on the streets as beggars. Was it better to be free and unable to provide for oneself or to be enslaved and have your needs met in exchange for the labor a person could provide for another? I opened my mouth to ask George's opinion, but he spoke first.

"I've received word that Lafayette has sent his son to live with us." George shook his head slowly as we walked down the street.

"Oh dear." The controversy over the Jay Treaty and the French reaction gave us both pause about welcoming George Washington Motier into the president's home. "I adore the young man, but is it wise to have him as part of our family?"

"I believe we need to find another place for him to reside." He glanced down at me and then back to the street ahead. "I propose we ask the Hamiltons to host him until the situation calms down or is resolved."

"He'd be near enough we could keep an eye on him without aggravating the ongoing debates. When is he due?"

"Sometime this spring." George squeezed my fingers and smiled at me. "I'll send a note to Alexander this afternoon."

It wasn't until April that the boy, along with his tutor, made the journey to Philadelphia. In short order he settled in with the Hamiltons and seemed to enjoy his stay with them. Naturally, we invited the Hamiltons to visit on a regular basis.

As we packed to make our annual trip home in June, a shocking event happened. One I had not seen coming. We had paused to enjoy a light supper the evening before our departure.

"I'm so pleased to be heading south to-morrow." I selected a bite of lobster and popped it into my mouth. "But I'll miss fresh lobster when we go."

George chuckled as he raised his wine glass. "Everyone will be glad for the respite of being on the plantation for a few months."

Doll rushed into the room, frantically looked about and then hurried to whisper in my ear. "Oney has left."

I frowned, not comprehending. "So? She likely had an errand to run."

Doll pressed her lips together and shook her head. "She packed a bag and walked out. She told me she ain't coming back, then opened the door and went."

Aghast, I sat at the table with my mouth open. She left? After we'd been so close and shared so much? Snapping my lips together, I looked to George. "What shall we do? Why would she leave me?"

I couldn't understand. I'd just informed her that her future was secured as I intended to give her to my granddaughter Betsy Custis when I died. She had smiled and thanked me for caring for her. As a house slave, she had an easy life among the finer accoutrements and furnishings. She received adequate nutrition and the added benefit of travel with the president and his family. Why had she left her comfortable home? Her mother and sister waited for her return to Mount Vernon. So she had left them as well.

George rose to his feet. "I'll send someone after her and then I'll be back."

"There must have been a man that seduced her." I shook my

head, dazed at the desertion. "There can be no other incentive for running away."

George sent men out to find her, but they never brought her back. We went home to Mount Vernon with one less servant. I was truly distraught, almost as much as when any of my children died.

I missed my maid, but the house teemed with family and friends and dignitaries throughout the following months. The Peters, Laws, Stuarts along with young Nelly, visited. As well, foreign dignitaries such as the minsters of Portugal, France, and Great Britain, and even a dozen Catawba Indian leaders spent time at the mansion-house during that summer and fall. All in all they provided a much welcomed distraction. And needless to say, I reveled in every minute. We were together and home.

---

In September, George went to Philadelphia again, this time to consult with Congress on policies related to foreign affairs. But the happy news that brought joy to my heart was that he also went to publish his farewell address. After finally being away from the government seat for a spell, he'd realized the strain he'd been under. Nothing and no one could convince him to even consider accepting a third term as president. He returned to Virginia to escort the family back to Philadelphia in October. The last time we'd make such a trip before retiring from public service. Huzzah! Soon we'd be officially retired to sit under our vine and fig and be left alone to enjoy our waning years in peace, entertaining our friends and family under the shady trees along the Potomac.

The final months of my imprisonment, those first several months in '97, came with bitter cold but also a host of events with friends and acquaintances all wishing to bid us farewell. A rather melancholy air hung over the plays and dinners and other functions we attended. We actually found ourselves enjoying the fun, and the house we stayed in stood only a few blocks from the New Theater. We also went to an amazing performance of tumbling on horseback and other equally thrilling but dangerous acts on horses. Indeed, we spent most of our time at exhibitions, lectures, assemblies, and formal addresses by many government leaders. And of course, we had our usual levees, dinners, and my drawing room each week to propel us through the months toward our freedom.

When Hercules ran away, I couldn't believe he'd prefer the uncertainties of fending for himself rather than having the security of serving the president's family. His departure felt much like a betrayal. We'd all miss his excellent meals, of course, but I simply did not understand. After the futile search for Oney, though, coupled with George's desire to ultimately free his slaves, we didn't bother trying to find him.

On George's sixty-fifth birthday an elaborate celebration provided entertainment for the entire city. The men of Congress each came to pay their respects. A thirteen-gun salute resounded through the heart of the city. The annual Birthnight Ball served as the high point of the season. George gave a toast to the dancers as was his custom and everyone applauded. I did as well, knowing the toast like the ball would be the last.

The day of John Adams' inauguration, March 4, 1797, I had a terrible cold with an awful cough so did not attend the formal release from our sentence. The next day at long last we prepared to set out for home. We loaded up two coaches with as much as they would carry. Children, aides, slaves, as well as our luggage weighed down the two vehicles. The remaining boxes, trunks, casks, hampers, and much more would be sent by boat. I wanted to arrive at Mount Vernon with all due speed.

However, our progress was impeded all along the way as crowds of people came out to greet us and say farewell to their retiring president. Various militias rode out to escort us, stirring up the dusty roads. Carriages and pedestrians surrounded us the entire journey. A week after we drove out of the capital, the coaches slowed and then finally stopped at our front door. Now our real life, the one we'd desired since the day we married, could begin.

# 23

Home never looked so good, despite its deteriorated state as a result of our long absence. We arrived on the fifteenth of March to the warm welcome of the servants. The first thing we did, while the servants unloaded the coaches, was take a stroll along the Potomac, hand in hand, rejoicing in our retirement.

The next day I began the lengthy but agreeable process of reorganizing the household. I'd decided to find a steward to oversee the housekeeping. At sixty-six, I no longer had the energy or desire to supervise the cleaning and polishing. I found a local woman who served the purpose, with Nelly working with her to learn how to manage a household. Nelly loved being what she called the "deputy housekeeper" and helped to entertain our many visitors with her singing and playing on the harpsichord.

George devoted his time to expanding the distillery output as well as the grist mill's capacity. He talked endlessly about the changes to the gardens and repairs to various buildings on the farms. Each morning, he rode out to inspect the progress and confer with the farm managers. While he took care of the necessary business for the day, Nelly and I entertained the steady flow of guests. I did a great deal of knitting or netting during the days of chitchat. Rarely did we sit down to dinner in the afternoon without at least one nonfamily member.

Inevitably, the conversations strayed to tales of the revolution or about the current strain between America and France. The same flow of visitors also brought a steady stream of news from various states and segments of society. See, just because we'd returned to our beloved home did not mean we had it all to ourselves. Far from it. Surprising news also arrived with each new group.

"What did you say?" Nelly's cheeks flamed as she stared aghast at the man across from her.

Our guest was quite flustered as well, having not anticipated the young woman's reaction. "Just that the Philadelphia gossips, if you can believe a word they say, think young George Lafayette lingers here so he can court you."

"Nothing could be further from the truth." Nelly huffed at the audacious rumor. "He waits for word he can return to his father, the Marquis."

That I knew to be true, since negotiations had begun to win our friend's freedom from prison in Olmutz. Nelly's vociferous protestations proved distracting though, and perhaps worth examining a bit more closely. Who *did* she find attractive? At some point, the young woman would be in search of a husband.

George's sister, Betty Lewis, passed in the spring. Her health had gradually deteriorated over several years of caring for his mother Mary, who suffered from breast cancer. We'd expected the sad news for some time. Her son, Lawrence, also suffered from failing health and melancholy, so we invited him to come live with us to help alleviate the burdens commensurate with entertaining at Mount Vernon. Our advanced age made it increasingly difficult to accommodate the early rising and late nights associated with proper hospitality. He arrived in late August and settled into our routine quite nicely.

I also invited my niece, the daughter of my sister Betsy, to come to Mount Vernon. About the same age as Nelly, Fanny would be a good companion for both of us. The young people cheered my days and made my heart light. They attended horse races and barbecues, dancing lessons and horseback excursions to neighboring friends. Their gaiety and laughter rang in the house as they related the tale of their antics each afternoon.

At dinner on a rainy fall afternoon in September, George cleared his throat to attract the family's attention. I'd noticed he appeared rather quiet and distracted but hesitated to trouble him with my concerns. He'd share what was on his mind when ready.

"I've received a note this afternoon." He glanced at each of us in turn, the table surrounded by our family. "My mother passed away yesterday."

I laid a hand over his and studied his expression. "I'm sorry to hear such sad news."

"She has left me a few things, sentimental items." George turned his hand palm up to clasp mine, warm and strong. "I suppose I'll have to go fetch them."

"She loved you in her own way." What more could I have said? We'd had a polite relationship but not a loving one. She'd respected and loved my husband, of that I remained convinced. Yet she seldom exhibited any overt affection toward him, especially in front of others. "I'm certain you'll miss her."

George nodded, his gaze pensive. "Indeed, I will."

Another life song ended on a sad note. I considered my dear husband for several long moments. The years had been kind to him, despite all of the stress and strain he was still a dashingly handsome man. At least to me. But we were both slowing down and I wondered how many more years we'd have together now that we had returned home. I prayed for many more so we could enjoy them in a peaceful ebb and flow.

---

In October, a rider brought a letter from Pennsylvania for George. He read it quickly, standing in the parlor where I worked on knitting socks, and then called out for George Lafayette. The lad hurried into the room.

"Yes sir?" Young George waited, hope bright in his dark eyes.

"I have happy news. Governor Morris has succeeded in winning your father's and the rest of your family's freedom."

"Excellent!" His grin revealed the joy filling him.

"I expect you'll want to sail for home soon?" My old man bobbed his head twice as a smile spread on his face.

"As soon as possible."

"I'll make the arrangements." George started to turn, but then stopped. "Will you be so kind as to stop on your way to New York to give Wash some money for his expenses? It would be a great favor to me."

"I'm pleased to be able to repay a small part of your kindness by doing so."

"We'll miss having you here." I smiled at the lad and he came to me to offer a brief embrace of his affection.

"Thank you for everything, Mrs. Washington. If you'll excuse me…"

"Go on."

Young George packed his belongings with joy, thrilled at the prospect of returning to his loving father's side. In short order, he and the tutor headed to New York. Our household was just a touch quieter without the youth's presence. Soon the noise level increased for a very different and troublesome reason.

The talk around the dinner table grew heated regarding the actions of France against American ships at sea. As the months passed and the tensions increased, I suspected another war threatened our country. President John Adams wrote to George frequently, and while I didn't read every letter, I knew what the man attempted to do: draw my husband deeper into politics. He said he merely needed my old man's advice and reputation to weigh in on the situation. As long as the president didn't need my husband to become involved in person, I'd not interfere.

We celebrated our thirty-ninth wedding anniversary in January 1798 with a small dinner party, inviting our neighbors and friends to Mount Vernon for the day. My new cook, though not as talented as Hercules, prepared a marvelous feast which everyone enjoyed along with the free-flowing Madeira. My contentment bolstered my elevated mood with my friends and family. Such was the life we'd come to enjoy and I prayed it would continue as far into the future as possible.

A few months later, my contentment ended. It happened while I was inspecting the flower gardens on a misty spring morning. I had just spotted a trampled bed of petunias, dog prints evident across the corner of the plot, when I heard George's footfalls.

"Patsy, I need to speak with you."

When I turned to peer at him, I could tell from his grim expression he had news I wouldn't want to hear. "Yes?"

"I know not how to tell you this except to simply say it." He hesitated, his gaze delving into mine, and then went on in a rush. "John Adams appointed me commander of the Army."

"He didn't." Shock reverberated in my heart, and I laid a hand on his arm to steady myself. Flashes of the past years spent at the rustic army camp and in the more refined lodgings of the presidential abodes blurred in my mind. Would he leave again? Be away for months on end if not years? He'd reached an age where I couldn't fathom his constitution surviving such an ordeal. I stared up at him and then slowly shook my head. "You've done your duty, my love. Pray tell me what you said to him."

"I've accepted his appointment." He laid a hand over mine and lightly squeezed.

"Oh. Then there is nothing to say." I pulled away, not able to fully give my approval to his actions. I'd gone along with his sense of honor and obligation for nearly forty years and now he wanted me to accept his decision to serve his country once again. Without even discussing the matter with me. He must have a good reason for doing so. I met his frown. "Why?

"I didn't want to, but felt it my duty."

I turned back to the garden, preferring to stare at the trampled flowers as tears threatened. My old man. How could George accept such a position again? Fury swept through me at his being drawn into what could become a nasty war against France. I heard his long sigh and his retreating footsteps but studied my flowers while I struggled to breathe.

He went to Philadelphia to organize the army, and stayed away for six long, wearisome weeks, before returning home. After that one trip, though, he managed to command from Virginia without acknowledging verbally the strain his absence had caused between us. Slowly the tension stretching taut abated as he remained on the plantation, but for how long?

---

Our family increased when Tobias moved back to Mount Vernon, specifically to live on Ferry Farm. I loved having so many young people surrounding me. Little had I anticipated the happy result of Lawrence Lewis's residence. He and my granddaughter, Nelly, became attracted to each other and chose to wed at Mount Vernon on George's birthday in 1799. The joy and hope surrounding the wedding further reduced the awkward strain and reminded us of our marriage so many decades before. Not all smooth sailing but we'd navigated the worst of it and could relax in the knowledge that we'd live out our lives together at Mount Vernon.

The wedding occurred after the evening candles were lit. George gave Nelly away, wearing his Revolutionary uniform at the bride's request. I couldn't have been happier for darling Nelly and her handsome husband. After the raucous wedding party, the couple departed on a trip to visit their other family members, including traveling down to New Kent and White House. They returned five months later.

Over breakfast the next morning, Nelly beamed as she stirred her oatmeal with a spoon. "We have an announcement." She waited for everyone to still and pay attention to her. "I'm with child!"

"That's wonderful!" I rose from my chair to hurry around the table to embrace her. "Another baby to add to our family."

"We'd like to live nearby, but are not sure exactly where to look." Lawrence sipped his tea and replaced the cup on the saucer. "Do you have any suggestions, sir?"

"We've been discussing while you've been away what to give you as a wedding present." George broke into a wide smile. "How about if we give you two thousand acres of land close to our house? You could build whatever style home you'd prefer."

"What an amazing gift." Lawrence sat back in his chair to regard George. He glanced at Nelly who nodded with an eager smile on her lips. "We accept."

I was overjoyed both by having another grandchild and that the newly married couple would remain nearby. The discussion turned to plans for which acreage, and how to clear the land to make room for an elegant home.

Fortunately, the army under George's command never took the field. Adams sent representatives to France to negotiate a treaty, which—thank goodness—was signed during the year. George officially resigned and I breathed much easier knowing he would not leave me, or ask me to follow him as I'd done before. I'd had entirely enough of camp life and only wished to be home with my family and friends.

George's brother Charles died in September, a distinct loss for my family. He'd been ill for several months, and spent much of his last days in extreme discomfort. George questioned his own mortality as a result of losing his only living brother. In fact, every death makes one think about the advent of the end of our own lives. George had intended to bequeath the gold-headed cane Benjamin Franklin had left to him to Charles. He decided to retain the gift for himself instead of giving it to any one else. I applauded his decision, as the cane had been a special remembrance of a very august man.

My health had many ups and downs. For years now I'd

wondered if I'd ever be in tolerable health. The colic came and went, bringing stomach pain and other unpleasantness. In October, I became so ill George sent for Dr. Craik not once but twice, trying to find some kind of relief. I retired to our bedchamber with Nelly, great with child, as my nurse. When I felt up to it, I read; when I didn't, I prayed. At one point, I wondered if I'd die. I'd had a good life, filled with loving family and caring friends. Indeed, my years had passed in such a different manner than I'd ever imagined when a young woman making her presentation to society. So much travel and adventure to recall as I lay among the quilts and bed linens. After several weeks, the pain and fever subsided and soon I could yet again count myself among the living. Could be near my husband and our entire family. That's where I knew I belonged always.

The sound of a new baby came to the house in late November. Nelly and Lawrence Lewis welcomed their new daughter, Frances Parke Lewis, after a long and painful lying in. Nelly had such a difficult time, the midwife ordered her to stay in bed for several weeks. I paid special attention to the instructions for her care, as her husband prepared to ride with her brother, Wash, to inspect his new property in New Kent County. The men left in early December, just as the cold settled in for the winter. The house seemed somewhat empty without their rousing tenor. Having Tobias remain to assist George with his correspondence, a never-ending task if there ever was one, also kept me from feeling abandoned by the young people. Before long we'd welcome back the adventurers, but until then we'd remain at home, warm and safe.

---

*Mount Vernon – December 1799*

The weather turned horrid on the twelfth, but George rode out on his usual rounds. I visited with Nelly and little Parke, assisting where needed and enjoying the love shared between mother and daughter. For a change, we had no visitors but had said a fond farewell to Bryan Fairfax and his family. The day wore on, the cold wind whistling past the shut windows and doors. As dinner time approached, I began to fret over George's absence. Had something happened to detain him? Just as the food was put on the table, he strode in, shivering in his wet clothing. Seeing the meal at the ready, he refused to change, but joined us to eat. I shot him a disapproving look. He merely shook his head with a wink and started to eat the hot food.

I observed his condition for the rest of the day, but he seemed to feel fine. The next morning, though, his cheeks were flushed and he sniffled repeatedly. Sure enough, he had the signs of a cold. I protested when he made to leave, to venture out into the snow falling softly to earth, so he could mark trees he wished to have cut down. Even though I tried to stop him, I knew he'd go out in spite of the worsening weather. Once he made a decision...

That evening, we sat by the fire in the parlor, sewing and reading. Tobias joined us, as was his custom. I was glad he'd returned to us after the upsetting failure of his business venture. At the start of George's second term as president, Tobias had gone to work for the Potowmack Company building a waterfalls in the Potomac river. A venture that cost him dearly in pride and monies. After a couple other stumbles in business, he'd come to visit us for a time. We were glad of his company and hoped to help him find a more suitable position.

George read from the paper, but his voice sounded odd. Instead of clear and strong, it sounded muffled, as though something clogged his throat and thus his speech.

"Darling, let me make you a throat syrup to help with your congestion."

"No, Patsy. I'll be fine." He snuffled and coughed. "It's merely a touch of the winter cold. It will run its course in due time."

"It's no bother." I prayed he was right and only suffered a

simple cold. "If you don't want one of my simples, then maybe some hot tea and honey to soothe the irritation?"

He forced a swallow and grimaced. "Very well."

I quickly provided the hot beverage and hoped it would ease his discomfort as we retired for the night.

Sleep took a long time to settle over me, listening to my old man's rasping breath at my side. The fire burned down until the room lay in darkness and cold seeped in to replace the warmth. I snuggled closer to George and he slipped an arm around me. With each rise of his chest, a sort of high whistle sounded in his throat. I didn't like the sound and longed for daylight so I could send for Dr. Craik. Slowly, I eased into sleep.

"Patsy..."

I opened my eyes to a still dark room at the strained sound of my husband's voice. "George? Are you all right?"

He shook his head, the bed shifting beneath us with his movement. "My throat hurts."

I sat up and looked at him, straining to see his features in the dimness. "I'll send for the doctor." I moved to leave the warmth of the bed, his welfare my only concern.

He grasped my wrist and pulled me back down, lifting the covers over me. "Stay here with me. Warm until morning."

"Let me retrieve one of my cordials to help until then." I moved again, to lift the covers but he stayed my hand. "George..."

"You'll...catch...a cold...if you get...up now." He swallowed and moaned with the effort, but tugged me down beside him. "Stay...with...me."

I sighed, reluctantly admitting defeat. I couldn't deny him. But the hours dragged past. We talked, or rather I did, about whatever I could think of to entertain him. About plans for Christmas day. About seeing the advent of a new year and a new century in only a few weeks. We'd lived through the change in the calendar and now the change from the eighteenth to the nineteenth centuries. I hoped so, at any rate. Then I chastised myself for thinking negatively, and redoubled my effort to stay calm and do what needed to be done. Whatever proved necessary to keep my husband alive and well.

Sleep slipped out the window to greet the slow arrival of dawn. I watched the dark pane, waiting for the first rays of sunlight which would bring my maid in to light the fire. Only then would I rise from the warmth of our bed, as I'd promised. At long last, the door opened and the girl eased in, heading to the fireplace. As soon as she'd put match to tinder, though, I called out to her. I'd waited too long already to wait for the flames to fully catch the wood.

"Fetch Tobias Lear, and hurry!"

I dressed myself as quickly as my shaking hands permitted, anticipating the imminent arrival of others. I needed to be ready to face whatever would follow. Steeling myself, I went back to George who had awakened at my words. I schooled my features into a calm mask, but he saw through it. He clasped my hand in his as Tobias rapped on the door and then barged in. I'd never seen such a welcome sight. I informed him of the situation, which he judged for himself in one quick glance. With a nod, he spun and left to summon Dr. Craik.

Throughout the day, people came and went in a blur of motion and sound. Ultimately three different doctors conferred on treatments. They bled my husband several times, and applied ointments to his throat, among other equally futile efforts. I studied him in silence, afraid to speak for the fear clutching my throat. Afraid if I allowed tears to fall, they'd never stop. I'd watched Daniel slowly suffocate from quinsy. I thought then I'd lived through the worst grief possible. I'd been wrong.

His breathing became more difficult with each passing hour, until he squeezed my hand to attract my attention from where I'd been staring at our joined hands, wondering how much longer I'd be able to hold his warm one in mine.

"I've two wills…" He swallowed, grimacing. "On my desk."

"You want me to get them?"

He nodded and rested his head back on the pillow. Did I dare to leave his side? Even for the few minutes it would take to retrieve the papers? What if while I was away... He made a gentle shooing motion with one hand, a half smile on his lips. I nodded and did as he asked.

When I returned and handed them to him, he skimmed their contents and then laid one on the bed. The other he handed to me. "Burn it."

Again, I followed his orders while he watched my actions. Then I resumed my seat by his side, gripping his hand, unwilling to let him go. "Fight for me, dear. Don't give up."

He shook his head and pressed a finger to my cheek. "I...may not...survive this. I'm ready.... We've had...a good...life. Don't be...sad."

"I love you." The concept of losing my husband that very day settled into my brain and shut down my emotions. I couldn't comprehend. He'd survived Indian attacks, every illness, the fighting during the war, the political intrigues of his presidency. Surely a cold and sore throat wouldn't rob me of my life companion. Tears pressed for release but I denied them.

"Where's Lawrence? Wash?" Each word emerged with audible pain.

"Still away to inspect Wash's property."

He closed his eyes, making anxiety surge into my throat. When he opened them again, I drew a breath. "Tell them...I love...them."

"I promise." I swallowed, and pressed my lips together, fighting the urge to sob. To wail at the sudden loss I faced.

My old man knew me too well. He laid a hand on mine. "We'll be...together...again.... I'll wait...for you.... Don't cry."

That's when I realized he'd given up already. Not as in quitting, but as in recognizing the battle had turned against him. Throughout the day doctors and family stopped in, but Tobias stayed with me. The only person who couldn't pay her respects was Nelly, as she remained under strict orders to stay in bed. It was for the best. She couldn't do anything to help, only rest as directed.

Later in the evening, with Tobias holding the great man's

hand, my husband drew his last painful breath. I'd moved to a chair placed at the foot of our bed, where I could be close while others came in to pay their respects. While I'd sat by his side, I made several decisions about what I'd do after....

At the sudden silence, I glanced up at Tobias. "Is he gone?"

"Yes." The single word preceded a choked sob. Tobias bowed his head and closed his eyes for a moment, saying a silent prayer on his friend's passing.

"'Tis well. All is now over." I studied the peaceful countenance of my husband, my mind a whirl of mixed emotions. "I shall soon follow him. I have no more trials to pass through."

———————————

I had Tobias move my things into the little garret room on the third floor, with instructions to close up the bedchamber in which George and I had spent so many happy nights together. I couldn't imagine every wanting to step foot in it again, to relive those wonderful memories without crying. Likewise I had his study shuttered, never to be used again. That was his private space and no one else's. The copyists would have to work elsewhere. Tobias and I functioned together over the next several days to summon the family and notify our friends. George's body lay in a mahogany casket for three days as he'd wanted. I went through the days like an automaton, dry-eyed and intent. More than once, Tobias looked at me as though he thought I'd break apart or burst into grief-laden wails. I refused.

On the eighteenth, four days after his death, the funeral took place. Nelly sat with me in my small room. I couldn't bear to go to the vault in the bitter cold to witness such a desperately sorrowful occasion as the burial of my spouse. I couldn't face any one. Couldn't cry or react to any one with anything approaching my former amiable self. My George. All I could think of was how alone I was now, lost and friendless without him.

A veritable crowd of people had gathered beginning in the morning. Uniformed militia marched from Alexandria, a band playing as they arrived. A procession formed on the portico, six honorary pallbearers and members of the militia carrying the casket to the vault. The cavalry led the procession, a soldier leading George's horse, its saddle painfully empty, while the muffled drums beat a steady rhythm into my broken heart. Through the cracked open window I heard everything on that cold crisp afternoon. Everything from the dirge to the minister's prayers, and then the volley upon volley of musket fire as select men closed and sealed the newly repaired door to the tomb.

I stayed away from the reception laid out in the large dining room following the burial. Facing so many people who all meant well by offering their condolences was out of the question with my mood so depressed and despairing. Without one whit of doubt, I would never be whole again.

# 24

*Mount Vernon – 1802*

Seventeen months of living in a fog of grief, loneliness, and even fear had been alleviated by only a few joyous occasions.

John Adams himself had visited and brought letters of condolence from him and Abigail. Such wonderful and dear friends they had proven to be over the years. After reading their very effecting remonstrance of their affection and sincere grief over the loss of such a great man, the tears I had refused insisted on making an appearance and flooded my cheeks. As I had thought would happen, I cried for quite some time before I could compose myself.

One request had been difficult to acquiesce to, but it had been clear to me the path George would wish me to take. I had very nearly memorized its contents from reading it so many times, debating my course.

Philadelphia, December 27. 1799

Madam

In conformity with the desire of Congress, I do myself the honor to inclose, by Mr William Smith Shaw my Secretary, a copy of their resolutions, passed the twenty fourth instant occasioned by the decease of your late Consort, General George Washington, assuring you of the profound respect Congress will ever bear, to your person and Character, and of their condolence on this afflicting dispensation of Providence. In pursuance of the same desire, I entreat your assent to the interment of the remains of the General under the marble monument to be erected in the capitol, at the City of Washington to commemorate the great events of his military and political life.

Renewing to you Madam, my expressions of condolence on this melancholy occasion, and assuring you of the profound respect which I personally entertain for your Person and character, I remain with great Esteem

Madam your faithful and<br>
obedient Servant<br>
John Adams

The decision proved tortuously difficult for me, knowing how much we enjoyed our home. George had desired to be buried at Mount Vernon, including specific instructions for the preparation of the vault to receive his body. Yet, he loved his country just as much. After four days of discussion with my family, I had Tobias draft a response based on our conversation.

Mount Vernon, December 31, 1799

Sir

While I feel with keenest anguish the late Disposition of Divine Providence I cannot be insensible to the mournful tributes of respect and veneration which are paid to the memory of my dear deceased Husband—and as his best services and most anxious wishes were always devoted to the welfare and happiness of his country—to know that they were truly appreciated and greatfully remembered affords no inconsiderable consolation. Taught by the great example which I have so long had before me never to oppose my private wishes to the public will—I must consent to the request made by congress—which you have had the goodness to transmit to me—and in doing this I need not—I cannot say what a sacrifice of individual feeling I make to a sense of public duty.

With greatful acknowledgement and unfeigned thanks for the personal respect and evidences of condolence expressed by congress and yourself.

I remain, very respectfully
Sir
Your most obedient &
Humble servant
Martha Washington

George's will included a provision to free his slaves, but only after my death. I'm sure he meant to provide the necessary manpower during my life to keep the plantation functioning. What he hadn't anticipated was the reaction of those one hundred twenty-three men and women to the prospect of freedom. After a fire at the mansion-house had been put out, I suspected the slaves had set it to kill me and win their freedom. Alarmed for me, my nephew Bushrod Washington urged me to free them as soon as possible. I agreed and as of the first day of 1801 they were free to choose where they wished to dwell. Some remained as free persons while the others left to seek their fortunes. I breathed easier.

Nelly and Lawrence had welcomed another little girl, Martha Betty, into the world last year, which of course made me happy. They and their children continued to live with me, helping me entertain guests and keeping me company. Tobias had been hard pressed to respond to the onslaught of mail and gifts flooding through our doors in remembrance of my husband, the "Father of His Country" as he'd been referred to for many years. I made time to feed and play with both the children and my parrots and birds, including my favorite cockatoo, kept in pretty cages on the portico. I'd taken an interest in the feathered creatures after the presidential years. Something about the chittering and preening of the birds soothed and entertained.

As the months passed, the flood of details associated with the passing of any plantation owner let alone such a famous and revered man as George dwindled to a trickle. As 1801 faded into 1802, I found myself feeling older and more frail. I chose to spend most of my time in my garret room, praying and reading, sometimes entertaining the young girls and teaching them how to sew. I had General Charles Lee make out my will, which in March 1802 I had Nelly copy over with a few adjustments to the bequests. Once witnessed, I put them in a safe place and waited.

So my story comes full circle. I knew I had to protect his reputation and our private lives. I decided to gather all of the letters George and I had written to each other from the days of our courtship until we'd returned home for good. I'd seen how people with evil intentions took events out of context and used them to lambast and pillory others. I'd not give them ammunition to besmirch George's reputation. Or mine, for that matter.

I pulled the chair closer to the fireplace. I had ensured no one would interrupt me or prevent me from doing my own duty. One by one, I fed the letters into the fire, using the poker to make certain no legible fragments remained. With each addition, I recalled the events and concerns of our joint life. Recalled the love we shared, such a deep and abiding joining of souls. Nobody possessed the power to remove our love from my heart. I didn't need written proof. I added another set of letters to the blaze with a smile.

---

On some days, I seemed to see George, leaning against the wall waiting for me to join him. Somehow I understood the time approached but had not yet arrived. My on-again, off-again colic had continued, with each episode seeming worse than the previous. In May, the bilious fever struck and had me in bed for two weeks. Dr. Craik came and stayed at my request. George's presence in the room, though nobody else could see him, reassured me even as I realized my own death loomed. I didn't fear it. Why would I? George waited for me like he had promised. Waited to carry me home with him.

The third week of my illness, I called my family together to say good-bye in case the end came during the dark of night. The minister prayed with me and served me communion to prepare me for the next phase of life. Death would be welcome, to take me home to my God and my husband. Would I be reunited with the rest of my family as well? I hoped I'd soon learn the answer.

Finally, my old man summoned me. Standing beside my bed, he smiled and held out his hand, motioning for me to rise and join him. At long last we'd spend eternity together. I closed my eyes a little before noon, a smile on my face, as I began my journey to my husband's side.

# EPILOGUE

Martha Washington died on May 22, 1802, at Mount Vernon. She lay in state in a white dress of her own choosing in a coffin displayed in the large dining room of the mansion-house. Her obituary, published in the *Alexandria Advertiser and Commercial Intelligencer*, provided a succinct description of her life:

> On Saturday the 22nd of May at 12 o'clock P.M. Mrs. Washington terminated her well spent life…. She was the worthy partner of the worthiest of men, and those who witnessed their conduct could not determine which excelled in their different characters, both were so well sustained on every occasion. They lived an honor and a pattern to their country, and are taken from us to receive the rewards—promised to the faithful and the just.

She and George lie buried side by side in a vault at Mount Vernon. Though Congress petitioned both of Martha's nephews, Bushrod Washington and John Dandridge, to allow George's remains to be moved to Washington, D.C., the requests were ultimately denied as George had specified in his will where he desired to be buried.

# WHO'S WHO IN
# BECOMING LADY WASHINGTON

*The real people and fictional characters (marked with an \*)*

Adams, Abigail "Abbie" – Friend of Martha Washington; wife of John Adams

Adams, John – Delegate; first Vice President; second U.S. President

Adams, Samuel – Leader of the Sons of Liberty

Alexander, William – Major General in the Continental Army

Arnold, Benedict – Major General in the Continental Army

Bache, Benjamin Franklin – Publisher of the *Aurora*; grandson of Benjamin Franklin

Baker, John – Dentist in Williamsburg

Bassett, Anna Maria "Nancy" Dandridge – Sister of Martha Washington; wife of Burwell Bassett

Bassett, Burwell – Husband of Anna Maria Dandridge Bassett; lawyer

Bassett, Burwell Jr. – Nephew of Martha Washington; son of Burwell and Anna Maria Dandridge Bassett

Bassett, Frances "Fanny" – Niece of Martha Washington; daughter of Burwell and Anna Maria Dandridge Bassett; wife of George Augustine Washington

Bassett, John – Nephew of Martha Washington; son of Burwell and Anna Maria Dandridge Bassett

Baylor, George – Captain in Continental Army; aide-de-camp to George Washington

Biddle, Clement – General in the Continental Army; George Washington's purchasing agent in Philadelphia

Biddle, Rebecca "Becky" Cornell – Friend of Martha Washington; wife of General Clement Biddle

Biddle, Thomas – Son of General Clement and Rebecca Biddle

Bouchard, Jean Pierre – French aeronaut who flew the first balloon in North America

Boucher, Jonathan – Reverend; John Parke Custis' school teacher

Braxton, Carter – Burgess

Broadwater, Charles – Burgess

Browne, Judith Carter – See Judith Carter Browne Lewis

Browne, William – Purchased Elsing Green; father of Judith Carter Browne Lewis

Byrd, Mary Willing – Wife of William Byrd III

Byrd, William III – Burgess; Colonel in Continental Army

Calvert, Benedict Swingate – Father of Charles Calvert

Calvert, Charles – Captain; Father of Elizabeth Calvert

Calvert, Charles – John Parke Custis' classmate; brother of Eleanor Calvert Custis Stuart

Calvert, Eleanor "Nelly" – See Eleanor Calvert Custis Stuart

Calvert, Elizabeth – Wife of Benedict Swingate; mother of Eleanor Calver Custis Stuart

Calvert, Rebecca "Becky" – Daughter of Benedict and Elizabeth Swingate

Calvert, Rebecca Gerard – Mother of Elizabeth Calvert

Carlyle, Nancy – Niece of Sally Fairfax

Carter, Charles – Burgess; Colonel in Continental Army

Carter, Charles – New Kent County Plantation Owner; potential suitor of Martha Custis

Carter, James – Doctor in Williamsburg

Cary, Robert – Factor in London

Conway, Thomas – Brigadier General in Continental Army

Craik, James – Doctor who visited Mount Vernon

Crawford, Valentine – George Washington's overseer and business manager for his Ohio lands

Cushing, William – Judge who swore in George Washington as first president

Custis, Alice – Slave; mother of Mulatto Jack, Daniel Custis' half-brother (*See* Jack, Mulatto)

Custis, Austin – Slave

Custis, Beck – Slave

Custis, Betty – Slave; seamstress

Custis, Breechy – Slave; waiter

Custis, Daniel Parke – First husband of Martha Washington; father of Daniel Parke II, Frances Parke, John Parke, and Martha Parke Custis

Custis, Daniel Parke II – Son of Daniel and Martha Dandridge Custis

Custis, Doll – Slave; cook

Custis, Elizabeth Parke – *See* Elizabeth Parke Custis Law

Custis, Fanny – Sister of Daniel Custis; daughter of John and Frances Custis

Custis, Frances "Fanny" Parke – Daughter of Daniel and Martha Dandridge Custis

Custis, George "Wash" Washington Parke – Grandson of Martha Washington; son of John Parke and Eleanor Calvert Custis

Custis, Hercules – Slave

*Custis, Jacob – Slave

Custis, John "Jacky" Parke – Son of Daniel and Martha
  Dandridge Custis; husband of Eleanor Calvert Custis Stuart

Custis, John IV – Father of Daniel Custis

Custis, Julius – Slave; manservant

Custis, Martha "Patsy" Parke – Daughter of Daniel and Martha
  Dandridge Custis

Custis, Martha "Patty" Parke – Granddaughter of Martha
  Washington

Custis, Molly – Slave; lady's maid

Custis, Mulatto Jack – Slave; waiter (*Note: not Daniel Custis' half-
  brother*)

Custis, Rose – Slave

Custis, Sally – Slave; lady's maid

Dandridge, Anna Maria "Nancy" – *See* Bassett, Anna Maria
  Dandridge

Dandridge, Bartholomew "Bat" – Brother of Martha
  Washington; son of John and Frances Orlando Dandridge

Dandridge, Bartholomew "Bat" – Nephew of Martha
  Washington; son of Bartholomew and Mary Burbidge
  Dandridge

*Dandridge, Billy – Slave

Dandridge, Colonel John "Jack" – Father of Martha Washington;
  commander of militia; Clerk of the Court; husband of
  Frances Orlando Jones Dandridge

Dandridge, Dot – Slave; laundress

Dandridge, Elizabeth "Betsy" – *See* Elizabeth Henley

Dandridge, Frances – Sister of Martha Washington

Dandridge, Frances "Fanny" Orlando Jones – Mother of Martha
  Washington; wife of Colonel John Dandridge

Dandridge, John – Nephew of Martha Washington; son of Bartholomew and Mary Burbidge Dandridge

Dandridge, John "Jacky" – Brother of Martha Washington

Dandridge, Martha "Patty" Washington – Niece of Martha Washington; sister of John Dandridge; daughter of Bartholomew and Mary Burbidge Dandridge

Dandridge, Mary – Sister of Martha Washington

Dandridge, Mary Burbidge – Wife of Bartholomew Dandridge; mother of Bartholomew, John, and Martha Dandridge

Dandridge, Nancy – *See* Anna Maria Dandridge Bassett

Dandridge, Old Sally – Slave; cook

Dandridge, Pansy – Slave; laundress

Dandridge, Unity West – Aunt of Martha Washington; wife of William Dandridge of Elsing Green

Dandridge, William – Brother of Martha Washington

Dandridge, William – Uncle of Martha Washington; husband of Unity West Dandridge; original owner of Elsing Green

Dinwiddie, Rebecca – Wife of Robert Dinwiddie

Dinwiddie, Robert – Governor of Virginia

Dunlap, William – Painting Tutor

Dunmore, John Murray – Fourth Earl of Dunmore (1730-1809); Last royal governor of Virginia; husband of Lady Charlotte Stewart Dunmore

Dunmore, Lady Charlotte Stewart – Wife of John Murray Dunmore; daughter of sixth earl of Galloway

Eden, Robert – Governor of Maryland

Fairfax, Bryan – Neighbor of George Washington; lieutenant in militia; justice for Fairfax County

Fairfax, Elizabeth – Wife of Bryan Fairfax; sister of Sally Fairfax

Fairfax, Lord George William – Neighbor of George Washington; husband of Sally Cary Fairfax

Fairfax, Sally Cary – Friend of Martha Washington; wife of Lord George Fairfax

Fauquier, Catherine – Wife of Frances Fauquier

Fauquier, Frances – Royal Governor of Virginia; husband of Catherine Fauquier

Franklin, Benjamin – Delegate and Diplomat

Fraunces, Samuel "Black Sam" – Steward; George Washington resigned his commission at Black Sam's tavern

Gates, Elizabeth "Betsy" Phillips – Wife of Horatio Gates

Gates, Horatio – Major General in Continental Army; served with George Washington in French and Indian War

Gibbs, Caleb – Captain in Continental Army

Gist, Nathaniel – Served with George Washington in the French and Indian War

Gooch, Rebecca – Wife of William Gooch

Gooch, William – Governor of Virginia

Grayson, Spence – Chaplain and Captain in Continental Army

Greene, Catherine "Caty" Littlefield – Friend of Martha Washington; wife of General Nathaniel Greene

Greene, Nathaniel – Brigadier General in Continental Army; husband of Catherine Littlefield Greene

Greene, Nathaniel Ray – Son of Nathaniel and Catherine Littlefield Greene

Hamilton, Alexander – Aide-de-camp to George Washington; Secretary of the Treasury; husband of Elizabeth Schuyler Hamilton

Hamilton, Elizabeth "Betsy" Schuyler – Wife of Alexander Hamilton; daughter of Philip Schuyler

Hancock, John – Lawyer; signer of Declaration of Independence

Henley, Bartholomew – Son of Leonard and Elizabeth Dandridge Henley

Henley, Elizabeth "Betsy" Dandridge – Sister of Martha Washington; wife of Leonard Henley

Henley, Fanny – Niece of Martha Washington; daughter of Leonard and Elizabeth Dandridge Henley

Henley, Leonard – Husband of Elizabeth Dandridge Henley

Henry, Patrick – Burgess

Howe, Robert – Brigadier General in Continental Army

Humphreys, David – Colonel in Continental Army; aide-de-camp to George Washington

Jack, Mulatto – Daniel Custis' half-brother; son of John Custis IV and Alice (Custis)

*Jacobs, Sarah – Midwife

Jay, John – President of Second Continental Congress; Ambassador to Spain; first U.S. Chief Justice

Jefferson, Martha – Wife of Thomas Jefferson

Jefferson, Thomas – Burgess; Signer of Declaration of Independence; third U.S. President

Judge, Oney – Slave; lady's maid to Martha Washington

Knox, Henry – General in Continental Army; husband of Lucille Knox

Knox, Lucille "Lucy" – Daughter of Henry and Lucille Knox

Knox, Lucille "Lucy" – Friend of Martha Washington; wife of General Henry Knox

Lafayette, George Washington Motier – Son of Marquis de Lafayette

Lafayette, Marie-Joseph Paul Yves Roch Gilbert du Motier de, Marquis de Lafayette – Served with George Washington during American Revolution; secured French support during the American Revolution

Law, Elizabeth "Betsy" Parke Custis – Granddaughter of Martha Washington; wife of Thomas Law

Law, Thomas – Husband of Elizabeth Parke Custis Law

Lear, Benjamin Lincoln – Son of Tobias and Mary Long Lear

Lear, Fayette – Son of Tobias and Frances Bassett Washington Lear

Lear, Frances "Fanny" Bassett Washington – Niece of Martha Washington; daughter of Burwell and Anna Maria Dandridge Bassett

Lear, Maria – Daughter of Frances Bassett Washington Lear

Lear, Mary "Polly" Long – First wife of Tobias Lear

Lear, Tobias – Secretary and Tutor; husband of (1) Mary Long Lear and (2) Frances Bassett Washington Lear

Lee, Billy (aka Will) – Slave; manservant to George Washington

Lee, Charles – General in Continental Army; prepared Martha Washington's will

*Lee, David – Friend of George Washington

Lee, Margaret Thomas – Wife of Billy "Will" Lee

*Lee, Melanie – Wife of David Lee

Lee, Richard Henry – Burgess; Colonel in Continental Army

Lewis, Betty Washington – Sister of George Washington; wife of Fielding Lewis

Lewis, Eleanor "Nelly" Parke Custis – Granddaughter of Martha Washington; daughter of John Parke and Eleanor Calvert Custis; wife of Lawrence Lewis

Lewis, Fielding – Husband of Betty Washington Lewis; George Washington's business partner

Lewis, Frances "Parke" Parke – Great-granddaughter of Martha Washington; daughter of Lawrence and Eleanor Lewis

Lewis, George Washington – Nephew of George Washington; son of Fielding and Betty Washington Lewis

Lewis, Howell – Nephew of George Washington

Lewis, Judith Carter Browne – Wife of Robert Lewis; daughter of William Browne

Lewis, Lawrence – Nephew of Martha Washington; son of Fielding and Betty Lewis; husband of Eleanor Parke Custis Lewis

Lewis, Martha Betty – Great-granddaughter of Martha Washington; daughter of Lawrence and Eleanor Lewis

Lewis, Robert "Bob" – Nephew of George Washington; husband of Judith Carter Browne Lewis

Livingston, Henry Brockholst – Lieutenant colonel in Continental Army; aide-de-camp to Benedict Arnold at Saratoga

Macaulay, Catharine – Friend of Martha Washington

Macaulay, William – Friend of Martha Washington

Madison, Dolley Payne Todd – Wife of James Madison

Madison, James – Signer of Declaration of Independence; Father of the U.S. Constitution; husband of Dolley Payne Todd Madison

Mason, Ann – Wife of George Mason

Mason, George – Burgess; neighbor of George Washington

Mercer, Hugh – Doctor; Friend of George Washington

Mifflin, Thomas – Quartermaster General in the Continental Army

Moody, Anne – Neighbor of John Custis

Moody, Matthew – Neighbor of John Custis

Morris, Mary – Friend of Martha Washington; wife of Robert Morris

Morris, Robert – Friend of George Washington; Governor of Pennsylvania

Mossom, David – Rector of St. Peter's Church

Mossom, Elizabeth – Wife of David Mossom

Payne, Lucy – Sister of Dolley Payne Todd Madison

Peale, Charles Willson – Painter

Peter, Elizabeth "Patty" Scott – Friend of Martha Washington

Peter, Robert – Friend of George Washington

Peter, Thomas – Son of Robert and Elizabeth Peter

Posey, Millie – Martha Parke Custis' friend

Powel, Eliza – Friend of Martha Washington; wife of Samuel Powel

Powel, Samuel – Friend of George Washington; Mayor of Philadelphia; President of the Philosophical Society for Promoting Agriculture

Power, James – Lawyer; friend of Daniel Custis

Randolph, Edmund – Friend of George Washington; Attorney General

Randolph, John – Burgess

Reed, Dennis – Son of Joseph and Esther Reed

Reed, Esther – Daughter of Joseph and Esther Reed

Reed, Esther de Berdt – Friend of Martha Washington; wife of Joseph Reed

Reed, George Washington – Son of Joseph and Esther Reed

Reed, Joseph – Friend of George Washington; Adjutant General of Continental Army; President of Pennsylvania Supreme Executive Council

Reed, Joseph – Son of Joseph and Esther Reed

Reed, Martha – Daughter of Joseph and Esther Reed

Reed, Theodosia – Daughter of Joseph and Esther Reed

Reinagle, Alexander – Music Tutor from Austria

Rumney, William – Doctor who visited Mount Vernon

Schuyler, Philip – General in Continental Army; father of Elizabeth Schuyler Hamilton

Smith, Nabby Adams – Daughter of John and Abigail Adams

Spotswood, Mary – Cousin of Martha Washington

St. Clair, Arthur – Major General in Continental Army

Steele, John – Captain in the Continental Army; captain of Martha Washington's Guard

Stephen, Adam – Major General in Continental Army

Steuben, Friedrich Wilhelm, Baron von – Prussian professional soldier responsible for training the Continental Army

Stuart, David – Second husband of Eleanor Calvert Custis Stuart

Stuart, Eleanor "Nelly" Calvert Custis – Wife of (1) John Parke Custis and (2) David Stuart

Thacker, Chickley Corbin – Minister who married George and Martha Washington

Thacker, Elizabeth – Wife of Chickley Corbin Thacker

Thompson, Charles – Secretary of Continental Congress

Todd, John – First husband of Dolley Payne Todd Madison

Warren, James – Army Paymaster; Speaker of the Massachusetts House of Representatives

Warren, Mercy Otis – Friend of Martha Washington; wife of James Warren

Washington, Anna Maria – Daughter of George Augustine and Frances Bassett Washington

Washington, Anne – Wife of Lawrence Washington (George Washington's brother)

Washington, Anne Lee – Wife of Augustine Washington (George Washington's brother); sister of Richard Henry Lee

Washington, Augustine – George Washington's father

Washington, Augustine "Austin" – Half-brother of George Washington

Washington, Austin – Slave

Washington, Bushrod – Nephew of George Washington

Washington, Charles – Brother of George Washington

Washington, Christopher – Slave

Washington, Elizabeth "Betsy" Foote – Wife of Lund
Washington

Washington, Frances "Fanny" Bassett – Niece of Martha
Washington

Washington, George – Second husband of Martha Dandridge
Custis Washington; first U.S. President

Washington, George Augustine – Nephew of George
Washington; husband of Frances Bassett

Washington, George Steptoe – Nephew of George Washington;
son of Samuel and Anne Washington; father of Anna Maria
Washington

Washington, Giles – Slave

Washington, Jane Butler – First wife of Augustine Washington
(George Washington's father)

Washington, John "Jack" – Brother of George Washington

Washington, Lawrence – Brother of George Washington;
husband of Anne Washington

Washington, Lawrence – Nephew of George Washington; Son of
Samuel and Anne Washington

Washington, Lund – Cousin of George Washington

Washington, Mary Ball – Mother of George Washington

Washington, Paris – Slave

Wollaston, John – Painter

Wythe, Elizabeth – Wife of George Wythe

Wythe, George – Burgess; lawyer

# AUTHOR'S NOTE

When I started to gather information about the life of Martha Dandridge Custis Washington, I discovered a wealth of historical details that were new to me and some which had been misrepresented in the biographies I read. I have done my utmost to ensure the story I've written is supported by historical references, typically more than one so that I have confidence in the accuracy and authenticity of the details of her life and times. The historical locations used as setting are, to the best of my knowledge, the places where Martha did in fact live or stay during her lifetime.

However, in a few instances I employed a bit of poetic license in order to highlight aspects of her personality and character not documented specifically in multiple sources. For example, I've included the playful horse race between Martha, Nancy, and Burwell to demonstrate the reputation she had for her horsemanship and to emphasize her spunk and playfulness even though sources do not indicate she met George Washington in that fashion.

Likewise, Martha's trip to Williamsburg to confront John Custis is my interpretation of how she might have given her "prudent speech" to him to convince him to allow Daniel to court her. Apparently what exactly that speech entailed is lost to the ages, so her conversation in this story is purely my speculation.

While no details exist as to Martha's presentation to society, research gave me the general idea of what such an important ball would involve. At the time of her presentation the Governor's Palace ballroom had not yet been built, so all major social functions were held in the upstairs meeting room of the Capitol building. In order to have the best idea of what the dancing might have been like, my husband and I took a dance class in Colonial Williamsburg. I also referred to a book about dancing and music in the American colonies.

Reading her surviving correspondence—she really did burn most of her personal letters before she died—yielded insights into her worldview as well her approach to her own life. The advice and expectations revealed in her letters to family and friends says much about who she was as a woman and as a general and president's wife.

Please note that the spelling of words has evolved over the centuries. I have attempted to reflect such evolution within this story, including newer words later in the text, in order to create the ambiance of the time period as well as I might. For example, "any one" remained two words throughout this period and "to-morrow" didn't tend to drop the hyphenation until the twentieth century; "fuss" didn't enter the English language until 1792 so doesn't appear in the story until the chapter dated 1794.

My aim was to provide as true and authentic representation of Lady Washington as I could, based on the many sources and impressions of others regarding her character. I trust she'd find it a close approximation of the strong, capable, fascinating woman she became throughout her amazing life. I hope you enjoyed getting to know this amazing woman as much as I did.

To find out about new releases and upcoming appearances, please sign up for my newsletter at www.bettybolte.com. I send out a monthly newsletter with book news to share with my readers, upcoming events and signings, and even a few favorite recipes, puzzles, and other doings!

I'd love to hear from you! Feel free to send me an email at betty@bettybolte.com, find me on Facebook at AuthorBettyBolte, follow me on BookBub, or connect with me on Twitter @BettyBolte.

You can find all of my other books on my website at http://www.bettybolte.com/books/.

Thanks for reading!

*Betty*

BETTY BOLTÉ is known for authentic and accurately researched American historical fiction with heart and supernatural romance novels. She has published more than 20 books of fiction and nonfiction topics. She earned a Master's Degree in English in 2008, emphasizing the study of literature and storytelling, and has judged numerous writing contests for both fiction and nonfiction. She is a member of the Romance Writers of America, Historical Novel Society, Women's Fiction Writers Association, Alabama Writers' Cooperative, and Authors Guild. Get to know her at www.bettybolte.com.